Praise for *The Struggle for Courage: In the Days of Jezebel*

"In *The Struggle for Courage: In the Days of Jezebel,* author Marilyn T. Parker has written a beautiful story about those innocently caught in Jezebel's crosshairs and the depth of love and sacrifice they encounter as faithful followers of Yahweh. Such a beautiful love story with an ending that left me with goofy happy tears. One of the best books I've read in a long, long time, and I truly hope there are more to come from this gifted storyteller!"

- DIANE MOODY, Amazon best seller and eight-time Amazon All-star, is the author of over 16 books, including bestseller *Of Windmills and War.* Diane and her husband Ken are the founders of OBT Bookz.

"In *The Struggle for Courage: In the Days of Jezebel,* author Marilyn Parker immerses readers in ancient biblical Israel during the rule of King Ahab. This gripping tale, which follows on the heels of her powerfully moving story of Leah, Jacob's first wife—*The Struggle for Love*—pits Obadiah, the governor of the palace, against the murderous Jezebel. This story of faith, courage, and love in a dangerous time presents a cast of riveting characters who must make hard choices—ones that have deadly consequences and cause great heartbreak. But through it all, there is joy and peace to be found in following God faithfully and courageously in the days of Jezebel."

- C.S. LAKIN, award-winning author of more that thirty books, fiction and non-fiction. C.S. teaches at writing conferences around the country. Her blog *Live Write Thrive* has been listed in the top 10 blogs for writers.

"With beautifully woven characters and a stunning narrative, The Struggle for Courage takes us through the story of Obadiah and Anna, two people who endure deep sorrow and heartbreak on the way to joy and redemption. Marilyn Parker has a gift for making Old Testament stories come alive, and this one shows us the relational, political, and spiritual realities of that time in a way few have mastered. A beautiful story filled with enduring truth."

- BETH LOTTIG, Owner of Inspire]

"The Struggle for Courage: In the Days of Jezebel. Such a timely novel. My favorite quote from the protagonist: *My life had been spent seeking courage, but what I found in the end was trust and surrender, which brought me to a place of peace.* Although Marilyn is a story teller, I believe God divinely inspires her imagination as she creatively pens the essence of the real story written between the lines."

-SUZAN CARTAGENA, author of *The God Connection* and *Identity Theft* is an author and international speaker. Her books have been translated into five languages. She and her husband, Micky, travel the world equipping pastors with the spiritual tools to bring victory to their churches.

Praise for *The Struggle for Love: The Story of Leah*

"I loved everything about this book. There was nothing to dislike. It was beautifully written, heart touching, tears flowing, stayed true to the Bible story, and one of the best books I have ever read. Thank you Marilyn T. Parker. I just ordered two more of your books."

- Amazon Customer

"OMG! this was the most touching story ever. I cried. I laughed. I wish everyone would read this book."

- Amazon Customer

"This was phenomenal. The writing painted all of the characters beautifully and enriched the story we all know and love."

- Amazon Customer

"I took a chance on a writer unknown to me and SO GLAD I did! This book is a phenomenal read!! The characters are so well developed and so real that you will feel what they feel and think that you are right there in the story with them! This gave me a whole new insight into the Biblical account and really fleshes out what COULD have happened in between the lines of the historical account from Scripture! You will not want to put this book down, but you also won't want it to end!! Very moving, extremely well written! You will not be disappointed!"

- Amazon Customer

The STRUGGLE *for* COURAGE

In the Days of Jezebel

THE STRUGGLE FOR COURAGE

Cover and interior by Roseanna White Designs

ISBN: 979-8-9857509-4-2

The STRUGGLE *for* COURAGE

In the Days of Jezebel

MARILYN T. PARKER

It was her laugh that settled it. The way it slithered through the air like a snake, tongue darting in and out. Jezebel had taken everyone Obadiah loved, and in doing so had left him with nothing to lose but his fear. He smiled at her robe-draped back as she passed. The queen would pay for her crimes. He would see to it.

CHAPTER ONE

Obadiah

Months earlier

I shouldn't be here. No one could expect it of me. No one did expect it of me. But I couldn't ask my friends to risk what I wasn't willing to risk myself.

I shifted the large bag of barley loaves to my other shoulder and looked back down the rocky slope. When we were young, Zim and I had disguised the narrow trail that led to this slit of an opening in the mountainside. We'd tugged small fallen trees and scattered several large stones across the path to divert other boys from finding the cave where we pretended to be kings plotting war or brigands looking for a place to stash our ill-gotten treasures. Yahweh had improved on our efforts. With a jolt of the earth the trail had become a field of rocky debris. Soldiers would have to leave their horses and approach by foot, allowing precious time for retreat into the tunnels. Why did that bring me no comfort today?

I pushed away the niggling thoughts that had scratched at my mind since I left the palace and ducked through the low opening.

My eyes adjusted slowly to the dim light. A salamander scurried across the uneven floor, hardly disturbing the chilly silence in its flight. The musty, earthy smell of the cave, along with the faint, sharp scent of rock, always reminded me of old parchment and iron-gull ink.

The cave had seemed much larger when Zim and I had played here as boys. I let out a breath of longing for happier times, when caves were for exploring instead of hiding prophets from a wicked queen. I put the bag down and kneaded the tense muscles of my neck, pressing my fingers into the knots.

My gaze rested on a tall staff leaning against the rock wall, worn where a man's hand had gripped it for many years. I pulled a long breath and let it stream between my pursed lips. "Jonathan? It's me. You can come out now."

In a moment, a yellow glow appeared at the dark bend of the chamber. It was another minute before Jonathan came around the corner, shadows dancing across his hoary head from the light of a flickering torch, a small band of bedraggled men and women, some with children at their sides, following.

A broad smile split his wizened face. "Obadiah. My young friend. It has been a while. We were beginning to wonder if you'd been hung from one of Ahab's rafters."

I tried to smile at the old man's attempted levity, but the corners of my mouth would not rise to the occasion. I'd actually spent a fair amount of time wondering if that would eventually be my fate and preferred not to be reminded of it.

Jonathan raised a palm. "Forgive me," he said, a mischievous sparkle in his eyes. "I have an unseemly sense of humor at times." He placed the torch in a niche carved into the wall and motioned to the outcropping of rock that broadened into a stony bench.

"That you have a sense of humor at all in these times is commendable, my friend," I said as we sat. I was certain it was Jonathan's sense of humor that kept him from madness, hiding in a cave for months on end. I could grant him a jest at my expense.

I lifted my chin toward the wall where the staff rested against the gray rock. Jonathan's gaze followed mine, and his wide smile collapsed into a thin line. He shook his head. "It's mine. I'm sorry, my brother."

The man was embarrassed. I didn't want to make him uncomfortable. He had enough to deal with, but such a mistake could cost him and the others their lives if Jezebel's henchmen were to find evidence of their presence here.

"It's all right, Jonathan. In the end, it's only Yahweh who protects us anyway," I said, hoping to ease the man's discomfort.

He nodded. "That is true, my friend, but in the future I will try not to make it so difficult for him."

I believed that Yahweh was our protector—in principle. But I sometimes woke in the night, cold with fear that I would fail these brave men and women and that I was putting the people I loved in danger by allowing them to feed the prophets Jezebel was so bent on killing.

"Do you have enough water? Joel or Zim will bring an amphora tomorrow. I hope it will be sufficient for a few days."

"It will be enough, my friend. There are not so many of us now. We are grateful for your help," he said, patting my knee.

One of the children moved closer, his hungry eyes fixed on the sack. "Forgive me." I motioned to Jonathan's wife, who was standing quietly by. "Please. Help yourselves." A wide smile, revealing her few remaining teeth, spread over her pleasant face as she picked up the bag, first offering a piece to me.

"No. No. I have eaten. Thank you." A stripe of guilt moved in my conscience. I was the governor of Ahab's palace, and few things from the king's table would be denied me—while my brothers, the prophets, lived with half-filled bellies and too little water because of the drought.

Martha handed a piece of bread to her husband and shuffled toward the back of the cave to distribute the rest to the others and to give Jonathan and me a private moment.

The strap was broken on one of her sandals. She had tied a length of cloth around her foot to keep the shoe from falling off as she scraped across the rock floor. I should bring some shoes. Why hadn't I thought of it before? And clothes. The edge of her robe was ragged. It had once been a fine garment, an unusual shade of red, almost the color of the ruby Jezebel wore on the too-long finger she loved to point at the victims of her diabolical fury. The robe was trimmed with intricate embroidery. A border of blue and bright yellow flowers on a white vine that meandered along the hem.

But it was threadbare now. And Jonathan's once-white tunic had turned a dingy gray. Anna would have an extra tunic for Martha. But Martha would just give it away, and I didn't know how I could inconspicuously bring clothing for them all. A hard lump formed in my throat.

"Are you sure you wouldn't like a piece?" Jonathan mumbled around a large bite of bread.

"No. Thank you." There was something I wanted to ask the man. Something that might prove sensitive. "I have a question, Friend."

The prophet swallowed and wiped his mouth with the back of his hand. "What is it, Obadiah?"

The air was thick as I sucked it into my lungs. I needed a wise word that I could hold when my thoughts swung dizzily in my head as they had been doing for some time now. I hoped Jonathan could offer one.

"Something troubles me. I mean no disrespect, but there's something I need to know."

"No offense will be taken, my brother," he said with a nod. "Say what you will."

I leaned closer to keep my voice out of range of those in the back of the cave enjoying their food.

"Some of the prophets take their wives and children with them. Others don't. Why … why do you choose to do so? Don't you think it dangerous?" I struggled to understand why these devout men would endanger their families. If there was some reasonable answer, I needed to know because I had my own decision to make.

"Ahh." he nodded. "I understand your concern. Many of the prophets take their wives with them. Others leave their wives and children in the care of family. Some choose not to marry at all," he said with a shrug.

"There is no right or wrong choice here, Obadiah, but I ..." He looked toward the back of the cave and again at me, his eyes soft over the crook of his smile. "I settled it when I finished my studies that I would not leave Martha behind. I need her wisdom. She often hears from Yahweh in ways I do not. It is not that I love my wife more than the other prophets love theirs." He winked. "Sometimes I'm tempted to send her back to her mother's house for a visit and forget to pick her up."

I couldn't help but laugh. The old man had definitely retained his sense of humor.

"It's a decision for each man to make," he said, his forehead settling into a thoughtful pinch. "But"—he placed a big hand on my shoulder—"I think this question is not about me and Martha. I think it's about you and Anna. When are you and Anna to be married?"

I ran my fingers through my hair. That was a question that required an answer soon. For years, Naboth had been expecting me to make an official offer of marriage, and I wanted to marry Naboth's daughter more than anything in the world. But every time we set a day to sign the betrothal contract, something happened in the palace that gave me pause. A rant, a threat, a servant alive one day and dead the next.

"In truth, we're not officially betrothed yet," I said, rubbing a finger over the bridge of my nose.

"Really? I'm surprised. We all assumed it was settled long ago. Have you changed your mind about Anna?"

"No. No!" I shook my head. It's only that I fear—" The word caught in my throat. Therein lay the problem. Fear. I had always known I would marry Anna. Zim and Anna's brothers had teased that she was too young for me to set my heart upon her. But I knew that a dozen years would be nothing between us when she was grown into a woman. What I didn't know was that my father would die, and, despite my youth, Ahab would make me governor of his palace in my father's stead.

"You have your father's exceptional ability to discern what needs to be done when no one else does, and to keep everything well ordered," he had said when he told me I was to become the new administrator. I had been shocked, uncertain I wanted the position, although intrigued by the possibility of following in my father's footsteps.

I wasn't Ahab's slave. I could have politely declined the offer and returned to my ancestral land. In theory. But refusing a king anything can be a precarious proposition. And something in me wanted to be the administrator of Ahab's palace. Organization and orchestration were the melody and harmony of a beautiful song to me. Instruments of joy and satisfaction.

"And I believe I can trust you as I trusted your father," Ahab had said.

Heat touched my cheeks. What would the king say of trust if he knew I had hidden dozens of Yahweh's prophets in the caves to escape his wife's murderous rage? And that I often fed them with bread baked in his own ovens?

"I know there is reason to be concerned for Anna's safety since she would be living in the palace, but Ahab seems to love you like a son. Is that not so?" Jonathan said, squeezing my forearm reassuringly. "The palace may be the safest place for you and a wife. Ahab would not likely let Jezebel harm the administrator he leans so heavily upon."

Perhaps Jonathan was right—but, to his question, I wasn't certain Ahab loved me like a son at all. He was possessive, and he had some strange affection for me, that was true. But Ahab had married a master manipulator. She turned the king whatever direction her evil designs required. He may not have participated in the purge, but he'd stood by while she killed hundreds of Yahweh's prophets. He said he could trust me, but could I trust him? I needed peace. Assurance that my bride would be safe. And in the house of Jezebel peace was difficult to come by.

Jonathan studied me for a long moment, the line dividing his fore-head deepening. "I see that you are troubled, my friend, and I do not dismiss your concerns. We live in a time of great wickedness, Obadiah. We want our lives to be normal, predictable. Safe." He glanced back at Martha, who was laughing with the other women. "I could have chosen to take my wife to a place where I could avoid risk and teach the law beside men that have chosen the 'safe' path—that doesn't incite people in high places to wish you dead," he said, with a quick lift of his brows.

"But if we always seek to avoid risk, our lives will be of little con-sequence." He leaned toward me, his kind eyes meeting mine full-on.

"However, that doesn't mean I do not fear for my wife. And my-self, for that matter. I do. But I try to trust Yahweh with my fears. He understands, Obadiah. Your life has been of great consequence be-cause you have risked it for me, and for Martha"—he waved toward the group at the other end of the cave—"and for them.

"Do you remember when Elijah went before the king and declared that there would be no more rain or dew upon the earth until he com-manded it? Yahweh spoke to him and told him to go and hide by the brook Cherith. He said there Elijah would drink from the brook, and ravens would come to feed him. You are our raven, Obadiah." His eyes glistened.

"When we would have surely died at the hand of the queen, you brought us, and so many more, to safety. And at great risk to yourself you have fed us, provided water. Yahweh chose you to protect His people. That you do it in spite of your fears is all the more courageous."

My eyes stung with the tears I was blinking back. I was ashamed that I had complained. *Yahweh, forgive me for my selfishness.*

"Yahweh will not forget your faithfulness to His servants. Perhaps it is Anna's destiny also—to risk herself for the safety of another. And perhaps not. But we all must trust Yahweh, whatever our duty demands."

I pulled in a deep breath. Was I trying to protect Anna from danger, to her detriment?

The sound of spilling rock cut through my thoughts. I put my finger to my lips and drew my sword, waving at Jonathan, who grabbed his staff and motioned for the group to gather their things and retreat to their hiding places in one of the tunnels. I had been followed! I didn't breathe for several long moments. What should I do? Hide with the others? No. If someone had seen me enter the cave, they would look for me and the others would be found. I had to stay where I was. My mind was whirling with thoughts of what I was going to say if it was Jezebel's soldiers. What story could I concoct that would account for my being alone in a cave?

I could say I had sensed I was being followed as I was riding about the countryside and ducked into a cave because rumor had it that the King of Syria was sending soldiers to spy out the land in preparation for war. That was true. They would probably believe my story. But had they seen me with the bread? That would be harder to explain. I gripped the hilt of my sword tighter. If I had to fight, I'd give it my best, but I was certain to end up dead in the process. The brush door I had carefully replaced fell away. Someone was entering the cave. My heart battered my rib cage.

What? "Anna?" I tried to blink the disbelief out of my eyes. I had given her strict instructions not to come to the cave again! "What are you doing here?"

"What do you *think* I'm doing?" she said, setting a large bag of bread on the limestone floor.

"I told you not to come anymore," I said, trying, but failing, to temper my tone.

"And you two!" Zim, my best friend, and Joel—who was the oldest of Anna's brothers—lowered an amphora of water to the stone floor, their eyes glued to my drawn sword.

"And what do you plan to do with that thing?" Joel said, pointing to the sword. "Pick my teeth?"

Heat flooded my face. I let out a breath and slid the sword into its sheath. Anna was looking at me like she could easily rip the skin off my body.

"One of you was supposed to come tomorrow! Too many at a time is dangerous. Why are you here, and why did you bring her?"

"I came with him," Zim said, pointing at Joel, who swatted away his finger. "Ouch! Why did you do that?"

"I will come when I feel the need, Obadiah. With your permission or without it!"

I lowered my head. "Anna, I just ..." How could I begrudge the extra bread that Anna brought? But I didn't want her to be here.

"Just what, Obe?" she said, standing as tall as she could but still forced to look up at me. "I know you think you are protecting me. But you have forgotten something! I am not yours to protect since I am still in my father's house. Still in my father's house, Obadiah!" Her wide green eyes sizzled with anger, a touch of pain in their depths. I felt foolish and petty, and I took her meaning. There was no betrothal contract that gave me the right to tell her anything. But what about the love she must know I felt for her? Did that mean nothing?

"Welcome. Welcome." Jonathan emerged and moved to greet the guests, giving me a kind look that said I should be quiet if I knew what was best for me. Jonathan kissed Anna's forehead. Color bloomed in her cheeks. Could a woman be more beautiful? She looked at me, and the stony veil fell back over her countenance.

Jonathan greeted Joel and Zim, thanking them for the water and inviting them to share some of the bread Anna had brought. "Thank you, but that bread is for you and the others," Joel said, embracing the older man. "I'm sorry to rush, but Obadiah is right. There are too many of us; we really shouldn't tarry." He turned to me, a smug turn of a smile on his handsome face. "Would you like to share a horse? Or do you want to walk all the way back to the creek bed where you left yours? If you're going to hide your horse, you really must find a better place, Obe." I gave him a stare that promised we would be talking about this later. Joel was my most valued friend after Zim, who would definitely hear more about this tomorrow.

I turned to Jonathan. "Blessings, brother. I will see you soon."

"Yes. We will continue our conversation then." He laughed, looking at Anna and the two men standing behind her. "I think it would be profitable."

Anna's brow slid into that deep line that divided it. She knew we had been talking about her. Now I would have more to explain.

I wanted to ride with Anna. Tuck her in front of me and let her lean on my chest, but I pulled myself up behind Joel. He was laughing beneath his breath. I could knock that laugh out of him.

"Just wait," I whispered. "I'll get the last laugh, you oaf."

I couldn't get Anna's eyes out of my mind as we rode. I was causing the woman I loved pain. I couldn't go on like this.

∞∞∞∞∞∞∞∞∞∞

Man

The man stepped back into the shadow of the wide oak trees where he'd been waiting for Obadiah to return. He'd followed the governor from the palace, a good distance behind. Obadiah had seemed in an awful hurry, looking back over his shoulder every little bit, like he hadn't wanted anyone seeing where he was going. The man had seen him lead that gray mare of his behind a thicket of small trees by the creek bed and take off on foot with a big sack over his back. Then he'd just disappeared.

The man knew Obadiah would have to come back for the mare. But he didn't know the governor would have company. He didn't recognize the men. He'd seen the girl. But where? She would be hard to forget. Obadiah was definitely up to something. He would find out exactly what, and then maybe Jezebel would set her sights on an easier target than that slippery fish she had sent him to catch.

CHAPTER TWO

Jezebel

What do you mean you couldn't find him? What good are you to me if you can't find one damnable prophet! Elijah is just a man. Not a god. It shouldn't be that difficult!"

The man was too stupid to be afraid. He just stood there, in Jezebel's private chambers, with its ivory inlaid chairs and Egyptian tapestries, his feet planted on the finely woven wool carpet without even the humility to feel out of place or worried that he had not accomplished the mission given to him. The queen wouldn't have been surprised if he had plopped down on the divan and put his feet up on the fur-covered stool. Of course, *he* would have been surprised if he had taken such a liberty.

Jezebel could barely endure the sight of the man. His flaccid jowls hung like empty saddlebags astride his pockmarked face. His smug smile made her want to slap it off of him. Why she'd commissioned this fool to find Elijah was beyond her comprehension now.

Her husband had sent messengers to all the surrounding cities, admonishing that none should harbor the prophet, and if any knew his whereabouts and did not divulge it, it would not be to their benefit—to say the least.

Jezebel had hired the imbecile because she thought going through less official channels might yield a quicker catch, but so far the idiot had not shown the adeptness of a blind man tracking a rat in a cave. It was Elijah who had brought on this dratted drought. But the mad prophet blamed it all on her.

Ahab should have seized the slimy fish while he had him, but he was too cowardly to do it overtly. Living with a coward could be exhausting.

The queen's gaze slid toward the eunuch standing at full attention by the entrance to her rooms from the hall. His intelligent brown eyes assured her he was listening for any indication she wanted the man dispatched. He lacked certain members that could make him a threat to Jezebel's privacy. A tongue for one. And he didn't hesitate on the rare occasions when she needed his large hands to wring a neck.

"The prophet's a ghost, my queen. It's rumored that he disappears in one place and appears in another." He shrugged. "How does one follow such a man? It is not possible. But I wouldn't worry, Your Highness," he said with such condescension it made Jezebel's shoulders stiffen beneath her royal robe. "I don't think the prophet will be bothering you anytime soon. He's probably all the way back to Tishbe by now."

Her brows rose. "Worry? You are the one who should worry! I don't long keep people in my employ who can't perform their duties." *And if you leave my employ, it will not be to find work elsewhere.* If the tiresome dupe wanted to keep his head attached to his skinny shoulders, he had better do what she commanded. She wanted Elijah dead. And the sooner the better.

"Your Highness, I will do my best, but we are on the cusp of war, and traversing the countryside can be dangerous. Benhadad would as soon slit the throat of a citizen as a soldier. It isn't safe."

"Benhadad is nowhere near the Jezreel Valley. It is rumor you hear. *And the king of Syria will be the least of your problems if you attempt to manipulate me.*

The man took a step back as though he heard her thoughts. Or did she speak them aloud? No matter. She was getting his attention.

"But ... uh, I have another bit of information that might interest the queen."

And he had not mentioned it straightaway? If he was playing a game, he had chosen the wrong partner.

"Well?"

"A few days past, while I was, uh ... looking for Elijah, I happened to see Obadiah riding away from the palace, in quite a hurry."

Obadiah. Now there was another thorn in Jezebel's flesh.

"And what is so strange about the palace governor taking a ride?"

she said, concealing her curiosity. Obadiah was up to something. She was certain of that. She suspected that he had warned off dozens of Israel's prophets when she'd set a trap to do away with the pests. She wanted them eradicated. They and their illusory leader, Elijah, were always speaking to her husband in the name of their god, accusing him of allowing her to pollute the land with Baal worship.

Pollute! What polluted Israel was its narrow-minded bigotry. Everything had to be done to the jot and tittle of their laws. Who could even remember them all? It gave her a headache to try, there were so many. Everything was unclean to these people. In Tyre they were tolerant of others' views.

"Go on, then—what was so exceptional about this ride?" she said, flipping a hand.

The man leaned in and lowered his voice; his breath smelled like a small animal had crawled into his mouth and died. Jezebel took a step back and covered her nose with the back of her hand. He was fortunate she needed him at the moment. Men had lost their lives for breathing their foul breath in the presence of royalty.

"Well, first thing, he kept looking over his shoulder, like he didn't want to be seen doing whatever it was he was doing. But I fooled him by staying far back and out of his line of vision so he didn't notice I was following him. And he had a big bag tied onto the saddle of that gray mare of his. The one with the black mane and white spots. Now, what is the governor of the king's palace doing toting around a big bag on the back of his horse? Huh?"

Did the man expect an answer? *Spare me, whatever god is listening to this moronic buffoon.*

Something soft rubbed against the queen's leg. "Ahh. There you are, Aste, my sweet." She reached down to gather her feline companion. "I wondered where you'd gone." She ran her hand along the sleek black fur of the gift her father had sent at the birth of her second son. Her father always knew how to pick a present.

She'd named her Aste after Astherah, the moon goddess, consort of Baal-Melqart. Another female who knew how to control her man. Aste nestled into the crook of Jezebel's arm, purring her contentment as the queen scratched behind the pet's pointed ears.

"And you didn't tell me about all of this because?" she said, focusing on the fool again. He reached out as though intending to touch Aste's head. The cat hissed a warning, and the man pulled back with a start. Good thing. Jezebel would have been forced to kill him had he succeeded. Some things just could not be tolerated.

"I planned to, my queen," he said, a wary eye to Aste as he spoke. "I was ... waiting to gather more information before I bothered you with it."

No. You were holding something back to negotiate with later.

The man aspired to take Obadiah's position as governor, and Jezebel had told him that it might be a possibility, or maybe she had promised him. Who remembers such things? The prospect of putting Obadiah in his place was a pleasant one, indeed. Ahab had no sense when it came to that man.

"So what did you discover in this game of hiding and seeking? Where did Obadiah go with this big bag?"

He shrugged his boney shoulders. "Well, I don't really know. Into a cave I assumed. When I caught up, I saw he'd tried to hide his horse behind a bunch of walnut trees, but walnuts don't provide much cover in a drought, and that spotted mare's hard to miss."

"The mare. The gray mare with the white spots," the queen said, trying not to roll her eyes. The man seemed very taken by Obadiah's horse.

"And this is the whole of your story?"

He shook his head several times, his thin brows arched high over his berry-sized eyes for emphasis. "No, my queen. Not by any means. I waited for Obadiah to come back. It was a while, but when he did, he was with some other riders."

"Other riders?" The tale was getting grander, but this could be important information. "Who were they?"

"Don't know that either."

Of course not.

"The girl looked familiar. I guess they all did, but I couldn't recall where I'd seen them before."

"A girl?"

"Yes. Pretty girl. Tall. Seemed upset with Obadiah. Giving him mean looks and such."

Hmmm. Jezebel couldn't put it all together at the moment—but she was certain the information would lead to something she could use to turn Ahab against the man he treated almost like a son. Better than a son, in truth. He didn't treat his sons very well at all. Not that Jezebel minded how he treated the sons of his other wives, who were mostly housed at the Samarian palace—but her sons were little more than a mild distraction to him. That had to change before Ahab chose an heir.

"You may go now." She had to think about what this information might mean and how best to use it for her purposes.

The man didn't move to leave. He settled his weight on one foot and then the other. He wanted her to pay him? He was fortunate she didn't have the eunuch throw him over the wall of her balcony, just for the pleasure of it.

"Your reward will be substantial if this information proves useful. And, eventually, there may be a certain position open that, shall we say, fits your skills."

The man's eyes assumed a mollified gleam. He took a step back and bowed deeply, directing a quick glance at Aste as he adjusted the lapels of his robe. He might be a perfect fit for palace governor. Jezebel needed a fool that she could manipulate. And Obadiah was no fool.

"Go." She pointed to the door that led to the stairwell connecting her rooms with her private garden. Her guards would show him out as they had shown him in. They probably thought she was having a tryst. It made Jezebel laugh. She was daughter of King Ithobaal of Tyre. Her father had not negotiated her marriage to the king of Israel those years ago for her to throw it away for a moment's pleasure. Some things were better than physical union. She stroked Aste's slick coat again.

<hr />

Eunuch

The room was warm, but the eunuch dared not wipe his brow as he stood at his station. The door behind him led to a long narrow hallway, which led to a second door and a second hallway, which opened to the wide corridor that led to the portico and air that didn't smell of strong perfume and deceit. He longed for a breath of it.

Jezebel had cut out his tongue. She hadn't done the deed herself, but she had wanted a Philistine for his size and strength. The eunuch had been brought to the palace with a group of slaves, and she chose him and a couple more out of the lot. And as if a tongue wasn't enough, she had watched with a small smile while the overseer of slaves took his manhood.

The eunuch breathed in a quiet breath. She needn't have worried. If Jezebel had been the only woman in the world, the eunuch would not have touched her.

Strange how people think that because a man has no tongue he cannot hear.

CHAPTER THREE

Anna

The market was already busy as Anna set up her booth for the day. Women wrapped in long lengths of cloth over their tunics towed children or bleating goats as they moved through the crowd, baskets precariously balanced on their heads or hanging at the crooks of their arms.

She hoped for a profitable day as she arranged the new vases and a couple of double-handled cooking pots she'd brought from the store of pieces she'd recently fired and painted.

The rattle of a cart drew her gaze back to the narrow stone road that separated the potters' booths from the cloth purveyors'. The donkey pulling it came to a stubborn stop just beyond Anna's stall. The beast's master yanked the rope, his language more colorful than the folds of dyed cloth stacked neatly on the stand across from Anna's. She felt heat moving up her neck from more than the weather. Anna's father had worried that the market might not be a good place for his beloved only daughter, since her brothers had all been too busy at the vineyard to accompany her. But she had always been of an independent nature, so he had agreed at the last that a little rough language wouldn't be her undoing.

"Anna, is it you?"

A twist of dread turned in Anna's stomach when she saw the young woman standing at her booth, two little boys clinging to her skirt and a sling over her shoulder in which lay a babe no more than a quarter year.

Fadima.

Fadima was a girl Anna's age from the gatherings both families had attended—before Anna's Father had been asked to leave for accusing the teacher of compromising the law to please the congregants. The girl had been betrothed to the butcher's son, who she bragged about as though he were a warrior wielding his sword rather than a pudgy-faced boy wielding a meat cleaver. But here the girl was, married and with three children already.

"Fadima," Anna said, nodding her head in greeting.

Fadima's tacked-on smile made her look the imposter Anna knew her to be. She tipped her head to the left and then the right, reminding Anna of a hungry bird sizing up its prey before lunch.

"I hardly recognized you," Fadima said, her tinny voice coming from somewhere behind her stiff lips. "You look ... different."

Old is what she meant. The girl looked at Anna's uncovered head. "And you have not married in all this time? I thought you were to be betrothed to someone from the palace. The cook, was it?"

Anna pursed her lips, knowing that her anger was barely hiding its face from the graceless girl.

She wanted to say she was too busy plying her trade to marry, but as much as the feel of clay taking shape beneath her hands filled her with a sense of power—that she could make something into more than it had been before she touched it—she would give up her trade in a moment for a husband and children. Not just any husband. A pot would be better company than many of the men Anna had met. She wondered if Fadima had married a pot in the form of a butcher boy. She was shamed by her attitude. It tasted of sour grapes, and no one knew better than a vintner's daughter that sour grapes were not at all appealing.

Obadiah was the only man Anna wanted to marry, and he was definitely not a pot. And he would not demand she stop making pottery, so she could have her trade and a family both.

But sometimes she wondered if the man truly wanted to marry *her*. She had been certain of it for years, but more and more he seemed to hesitate, making one excuse following another for why he had to put off signing the marriage contract yet another month, another year. She believed he hadn't signed it because it must be fulfilled within the time agreed upon, and he wouldn't be able to offer any more excuses!

"Or was it the baker?" Fadima said, her voice a scratch in Anna's ears.

"No. It is the governor of the palace I'm to marry," Anna said with a stitch of smugness.

Fadima's beady eyes centered on Anna's uncovered head again. "Oh, and you are betrothed? When does the betrothal end? I hope to be invited to your wedding."

"Excuse me, young lady."

An elegant woman dressed in a finely woven robe with intricate gold stitching at the neck lifted a vase from the table. "What a lovely piece. So delicate. So thin. And the glaze. Beautiful." She turned toward Fadima. "Don't you think so, my dear?"

Fadima looked at the vase for a long moment, then shrugged, the fake smile slipping into a straight line.

"I'm sorry, Fadima, but I must take care of my customer. It was nice to see you again," Anna lied. It was not nice at all.

Fadima grabbed the hands of her two small boys and turned toward the road without a word.

"Sour little lady, isn't she?" the woman said as she watched Fadima half-drag her boys away.

Anna giggled and raised an eyebrow. "I really don't think I should comment."

The woman smiled and gingerly laid the urn on the counter, then stepped back to get a wider look. "And you are the artisan?"

"I am," Anna answered. "It is one of my favorite creations." Anna wasn't used to touting her own work, but if she was going to be a businesswoman, she was going to have to learn.

"That's amazing. At first I assumed you sold for a master craftsman." The woman's gaze settled on Anna's hands. "But you have the hands of a potter."

The heat Anna had felt earlier settled in her cheeks. That was the only thing about being a potter she didn't like. Her hands were always red and rough from the clay. She slipped them into the folds of her tunic.

"It's a compliment, my dear." The woman smiled and patted Anna's arm. "You should be proud of yourself. So few women your age do more than care for their husbands and children. Don't misunderstand. I have four wonderful daughters and a husband I love very much, although … he is often away." Sadness touched the woman's beautiful brown eyes for just a moment, and then she smiled brightly and Anna wondered if it had been her imagination. "But there is something inside me that is only satisfied by creating beautiful things," the woman said, running the flat of her center finger around the rim.

"You are an artisan then?" Anna asked.

The woman laughed. Her laugh was lovely. Like a wind chime.

"No, my dear. Not in the way you are. I have no talent for actually creating something as lovely as this vase. But I have an eye for color. For lines and curves and textures that, when put together, become a piece of art in themselves." The woman carefully placed the creation on the table. "If you will set this aside for me. I'll send a servant to fetch it tomorrow. It will be perfect for an arrangement I'm working on now."

"Don't you want to know the price?" Anna asked. The woman was wearing expensive clothing, but Anna couldn't imagine anyone not asking the price of an item they planned to purchase.

"Oh, yes. The price." The woman reached into a pocket sewn into her robe and pulled out several coins. "Would this suffice?"

Anna's tongue stuck to the roof of her mouth, but she managed to nod.

"Then I'll send my servant to pick it up in the morning."

"Thank you!" Anna said, stunned by the woman's generosity. "Oh, what is your name? You didn't say."

"I am called Lillian."

"Thank you again!"

The woman smiled and turned toward the booth of colorful fabrics Anna had compared to the man's foul language.

"The piece was worth the price. Your work gets more beautiful by the day."

Anna jumped at the sound of Obadiah's voice. She hadn't seen him approach the booth. But there he stood, with Zim beside him, his gaze intent on her, the permanent crease between his brows—etched by continual worry, in Anna's opinion!—a little softer than when she'd last seen it.

Anna was angry with her heart for beating an irregular rhythm when she saw the depth of Obadiah's dark eyes, the strong slope of his jaw, the small curve of a smile on his handsome face. She'd loved him since she was a little girl playing in her father's vineyard. But sometimes, she could ... oh, she couldn't even think of the words for it, he so exasperated her!

"Good morning, Zim," Anna said, ignoring Obadiah altogether. Zim mumbled a greeting, looking sideways at his best friend, a tease in the turn of his mouth. Obadiah shot him a chastening look and drew in a deep breath.

"Would it be possible for you to take a short walk with me? Zim can watch the booth for a few moments," Obadiah said, slapping Zim's arm a little too hard with the back of his hand. Zim rubbed it and gave his friend a sardonic smile.

The camaraderie between the two and Anna's brother Joel always made her a little wistful. She had no such female counterpart. She was her father's only daughter, and sister to three rowdy brothers—whom she loved desperately but who hadn't taken wives yet, so Anna didn't even have a sister-in-law to call a friend. And since her mother had died birthing her, she was the solitary female in the family. *Maybe that's why Obe hesitates to marry me,* she mused. Maybe she wasn't feminine enough, having been raised with boys. Or perhaps he thought she lacked beauty, which she believed was the case. Something was keeping him from signing the betrothal contract.

"I don't know. I'm rather busy right now," she said, offering what she hoped was a withering glare.

"Please, Anna. I really need to speak to you," he said, a gentle plea in his eyes. "It won't take long. I have to return to the palace soon."

Zim, who was now smiling so wide two deep dimples creased his cheeks, seemed to be enjoying his friend's uncomfortable predicament.

"I suppose I can spare a few moments," Anna said curtly, "if Zim doesn't mind."

Zim bowed his head, then wiped an errant strand of dark hair out of his eyes and slipped onto the stool. "It would be my pleasure."

"If anyone has a question, just tell them I'll be back shortly."

Zim nodded, the mischievous smile still lighting up his face. Anna tucked the coins into her sash and started walking, not waiting for Obadiah to lead the way.

The donkey had given up his stubborn streak and moved on, but the road was now filled with a small flock of bleating sheep led by a boy far shorter than the hooked staff he carried, and a young girl, a sister by the look of her, catching the dawdlers at the rear. Anna found her way around the edge of the white lumps, her chin set like the bow of a ship slipping through the sea of shoppers.

Obadiah stepped to her side. His nearness made her heart pick up its angry pace again. She matched her stride to the beat of it.

"Whoa," he said, slipping his hand through the bend of Anna's elbow. "I asked you to walk with me, not run a race."

Anna stopped in the middle of the road, letting the crowd go around her, arms stiff at her sides.

Obadiah regarded her for a long moment, his visage humbled and tender. Anna's determination to keep her ire intact began to slough away. She hated that the man could manipulate her emotions with those plaintive looks.

"I'm sorry, Anna ... for the cave. I didn't mean to react so angrily." He took her by the arm gently and resumed walking. She wanted to stay angry at him, but his touch melted her resolve.

They walked in silence for several minutes. Obadiah led her to a place behind one of the vegetable booths where a large tarpaulin offered some privacy and turned her toward him. His eyes were soft with ... something. Anna lowered her head so he couldn't see how deeply those eyes affected her. She didn't want to forgive him so easily. Let him work for it!

"Anna." He lifted her chin with two fingers, a tenderness that contradicted the strength of the man in the gentle touch of them. "I love you. You must know that. I only want to keep you safe."

Her throat thick, she could barely swallow. Was it truly that Obadiah wanted to keep her safe? There was some comfort in the thought of it, but she wanted more than safety in life. She could stay in her house and close the door to the world, and she would probably be safe. But she wouldn't be happy. *Shouldn't my happiness be as important to Obe as my safety?* More? Or was it all an excuse? She was tired of excuses.

"I was speaking to Jonathan about ... about us when you burst into the cave. About his wife," Obadiah said, rubbing his thumb along her jaw. "I asked why he brought her with him when they could be taken by Jezebel's men at any moment. He said he didn't want to leave his wife behind. He needed her, so he chose to keep her by his side." Obadiah took a breath and let out a whistle of air through his lips.

"I've been considering his words for several days, and I've decided I don't want to wait any longer. I need you, Anna. As Jonathan needs Martha. I have been irrational to let my fears rob us of a life together."

He got on one knee and grasped Anna's hands with both of his, his eyes gentle and dampened with deep emotion. "I know this is not the best of places to do this, but I don't want to wait another minute. I love you. I want you to be my wife. As soon as possible. Will you marry me? That is, of course, if your father will still give his blessing. I wouldn't blame him if he didn't, but I'm rather sure he will," he said, a muscle in his cheek tugging his mouth into a sideways grin.

Did Obadiah just say he didn't want to wait any longer? Or were Anna's ears clogged? He did. He said it … but could she believe it? Or was this another maneuver to keep her on a string like a fish you didn't want to get away but didn't want to commit to cleaning and cooking either?

Her heart began to pound, but was it for joy or for fear that this would be another empty promise? Anna wanted to believe that Obadiah loved her. No. She knew he did. And she knew there was no other woman that he would prefer above her. But did he really want to be married at all? She hadn't considered the possibility before that moment. Was his reticence to marry due to having to share a wife with his work, which he clearly loved? Was his fear about the palace more that he wouldn't be able to be a loyal servant of the king and a loyal husband at the same time? Or did he think a vintner's daughter would be an embarrassment at court?

"Anna?" The joy on Obadiah's face turned to confusion and concern. He stood to his feet, still holding her hands tight in his.

"What's wrong, Anna? I … I thought you would be happy. I'm sorry. Did I assume wrongly that you wanted to be my wife?"

She raised her gaze to his. His brow was pulled into that same deep line dividing his forehead, his eyes filled with what looked a little like fear. He did love her. He didn't want to lose her. But was that enough for him?

Anna lowered her head. "I don't know, Obe. I'm confused."

He took a step forward. "You're confused as to whether or not you want to be my wife?"

She shook her head. "No. I've always wanted to be your wife, Obe.

But have you always wanted to be my husband?" He blinked hard. "Do you really want to be married? To anyone?"

"Anna, I have wanted to be your husband since you were a little girl making mud pies."

Anna tried not to laugh. She remembered trying to feed the small round mounds of damp dirt to Obadiah when she was six or seven years old. He would pretend to eat them then toss them behind his back, but she was not to be fooled.

"You don't like my mud pies! You didn't eat them. You just threw them away," she'd said with a puckered bottom lip. He had hesitated a minute then reached for the one she was holding and shoved it in his mouth. Anna could still see the look on his face as he tried to swallow the mud pie. He ran to the stream, spat out the dirt, scooped up the water in his hands, and drank and spat again.

That could have been the moment Anna decided she wanted to be Obadiah's wife. When she got older, of course. But it had been so long in the waiting. She was having difficulty trusting that this time would be any different than the last, what? Ten times?

Anna looked at the ground, and he let go of her hands and took her by the forearms. "Anna, I know I've let you down. So many times, but I hope you can believe that not one of them was because I didn't love you, or because I didn't want to marry you. You are more important to me than my position, than anything. It's been fear that has stopped me from making you my wife, Anna. Fear that I would lose you if I brought you into the palace. And that fear was not without merit. The palace is a dangerous place, but I've determined that I won't let that fear rule me anymore." He touched her cheek. "So, one more time, Anna. Would you … please be my wife? If your father agrees, of course."

Anna didn't look at him. Did she want to take the chance that her heart would be hurt by another delay? That he would find another excuse to put the wedding off? So what were her choices? To send him away now and regret it the moment she did? Or to trust that he would follow through this time? If truth were told, she had no choice. She loved Obadiah, and she didn't want to marry anyone else—not that there were men lining up to ask for her anyway. She looked into his eyes for a long moment.

"When? When will you sign the betrothal contract, Obe?"

"Tomorrow. Tell your father that I request a meeting with him an hour before sundown for the purpose of signing the contract. Do you think he can have it prepared by then?"

"I think he's had the contract in a basket since I was twelve. Of course, it could be faded and tattered by now, since I am long past twelve," she said sarcastically.

Obadiah grinned. "Not too long past twelve."

"Eight years. Eight years past twelve, in case you don't remember how old I am. I'm reminded every time I look into the polished brass."

Obadiah threw his head back and laughed. "Anna, you are more beautiful right now than you have ever been, and that is a feat, because I thought you were the most beautiful thing I had ever seen the day you almost killed me with that mud pie."

He remembered the mud pie. She was surprised.

"There will be no time to prepare a feast."

"If that is important to you, we will wait, but we will have the grandest feast Jezreel has ever seen at our wedding. Your brothers can witness the signing in your home." He moved closer, cradling her face in his smooth hands. "Tomorrow I will sign the contract. And you know what that means. We will be married in the eyes of the Law. You will be my wife, only separable by death or divorce, and I will beg for the shortest betrothal possible. I think your father will agree."

Anna's heart filled with love for Obadiah. She had to trust that it would be different this time. She had to believe that he truly wanted to marry her and that he would not hurt her again.

"I think I could convince him if he thought otherwise." she laughed. "I love you too, Obe. I want nothing more than to be your wife. Yes, I will marry you."

A crooked grin stretched across his face. He bent and kissed her forehead, lingering for a long moment.

"I'd like to give you a proper kiss, but I will have to wait. Not long though, and I think the wait will be worth it."

"You *think* the wait will be worth it? Maybe I should change my mind right now."

"I know it will be worth it," he said with a chuckle. "I have been dreaming about it all these ... how many years did you say it has been?"

She smacked his arm.

"But I can't think about it too much, my love, without having to take a trip to the river."

Anna felt her cheeks bloom with warmth.

He whispered, his voice raw and full of promise. "Tomorrow, Anna."

Tomorrow. Anna's feet hardly touched the ground as she and Obadiah walked through the market, the back of their hands touching discreetly. He left her at the head of the path between the weavers' booths and the potters' since he had to return to the palace. She almost danced the short distance back to her own stall. As soon as it was in sight, she saw Zim, the smile gone from his face. Her heart plunged.

"I closed the curtain. I was just gone for a minute, Anna. I swear it. I had to …" His face turned a blazing red. "When I came back I found it lying on the table as you see it.

The piece the woman had purchased was scratched down the center. It had been done with a knife. This was no accident. No child's prank. Was it Fadima? Why would she do this? Why would anyone do this? Nothing else was touched. Everything was as she had left it.

"I'm so sorry, Anna. Obe will have my hide for this." She shook her head. "No need to tell him." It would just be something else to upset him. And she wouldn't let that happen right now. Not until that marriage contract was signed! Not ever, if she could get away with it.

"Don't worry, Zim. I have similar pieces at home. I'm certain the woman will be happy with one of them."

But why? Why? That was the question.

◇◇◇◇◇◇◇◇◇◇◇◇

Man

The man put down the garment he had been feigning interest in. He thought he'd recognized the girl. The daughter of Naboth, that owned the vineyard behind the palace. And she seemed to be quite attached to Ahab's governor. He couldn't help himself when he saw the skinny one leave the booth unattended. He would never think of stealing the vase. He just wanted to see Obadiah's face when he returned with the girl. Make the pompous governor worry about her a bit. But Obadiah didn't come back. Oh well. He'd soon be taking the governor's job, and he'd have plenty opportunity to mess with Obadiah's mind then.

CHAPTER FOUR

Obadiah

The steam from the roiling cauldrons hit me in the face as I walked into the wheel shop. Almost immediately I felt the sweat gathering on my brow and soaking the underarms of my garment. I would have to change my tunic before I met with the king, but I had to tell Zim about Anna and me. I had hardly slept at all the night before. But when I did, my dreams were sweet.

It was quite a process, making a wheel strong enough to pound the earth behind a pair of warhorses. The wood was boiled and bent and fitted to a mold to ensure a perfect round. Zim was one of the best wheelwrights employed by the palace. Not that he got the credit he deserved.

Zim looked up from the chariot wheel he was repairing, dark curls clinging to his forehead, a wide smile unfolding across his red face. He raised a finger to let me know that he would be with me in a minute.

The rhythmic sound of hammers meeting the metal that would become fittings and rims for the wooden wheels, and the pungent odor of treated animal hides being cut and shaped into harnesses brought back fond memories of my childhood.

Zim's father had been a palace wheelwright before him, as mine had been the palace governor. As boys, we'd spent many happy days in this shop. Zim's father made us toy chariots with miniature six-spoked wheels that we harnessed to dogs and raced through the palace grounds, causing more than a little chaos with the staff. A man could have no better friend than Zimiric ben Salmone. I couldn't wait to tell him the good news.

"Good to see you, friend," Zim said as he dragged his sleeve across his forehead and stretched, rolling his shoulders and twisting at the waist. What Zim did was hard work, but there was an art to it that brought him great satisfaction—without the stress of palace intrigue. Sometimes I envied his simple life. But at this moment I envied no one. I was blessed above all men.

"I'm going to do it," I said, sure that my smile would crack my lips, it was so wide.

"Do what?" He laughed. "It must be important if it brings you to the wheel house when the wood is boiling. You look like the fish I had for supper last night."

"Sign the marriage contract. Tonight." Just hearing my own words brought a surge of gladness to my heart.

Something indiscernible slid across Zim's eyes. The brightness that lit his face had gone gray for a flicker of a moment. Did he not approve? Of course he approved. Zim knew how much I loved Anna. He would wish only the best for me. And Anna was the best a man could hope for. She was a woman of profound faith and fearless resolve. She didn't hesitate to speak her mind no matter the consequence. An attribute I admired because I often lacked such courage myself. I didn't deserve her, but in a few hours I would sign the papers that would make her mine forever.

"Tonight?" he said, lifting his dark brows in surprise.

"Tonight." I could hardly contain the swell of joy I'd felt from the moment I'd finally put aside my fears and made the decision.

"Well, that's a surprise." He mopped his sweaty forehead again. "I was beginning to think you'd never get around to it."

"You aren't the only one." I could see Naboth's thin-lipped frown the last time I'd postponed signing the contract, and Anna's relief when I'd told her the wait was finally over. Why *had* I waited so long? I couldn't fathom an answer now.

"I can no longer let my fear of Jezebel rob me of a life with Anna, Zim. I talked to Jonathan. If he can lead about a wife in such times, I can do the same in the palace. I know how much Jezebel hates me, but I have Ahab's favor, so—as Jonathan said—the palace may be the safest place to be."

"Have you cleared it with the king?"

"No. I'm headed there now for my weekly meeting with him. I'll broach the subject then. After I change," I said, laughing and pulling the neck of my tunic to let in some air. "But he has known for a long while of my intention to take a wife. He asked me a few weeks ago what had become of my plans."

Zim walked toward me, a genuine smile sliding over his face. We embraced, further soaking my linen tunic, but I didn't care. He held me out by my forearms and gave me a little shake. "It's about time. If you'd waited any longer, I would have had to do the duty for you. Blessings to you and Anna both."

"Thank you, my brother. You can say a prayer for me that Jezebel is not taking lunch with the king today. She always gives me indigestion."

I settled onto one of the elaborately carved chairs in the anteroom, clutching the scroll I would use to give my official accounting to Ahab over our weekly luncheon. This tradition rarely adhered to any sensible notion of lunchtime; my stomach growled impatiently. However, the thought of a slip to the palace kitchens was out of the question. I needed to remain at hand. This was my only opportunity to talk to the king before my meeting with Naboth. My stomach could wait.

I lifted my fingers from the arms of the chair and wiped my hand on my robe. I despised these chairs. They were covered in the fur of exotic cats, the spoils of one of Ahab's staged hunting ventures, where the hapless creatures were driven into a corner with no hope of escape. The sport of killing such defenseless animals baffled me.

Despite the veneer of favor Ahab extended toward me, I knew all too well that he wouldn't hesitate to plunge a sword into my heart if he detected even the faintest hint of betrayal. And if word ever reached him about the cave ... he would most certainly feel betrayed.

The burdens of the past years had begun to wear me down, but I determined that such days were behind me. I was going to live my life with Anna in peace, regardless of the palace's relentless machinations. Everything would work out. My stomach twisted into a tight knot.

I rose to my feet as the towering gilded door groaned open. Beniah, one of the king's personal guards, gestured for me to enter the private dining hall. There was a heady merging of smells in the room. Spices and herbs and roasted meat mixed with the oils used to keep the wood from drying out in the warm weather. It would be a comforting odor if it were not associated with my meetings with the king.

Ahab sat at the intricately carved table, indulging in the opulent feast spread before him, framed by four grand arched windows. I imagined *his* stomach was not growling.

I put one knee to the floor and bowed, waiting for permission to rise. I knew every tile of the inlaid floor beneath me. Ahab chose not to prolong my prostration today. Occasionally he would leave me in that position for several minutes, just for the entertainment of it. But he didn't seem to be in the mood for games today.

"Come. Eat." He tore off a chunk of what looked like roasted duck. I nodded and took my seat across the table, my stomach rumbling again.

Ahab's servant set a plate of food in front of me and retreated to the corner pillar where he watched for the slightest sign the king was in need of anything. To miss Ahab's signal could cost the man much, depending on the king's mood at the moment. I watched the king's mood as well. I hoped for a good one.

Ahab dabbed his mouth with a linen napkin. He was not a peculiarly handsome man. He had the look of a mongoose, his eyebrows half circles over wide eyes, his nostrils perpetually flared above a small, narrow mouth. He lacked the ominous mien of a wicked ruler—but one should not be misled. More than once I'd seen a mongoose grapple a large snake and bring it to a quick end with its small, sharp teeth. Ahab was not to be underestimated.

"And how runs my palace since we last spoke, Obadiah? Like a finely tuned instrument, I am certain, with you as conductor. I really don't know what I would do without you. You are even more efficient than your father, God rest his soul."

A memory emerged of my father, his gentle eyes a sad shade of gray, whispering a prayer for Ahab.

The Law commanded that men honor their rulers. My father had told me at his knee that regardless if the king is honorable or not, he is nonetheless the king, and we should honor him as such. Not for the man he is but because all authority comes from God. I struggled with those words when I first took my father's place as governor, and I struggled with them still.

Ahab spoke the name of Yahweh. He was descended from faithful Abraham, claimed the Lord as his creator yet bowed his knee to the Baals in the temple he had built for them at Jezebel's insistence. What I felt in my heart for Ahab was far from honor. My father would be disappointed, I feared.

"Well?"

"All is well, my king." I unrolled the scroll on which I kept a record of palace business. "The renovation of the west stables is on schedule. I have ordered all the tapestries to be cleaned in the east wing, which will take some time. I've—"

"Enough," he said, waving a hand. "Is there anything on that scroll that I really need to know? Anyone needing to be thrown into the dungeons? Hung?"

I forced a lump down my throat. The king began to laugh. "I'm jesting, Obadiah. You would probably not tell me if there were. If there's nothing more important than tapestries, enjoy your lunch."

I ate in silence as the king prattled on about a possible threat from Benhadad, the king of Syria, waiting for the right moment to inform him about my upcoming marriage.

I hadn't finished half my plate when the king arose. "You may go, Obadiah."

No. I couldn't go. I needed to talk to him. I stood quickly. Too quickly. My head began to spin. "My king, I ... I need to tell you something ... ask you something."

"Can it wait until next week?" he said, irritation in the pinch of his brow.

No it can't. "Of course, my king. If you please. But it's a matter that will cause me some difficulty if it is not addressed today."

The king plopped back into his chair and waved a hand. "Sit. Sit."

"Yes, my king." I seated myself slowly. Praying beneath my breath that Ahab would not let his irritation taint his judgment.

"Well?" Ahab said, "what is on your mind, Obadiah? Be quick with it."

I took a deep breath. What would I do if the king refused me? I wasn't his slave. I could resign my position. But the king would be insulted, and insulting a king was seldom a prudent course of action. *God, be merciful.*

"You remember I told you some time ago that I wished to marry?"

He nodded, shifting in his seat.

"Well, I am supposed to sign the marriage contract today—this evening—and I felt it my duty to inform you first."

Ahab pounded the table, making me jump almost out of my seat.

"Wonderful! It's about time!" He rose from his high-backed chair, came around the table, and slapped my back. "You need a wife. I was about to offer you one of mine." He raised a brow. "You can still have one if you prefer."

I felt the blood draining from my head. He wouldn't? Would he?

"I'm jesting, silly boy. You must have the wedding here. You know how the queen loves weddings."

My lunch turned to a sack of stones in my stomach. I knew how Jezebel loved weddings—and funerals. A year ago one of her maids had fallen in love with a steward. The man had been caught with a fork from one of the queen's own sets of silver. Everyone expected Jezebel to have him hanged immediately, but, instead, she planned a grand wedding for them, with a band of musicians and food fit for the queen's own table. As soon as the wedding feast was over, she had the man tied to a horse and dragged along the palace drive. His body was tattered by the time he'd made the first round. Then she gave him a funeral fit for a nobleman.

The maidservant, not able to hide her grief, wept incessantly. The queen, thinking her ungrateful, had her run through with a sword and gave her a funeral just as grand. They were both buried in the graveyard reserved for royal cousins and relatives of lesser degree. No. I didn't want Jezebel to have anything to do with my wedding.

"I will discuss it with her, my king, but she's a modest girl. I rather think she will prefer something less grand."

"As you wish, Obadiah, but you will move into larger apartments. You can't take a wife into that tiny hole you stay in."

That tiny hole was a suite of two large rooms. But I dared not refuse the king's generosity again. "Thank you, my king. I'm certain my bride will be thrilled."

Of course, that wasn't true. Anna and I hoped to be allowed to live outside the palace eventually. My ancestral land was only a short distance. I paid servants to run it since I was the only living heir. But that was a request for another day. I was fortunate my announcement had gone so well.

~~~~~~~~~~

When I had backed through the tall door, I turned to see Jezebel standing a short distance away, her eyes trained on me. Something in her gaze sent shivers down my spine. A headdress I always thought resembled an upside-down bowl covered with gold leaves sat on her head, gold bands woven through her fiery-red hair. A regal blue robe hung loose over her thin frame. My heart thumped so fast, I was certain she could see it beating in my temple. I took a knee and stared at the stone floor. She moved close enough for me to see the tips of her lapis-studded shoes peeking out from her elaborate gown.

"My queen," I stammered, struggling to keep my voice steady.

"Rise, Obadiah. I was looking for you," she said in a honey-sweet voice. "There's something I want to show you."

I rose, apprehension and confusion rioting in my head. *What is this?*

"Come," she said, taking my un-offered elbow and turning down the long corridor that led to the portico where Ahab addressed the public in the courtyard below.

Jezebel had never exhibited such familiarity. Her disdain for me was undeniable, and yet here she was, her arm tucked into mine as though we were old friends taking a leisurely stroll. But we were not friends, and her proximity made my muscles draw into tight coils. She was so close I could smell her soap lying under an air of spicy musk with a touch of cardamom and cinnamon.

The guards' eyes went wide as we made our way down the long, broad hall lined with arched doorways and candles burning in gold sconces.

"We don't know each other well enough, Obadiah."

I thought I knew quite enough of her. I wished I didn't know the woman at all.

"You have my husband's favor. He extols your virtues frequently," she said brightly, squeezing my arm. "He speaks of your father's loyalty and your own. Loyalty is a quality he values." She paused, her black gaze penetrating. "A quality I value as well."

A servant girl, who occasionally liberated leftover bread from Jezebel's feasts and discreetly offered it to me or one of the few servants who knew I was harboring the prophets, emerged from one of the arched doorways, bearing a tray of half-eaten fruit.

She stood stock-still for several long moments, her mouth sagging like it had lost a screw. I willed her to retreat before Jezebel took note of her and sought her out later. She snapped her mouth closed and stepped back through the doorway. I steadied my breathing as best I could, but I feared Jezebel could feel my heart pounding.

"I'm a loyal wife, Obadiah. And my husband is loyal to me. Not for my beauty. I've never been much to look at, as I'm sure you would agree if you dared," she said with a snicker.

I felt my face flush.

"My own mother was ashamed of me. She was a beautiful woman, and she was embarrassed to have a child with such a long nose and bright-red hair. But my father—" Her tone changed. "He wasn't much of a father. Royal fathers seldom are. However, he recognized that I possessed a gift, a gift that could be exploited for his gain and mine if he could marry me off to the right man."

The conversation was taking a turn I did not like. All of this personal information. If Jezebel regretted having told it in the morning, she would have another reason to try to get rid of me. But she showed no hesitation, just prattled on like a common wife gossiping with a friend. My arm ached from the taut muscles that held it at Jezebel's disposal.

"Ahab is the ideal husband, you see. He's just weak enough to require my assistance occasionally, yet not so feeble as to be tedious. I have an aversion to tedium. In fact, I had my childhood friend fed to the crocodiles because she was dreadfully dull." She giggled.

"Watching the crocodile drag her underwater was far from dull." Her lips curved into a pout. "I did miss her, however."

Nausea churned in my stomach. What was the purpose of all this? Why was she sharing these details with me? It certainly wasn't an attempt to forge a friendship.

She looked at me thoughtfully. I tried to keep my eyes fixed on the two massive doors at the end of the corridor, but I could see her in my peripheral vision, taking my measure, the corners of her thin, red mouth curled upward.

"You are anything but dull, Obadiah," she said. "There's something intriguing about you, like layered rock. It makes one wonder what lies beneath the surface." She cocked her head to one side, looking rather like a bird assessing a worm.

"Do you like my pendant?" she said, slowing her pace. "It's quite unique."

I stole a glance at the necklace hanging around her narrow neck. Her long, thin fingers caressed it, much like one would stroke a cherished pet. The central stone was a dull white, almost gray. It appeared to be ... a bone? Lapis and emeralds encircled it, and it hung from a gold chain.

"When my mother died—or, more accurately, was murdered—I requested one of her bones. I had it fashioned into this pendant. Would you like to know why?"

I remained silent, my heart racing. She didn't wait for my response.

"It wasn't because I missed her or desired to keep a part of her close to me." She laughed, a chilling sound that scratched its way down my spine. "I wear my mother's breastbone around my neck as a reminder that I am stronger than she was."

Her eyes darkened, and her nostrils flared. "For all her condescension, she was too feeble to secure her place in my father's kingdom. He had her executed because the mere sight of her sickened him. She was too arrogant to see it coming."

If Jezebel intended to shock me, she had succeeded.

She leaned into me, her arm still linked with mine. "But I apologize for casting a pall over our pleasant conversation. Let's return to my story. The king didn't marry me for physical pleasure, Obadiah. He has many women who can provide that. However, none of them possess my unique abilities."

A bead of sweat trickled down my temple, but I dared not wipe it away.

"He married me because I can make him powerful. More powerful than any king before him."

As we neared the end of the corridor, my heart began to slam against my chest. The massive cedar doors carved in intricate design, flanked by two stone-faced soldiers, seemed suddenly hostile. Jezebel turned to me, eyes narrowed into thin slices of hatred.

"So you see, Obadiah, it doesn't matter what my husband thinks of you. It's what *I* think of you that matters."

The guards tugged at the large polished-bronze handles. The two heavy doors creaked open. Jezebel let go of my arm as we stepped outside onto the portico and through the wide arch that framed the entrance. A waft of cool air brushed my sweaty forehead.

Only a few of the king's subjects were present in the stone-paved courtyard at the bottom of the grand staircase lined with clay pots filled with blooming plants. A group of elderly men, too frail for labor or trade; a few women, one with a child turned into her skirt, a hand on the child's back and the other hand covering her own mouth—every gaze was directed behind me, just above the arch. I turned to look. Something caught my eye. Something overhead. Two shapes dangled from long ropes fastened to the bar beneath the upper-story windows, where the king's banner usually hung.

However, there was no banner now.

Two pairs of feet pointed downward, one with a sandal secured by a frayed cloth.

My eyes traced the hems of a drab gray tunic and a ruby-red robe adorned with intricate embroidery—a border of blue and vibrant yellow flowers on a meandering white vine along the ragged hem.

I didn't want to let my eyes travel upward. I didn't want to see the long ropes tightly cinched around those precious necks.

But I had no choice.

Jonathan.

Martha.

My knees gave way, and an unfamiliar guttural sound escaped my chest, rushing past my lips.

"Thank you for accompanying me, Obadiah," the queen said matter-of-factly. "Perhaps we can do it again—soon."

The flop of her shoes echoed against the unfeeling stone floor as she walked back into the palace.

I pressed my face to the ground and wept.

CHAPTER FIVE

Obadiah

Anna set a tray of bread and cheese on the table between Naboth and me, fire burning in her eyes. I didn't blame her. I had missed my meeting with Naboth the night before. I hadn't even sent word until long after the appointed hour. I had gone to the cave to see if the rest of the group had fled or if they still hid in the tunnels.

They were all there. Jonathan and Martha had sent them to their hiding places when they heard several horses approaching. By the shouts and the spilling of the rock, the couple knew it was not friend but foe that would enter the cave in a matter of a few short minutes. They set aside the brush that covered the narrow entrance and walked outside to stall the soldiers, giving the prophets and their families time to escape into the tortuous turns of the tunnels.

We wept together, arms over shuddering shoulders, a circle of grief. I led them to the other cave, where I had hidden fifty prophets until they decided to chance a return to the hills east of the Jordan River. I had to find a place for the rest somewhere further from the palace. There weren't that many, mostly families with children that had chosen to stay in the relative safety of the cave—but it wasn't safe anymore. I only prayed I wouldn't discover them hanging in the portico tomorrow.

I smiled at Anna, but I knew my smile was feeble and didn't ease the turmoil in her heart. *Anna.* I wanted to reach up and touch her cheek and tell her that I loved her more than life—but I couldn't. It would sound hollow in her ears. And in her father's.

"Thank you, Daughter." Naboth nodded, his face drawn. Anna left the room and closed the door with a *thud.* I stared at the carved-wood door as it rocked on its hinges. I had disappointed Anna again. My heart ached.

Naboth bowed his gray head and prayed the blessing of the bread, tore the barley loaf, and handed a piece to me. His hand was scarred and stained from a lifetime of tending the vines. Even before I'd fallen in love with his daughter, Naboth had welcomed me to his table alongside his own sons. Had taught me about vines and soil. Had mourned with me when my father died and prayed for me when I assumed the governance of the palace at such a young age. I admired him. I didn't want to see displeasure in his face. But how could it be otherwise?

The warm scent of yeast in the bread set my mouth watering. I didn't remember when I had eaten last. At Ahab's table I guessed. But I didn't put the bread to my lips.

Naboth laid his own piece on the clay plate and looked at me, eyes a mix of anger and sadness. "Tell me, Obadiah. What is it that you have come here to say?"

I drew a deep breath. I didn't want to say it. I knew the words would not be met with understanding from father or from daughter, and I didn't blame either.

"Naboth ... I think I may have to postpone the betrothal again."

I held the man's gaze for a long moment, watching as his jaw tightened beneath his thick beard. His head moved almost imperceptibly from side to side.

"Not again, Obadiah."

"I'm sorry Naboth. It's not what I want. It's just that—"

"No more excuses, Obadiah."

I blinked. "It's not an excuse, Naboth. I promise." The word hung heavy in the air between us. I had already broken my promise. What good was another now?

I shook my head. "I can't take Anna to the palace, Naboth. Jonathan and Martha. It ... It isn't safe. When I next meet with Ahab, I plan to ask him to let me live on my ancestral land. It's not far. I could travel between there and the palace." I raised my shoulders. "I could leave her there with servants for a few days at a time if necessary."

"And do you think Ahab would allow it?"

I sucked a breath. "I don't know. But given enough time, I believe I could convince him of it." I threw up my hands. "Or I could just quit and be done with the palace altogether." But Naboth knew as well as I that Ahab would not allow me to leave that easily.

He worked his forehead with his fingers. "Do you love my daughter, Obadiah?"

The question felt like a slap. "Yes. I love her very much. I thought you understood that, my lord."

"I do understand, Obadiah," he said, placing his palms gently on the table. "But I am a father. When my daughter feels pain, I feel pain. It has been years that she has waited for you to find a convenient time to marry her. Most young women her age have several children already."

I closed my eyes against the sorrow in Naboth's face. I loved this man. And I loved his daughter. How was it that I could love someone so much and cause them so much pain? "You must know that I would marry her at this very moment if I could be certain she would not come to harm."

Naboth leaned forward and placed his weathered hand over mine. The warmth of it comforted me. I wanted to hang on to that comfort.

"Certainty is not something given to man, Obadiah. There is risk in every part of life. I know it well."

A shadow of something that I didn't understand passed through his eyes.

"You are a good man, and I have always been grateful that you would someday be my son-in-law. I know how much my daughter loves you. She would risk worse than Jezebel to be your wife."

"But aren't you afraid for her? Living in the palace with such wickedness?"

"Yes. Of course I am afraid for her," he said, leaning back in his chair. "But she would have you. And I believe you would protect her with your own life. There are other risks. I want to see my daughter safely married before ..." He pressed his lips together, holding back something.

"Before what?"

"Never mind," he said, letting his shoulders fall with a long exhale. "I'm sorry, Obadiah, but the betrothal can be put off no longer. You must decide. If you truly think she will be in grave danger at the palace,

I will accept that. But if you want to marry my daughter, you must make a decision."

"I want to marry Anna, Naboth. I don't need to make a decision about that. I decided years ago. I'll be praying about what to do. I'll find some way to work this out, Naboth."

"No, Obadiah." Naboth's chest rose with a deep inhale of breath. He pressed his lips together and let it out through his nose. "You must decide today. Now."

What? I felt the earth begin to shift.

"You must decide now. Before you leave this room." He tapped a long finger on the table. "I must know that you are going to marry my daughter. That the betrothal period will begin today." I stared at Naboth. Surely he didn't mean I had to sign the contract at this very moment. I needed time to make arrangements. Find a solution to keep Anna safe. I felt the thread that bound me to Anna fraying beneath my grasp.

"Today? Naboth, I—"

"Today, Obadiah. It must begin today. You must make up your mind now."

I couldn't breathe. How could he expect me to make such a decision this very minute? If we just waited a little longer, maybe something would change.

"Naboth, please."

The man stood. I rose from my chair, all sense of the solidness of the floor beneath my feet gone.

"Now, Obadiah. Yes? Or no?"

He couldn't ask this of me! To say yes would be to put Anna in great peril. To say no was unthinkable.

"Naboth—" I pleaded with my eyes.

"Yes or no, son," he said, raising a palm.

My heart began to rip and tear and leak into my chest. *Yahweh! Please.* I couldn't give Anna up. I couldn't walk away from this place knowing that she would never be my wife. I couldn't do it!

But I couldn't subject her to Jezebel's diabolical whims either. I couldn't fear every day that I would see her hanging from a rafter or lying on a stone floor with her life blood pooling beneath her. I couldn't do what Jonathan did and face the possibility that she would be taken from me. Raped. Or slaughtered.

I swallowed a deep breath, my eyes locked with Naboth's for several long moments, then bent my head. "No. I can't."

Sadness swept over Naboth's sun-dried face. "I understand that you think you are doing what is best for my daughter, Obadiah." He shook his head. "Perhaps you are, but I must see her safely married. I will let it be known tomorrow that Anna is available to wed. Others have asked. I've never even considered anyone but you because I know that you fear God and you love Anna—but there will be another, who will love her and care for her. And maybe you are right, and it is better that she wed someone not under Jezebel's gaze." He took my hand in both of his and gripped it tightly. "I'm sorry, my son."

I nodded, my eyes watering. "She deserves a good man, Naboth. I'm sure you will see to that."

Naboth nodded, his face painted in sadness.

As I closed the door behind me, Anna looked up from stirring a pot of stew on the stone hearth in the kitchen area. I wanted to go to her. Take her in my arms and cry into her hair. But I couldn't do that. It would not be fair. She turned back to her stew, and I walked away.

I picked another blade from the patch of sparse grass growing next to the large rock I had been sitting on for the last hour. It had been a week since I'd left Naboth's table. Every day was worse than the day before it. Every moment I could see Anna's back to me as she stirred the stew on the stone hearth. I hardly had the strength, mental or physical, to perform my duties.

This place in a gulch behind the stables was where I used to sit as a boy when I had to think things through. I'd spent a great deal of time on this rock when my father died, Zim on the one across from me, just being there until the tears came and he scooted beside me crying himself. I had done the same for him when his father died.

The sound of footsteps slipping on the loose rocks brought my head up. Zim was coming down the hill. I blew out a long breath. Only Zim would know to look for me here. But I didn't want company at this time. I just wanted to be alone with my misery.

"Obe ... I've been looking for you," he said wiping his hands down the front of his work-stained tunic. He must have heard. I hadn't told him. Told anyone.

I motioned to the flat rock across from me. "Sit if you like. I'm not good company at the moment."

"No, I I ... don't have long. I have to get back to the wheel shop. Uh, I need to talk to you."

"Then sit. I'll get a crick in my neck looking up at you this way."

Zim sat on the rock, scratching his neck, staring at his sandals.

I rubbed my hand down my face. I hoped my eyes weren't red. I had mourned when my father died, felt sorrow and pain that threatened to choke me to death—but this was worse than mourning the dead. I couldn't have stopped the fever that burned the life from my father's body, but I could have stopped this. Was I wrong? Did I do this out of cowardice? Fear? How could I give her up? But how could I deliberately put her in danger?

"You heard?" I said to the ground beneath my feet.

"Yes."

I let out a long sigh. "I'm sorry I didn't tell you, Zim. I just ... thought that if I didn't say it aloud, maybe I could believe it wasn't true." I shook my head. "Then he has spread the word already?"

"Yes."

"I don't understand," I said, biting back tears. "I know I've put it off so many times. But he knows I love her, Zim. Why couldn't he wait? Just a little bit longer."

"Obe ..."

"I had to do it, Zim. Jonathan and Martha ... I just couldn't take the chance. Jezebel has shown herself more wicked than even I could have believed. How can a woman be so heartless, Zim?" I said, looking my brother in the eye.

He dropped his head. "I don't know." We sat in silence for a long moment.

"Obe ... I really need to tell you something." Zim's face was a blood-less shade of gray.

"What's wrong, Zim? Is it Anna? Has something happened to her?" My heart was battering my chest.

"No. Well, yes, I guess. Nothing bad. Uh, at least I don't think it's—"

Zim stood and wiped his hands on the side of his tunic again. I stood also, my heart kicking up another beat. "What is it, Zim. Tell me."

He took a long breath and fixed me with a determined gaze.

"I asked Naboth for Anna's hand, and he accepted my offer."

I furrowed my brow. I must have heard him wrong. "You did what?"

He straightened his shoulders. "You heard me, Obe. I'm going to marry Anna. I would never have tried to separate the two of you. But you gave her up. It was your choice. So I chose to follow my own heart, Obe."

I didn't think about what I did next. I just slammed a fist into Zim's jaw.

He hit the ground with a thump and a groan. His mouth was bleeding, his eyes wide as he stared up at me.

"You didn't have to do that, Obe."

"And you didn't have to jump in the moment I called it off!"

Zim pulled himself up and wiped his mouth with his hand. He looked at the blood then back at me. "If I had waited, Naboth would have given her to someone else!"

He raked the soiled hand through his hair. "I'm sorry, Obe. More sorry than you could imagine. But I love her. I've always loved her. If you'd paid the least bit of attention, you would have known that. But you didn't! You don't pay attention to anyone but yourself! You certainly don't pay attention to Anna! If you did, you could see how hurt she's been. How hard all of this waiting has been on her!"

I heaved a deep breath. Did he think I didn't care? That I didn't know it was hard on Anna?

"And how hard do you think it would be for her to be at Jezebel's mercy! You work for them too! You're putting her in danger by this! Don't you care about that?"

"I don't live in the palace. There would be no need for her to be around the queen. Jezebel doesn't know I exist. I will protect her with my life, Obe. I promise you that."

Tears brimmed in Zim's eyes. "You are my friend. I don't want to hurt you. But you chose, Obe. You chose to let her go. I didn't make you do that. Nobody made you do that. It was your choice, and I know you did it because you love her. But I chose too, Obe. I chose to marry the woman I've loved since we were children. And I won't apologize for it."

I felt bereft. Angry. Abandoned. By Naboth, who couldn't see fit to give me at least a few more days. A week. To try to figure things out. And now by Zim. Why would he even think of asking for Anna, knowing how much pain it would cause me? Wasn't there some sort of code of brotherhood that forbade it?

I bit my lip. "Just go, Zim."

Grief washed over his face. "I'm sorry, Obe. I truly am."

I watched Zim as he trudged up the hill toward the wheel house. I was deeply ashamed of myself. Intensely angry that I could be so selfish. A better man would be happy that Anna would have a husband as good as Zim. But I was not a better man. I could raise no feeling of gratitude that my best friend was going to marry the woman I loved. And I could not wish my brother happiness. My heart seemed to cave in on itself.

CHAPTER SIX

Kenen

"Good morning, Kenen. It is good to see you will be joining us today," Lemech said, a snit of sarcasm in his tone.

Kenen dipped his head toward the barrel of a man planted heavily on one of the stools sitting just inside the city gate, his fine linen tunic rucked to his splayed knees as he leaned toward the man sitting across from him. *Lemech, Lemech. Too much time at the table this week?* The council was going to have to provide the man a sturdier stool if he continued to expand at the present rate.

The other city officials, dressed in equally fine, but considerably smaller garments, met Kenen's eyes with a nod and continued their conversations. Snobs. He had never quite felt a part of this group, even though he'd sat among them for more than twenty years. He missed more sessions than he should, he supposed. He found the pomposity of the procedures tiring, and the people even more so.

Kenen was not born to the position as many of the men on the stools had been. His father was a middling merchant. Not without success in his trade but not with enough to gain a place of significant prestige among his peers. Something the older man must have craved since he was so intent on his son achieving the status, he devised a plan to get him there.

"You need a woman of grace and beauty—and money—if you're going to rise in politics." So by some artful maneuvers he'd arranged a marriage for Kenen with the daughter of a prominent businessman.

Lillian's father owned several herds of camels and a sizable fleet of flat-bottom boats on which Kenen's father transported his goods up the Kishon River.

"A marriage made in heaven!" his father had said when the betrothal contract was signed.

Kenen had been less than enthused about the situation, but, as it turned out, Lillian was truly a woman of grace and beauty, and he had fallen fully in love with her from the first day they wed. With her wealth and Kenen's hard work, he had risen to the position his father had desired for him, but men like Lemech had long ago disabused Kenen of the idea that politics was more than a brutal contest of who could tromp on the most heads on their way to the top. Lemech was a real head-tromper.

Kenen pushed out a long breath. He wasn't exactly proud of his own actions. And as much as he despised Lemech and the others, he'd done worse. His upward path had exacted a high price in pain from his wife. He had hurt her in unforgivable ways. He would do anything to go back and undo it all, but no one gets to do that. And he didn't deserve it anyway.

Indistinct voices floated over the stone wall: vendors and impatient donkeys both braying their discontent that the city gates were not yet open. Six armor-clad soldiers on the second-story roof of the gatehouse shouted down at the crowd to hold their peace, that the sun was barely up.

The wooden double doors were the height of six men but narrow. So when the gates finally ground open, the citizens who lived on the outskirts of the city, eager to ply their wares in the marketplace or be the first in line to purchase the best of the day's goods, pressed through with little consideration for where their donkeys stepped or who might be in front of them. *Strange how a line brings out the worst in people.*

The line thinned to a trickle of older men and women leaning hard on one leg or another to ease the pain in their aging joints and younger women with babes strapped to their breasts or backs—and behind them a man dressed in a fine but simple robe.

Naboth.

Kenen chuckled. Lemech was always unhappy when Naboth joined the group. And Kenen was always happy to see Lemech unhappy, so this could be an amusing day after all.

Naboth was an elder of the city by right of his ancestry, his father having been a nobleman of good reputation before him and a producer of the finest wine in the Jezreel Valley and beyond. The son could lay claim to both counts. But Naboth took the Law's command to have no gods before Yahweh seriously, and he had no compunction against making his opinion about the increased integration of Baal worship known. And since Lemech and much of the council walked the legendary fence on the issue, not wanting to seem intolerant or out of step with the population—or the queen—Naboth was not their favorite member.

"Forgive my tardiness." Naboth tipped his head toward Lemech, who grunted his acknowledgment of the vintner. Lemech only held the position of head elder because Naboth didn't challenge him for it. The elders of Israel were supposed to be chosen for their wisdom, leadership, and integrity, with consideration to how long they had served. Naboth outranked Lemech on all counts, especially integrity. But Lemech took the ground and no one challenged him, least of all Kenen. Let the fat man have it. Kenen had no desire to lead the group. He only sat in the council because it gave him the prestige necessary to succeed in business.

One of the younger members offered Naboth a stool and then sat on the hard ground. One never knew who or how many city fathers would sit in the council on any given day, so deference was given to the members according to age and long standing.

Naboth was of a certain age, but he was not a weak man by any means. He worked his vines, not hiring a manager like many successful vintners did. He and his sons did most of the work as Kenen understood it, hiring seasonal help when needed. Naboth made Kenen uncomfortable at times but he counted him an upright man, if a bit overzealous.

The first business of the day was to witness the transfer of land to a kinsman redeemer on behalf of a widow whose husband had died, leaving her with no son to inherit the father's land and care for her in her old age. The man's brother had abdicated his right to redeem his brother's land *and* his wife, having a wife of his own who had no desire for a beautiful young woman to share her household. A cousin next in line agreed to fulfill the duty prescribed in such cases. The brother took off his sandal and tossed it on the ground as a sign that he would not redeem the land—or the wife—and the next in line was free to do it.

Crying and angry voices turned Kenen's head toward the gate where a woman was being pulled through the opening by a furious-looking man, followed by a more subdued younger man who could pass for a brother if he wasn't one. Kenen recognized the angry man as a caravan master, hired to lead travelers and merchants eastward along the trade routes through Megiddo and Beth She'an and sometimes as far as Damascus. Kenen didn't know him personally, but judging by the fire in the man's eyes and his anger-contorted face, it was just as well that he didn't.

This looked like an adultery case. Kenen's breath slowed almost to a stop, making his head feel light and his face pulse with heat. He didn't like these cases. They almost always ended in a stoning.

The man shoved the woman, causing her to fall hard on her knees. But she was up in a moment, her colorless lips pressed into a hard line.

"She's an adulteress! I caught her in the act! I want her stoned, now!"

Sweat trickled down the sharp angles of the woman's face, but defiance purled in her narrowed eyes. "He's lying!" She slapped her chest. "I am the one who caught *him* in the act of adultery! In our own bed! He's trying to be rid of me so he can have his, his—" The woman swallowed the word that was obviously on her tongue, probably considering it would not help her case to appear vulgar before the court.

"That is a ridiculous accusation, and I have another witness!" the man said, pulling the younger man forward. "He saw her. In the bed. With another man."

The witness grayed a shade but nodded wordlessly.

"Not true! He wasn't even there, and if he had been, he would have seen his own brother beneath the blankets with someone other than his wife." She met the brother's eyes with a plea. The man ducked his head.

As the accusations flew back and forth, a knot tightened in Kenen's stomach. The accused woman's defiance clashed with the fury of her accuser, and the weight of the impending judgment ignited the air. *Why didn't I stay in my bed today?*

Lemech pulled himself up from his chair and tugged his tunic over his belly. He addressed the brother of the accuser. "You were there? You saw this woman in her husband's bed, committing an act of adultery against him?"

The brother's color had turned from white to a sickly yellow. Kenen thought the man might actually lose his morning meal.

"Well, speak up, man!"

"Yes, I ... saw her."

"Where did you see her?"

"In their ... bed."

"And what was she doing?

"She was ..." He raised his palm. "She was doing what she is accused of. I'd rather not go into the details."

"There's no need. We understand the situation. Do we not, brethren?" Lemech looked at the circle of judges. Most nodded heartily. A few did so with lowered eyes. Probably guilty of the same crime. His gaze landed on Kenen. Kenen didn't nod, averting his eyes from the man, telling himself that Lemech didn't ask him directly so he didn't have to protest against this charade. He could just stay quiet and this storm would blow over. Shame nipped at his excuse. He needed to speak up. Now.

Lemech faced the crowd that had gathered in the courtyard, straightened the edges of his robe, and spoke in that pompous voice he thought lent him an air of authority but truly just made him sound like one of the street vendors.

"This woman has been accused of adultery in the mouth of two witnesses. She shall be taken out of the city and stoned." The husband's lips twitched up in satisfaction, and he spat on the ground at his wife's feet. "And good riddance."

What? Slow down, Lemech.

"Hold, Lemech."

Kenen was relieved to hear Naboth's voice lift on the air. All eyes turned toward the vintner, who had stood, his body and his voice emitting the authority of his years as a judge on the court. Naboth stepped forward.

"I would like to speak." His voice was calm but commanding, cutting through the murmurs of the crowd.

Lemech rolled his eyes but waved a hand, granting permission.

"What if this woman speaks the truth?" Naboth continued. "We all know that false accusations are not unheard of in these matters. Should we not investigate further before condemning her to death?"

The crowd went quiet, the chatter replaced by a tension that thrummed through the air. Lemech's face darkened with irritation. "Are you suggesting we doubt the word of her husband and a witness?"

"I am suggesting we seek the truth," Naboth replied. "And that we remember the commandment against bearing false witness. Let us question the witness further and see if his story holds."

Kenen looked at Lemech. The man's gaze had hardened, his lips a thin line of impatience. He didn't like the vintner, and it showed. "We have the testimony of two witnesses, Naboth. And the woman was caught in the very act. That is sufficient under the law."

Naboth shook his head, his eyes narrowing under his heavy brows. "Is 'sufficient' enough when the woman's life is at stake? Are these witnesses impartial?" he said, spreading his hand toward the woman's accusers. "Are they beyond reproach? Forgive me, but it seems to me that one of them bears a vested interest in the outcome of this trial."

And a vested interest in someone other than his wife.

A hum of questions rippled through the crowd, heads turning toward the accused man and his supposed witness.

"The man who stands before us," Naboth continued, his voice steady despite the tension sparking in the air, "is not merely a bystander. He is a relative of the accuser. Can we truly trust his testimony, knowing the ties that bind him to the man?"

Kenen thought the vintner made a valid point, but Lemech scoffed, his disdain palpable. "We must uphold the law, Naboth. It is not our burden to chase after every small detail. The men are members of our community."

Kenen shook his head. *And the woman isn't?*

"But we must question their integrity! We cannot allow our judgments to be swayed by the biases of those who seek to manipulate the truth for their own ends. The law was not given to Moses to be used in this manner!"

The accused woman, her eyes ablaze with defiance, seized upon Naboth's words. "He speaks the truth!" she cried, her voice ringing out above the tumult. "My husband seeks to rid himself of me, not because of any sin of mine but because of his own guilt!"

A tense silence descended upon the assembly, the weight of Naboth's protest echoing in the air like a solemn dirge. But Lemech remained unmoved, his resolve unshaken. "We must uphold the Law," he repeated, his voice a grim pronouncement of finality. "Justice demands it."

Kenen could see it coming. Lemech had said the wrong thing, and Naboth was not going to let it pass. "If you are truly concerned about upholding the law, Lemech, why do you wear an amulet meant for the worship of gods strictly forbidden by it?"

Kenen couldn't believe that Naboth had openly accused Lemech of idol worship in the presence of all these witnesses. Lemech's plum-colored face contorted with hatred for the man.

"I will have no part in this." Naboth turned toward the gate. The entire assembly stood in silence, watching the vintner's back as he retreated. When he had passed through the narrow gate, Lemech commanded that the woman be held in one of the gate chambers until the "field of stones" could be prepared.

Kenen decided he would find some way to excuse himself from the spectacle. Who was he to be throwing stones at anyone?

CHAPTER SEVEN

Anna

Anna's thoughts wandered to Obadiah as they often did as she squatted before the potter's wheel, her damp hands guiding the curve of the clay. Mesmerized by the steady *whirr,* she would have conversations with him in her mind. Arguments. She'd tell him what a coward he was at heart and how much she hated him for abandoning her. And then she'd tell him how much he'd hurt her—and how much she'd loved him. Still loved him. And how much she hoped he rotted in Hades. The imaginary conversations always ended in tears.

But no more. It had been almost three months, and Anna wouldn't shed another tear, she told herself.

In a few months she would marry Zim and move into the old stone house he had repaired. Anna's father had asked him to live at the vineyard, since his own ancestral land was run by his two older brothers. Zim had chosen to become a wheelwright like his father and leave the working of the land to them. He slept in a small shed attached to the wheel shop and only went home to visit on occasion. So, of course, they would live at the vineyard. In the house where Anna was born.

The vessel on the wheel would sit on Anna's own table when she'd fired and painted it. Maybe it would hold some of the purple and yellow flowers that had defied the drought.

The betrothal period, which was most often a year, had been cut by half. Anna's father seemed in a hurry to see her wed. She thought maybe he was ill and had hidden it from her and her brothers, but he seemed well enough. Perhaps she made more of it than it truly was, but she still felt there was something that had driven his haste.

The old house was set on a rock foundation, sturdy and solid. Zim had cleared the land of undergrowth and fixed the shutters that hung sleepily over the small windows. He had never let Anna inside, although she'd begged incessantly, but she'd seen him make a lime-wash mixture to paint the aging plaster, and he'd been working on some things at the wheel shop in what time he could call his own. He'd made some shelves to hold the pots and bowls Anna had been making, and she'd seen some drawings of a table with chairs he'd sketched on a flat piece of wood. It was much grander than she would have expected for their humble home. Zim did with wood what Anna did with clay.

Anna and Zim had both turned crimson when her brothers teased about the wooden frame he'd built to keep their wool mattress off the ground. "Are you sure it's sturdy enough?" Joel had said with a sly grin. "I wouldn't want it to break at an inopportune time." Anna threw a clod of dirt at him and tramped back to the house, her ears burning with her brothers' laughter.

The thought of her upcoming wedding brought Anna both joy and pain. She would be married. She would lie with her husband and bear a child—children. But the man in her bed would not be Obadiah. And the children of her womb would not be his. Tears tried to gather in her eyes again, but she stuffed them back. The time for tears was over.

"That's going to be beautiful."

Zim's voice startled her. *No!* She pressed her clay-covered fingers to the top of her head as the pot spun into a misshapen mass. Anna stared at the blob, aggravated and disappointed as it rode the wheel to a stop.

"I'm so sorry, Anna. I shouldn't have said anything until you were finished. I was just ... caught up in the beautiful shape the piece was taking."

She pushed herself to her feet, wiped her clay-covered hands on her smock and picked what clay she could feel out of her hair. "It's all right. I'll rework it later." Of course, it would never be the same. No two pieces ever looked exactly alike, and she had been so happy with the curve.

A touch of red colored Zim's cheeks. Anna felt sorry for him. She had made him feel worse by her reaction. It was just a pot. She gave him as much of a smile as she could marshal.

Zim's boyish good looks were nothing like the solid lines of Obadiah's face. Where Obadiah had a strong, heavily bearded chin, Zim's was narrow with little more than a wisp of stubble. But Zim had laughing eyes, where Obadiah's were always shadowed by deep thoughts. He wore a perpetual frown, though it didn't make him any less handsome.

"It's alright. Really," Anna said, offering a genuine smile this time. The knot of embarrassment loosened on his visage. He smiled that wide, pleasant grin that made his face light up. His smile was warm. There was a sense of safety in it.

"Could we take a walk?" he said, gesturing toward the door. "I already asked your father, and he said not to go further than the treading floor."

That Anna's father allowed them out of his sight was a testament to his confidence in Zim. Her three brothers were a little less gracious. They loved to threaten Anna's betrothed with something she could not speak of if he treated her dishonorably in any way. Not that they really believed he would. They were all friends. Had been since they were children, but that didn't make them less protective of their only sister.

Anna nodded and pulled off the outer smock she wore when she was working with the clay, washed her hands in the basin sitting by the wheel, and picked more clay out of her hair.

Neither of them spoke as they walked down one of the rows of grapevines. Anna loved these climbing shrubs. They were not majestic like the walnut trees or the olive. But they were unequaled for the sweetness of their fruit. And her father's vines bore the best grapes in all of Jezreel. She and Zim would share a cup of his finest wine at their wedding while the words of the marriage blessing were spoken over them.

Zim's forehead took on a crease. It was obvious he had something on his mind and was looking for the courage to frame it on his tongue.

Anna wished he'd just spit it out. She wasn't one to hold back much of anything. Something her father found exacerbating at times. Something Obadiah had always admired—he'd said—since he was so slow to speak.

They passed through the vines and emerged at the rectangular treading floor cut into an outcropping of bedrock and sat on the stone ledge. The dredges of the last treading stung Anna's nose. The stone floor sloped toward a drain where the juice ran into another, smaller vat and the skins and bits of leaves left on the floor were gathered and left to rot and leach back into the ground. The odor was strong but sweet. She loved the smell. This was one of her favorite places to sit.

Zim was still struggling. Anna decided to put him out of his misery. "What is it, Zim?"

He ducked his head and drew a deep breath. "I... I have something for you. A gift."

"A gift?" He had already given her a betrothal gift. It was a beautiful chest he'd carved out of black walnut, which was far more expensive than he could afford, she was sure. That was all that was required. He needn't give her another.

"Yes, a gift—but it's not valuable," he added quickly. "Worth nothing at all in coin."

He pulled a necklace over his head and placed it in Anna's hand. It was still warm from lying next to his skin. It was just a pretty rock, gray with swirls of orange. It had been put into a pewter setting, a small loop welded to the top with a thin braided cord through it. She looked over at him, puzzled. His face was full of some deep emotion she didn't understand.

"My mother gave me the rock shortly before she died. Her health was deteriorating. We all knew she would pass soon." His throat moved. "We were walking in the garden, and she picked it off the ground. She told me to keep it, as a reminder that Yahweh was the Rock of Israel. That He was my Rock in times of trouble, and I should always trust Him to do what was best for me." He took a long, deep breath. "I would hold it at night after she died. It made me feel better. Like my mother was still close. Like Yahweh was close. When I was older I molded a setting for it and wore it around my neck. I often find myself holding on to it when I pray."

Anna turned the stone in her hand. "Zim ... I can't take this. It means too much to you."

His dark eyes glistened. "Not as much as you mean to me, Anna. I have the memory. I won't forget. But I want you to have it, even if ...."

What was he talking about?

"Even if what, Zim?"

He gulped and stared at his sandals for a long moment. "I want to set you free, Anna ... if, if that's ... what you want."

Anna's brows flew together. *Set me free?*

"These months have been the happiest of my life, but I've seen the pain in your eyes. I know you are still in love with Obe."

Heat spread up her neck.

Zim turned toward her. "I can break the betrothal. So you can be with him. I would let it be known that I found no fault with you. That you had done nothing wrong." He rubbed his forehead. "Maybe I could say I had been unfaithful, and I didn't want to spoil your bed with my sin."

Anna stood quickly and looked down at him. "Zim! You would be stoned if you did that!" *What was he thinking?*

He stood and let out a breath. "Well, maybe I could feign an illness. Say I'm dying, and I don't want to burden you with my care. I'll think of something, Anna. Something that won't cast you in a bad light. I'll take whatever blame comes. I just want you to be happy."

Anna didn't know what to say. She couldn't believe that he would even think of such a thing! Did he want to be rid of her too? She looked into his face. It was lined in places she had never seen it lined. The perpetual smile swallowed by ... what *was* this? Anger started in the clench of her fists and spread through the rest of her like a wind-whipped flame.

She leveled her narrowed gaze at him. "Zim, do you want to marry me?"

"Do I want to marry you?" He looked dumbfounded. "I've wanted to marry you since the first moment I saw you," he said, wiping that stubborn piece of hair off his forehead. "But Obe—he was so much stronger and braver. More of a man. I stood by and said nothing. I was a coward, Anna."

Anna wanted to explode. What was this man thinking? She shook her head and raised a finger.

"First of all, Obe may have been stronger, but he was not braver." She glowered into his troubled eyes. "You are not a coward, Zim." The breath went out of her. She studied the ground for a long moment, searching in the sandy soil for the words that would soothe her betrothed, but the truth was needed. The plain and simple truth. "Zim, I love Obadiah. I have loved him for as long as I can remember." Zim's throat moved as he swallowed the hurt she knew the words brought him.

"But Obadiah chose to let me go." She heaved a sigh. "I know he thought he was doing the best for me. But he didn't give me a choice. He made the choice for us both." Her eyes locked on Zim's. "He didn't trust me. He didn't trust himself. In some ways, I think he didn't even trust Yahweh. I would have gladly died at his side, like Martha died at Jonathan's. But he took that decision away from me."

Anna reached up and touched Zim's face. The stubble of his beard soft beneath her fingers.

"So I'm making another decision. One I make of my own accord. *My* decision. This is what I choose. I choose to be your wife. To give you my body and my devotion—and, if you will be patient, to give you my love. All of it. I want to be your wife, Zim, so stop this foolishness."

She put the necklace over her head and dropped it beneath her tunic where it would lie against her skin as it had Zim's. She stepped toward this man who was to be her husband. Her heart was full. She put her arms around his neck and reached up to kiss him. He leaned into her kiss, slipping his arms around her waist. Returning it with love and tenderness and passion.

"Whoa!" she pulled away, chuckling. His eyes were bright with joy. "You still have my father and brothers to answer to."

He laughed and pulled her to his chest, burying his face in her hair. "I will wait. But not so patiently, I'm afraid."

◇◇◇◇◇◇◇◇◇◇◇◇

Obadiah

I was saddling Gray when Zim came into the stable. It had been some time since my best friend had delivered the news that he was going to marry the woman I loved. We had parted poorly. I looked at his chin for signs of the blow I'd dealt him. If there had been any real damage, it had healed. I was glad. I wouldn't want to leave a scar as a reminder of that terrible day.

"Zim." I offered in acknowledgment of his presence.

"Obe."

Awkward silence filled the space between us. How do you begin a conversation when the last one was so painful?

Gray snorted a greeting, and I threw the saddle over her back and cinched it securely, wanting to escape but knowing I needed to settle some things with Zim.

"Going for a ride?" he asked.

"Yes." I drew a deep breath. "Would you like to come along?"

Zim's eyes looked at once excited and trepidatious. "Yes, I'd love that."

I motioned to the next stall. "Saddle the bay."

From the rise of the palace hilltop, we looked out toward the Jezreel Valley lying between Mounts Gilboa and Hermon on the east and Mount Carmel on the west. The valley had been a variegated blanket of greens and yellows threaded with silver streams before the drought, but the drought had dried it into drab shades of brown, splotches of gray, and bits of faded green here and there.

The sense of serenity the vista had always inspired belied the history of the wide depression. More blood had been spilled in the Jezreel Valley than any place in Israel. King Saul had fought and lost to the Philistines here. Jael had a put a tent peg through Sisera's head, fulfilling the words of Deborah, a female judge of Israel, that the battle would be won at the hand of a woman because the men had refused to lead. Whoever thought that Israel's women were weaklings hadn't known Jael or Deborah. Or Anna. Deborah would have nothing on Anna if Anna were forced into such a role. *Lord, how I miss her.*

Gray pawed the ground, her ears pointing forward, her tail swishing happily from side to side. It had been far too long since I'd ridden her. I put my foot in the stirrup and pulled myself up.

"The creek?" I asked.

A huge smile spread over Zim's face. "Of course."

As children Zim and I had spent many an afternoon sitting on the grassy shore of one of the myriad creeks that ran from Mount Gilboa to the north into the Kishon River. Our mothers had both died in childbirth. Zim had two, much older brothers, Eber and Nathor, who were born of a different mother who had died of a fever when the boys were approaching manhood. The brothers worked the family's land, a good distance from the palace. They were good men, and Zim loved them, but they were far removed from his daily life, whereas Zim and I had spent almost every day of our boyhood together.

Many of the women of our acquaintance had offered to take over our guardianship while our fathers worked. Almost all of them with a thought to becoming a more permanent part of our families. But to the women's dismay, neither of the men was looking for a new wife, and both were satisfied that when we were together we would take care of one another.

When we were away from the city gates, I gave Zim a warning smile and kicked the mare into a gallop just as Zim let out a hearty, "Hah!" and did the same. There were three sounds that set my senses soaring when I rode at a gallop: the rhythmic drubbing of hooves hitting the ground, the huff of the horse's heavy breathing, and the haunting sound of displaced air whistling by, pulling at my tunic, smoothing my hair back with an invisible hand. It was like floating as I stood in my stirrups, leaning low over Gray's neck, just close enough to feel the gentle rise and fall of her gait without disturbing it.

I was leading when we approached the big stump that was our marker. I dug my heels into Gray and cleared the stump by half a length. Zim slithered around it, a short distance behind. We were out of breath, but we were laughing. A deep, hearty laugh that comes from doing something satisfying with someone you care about. And I did care about Zim. Nothing could keep me from it. Not even the ache in my heart for Anna.

Still grinning, we threw the reins over a dry branch and walked to the shore. The drought had changed our favorite spot. The water was so low there would be no swimming, and the grass was mostly parched with a few thin patches of green at the creek's edge. But we were used to the damage the drought had done to the normally fertile Jezreel Valley. Our memories could fill in the missing fishing poles and the stippled flesh from the first dive into the cold water.

We found a pair of good-sized rocks where we used to sit with our poles of sticks and strings and dangling homemade hooks and sat, looking over the few places where the water trickled over the smooth stones and pooled in what had been the deepest part of the creek.

"I've never been able to beat you at anything." Zim laughed. When the words settled in the air between us, the smile slipped and I knew he would like to recall them. He *had* beaten me at something. The most important thing of all.

Zim dropped his gaze. "I didn't win Anna, Obe. I got her by default. I wouldn't have had a chance if you had still been in the race. She would be marrying you. Not me. I'm second best, Obe. I know that."

We sat in silence for a few long moments. I wanted to let the words stand—that Zim *was* second best, and that he *wouldn't* have had a chance with Anna if I hadn't let her go. But I couldn't. I heaved a breath and sighed it out, drawing my hands over my face and letting them drop to my lap.

"You're second to no one, Zim," I said, my shoulders slumping. "I've thought a lot about what you said that day. You were right. I *am* selfish. I don't see what's going on around me. All these years, and I didn't know that you ... that you were in love with Anna."

I raised my eyes to his. "Why didn't you tell me?"

Zim shrugged. "What good would that have done? Anna loved you. You loved her. I accepted it. What else could I do?"

He was right. What good would it have done? I wouldn't have given her up just because Zim had a crush on her. But maybe I could have been a little more considerate of his feelings. No. It was best he hadn't told me. It would have ruined our friendship, and Zim still wouldn't have been the better for it. Anna would still have chosen me. *I think.*

But maybe if she had known Zim loved her. If she'd known she had a choice ...

I sat on the rock, looking out at the dry creek bed, hoping I could find the courage to say what must be said. Once the words were out, they could not be recalled, and they were going to change things forever.

"I know you didn't want to hurt me. I know that if you hadn't asked for Anna someone else would have. Probably someone I would have hated." I curled my lip. "No, *certainly* someone I would have hated," I said with a feeble laugh. "But I can't hate you. No matter how hard I try."

I let my eyes find his and looked into them for a long minute, wanting him to understand the magnitude of what I was going to say. "But nothing can ever be the same between us. You're my brother. I love you." I tried to swallow the knot in my throat. "But everything will be different—because I will always be in love with your wife."

Speaking the words aloud was like ripping a barely formed scab off a wound. I would always love Anna.

"You won't be able to abide that. And neither will I."

Zim studied the dry ground for several moments. He had to know that I told the truth. We could never have the bond of our youth. It would be too much to bear for both of us.

"Well, that makes things a little more difficult, Obe. Because I came here to ask you something."

"What?"

He rubbed the back of his neck. "I want you to act as friend of the groom at my wedding."

What! I jumped to my feet. What was he thinking? "Don't be ridiculous. How could you ask such a thing of me? Aren't things hard enough as they are?" Why would he even think of putting me through that?

He stood, his face a plea. "I can't get married without you by my side, Obe."

I couldn't believe it! My lips pressed into a line that must have been almost as narrow as my anger-slit eyes. "Well, I guess you just won't be getting married then, because I will absolutely *not* be your friend of the groom! I've got to get back to work. Let's go."

We rode back to the palace in silence. How dare Zim even ask me to do such a thing? It was cruel. I didn't care what he said. I wasn't even going to be at that wedding, let alone as friend of the groom. He could get one of his *real* brothers to do it.

CHAPTER EIGHT

Anna

Anna missed the mother she had never known. Her father's cousin Zadah had done a mother's night-before-the-wedding duty. But it was awkward and terrifying, to tell the truth. Zadah had stuttered and stumbled through the mechanics of the marriage act and how I should not hold my breath, as it only intensified the pain.

"Try to relax, my dear. It won't last long," she'd said, patting Anna's hand. By the time she'd ended her speech, they were both as red as kindled fire and almost as warm. Anna was wondering why she had ever wanted to be a wife. Surely, it wasn't *that* disagreeable! She remembered the kiss she and Zim had shared at the treading vat and the few they'd stolen since. The warmth in her belly had been pleasant. More than pleasant. But Cousin Zadah made it sound like it was torture that awaited Anna on her marriage bed. She hoped Zadah didn't speak for every bride.

"You look nervous."

Anna turned to see Lillian standing in the threshold of the chamber, the woman who had purchased that first vase in the marketplace. She had come back for another and another after that, and one day Anna blurted out that she was getting married in a month and would Lillian come, please? Anna had few female companions, since she was raised with brothers and lived at the vineyard most of the time, and no female relatives but Zadah, who she feared would not be the attendant she had dreamed of as a young girl. Lillian said she'd be delighted, as they had become quite good friends.

"I brought some more guests." The fine lines at the corners of

Lillian's bright eyes only made her more striking. "I hope you don't mind." She motioned several young women forward and gestured as she introduced each one. "My daughters Mara, Hadassah, Miri, and Dorcas, and two of my granddaughters, Josephine, and another Anna." They all smiled the same beautiful smile. Anna's heart swelled with thankfulness.

Anna's family owned another home inside the city gates. It was a very short walk to Jezreel, but they spent most of their time at the house at the vineyard, especially during the growing season, since the vines needed to be constantly examined for blight and climbing cutworms or beetles. In the winter, when the plants were cut back and stripped bare, they would spend more time in the city, but Anna had never really made many friends, unless one wished to consider Fadima a friend, and Anna didn't. However, everyone loves an occasion. There would be many townsfolk following the groom and his men along the path from the Jezreel house to the vineyard house where Anna would be waiting, and then to the house Zim had prepared for her. But only Cousin Zadah had come to help Anna, and she seemed relieved enough to step aside.

"And we brought gifts!" the other Anna said, brown eyes sparkling.

"But first things first!" Dorcas—or was it Miri? No. Dorcas laid an ornate box on the table and pulled out a chair for Anna to sit.

Zadah had nervously helped with Anna's *mikvah* so she was both ceremonially and physically clean. The girls descended in a flurry, laying jars and bags on the table. One of the girls opened a narrow flask, and the sweet aroma of rose oil with what Anna thought was a hint of aloe and the woody scent of myrrh filled the room. It was no doubt expensive. Anna was overwhelmed by their generosity. They rubbed it on her arms and neck and her roughened potter's hands. Miri knelt and massaged her feet with it and, with a giggle, raised Anna's skirt and rubbed the concoction on her legs, then painted her toenails with henna.

Mara studied Anna's face for a long moment, the corner of her mouth pulled up in a contemplative twist, like an artist looking at a blank canvas, deciding what to create. In a few moments time she had applied a generous amount of cosmetics to Anna's face.

"Not too much?" Anna asked Lillian tentatively.

"Trust me," she said, nodding her approval. "The girls are masters of kohl and color. You look stunning."

Stunning? Anna doubted even these young women, so obviously skilled in the feminine arts, could accomplish that.

Hadassah created a web of braids at each side of Anna's head and fastened them at the back with the jeweled hairpins that had belonged to Anna's mother. She was glad that Hadasah let the rest of her hair flow to her waist. Zim would like that.

She stood, and the others wrapped an exquisite length of soft blue material with gold threads in the weave around the simple white gown Zadah had recommended to Father.

"You don't want her to look like you're made of money," she'd said.

Father had asked Anna what she wanted, and she told him the gown was perfectly fine. He had no idea what fashionable attire was for such an occasion since he paid little attention to women's clothing. He would have given Anna anything she asked, as happy as he was to see her getting married. But, without attendants, she would have had a hard time dressing anyway, so keeping her clothing simple seemed best. But now she was being attended to in a manner she would never have dreamed, and her clothing was far from simple.

Father had retrieved her mother's wedding jewelry from the wooden chest in his chamber where he kept it, along with the exquisitely embroidered *mitpahath*, the head covering her mother had worn at their wedding. When Anna was a little girl, he would allow her a peek into the chest from time to time, with the assurance that it would be hers to wear and pass down to her own daughter someday.

She ran her fingers over the gold bracelet on her arm. He had had it engraved with *Mazal Tov, my beloved Anna*, and presented it with a kiss to her forehead and a tear trickling down a crevasse of his lined face.

The girls girded Anna's waist with a beaded belt of so many colors that they melted into a shower of iridescence.

"Thank you," she said to Lillian, trying to hold back tears lest they ruin all the girls' hard work. Lillian kissed her on one cheek and then the other.

"You are most welcome, dearest. I am honored that you allowed me this pleasure."

A servant girl pushed the wooden door open. "I see the lamps! They're coming!"

Anna's stomach turned over in a quick movement that made her fear her supper would land at her feet. But no. She hadn't eaten anything since her small morning meal. And now it was too late. Her husband was coming for her. Food would have to wait. She took a few shallow breaths until her lungs let loose the air they were holding hostage. She hoped she wouldn't faint under the *chuppah,* or, worse, in her wedding bed. If she did, she would never tell Zadah. It would be added to her tale of terror if she ever attended another bride.

"Hurry," Lillian said, setting Anna's new sandals on the ground before her and steadying her as she stepped into them and slid her red-tipped toes to the end. No one had ever colored her toenails. She could hardly take her eyes off them. She picked up the delicate head covering and looked at Zadah. "Would you do the honor, Cousin?" Zadah blinked back tears, took the long veil in her hand, and pulled up a stool since she was short, and Anna was anything but. "Would you help me, please?" Zadah said to Lillian. A beam of pleasure lit Lillian's face as she took a section of the fine cloth in her hands.

The room grayed as they lowered part of the covering over Anna's head and spread the rest over her shoulders and back, letting it hang to where it almost touched the floor. She was glad that she could see through it, though faintly. The last thing she wanted was to trip and fall into a heap on the ground. Anna wasn't known for her gracefulness. And she wanted to see Zim's face. See the laughter in his smile. And her father's face, which would be damp with tears and bright with joy.

Lillian laid a garland of grapevines atop the veil and fastened it with several sparkling hairpins. The grapevines were Anna's idea. Flowers were scarce in the drought. The few sturdy wild ones that had been growing in the garden beside her house had begun to wilt under the warm sun. But the grapevines were her family's livelihood, and she was happy to honor their significance. And they were beautiful despite the dearth. Hardy plants that searched deep in the soil for their sustenance. Anna wanted to be like them. Strong and fruitful.

"Have you had anything to eat?" Lillian said.

Anna shook her head.

"Zadah, could you get Anna a small bite of bread?"

How did Lillian know she hadn't eaten? Anna was so grateful. The thought of fainting was terrifying. Zadah fetched a piece of barley bread wrapped in a cloth and gave it to Lillian, who broke off a small piece and handed it to Anna beneath the veil.

"Just a bite or two."

From a distance, a thin wave of sound seeped through the shuttered windows: cheers, shouts, women clapping and making undulating intonations with their tongues. The noise grew louder as the group grew closer, then went to a quiet murmur as a strong voice bellowed above them all. "The bridegroom cometh. Come you out to meet him."

Anna's breath caught for a long beat. The voice was Obadiah's, as she knew it would be, since he'd finally agreed to be friend of the groom. An echo of longing wormed its way into Anna's consciousness. She had loved Obe most of her life. She had always thought it would be Zim making the pronouncement, standing beside Obadiah as he waited for her to open the door and become his bride. She still couldn't take it in—that she was not marrying Obadiah today—that she was marrying his best friend instead. Anna stood straight and forced herself to take a deep breath. Yes, Obadiah's choice still hurt. She didn't know when that would end. But she had come to love Zim. Truly love him. And she would not divide that love. It belonged to Zim alone. She would always care for Obadiah. But the love was changing to the affection due a dearest friend. He was that. Obadiah. A dear, dear friend. And that was what he would remain.

<hr/>

Obadiah

So here I was, standing outside Anna's doorway with Naboth and Zim, calling her forth to become my best friend's bride. Zim had just not given up. How could he expect me to do such a thing? It was as if I had lost an arm in losing Anna, and now he wanted me to watch while he cut off the other one.

But we were brothers, just as truly as if we had come from the same womb. I was trying to be happy for him. I had come to the conclusion that if I couldn't marry Anna, I should be glad it was a man I knew and trusted. I supposed I trusted him. I trusted him as much as a man *could* trust, in the present situation.

I was certain that he would care for her as the treasure she was, so I reluctantly agreed to perform the duty of the groom's friend.

The crowd behind us erupted into shouts and joyful laughter as the door to the old stone house creaked open. I held my breath, hoping to keep my emotions under control. Her cousin Zadah was the first to appear in the doorway, dressed in the same plain robe you might see her in at the market on any given day. I pitied Anna if the old woman had been her only help on her wedding day. But, to my surprise, several women made their way through the narrow door. First: a woman of middle age, striking in an emerald-green gown, her hair pulled up in the fashion of women of means. It took a moment for me to place her. She was the woman who had purchased Anna's vase that day at the market. And younger women, all beauties, smiling and laughing, their faces glowing with excitement. I didn't know any of them, but my heart thanked them for making this day special for Anna.

My knees turned to water when I saw her in the doorway. I forced myself to breathe evenly so Zim wouldn't notice my reaction. I could hear the small gasp as he sucked air into his lungs.

She was veiled in a delicate *mitpahath* that caught the light of the torches dispersed throughout the crowd. She was an apparition, too beautiful to be real. I couldn't see her face, but I didn't have to. It was imprinted on my soul.

Anna had never thought herself beautiful. She often deprecated herself. I had never been able to understand it. She was exquisite. Tall and lissome and full of a vivacity that revived everything around her. I had always envied her mettle. She was fearless. She could never tolerate a bully, even as a child. Once she hit a boy who was tormenting his fellow with unkind words. The boy was so stunned he just stared at her, holding his hand to his cheek. For days he followed Anna around like a gangling pup, enamored with this towering creature who had put him in his place—until I caught him behind a booth one day and told him if I saw him near her again, I would tell everyone he'd been properly put down by a girl. Even then I hated competition.

Naboth went to her and enfolded her in his arms for a long moment. He kissed the top of her head and helped her into the *aperian*. I could see the sheen of tears in his eyes as four men in identical wedding garments lifted the long poles of the conveyance upon their shoulders and began carrying Anna down the wide path alongside the vines that led to the house at the end of the vineyard. Zim and I followed, then her father and her brothers, Zim's brothers, and a good portion of the city of Jezreel, it seemed. A small clutch of the city's noblemen and priests whom Naboth had often chastened for their compromise of the Law followed as close to the front of the line as they could get without supplanting the wedding party. I guessed not even their scorn for the father of the bride could keep them from making an appearance at such an occasion.

Naboth had spared no effort. Lamps burned everywhere, lighting the paths around much of the vineyard. Illuminating the large tent that stretched its corners from the end of the vines almost to the dooryard of Zim and Anna's house.

A stitch of guilt struck me. Had I accepted Zim's request earlier, I would have been there to help him prepare his home since his father was dead and his brothers too far away to do much. What kind of "friend of the groom" was I?

I hadn't eaten. I often forgot to eat these days. The succulent scent of lamb and fatted calves roasting on open pits hung in the night air. I would eat tonight. And smile. And mostly I would drink. Several tall clay jars of what I knew would be Naboth's finest wine sat solidly along the edge of the tent with a dozen men standing ready to serve it to the guests. And that would be just for tonight's feast. Six more days of this. Yes. I would definitely drink.

From the tent, men plucked the lyre and the harp and blew into flutes and other instruments. Later there would be joyful song and lively dancing, timbrels and trumpets. I grew more and more melancholy just thinking about it. I wondered if the true reason I'd yielded to Zim's begging was some senseless hope that Anna would stop the ritual and tell everyone she couldn't be Zim's wife because she still loved me.

Anna and Zim stood under the *chuppah*, ready to receive the wedding prayers and drink the covenant wine. Then they would go into the bridal chamber Zim had prepared in the house and consummate their marriage and rejoin the feast to celebrate with their guests.

From my place outside the canopy, I thought I saw her turn her veiled head ever so slightly in my direction. I was almost sure she was looking at me through the thin cloth.

Anna. I'm sorry. I was so foolish to let you go. Please don't go into that room, Anna. Don't give yourself to Zim. I love you. I wanted her to call it off and say that she would wait for me for however long it took. I hoped my eyes spoke how much I loved her. How sorry I was for hurting her—but she wasn't looking at me now. Her head was tilted toward Zim, and he was smiling down at her, his eyes full of love.

I found a place at the edge of the tent, apart from the revelers, some of whom had already had too much of Naboth's wine. He was walking toward me. I tried to rearrange my thoughts, fearing they would show on my face and Naboth would see them and reprove me. But that wasn't what happened.

"Thank you for serving as Zimiric's friend, Son. I know how difficult it must be for you."

That Naboth would still call me "Son" brought tears to the back of my eyes.

"You know I would have waited if I could have," he said, sympathy laced in his aging voice.

In truth, I didn't know why Naboth had seemed in such a hurry. A few more weeks? Months? Even a year or two. What worried Naboth so much he couldn't have been patient a while longer? There was more to it than he was telling.

"I understand why you said no, Obadiah. I know you were doing what you thought best for Anna—as was I." He clapped his hand over my shoulder. "Which one of us was right will soon be revealed, I fear."

"What do you mean, Naboth?" What was it that made Naboth so anxious to get his only daughter married?

His gaze flicked to the noblemen sitting in an honored place at a table covered with a linen cloth and heavy-laden with every sort of fruit and nut and cheese, small loaves of barley bread in woven baskets, and a large tray of spit-roasted lamb and goat, sipping their host's best wine with appreciative looks on their bearded faces.

"Never mind me," he said, "I'm just an old man rambling about nothing, Obadiah. Don't give it another thought."

But it wasn't nothing. I was certain of that. I just didn't know what it was. I looked back toward the men. What would they have to do with Naboth's rush to get his daughter married? I wanted to find out.

The music stopped. The revelers were clapping and cheering. Zim had Anna by the hand and was leading her into the house.

I bit my lip, the metallic taste of blood slick in my mouth. Suddenly I was filled with the deepest shame. Anna would be guilty of adultery if she left Zim for another man. I knew that. Why would I even entertain such folly? I was losing my tenuous hold on reality. I had made my choice, and as much as I might doubt the wisdom of it now, it was done. Anna was going into that house to willingly give her heart and her body to Zim.

She wasn't mine. She never would be.

I didn't remember how long I stared at that closed door, rummaging through memories of Zim and me as we were growing up. As soon as our daily work was done we would meet at the wheel shop and head on some adventure or another. Nothing ruffled Zim. Even when I fell into one of my darker moods, Zim was there to encourage me. I didn't know what my life would have been without him after my father died.

I felt tears fighting for the freedom to spill down my face unabashedly. Would I really cause such pain to my dearest friend? If I would, I was an unworthy friend, indeed. But Zim had always been the better friend. The better man. I could see that now.

Zim had been right when he said I didn't pay attention to anyone but myself. I'd never one time noticed how much he cared for Anna. We had always been together: Anna, Zim, and me. Zim was our chaperone. Always with us but ever the third wheel. How it must have hurt him to love Anna as he did and watch me in the position he longed for, the man she had set her affection upon.

Oh, Zim. I'm sorry, my brother. I hoped someday I could earn the loyalty he had given me so freely through the years.

Yahweh, forgive me. Help me be a better man than this.

Something moved inside me. It rose from some obscure place where it had lain hidden for too long. A resolve. A new purpose to replace the old that was so deeply rooted in selfishness. I would be a sentinel to watch over these two souls. To pray for them, that God would prosper them. To stand in the way of any who would seek to separate them or bring them harm. And when they had children, I would do the same for them. I would be their Uncle Obe and provide in any way I could for their happiness and well-being. I breathed a long sigh of relief. For the first time since I'd sat at Naboth's table and told him I would not sign the betrothal contract, I had a measure of peace.

Sometime later the door opened just a crack, and Zim laid the white cloth on the table prepared to receive it. It took a moment for my feet to get the message to move. I walked slowly to the table outside the door and collected the cloth, as was my duty as friend of the groom. The red stain, bright against the white cloth, was the seal of my determination. I walked back to where Naboth was standing and handed it to him. He received it with tears in his eyes.

"Thank you, Obadiah. Would you hold this for just a few moments? There's something I have to do."

Naboth turned toward the table where the city fathers sat enjoying their food. He squeezed my arm and walked toward them.

At that moment I included Naboth in my vow. I would guard this man's life and well-being with my own. Whoever set out to hurt him would have to deal with me.

CHAPTER NINE

Kenen

N aboth puts on quite a party," Lemech said, forking another huge bite of lamb into his mouth. Kenen nodded, sipping Naboth's exquisite wine from a clay cup. Watching Lemech eat would have spoiled Kenen's appetite if the lamb had not been so succulent. It was a beautiful evening for the occasion. The air was infused with the earthy aroma of grapevines mingled with the sweet fragrance of the olive-oil lamps swaying in the gentle breeze. From tall poles, the lamps cast a warm golden glow over the rows of vines stretching to the far end of the vineyard.

Kenen scanned the other side of the tent for his wife. She was laughing with their daughters, sitting on plump pillows, their food spread before them on a brightly colored mat. The sight warmed his heart. He was glad to see she wasn't sulking. Lillian seldom sulked, but he feared she might feel slighted since Lemech insisted the men of the council sit together without their wives. It was a common practice but not one Kenen would normally adhere to. He enjoyed his wife's company and adored the chance to spend time with their daughters. As for enjoying Lemech's company? Not so much.

He couldn't help wondering why Lemech had insisted they all come, and as a group, since the man clearly held little affection for the vintner. Naboth was a pebble in Lemech's sandal. Kenen agreed that the man *was* sometimes a source of irritation, but he was also a man of no small influence in some circles. And Lemech was a person who enjoyed being seen, and the heavens forbid that anyone assume Naboth had slighted him.

Lillian must have felt Kenen's perusal because she turned her eyes toward him. She smiled pleasantly enough, but he knew she was not happy with the seating arrangement. He would buy her a little gift in the market tomorrow. It needn't be large. It was the thought that counted in Lillian's mind. But Kenen had much more than a seating arrangement to make up for concerning his wife.

At the far end of the tent, the father of the bride seemed engaged with Obadiah, the palace administrator. *So Naboth has friends in high places.* The governor was known to have the ear of the king. Kenen had met neither administrator nor king and wasn't the sorrier for it. Ahab was not a man you wanted to be closely associated with. Or that *Kenen* wanted to be closely associated with, at least. Lemech would, no doubt, be happy to be personally acquainted with the sovereign, but the king of Israel was a man of many moods, and his wife was, well, his wife was rumored to be quick with her judgments. Kenen would not want to be the recipient of her ill temper. Better to be out of the limelight where the king and queen were concerned.

Lemech tapped Kenen's arm. "Look who is coming to pay his respects." Kenen looked back toward the place where he had seen Naboth and the palace governor in conversation. Naboth was walking toward them.

Lemech leaned back in his chair. He seemed to be of the mind that Naboth was coming to show him some special honor, but the look of concern on the governor's face as he watched the vintner's approach made Kenen think that Naboth had something else to discuss.

Naboth nodded respectfully. "Friends. It is good of you to join the celebration of my daughter's marriage."

Lemech straightened his back and nodded at their host. "How could we miss this exquisite wine, Naboth?" he said, raising a cup. "Your vintage is the best in all of Samaria and beyond."

Lemech was spreading the flattery thick. If Naboth could hear what Lemech usually spoke of him, he might not be so gracious. Lemech took another sip and set the cup on the table. "And of course we wish to share in your happiness, uh, but I'm afraid I don't know your new son-in-law. Who are his parents?"

If Lemech was trying to insult the father of the bride, he was not successful. Naboth seemed proud when he nodded at the bride and groom sitting at the main table, their heads together sharing a private word and a smile.

"Zimiric's parents are no longer living. His father was a wheelwright in the palace wheel shop, as is he. He is of the tribe of Ashur, a fine young man who I believe will make my daughter very happy."

"Oh," Lemech said, a little curl to his lip. "A wheelwright. That is certainly an important skill in these uncertain times."

"Yes, it is," Naboth said, not letting Lemech's veiled insult stir his ire. Although well-to-do, the man clearly cared little for station. His daughter's happiness seemed paramount. Kenen knew how girls could pierce a man's tough veneer and turn him into mush.

Greetings over, Naboth's face sobered.

"I'm afraid I have a favor I must ask of you, Lemech."

"A favor?"

"Yes, but a bit more than a favor, I suppose. I must insist that you remove the icon from your neck."

Kenen looked between the two men. Naboth's face showed no anger. But it was clear he meant for Lemech to comply with his demand. A glance at the other men revealed no such ornaments around their necks. They often wore ones similar to Lemech's but probably had the good sense to leave them at home. I hoped that Lemech would have the good sense to do as Naboth asked.

"Or, you may put it beneath your tunic, where it will not be seen. That way no one else will be contaminated by its presence. The sin will be yours alone."

Anger flashed over Lemech's face. He obviously dismissed the notion of being asked to remove the idol as absurd. Heat crept up Kenen's neck. Lemech was going to embarrass them all. The man didn't have a hint of humility in his rotund body.

"That is ridiculous! I will do no such thing! How dare you treat a guest in such a manner!"

Naboth bowed his head. "It pains me to do so, I assure you. I would not have my guests feel discomfort. But I cannot allow you to wear ... *that* at my daughter's wedding. You know my stand, Lemech. Why would you dishonor me by sporting an idol around your neck at such a happy occasion?"

"It is my business what I wear!" Lemech said, his chest expanding with arrogance, chin lifted in haughty defiance.

"No. I'm sorry, but it is not. It is an affront to me, but, more than that, it is an affront to Yahweh. I want you to stay, but if you will not remove it or hide it, I must ask you to leave."

Naboth turned to the rest of us. "I'm sorry for the attention this draws to you, my lords, but I cannot let this pass. Forgive me for any discomfort, and please know that you are welcome to stay."

Kenen lowered his eyes. What an imbecile Lemech was to wear such an amulet in Naboth's presence. The least he could have done was hide it beneath his clothing if he couldn't go without it for one evening. Even now. How hard would it be to just drop the thing down the neck of his robe? Kenen was getting tired of Lemech dragging him into conflicts that were not his own. He wanted to just resign his position on the court. But at what price? He would lose everything he had worked for. But Lemech was pushing him too far. One of these days Kenen would put the man in his place.

Naboth had kept his voice down, but the people near us could see something was amiss. Lemech stood, anger rising in him like a pot of bubbling stew left unattended over the open flame, its contents threatening to boil over and create a mess for the rest of us to deal with. "It was my mistake to attend the nuptials of the daughter of such a man as you. It was beneath me. Let's go, Kenen."

When Kenen didn't rise, Lemech's face contorted even further. "Now!"

Fury roiled through Kenen. Lemech had no right to demand anything of him. He wasn't the man's servant! But Kenen didn't want more of a scene. It was a wedding, and he didn't want to mar it for the bride and groom. He looked toward his wife. She was talking with some other women, unaware of the discourse. She had taken a conveyance to the bride's home. From there, she and the girls had walked with the revelers. She would expect to walk back with them. Kenen stood and nodded at Naboth. "I think it is better that we go. Thank you for the delicious meal, and the superb wine."

"I'm sorry, Kenen. I did not wish to disturb your evening. Forgive me. But I could not let this pass."

Lemech glowered at Naboth. "I am afraid you will regret this night, Naboth."

It sounded like a threat. Kenen wished that both men would just let their differences go, but neither was the kind of man to do so. Lemech walked toward the trail that would lead them out of the vineyard, Kenen and the others following. Worry stirred in Kenen's gut. Lemech's threat was not to be taken lightly. He hoped Naboth understood that.

CHAPTER TEN

Obadiah

A band of blurred light peeked through my half-opened eyes then faded to darkness as my mind slipped toward sleep again. I was almost there when the sound of my breathing lost its rhythm and stirred me. What was that noise? Was someone knocking? *Go away. Let me sleep.* The knock was louder now.

As the fog began to lift, reality descended like a sack of stones on my chest, as it had every morning since Anna and Zim's wedding, nearly four months ago. But every day the burden had gotten a stone lighter. I would never have Anna. She was Zim's. But I had accepted it, and I would do everything in my power to support them.

"Obadiah!" The voice was louder now. There *was* someone knocking.

"Obadiah! The king wants to see you. Now!"

I groaned and forced my eyes open, looking up at the gilded chandelier. It held no candles. I wouldn't put the servants through the task of lighting them and snuffing them out again like they did each day in most of the rooms in use by the king and queen. I wouldn't even be in these rooms if I'd had a choice. Or wear expensive clothing. Or—"

"Obadiah! Please!"

"I'm coming! I'm coming!" I pulled myself up and slid a tunic over my head. This was my free day. But that never kept Ahab from calling me from my bed when he pleased.

I tugged at the heavy door and looked out through bleary eyes. It was Beniah, one of Ahab's servants, his long, narrow face stretched longer by the lift of his brows and the downturn of his thin lips. The scent

83

of mint leaves and soap slipped through the open door. Ahab couldn't abide foul odors about his servants. Bad breath could send a servant to work at the latrines, where they would get their fill of unsavory scents. Which reminded me that my own breath was probably not pleasant at the moment. I opened the door wider and took a step back.

"What is it, Beniah?"

He gave a quick nod. "The king says for you to come now. Meet him in the small dining room and come dressed to ride."

Dressed to ride?

I ran my hand through my hair. It needed a wash. "Did he say where we were riding to?"

"No. Just that you should make haste."

I nodded. "Thank you. I'll dress and be right there." No hair washing or beard trimming this morning. But I would put several mint leaves in my sash. At the least, my breath would be fresh.

"Please hurry," the man implored. "He's in a terrible humor. You know what he might do to me if you tarry too long."

"Don't worry. I'll just be a few minutes."

I shut the door and hurried to the chest where my riding clothes lay neatly folded. I knew what the servant meant. Ahab often took it out on his messenger if his orders weren't obeyed immediately.

My heart was beating fast when I reached the door of the well-appointed room where Ahab sometimes took his private meals. I caught a quick breath before I knocked. The door groaned open, and the stiff-lipped guard stepped aside to let me enter. The room was a fraction of the size of the main banquet hall but big enough to feed a great many guests. The king always looked very small when he dined alone in it. Not something I would ever tell him.

He was sitting before a table spread with fruits and pastries, several varieties of cheese and meats, breads of different grains, and a silver flask of what I knew was fine wine. Every time I saw Ahab's bountiful table I thought of the prophets and their families with barely enough to keep their stomachs quiet. When the king had eaten all he wanted, the servants would gather the trays of mostly untouched food and dump them in the refuse buckets, lest the next day the king claim to recognize a piece of bread or meat he had been served the day before and accuse them of trying to poison him with spoilt food. A few servants dared to stow away some for their own use. Some hid the bread in a storage room until they could discreetly give it to me for the prophets. It was a brave thing for them to do. I prayed that they would never be caught. It troubled me that so many knew what I was doing. My secret wasn't much of a secret anymore.

I wondered if the king had felt a pang of hunger in his entire life. Not likely.

He was dressed in simple clothing. He could have been mistaken for a servant if one didn't know his face—or failed to notice that he was sitting in the king's chair, eating from the king's table. Why was he dressed this way?

I knelt on one knee. "My king."

"Rise. Rise," Ahab said, an aggravated edge in his voice. He had often told me not to waste his time with all the bowing, but once, when I took him at his word, he derided me sharply for it. So now I bowed anyway, thinking it was better to suffer from showing too much respect than from not showing enough. This *friendship* Ahab held with me was a tenuous thing, like walking across a swinging bridge with no rope and nothing to hang on to if you made a wrong step. I mostly feared Jezebel would put a word in Ahab's ear that would cause him to give me a little push. Thus far she had not succeeded, but I was not truly Ahab's friend, and I was careful to watch where I walked.

"You're late!" he said around a mouthful of bread. It seemed kings weren't taught that talking with your mouth full is not pleasant for the people forced to observe it.

"I'm sorry, my king," I said as I pulled myself from the floor. "I was sleeping soundly, and the servant had difficulty waking me." I wanted to make certain that no blame came to the man.

"Let's go," he said, wiping his mouth with a cloth and laying the half-eaten loaf on the table. I considered asking him if I might take a piece of bread with me since I'd had no time to eat but thought better of it.

The stable hand saw us coming and hurried toward the king's steed.

"No. Saddle the chestnut," Ahab said with a nod to the animal. That was strange. Ahab seldom rode anything but the big black warhorse.

I would saddle my own horse. It was early, and no one had expected the king to ride today, so there was only one attendant in the stable. I looked around for the big gray mare. "Where's my horse?"

The man looked at me quizzically. "Your friend hasn't brought her back yet."

My friend?

"What friend?" Who would borrow my horse? Zim? I didn't think so. Zim would be working. And he'd never borrowed the mare before. The stable hand paled several shades.

"Your friend. He ... said you told him he could borrow her whenever he pleased."

What?

"What's going on? I asked for the chestnut," Ahab said, his face darkening. His mood was worsening by the moment.

"Get the chestnut," I whispered. "Now. And don't ever let anyone take my horse unless you hear it directly from me." I saddled a bay and mounted as the man gave Ahab a foot up and strapped a skin of water to the saddle. He strapped another to mine and stood back, nervous that he'd been so unwise. When I returned—from where, I had no idea—I'd find out who had borrowed my horse without my permission.

When we were out of the stable, Ahab turned the chestnut in a slow circle, looking out over the thirsty valley. The lines in his forehead deepened, and the muscles bunched on the side of his face like little pouches as he clenched his jaw. "Curse you, Elijah!" Ahab spat, his voice slashing through the air like a sword. "Curse you for what you've done to us. Anyone found aiding or sheltering you will meet a fate worse than death."

A chill slid down my spine. In that moment I was reminded that no one, not even I, was safe from the fickle storm that ebbed and flowed in Ahab's head.

"The desert is to the east. No use looking that direction," he said, everything about him tight and rigid, like a coiled spring. Ahab's demeanor was making me nervous. What were we looking for?

He waved a hand. "I'll go to the north; you to the south. Check all the springs. Hopefully, we can find grass enough to save some of the horses and mules. Benhadad *will* attack. I'm certain of it. And if he does it sooner rather than later, we won't even have enough beasts to bear the supplies."

The king was right. There was water enough from the subterranean springs and deep wells near the palace to support grassy areas for the king's personal animals and water for them to drink. The same springs watered Naboth's vineyard, which was why his vines were not withered. But grass to feed the rest of the livestock was sparse, and many of the animals had died.

And the king was correct in his concern about the possibility of war. Last year's defeat of Benhadad had been a matter of miscalculation by the Syrian king. And Ahab's relationship with the leaders of the many city-states surrounding Samaria was worn thin by abdication of his power to Jezebel. They feared it was a foreign woman who truly sat on the throne in Samaria. They were not far from the truth.

But surely the king knew that every foot-span of the Jezreel Valley had been searched for such streams. And was he saying that he would go out into the countryside alone? His choice of humble clothing and a horse less recognizable than the black might disguise him from a distance, but anyone coming close enough to see his face would know him. It was a risk he should not take!

"My king, surely there is a contingent of soldiers that will accompany us? Perhaps you have already sent them ahead? Or are we to wait here for their arrival?"

Ahab's mongoose eyes locked with mine like the small, but dangerous, wide-eyed animal sizing up a snake in the grass he was ready to pounce upon.

"You are afraid, Obadiah? I never took you for a coward. But perhaps I don't know you at all," he said, his unblinking stare making my eyes itch. Ahab was in a volatile state. I should have held my thoughts, but I could not.

"It is not for myself that I fear, my king." I spoke the truth. I would be in little danger by roaming the hills of Jezreel, but there were many, even some followers of Yahweh, who would think they did Yahweh a service by terminating the man who had profaned the worship of the one true God. My father had taught me to honor the king. I was trying to do that by discouraging him from this frivolous disregard for his safety.

"I only fear that you put yourself in harm's way."

His wide eyes finally blinked, and he seemed to come out of the angry stupor that had possessed him.

"I'm not senseless. There are always eyes on the king. That you cannot see them is only a tribute to their talents. But I sometimes wonder if my greatest danger is not from those closest to me, governor."

Unease prickled the back of my neck. *Governor.* He seldom addressed me by my title. I had no doubt that Jezebel was a constant buzz in the king's ear where I was concerned. It seemed only a matter of time before she had the proof she needed to bring me to the king for judgment. A judgment that would be swift.

He turned the chestnut toward me. "Well, go on! If we've found nothing by noonday, we'll meet back here and make a note of what areas we've covered and try again tomorrow."

I bowed my head. "As you say, my king." I turned the sinewy bay toward the south, thankful to ride away from the man.

<hr/>

Sweat salted my eyes. Swiping them with the sleeve of my tunic made them sting all the more. The sun was almost at its pinnacle, and I had found nothing but sun-cracked stream beds and parched fields. I would have to turn back soon to meet the king at the stables. I hated to think what kind of mood I might find him in if he'd found nothing as well. And the mare had better be there when I returned.

Something caught my eye. There was a man on the dusty trail ahead. Probably just a lone traveler, but I touched the hilt of my sword to reassure myself it was safely in its scabbard. As the figure drew closer, I saw it was a wild bush of a man, with baked skin and long, frizzed hair. The animal skin slung over his shoulder was belted to his worn knee-length tunic, and he leaned on a tall gnarled staff.

Elijah!

I dismounted and fell to my knees, bowing my face to the dry ground. "Is it you, my lord Elijah?" I had never met him, though messages had been relayed between us from time to time through the prophets. I'd heard of his wild hair and his rugged clothing. It must be him. I could hardly believe that I would just come across the famed prophet of Israel while wandering through the countryside looking for grass. Thank Yahweh Ahab had chosen the opposite direction.

"It is I. Get up from the ground, son. Save your bowing for Yahweh and the king."

I scrambled up. Elijah was looking at me, a quizzical furrow in his brow.

"You know who I am," he said, leaning hard on his staff. "Who are you?"

I lowered my head and placed my hand over my heart in greeting. "I am Obadiah, governor of Ahab's palace, my lord."

His dark eyes lit, and the straight line of his mouth pulled into a wide smile that looked painful on his sun-baked face but unpretentious and kind. This was not how I'd pictured the fiery prophet who had stood in the presence of the king of Israel and pronounced that not a drop of rain would fall in Israel except at his word. He seemed so ... human.

"Ahh, yes." Elijah nodded. "I am happy to finally meet you. Are there still many prophets in your care?"

"Not as many as before—since Jonathan and Martha—" The familiar grief choked off my words. I wasn't certain if Elijah had known the couple, but I was certain he'd heard of their sacrifice for their fellow servants of Yahweh.

He nodded, sorrow in his rugged face. "They are sorely missed. But we can only hope to follow their example. To give your life for another is the greatest sacrifice. They will be rewarded."

Give my life for another? Could I do it if called upon? Could I give my life for Zim? For Anna? I thought I could do that. But what about someone who didn't deserve it? What about the king? Could I give my life for Ahab? We don't really know our own hearts until they're beckoned to action. I'd learned much about my heart when Zim told me he was going to marry Anna. The things he told me hurt, but they were true. And I was trying to become a better man.

"Sit with me, Obadiah." He lowered himself onto a large, smooth rock where a blue-green lizard sunned himself.

"Are you thirsty, my lord?" I pulled the water skin off the bay.

"Yes. Thank you. I just drank the last of my water. Your offer is most appreciated."

I passed him the skin and sat on the rock beside him. He took a long drink and handed it back to me.

"No. You keep it, my lord. I will be returning to the palace soon."

He nodded his thanks, but did not turn to look at me when he spoke again "And you will be seeing the king?"

Something in Elijah's words gave me pause. Did the prophet want me to take a message to the king? To even mention that I had seen Elijah and hadn't somehow apprehended him, would put a noose around my neck. I scanned the horizon, suddenly afraid that I might see Ahab leading a charge over the ridge, one of his *invisible* soldiers having seen the prophet and informed the king that his enemy was just over the hill. There was nothing but sizzling sand and gray rock, but my heart still beat wildly.

"Yes ... we are to meet at the gate. We have been looking for streams of water where there might be some grass for the horses," I said hesitantly.

Elijah took another drink and wiped his mouth on his sleeve; a small smear of blood stained the garment. His lips bled from the deep cracks. "You needn't look any further. By dusk tomorrow the ground will be soaked with rain."

Rain? My brows reached for my hairline. Did I hear the man correctly? An end to this wretched drought? I wanted to ask him how he could be certain, but if he had stopped the rain with the word of his mouth, it seemed logical that he could start it the same way. Thank Yahweh!

The prophet put his large hand on my knee. "Obadiah, I want you to find the king and tell him to come to me here."

What? My mind reeled. A shiver ran down my spine, the hair rising on my arms like little soldiers standing at attention. Ahab was already eyeing me with suspicion. And after his promise to annihilate anyone who aided or abetted the prophet? I had heard the stories of how the Spirit had transported the prophet from one place to another. If I were to tell Ahab to come with me to where Elijah awaited him, only to find the prophet gone when the king arrived, who knew what he might do in his present state of mind.

"I'm sorry, my lord, Elijah, but I ... fear to do so could ... be dangerous." *It could be more than dangerous. It could be deadly.*

"And why is that, Obadiah? I have been told that you have the king's favor. Is that not so?"

"No one has the king's favor when it comes to you, lord Elijah. There isn't a kingdom to which Ahab hasn't sent out search parties looking for you. And if they said they didn't know where you were, he made them take an oath to it or suffer his wrath in whatever way he could make their lives miserable. Just this morning he threatened death to anyone who helped you, and—" I stuttered, "Th-there are rumors that sometimes you are in one place and then ... suddenly in another. If I bring Ahab and you are gone, that would not bode well for me."

"Don't concern yourself, Obadiah. As the Lord God lives, I will surely show myself to Ahab today."

I was still afraid. I knew the prophet could see it, and it made me ashamed. I felt like a coward.

"Obadiah, don't be ashamed of your fear. No one is more afraid than I."

I furrowed my brow. "You, my lord? Surely not."

"I live in constant fear, my son. It has become my faithful bedfellow at night and my constant companion by day. Sometimes I feel like I am the only prophet left who Yahweh requires to speak to kings on His behalf, and I am the most fearful of them all."

I had a difficult time believing the truth of his words. A man who would face an angry king without as much as a sword could not be so fear-ridden as that, but he wouldn't lie to me.

"Fear and cowardice are not the same, my friend."

Did he read my thoughts?

"You are a very brave man, indeed. You have risked your life for the Lord's prophets. That you are afraid of Ahab and Jezebel is to be expected. I fear them, but I try to keep my thoughts on Yahweh. He is our strength. We have none of our own."

I nodded in agreement. I certainly had no strength I could call my own.

The prophet sighed heavily. "That Ahab has allowed his wife to openly worship Baal and built her a temple in which to do it is a most egregious sin, exceeded only by the fact he worships in it himself. It's like spitting in the face of Yahweh, yet so many of our people think nothing of praying to Him in one breath and Baal in the next. Jezebel has incited Ahab to cause Israel to sin, and our history tells us what happens when one does that. Ahab will pay a heavy price eventually, as will his wicked wife."

Tears pooled in the prophet's eyes. "I saw it—them. Like you saw Jonathan and Martha. I saw the heads of the prophets. Hundreds of them, on stakes, lining the road to the school." The tears escaped and coursed down his craggy face. My eyes flooded as well as I recalled the cries of those who had been trapped in Jezebel's snare. I didn't see them meet their end. I was leading those I could to the caves. But I'd heard the terrible tale of what happened to them.

"I walked between the two rows of tall spikes lining the road to the school, looking up at the brave faces distorted and discolored by a cruel death. Many of their eyes were still open in shock. I couldn't turn away. I looked at each one. I owed them that honor—to look with my own eyes upon the sacrifices they had made to open their mouths against evil."

He shook his head, tears coursing down his sun-beaten face.

"They will receive the reward due them, but I will never get the sight out of my mind. I often see them in my sleep and wake in a wailing lament. Hundreds of heads of men and many of their wives and children." He dragged the sleeve of his dusty tunic across his dripping nose. "Yahweh does not let such wickedness go unpunished. Jezebel will pay. As will her weakling husband."

The prophet let out a long breath. "But they will answer to Yahweh. Not to me. I am only a voice crying out against evil. I am not the sword of the Lord. That is left to others."

He pulled himself up with his staff, his chin trembling. "It is Israel that my heart is shattered for, Obadiah. How will she escape the righteous judgment of our God? His wayward children. They go limping between two opinions. How can they turn their heads at such evil and pretend they do not see?"

The question lay like heavy bricks on my back. How indeed?

CHAPTER ELEVEN

Obadiah

I allowed the bay to drop a half stride behind the chestnut for just a moment and looked behind me. The land was flat for some distance, and no soldiers were in sight. Unless Ahab's guards were *literally* invisible, no one followed. Perhaps there were no soldiers and the king just wanted a day alone, away from Jezebel. Who could blame him for that? But I would not abandon the possibility that someone followed our tracks from afar.

"You wouldn't be leading me into a trap, would you, Obadiah?"

I sucked a shallow breath. Ahab had been at the gate, waiting for me when I arrived with Elijah's message. I had been surprised that he had agreed, without protest, to allow me to lead him to the prophet. He was almost docile as the chestnut plodded beneath him. Ahab was a man of wide mood swings, as the day had already demonstrated, and I didn't want to get caught on the downside of one now, but there was something pitiable in his voice. Like he would be disappointed if I'd betrayed him. I had to admit that there was something in me that enjoyed Ahab's approval. That reveled in being the man the king trusted. As though that made me special. Ha! Special like the spider's favorite fly. What good man would want the favor of a wicked king? Elijah surely wouldn't seek such an honor.

But wasn't it possible I'd been put in my position for such a time as this? Honor the king. Isn't that what Yahweh commanded? David honored King Saul, even though the prophet Samuel had anointed David to take the crazed king's place. David could have killed Saul several times and taken the throne of Israel that was his by the word of God to

Samuel, but he didn't. And when a man came to David saying he had finished Saul off, David asked him, "Why weren't you afraid to touch God's anointed?" and promptly had the man executed. David tore his garment and mourned for Saul. God exalted David to the throne, but David had not dishonored the former king by touching the anointed of God, no matter how wicked the man was. Would I mourn Ahab's death? I didn't see how it could be so. I was not David.

"No, my king. I assure you, it is no trap."

Ahab's shoulders loosened a bit. I exhaled the breath that I'd been holding. He did trust me. But still—for some reason—that filled me with shame.

Ahab followed me to the place where Elijah waited, tall and thin, his worn staff in his hand. He hadn't been spirited away. I breathed a sigh of relief.

Ahab did nothing but stand and stare at the prophet for several long moments before he spoke. "Is it you, you troubler of Israel?"

"It is me, Ahab. But I am not the troubler of Israel. You and your father before you have that distinction."

Ahab swept a hand through the air as he looked around. "And you, yourself, have not troubled Israel? You shut up the skies and let the earth turn to useless dust! People have died from hunger, you know," he chided. "And the animals? All because you just couldn't live and let live. You had to have your way, no matter what it cost."

I could see a flicker of grief in Elijah's eyes. It was difficult to understand why the innocent suffered with the guilty. But *was* Israel truly innocent?

The prophet sighed, his eyes closing for a long moment before he spoke. "Yes. I know people have died of hunger. I weep for those who suffer. But you see, Ahab, it was not in my power to stop the suffering—it was in yours."

Ahab's head jerked back as though he had been punched. I pondered the prophet's words. What did he mean that it was in Ahab's power to stop the suffering? Elijah said that it would rain tomorrow. Was that not in his power?

Elijah moved his head from side to side. "If you had fallen on your face before Yahweh in repentance. If you had torn down the temple of Baal stone by stone and burned the remnant to the ground, forsaking

94

all gods but Yahweh. Then. Perhaps. The God of Israel would have sent His rain to water the earth again. But you did not. I cannot stop the rain or start it again, king. Only God has such power. It was only as I met Obadiah in the desert that I heard Yahweh's voice."

The skin on my arms stippled. Yahweh had spoken to Elijah in my presence, and I had not sensed it.

"He told me to speak these words to you. 'Now, therefore, gather all Israel to me at Mount Carmel, and the four hundred and fifty prophets of Baal who eat at Jezebel's table. We will see who is the God that rules the fire and the water—the God of Israel or the gods you have prostituted yourself before.'"

I didn't go with Ahab to Mount Carmel. He didn't ask and I was glad. I spent the next morning at the cave, relaying the exchange between the king and Elijah to the prophets who still sought refuge there. It would rain this day. Elijah had promised. There would be no more need for hauling water. The natural cistern in the rocks would store the precious fluid, and the prophets could drink their fill. But would it be safe yet for them to leave? I thought they should stay in the protection of the cave with their young and their old for now. I would try to secure places for them a good distance away. It was still not safe for a prophet of Yahweh to be found wandering the countryside.

When I returned to the palace, Jezebel met me at the entrance. I was surprised she was not at Carmel with Ahab. He probably made her stay back to avoid a confrontation between his wife and Elijah. If so, it was a wise choice. Jezebel would not have been silenced before such a crowd.

"Where have you been, Obadiah?"

I bowed my head. "I have been seeing to the business of the king." It wasn't truly a lie. I had been discussing the possible outcomes on Mount Carmel today.

Jezebel's eyes lit like they were not reflecting the light from the torches but a flame from within.

"I thought you would be at Mount Carmel with the rest of the Israelites, watching Lord Baal destroy your prophet friend. I heard you met

Elijah by chance on the road. What a fortuitous coincidence for you. It seems you are friends with many unsavory characters."

For some reason, Jezebel's threats didn't frighten me today. Maybe they would tomorrow. But today I felt a strength I had not felt for a long while. I stood tall as I addressed the queen of Israel.

"Yes, my queen. I know many unsavory characters. But friends?" I shrugged. "Only a few. Is there something I can do for you? If not, I must be about my duties."

Her eyes narrowed. "Yes, Obadiah. Your duties. To the king."

She turned aside and walked down the long hall to the arched door that led down a private hall to her private quarters, her head high in the air. I almost laughed aloud at the thought that scurried through my mind. Her nose was turned up so far, if it rained she might drown. And it would rain today. Elijah had promised.

It was late in the day before I smelled it in the air—rain. And then it poured as if all the rain from the last three years had been released in one instant. I walked out onto the portico, my heart filled with awe, and raised my hands and let the water splash on my face. I had avoided the portico since Jonathan and Martha had died here, but today was a victory, and in some strange way I thought I was sharing it with them. When I turned to go in, Jezebel was standing under the overhang, a menacing smile curving her red lips at the corners.

"Lord Baal has prevailed, Obadiah. He has brought rain to the realm of Ahab."

I bowed, a single shallow dip of my head. "It is true. A god has brought rain. We will soon know whose god it was."

When Ahab returned, his hair hanging in sodden strands, his robe dripping on the mosaic tiles, it was obvious whose God had brought the rain. He wore defeat like the water-logged garment on his back.

I made myself small behind one of the columns as I listened to Ahab relate the day's events to Jezebel. Elijah had poured water over the altar, yet Yahweh had brought fire from heaven to burn up the drenched sacrifice while the prophets of Baal wailed and cut themselves for nothing. Oh, how I would have loved to see it for myself. Over four hundred prophets of Baal had been destroyed.

The shriek that erupted from Jezebel's mouth sounded unearthly, like some creature from the underworld. She screamed for a scribe and a messenger to take a letter and deliver it to Elijah.

"Write it down!" she shouted. The poor scribe was shaking so hard, I thought he wouldn't be able to write and he would lose his head right in the anteroom.

"To Elijah the Tishbite, from Jezebel, queen of Israel. As you have done to the prophets of Baal, so may the gods do to me and more also if I do not make your life as the life of one of them by this time tomorrow."

The next day, I heard that Elijah had fled the land in fear of Jezebel. I didn't judge him as some did. As the prophet had told me, fear and cowardice were not the same thing. We would be hearing from Elijah again—I was certain of it. I wondered if Jezebel had not spoken a curse on herself. By her own words, she'd promised the fate of her prophets and worse would be her own. The hair rose on my arms.

<hr/>

Jezebel

It had rained steadily since the debacle at Mount Carmel. Heavy gray clouds had unburdened themselves over the royal carriage from Jezreel to Samaria. The roads were all but impassable. But the large company of soldiers that transported Jezebel to the capital knew they must defy the elements—and if necessary, the gods themselves!—if they wanted to live another day. The queen had to get to the temple and inquire of Lord Baal just where he had been when her prophets were entreating him to burn up a solitary bull! And the rain! How was it the grizzled old prophet could command it to rain, and the king of Israel had to outrun the storm in his chariot! Her blood boiled in her veins, but it didn't make her any warmer.

The carriage turned onto the stone-paved road that led to the temple. Jezebel tucked her chin into the fur collar of her robe. It was no dryer in Samaria than it had been in Jezreel. Water pooled beneath the elm trees lining both sides of the road, the trees already standing taller with their three-year thirst sated. The queen had instructed the gardeners to see that the trees were adequately watered, but she could hardly have punished them when there was no water to be had. It was Elijah she wanted to punish. And the day would come.

The crowd lining the roadway was thinner than Jezebel had seen it since the day she first rode through the Arch of Baal with Ahab. Maybe a hundred or a little more. Perhaps the cold and the damp kept most in the shelter of their homes—or perhaps it was the sound defeat at Mount Carmel. *No one likes a loser.*

To the contrary, the dedication of the temple of Baal had been a grand affair, with teeming crowds cheering and throwing flowers. A joyous occasion, except for the few narrow-minded Yahweh worshipers, and that abominable Elijah and his ragtag minions, shouting their condemnation of the temple. *The man spoils everything by his very presence on earth!* Ahab had built it so his queen could worship the principal deity of her homeland. And after much cajoling, he had worshiped there himself. And if some Israelites wanted to add Baal worship to their worship of Yahweh, Jezebel welcomed them with open arms. Baal was inclusive, not like the prophets of Israel, who thought it blasphemous to join in the worship of another god.

The queen's spirits rose with her reverie. That day the sun had shone bright and warm on the newly completed edifice, bathing the limestone in hues of gold and brown. The Arch of Baal stood on its own, detached from the temple like a bowlegged Nephilim ready to stomp out all unworthy to enter.

The Israelites had stood in long lines with their calves and their goats, eager to sacrifice at the altar of the storm god.

Of course, Jezebel knew they were not coming out of true devotion. The Israelites were ever the opportunists. All it took was convincing a few people in high places to walk the stone road. A few priests, a few noblemen, and all of Samaria trotted behind.

For most Israelites it was an economic decision. Ingratiating themselves with the higher echelon. It was not beneath their mores to visit the temple prostitutes either. Self-righteous actors! Jezebel had seen them lined up, shekels in hand—and seen them leave, their damp faces flushed with pleasure.

And the Israelites took into account that the nations around them revered Baal as the bringer of rain in its season. Why tempt fortune? They would play it safe, just in case.

Bringer of rain. Hmph! Jezebel was going into the temple that she had built for the god and confront him face to stony face about that! But, right now, she needed to turn the mood of the people following the carriage as it approached the edifice. She pounded on the door, a signal for the driver to stop.

Soldiers drew close as the Queen of Israel stood at the center of the Arch. She motioned them back. Only the Philistine eunuch stayed a step behind her should she need him, but Jezebel wanted no show of force today. The people were stupefied to see her standing in the downpour. At this point she cared little that her hair hung in sodden red strings below her headdress or that her royal robe mopped the cobbled stones.

"Go home to Tyre, harlot! We don't want you here!" snarled a man not more than five paces from the queen, his bristled chin raised in defiance. Jezebel met him with a steady gaze and made a small quelling motion for the guards to stay in their places. She would have enjoyed letting them hang him from one of the tall elms that lined the road, but that would not sit well with his comrades. She raised her hands and the crowd silenced so one could hear only the steady thrumming of rain on the smooth rocks.

"Give thanks, my people." She cupped her hands and let the water gather in her upturned palms. "Give thanks. Lord Baal has poured out rain on our land. He has stopped the drought brought upon us by the false prophet, Elijah!" *An untruth about who brought the rain but a necessary one.*

Some among the crowd turned their faces to the darkened sky and cheered, chanting "Praise to Baal, God of Thunder, who has brought rain to our land again!" But there was an angry murmur rising over the pelting as many began to shout, "Yahweh brought the rain through the prophet Elijah. The prophets of Baal could not force a drop of liquid from the sky! Yahweh is God!" they cried.

Jezebel sucked air through her flared nostrils but kept her mouth clamped shut. She would remember them. But now was not the time for retribution.

The frustrating thing was they were right. At least the part about the prophets not bringing the rain. Ahab had watched the whole thing from his chariot on the hilltop. Elijah had called down fire from heaven to consume the sacrifice. And then he sent word to the king to get off the hill because a torrent was coming. Ahab had laughed until he heard the first clap of thunder. He was nearly cut off by the flood. The prophets of Baal had stood by while Elijah called down fire and then the rain! If the people hadn't killed them, Jezebel would have done it herself.

One man grabbed another by the neck of his robe, their hooked noses almost touching. Bedlam broke loose in the drenched crowd. Men raising their fists against one another. The eunuch grabbed Jezebel's arm as the bearded man who had shouted insults moved toward her. Her feet slipped, and the soldiers pulled her through the arch and into the outer court of the temple and took their places at the entrance of the god's throne room. The queen's heart was still hammering in her ears when the guards opened the wide doors. She caught her breath and straightened her robe. The man would be in chains before nightfall and headless before morning! No one could expect the queen of Israel to let such an act go unpunished.

In the innermost chamber, candles on gold stands cast ghostly light across the walls made of large highly-polished cut stones. Despite the fire burning in the pit in front of the god, Jezebel shivered at the chill captured by her damp clothes. She would be glad to be delivered to her brazier-warmed rooms in the Samarian palace! But she had a message to deliver first.

Arches on either side of the room opened to halls that led to the priests' private quarters and rooms that not even Jezebel had been allowed to enter, not that she wanted to. Better not to know what the priests engaged in behind closed doors.

Thin whorls of smoke rose from shallow bowls of incense sitting on a stone altar. The cloying scent made her eyes itch. Did the gods actually enjoy such overpowering odors? But, of course, they didn't actually breathe the obnoxious fumes, so it mattered not to them how their worshipers suffered.

The sacrificial bull already rested on the outstretched arms of the statue of Lord Baal. Two white-robed priests began the incantations, their voices high and tinny as they chanted, entreating the god to accept the offering on the queen's behalf. They stepped aside, and the god's arms lowered until the bull rolled off them and into the fire pit below, stirring sparks and a burst of flames and sending a welcome waft of warm air Jezebel's way. Of course, everyone knew the arms were operated by unseen priests behind the statue, but the effect was impressive all the same.

The smell of singed hair hung heavy in the air of the innermost chamber until the fire made its way to the flesh of the animal and the scent of roasted meat filled the room. It made Jezebel hungry. The bull was an offering to Lord Baal, but it was the priests who would eat it.

The queen motioned the priests to leave. They backed out of the holy place with their heads bowed, leaving her alone with the mighty storm god, who sat on his bronze throne, that silly cone of a cap on his head, a pair of bull horns protruding from beneath it.

Jezebel curled her lip. *Mighty storm god.* He hadn't looked very mighty at Mount Carmel yesterday, but she bowed at the waist for a long minute. Gods could take it personally if not paid the proper respect, and she didn't want to push him *too* far. When she brought herself upright, Jezebel thought she saw a smirk on the statue's face. A reflection of the light? Of course. Bronze statues don't smirk.

"Ahem," the queen said, lifting her chin. She wouldn't grovel, even in the presence of a god. She was the queen of Israel, and she wanted the god to remember it!

"I hope you are enjoying the temple I built for you, Lord Baal." Best to remind him from the outset that he wouldn't be sitting on that throne if she had not convinced her husband to build this house for him. And did he know how many problems his house had created with the few faithful Yahweh worshipers? And what about the crowd outside that would like to see him dragged from his perch and melted down for pots?

"If I may respectfully inquire, Lord Baal," she said, raising a brow, "Where were you yesterday when four hundred and fifty of my ... *your* prophets were slaughtered?"

Elijah had taunted the prophets of Baal when they prayed and danced around the altar from morning till noon and still no fire had appeared to burn up the sacrifice.

"Pray louder," he'd mocked. The thought of it made Jezebel's blood sizzle. "Maybe he's sleeping, and you need to wake him. Or maybe he's relieving himself, or he's gone on a journey," Elijah had taunted.

I hate that blasted prophet!

The prophets of Baal had cut themselves until blood soaked their bodies and not a single spark appeared. And then Elijah poured water over his sacrifice and called down fire, and the whole thing burned up in a minute. And after that, he made it rain!

"Not that I'm chiding you, Lord Baal," she said through tight lips. "Perhaps you had something more important to do than defend the eminence of your prophets." *Or your queen!*

The sacrificial bull on the altar sizzled, the fat popping in the intense heat of the flames. A sudden, sharp crack echoed through the room as a piece of the bull's flesh burst forth, narrowly missing Jezebel and landing with a hiss on the stone floor. Jezebel flinched, a momentary flicker of panic thrumming throughout her body before it was replaced with a swell of fury. Was that a peace offering from the god?—or was he trying to maim her?

"Maybe I should have built a temple to one of the female gods!" Jezebel said beneath her breath. Asherah, mother of the gods, including Baal? But Asherah prostrated herself before Baal's father, El, whenever she entered his presence, and Jezebel couldn't build a temple for a goddess who would lower herself to the floor and give her husband a chance to walk on her, so she had erected a likeness of the goddess on a pole near the temple.

Or maybe Anat. But Anat was probably a little too violent to suit the Israelite women. She was accused of splitting another god with a sword and grinding him up with a millstone. And Baal was leader of the pantheon, so it would not suit to build a temple to a lesser god.

Jezebel studied the eyes cut deep into the large bronze head. They drooped at the corners, making the god look tired. She mused that the artisan could have made them a bit more intimidating. The piece of meat was still smoking on the stone floor. *Maybe I should just leave and let Baal work it out himself.* She wasn't getting anywhere. She would send another prize bull or two. Or ten if necessary. Maybe that would get his attention. She was tired and wet, and she wanted her rooms and a warm supper.

Jezebel bowed in obeisance and walked toward the entrance, waving off priests that suddenly appeared to see her out. She shook her head and moved on, trying to maintain some measure of dignity in her disheveled state. When she was almost to the wide doors leading to the outer court, she felt the brush of a hand on her shoulder. She jerked around, ready to rebuke the priest who dared to touch her, but the priests were gone, as she had ordered. Only the bronze statue sat at the far end of the chamber, the waning fire at its feet. And, of course, the Eunuch standing by the door at the back of the holy place.

Jezebel was suddenly warm, sweat beginning to dampen her forehead. Her feet didn't seem to want to move, as if they had a mind of their own. The barest breath of air touched her ear.

I have work for you to do. Do not fail me. I will make your name live on through the ages.

She turned to the image of the storm god once more. Was he speaking to her? The voice didn't seem to come from him at all. It was close, very close. But it must have been him. Who else?

Eunuch

The eunuch stood in the shadowed recesses at the back of Baal's throne room, the oppressive atmosphere pressing down on him like a physical weight. The acrid sting of incense mixed with the cloying scent of burnt offerings created a fog that clung to his senses, making his head feel like it might pop and splatter over the tiled floor like the sacrificial meat had done a few moments before.

As Queen Jezebel's sharp, demanding voice had echoed through the vast hall, he had felt a chill creep up his spine, dragging a growing sense of dread. The flames from the firepit danced on the bronze statue, making the eyes seem to follow Jezebel's every move, an unnerving shift that made the hair on his arms stand on end.

There was something malevolent in the room, and it wasn't anything made of wood or metal. The eunuch had often sensed that there was some unearthly power working in the queen. No one could be so evil without some foul spirit pulling at the strings like a puppeteer making a doll dance. He felt watched, scrutinized by something unseen, its intentions unknowable. The queen approached and he followed her through the tall doors, thankful to breathe some fresher air.

CHAPTER TWELVE

Anna

The sky was bright and brisk. Today was the first clear day since Yahweh had opened the heavens at Elijah's command. Anna breathed in the fresh scent, ecstatic that the drought was over, even though dealing with the mud was a challenge. She set her basket at the door of her house and slipped off her sandal and put it to her nose. She thought it still smelled faintly of vomit although she'd washed it thoroughly at the well. Probably just the memory of it. Not that she minded. She breathed into her hand, but the sprig of mint she'd plucked from her dooryard had covered that well enough.

Joy was bubbling in Anna's chest, and she couldn't stop smiling. She pressed her lips between her teeth and drew a huge breath through her nose. This was the fourth morning she'd lost her morning meal, and her blood should have come many days ago. *Blessed be Yahweh!*

It had been over four months since she'd stained the wedding sheet. She had begun to fear she might be like Rachel, who'd watched her sister bear son after son before she bore her own.

Zim would be so happy. He had been watching her courses closer than she did herself. Her face had reddened each time he asked when her blood was due. Anna thought they had not been married long enough for such familiarity. But he'd been out of bed before dawn the last few weeks. With the imminent possibility of war with Syria, production of chariot wheels had increased. He'd been so busy, he must have lost count. She was glad because now she could surprise him with the wonderful news. Zim would be a good father. He was a good husband.

Anna left her shoes outside and opened the door to see Zim sprawled across the bed at an odd angle. His work tunic was lying on the floor where he'd slipped out of it. He was wearing nothing but a loincloth. Heat touched her cheeks, both from embarrassment and from other things. He stirred and turned his head in Anna's direction, blinking his beautiful black eyes into focus. He'd been working so hard, he must have been allowed a short day at the wheel shop. The corners of his mouth turned up in a sleepy smile.

"Hello," he said in a low voice that turned up the temperature in Anna's cheeks.

Suddenly, she was as abashed as she had been when he led her into the bridal chamber. Zadah had frightened her so, she was as nervous as a flame flickering in a draft when Zim took her to bed. He had been gentle, but the whole experience had been almost as Zadah had described, though not as painful as she made it out. But it was not without tenderness as they both worked through the awkwardness of it all. But four months had made a great difference, and Anna had come to find pleasure in her husband's embrace. A great deal of pleasure.

Zim patted the bed next to him. Heat flooded Anna's face again. She hoped he wasn't suggesting anything because she was self-conscious and still preferred the cover of darkness. And, besides, she wasn't exactly sure if he'd want to after she told him the news. Once a woman was with child, would a man still want to couple with her? Anna wasn't exactly sure how things were done, and she had no woman to ask.

Sensing Anna's embarrassment, Zim pulled himself up on the edge of the bed and gave it another pat. "Just come sit by me for a moment. I have to go back to the shop soon. I had a chance to slip away while they cleaned the boilers."

"I'm with child." The words just tumbled out of Anna's mouth without preamble. She wanted the moment to be so special, and that was all she could say?

Zim's jaw dropped, and for a long moment Anna thought her declaration had sent him into shock. Then in one long leap he was off the bed and holding her so close to his chest she couldn't get a breath.

"Oh, I'm sorry," he said, suddenly as serious as a cat hovering over kittens. "Did I hurt you? Are you well? Come sit on the bed. No. Lie down. Are you tired? Hungry? What can I do to help you?" His words fell over one another and spilled into a throw-back-your-head chortling that lit up every part of his handsome face.

He gentled his arms as he held her close and whispered in her ear. "You have made me so happy, beloved." Then he found her lips with his and kissed her with such tenderness, it brought tears to her eyes.

In a few minutes Anna knew the answer to her question about whether men wanted to couple when their wives were pregnant and had completely lost her aversion to the light.

The marketplace was not so crowded as it was the last time she'd come. At the cloth purveyor's booth two women held up a length of dyed wool, a pretty green that looked like the grass after the rains. Anna could hear a man bargaining with the fish merchant from the other end of the street. Apparently the customer thought the fish was not so fresh and the indignant merchant swore it was caught only this morning. Only a smattering of shoppers perused the booths. But it was still early, and Anna was so happy she hardly cared if she sold a thing. She took a worn wool cloth from the basket behind the wooden counter and began wiping down the pottery she had brought to sell for the day.

In truth, she hadn't brought it herself. Zim had insisted that Joel accompany her and set up the booth, since he was unable to do so himself. Her brother had been given strict orders that his sister was not to lift as much as a pot. Of course, within hours of Anna telling Zim about the baby, he had announced it to the whole family and who knows who else. He'd probably told the goats and the sheep and a few hens to boot. Anna would have preferred a few private days between them before the teasing started. But Zim couldn't have held it in if he tried. Anna had never seen a man so ecstatic.

As she polished a vase similar to the first one Lillian had purchased, the one that was scratched when she returned to the booth, her thoughts drifted back to the joy of that day. Obe had finally proposed. She was happy. Truly happy. But that happiness had been scarred—just like the vase. *Is joy always followed with pain?* An uneasiness wormed its way into her mind, but she quickly pushed it aside.

A man was approaching Anna's booth. She laid the cloth beneath the counter and stood up straight. He was a stranger to her. His long face reminded her of a donkey her family had once owned. She chided herself for being so unkind, but there was an undeniable resemblance, except the donkey didn't have jowls that hung like saddlebags on either side of its face.

"Good day," the man said, looking at her through small round eyes. "It's a fine collection of pottery you have here." His voice was oily and ... strange. She was wary of the man.

"Thank you," Anna replied cautiously, not liking the way his gaze lingered on her.

He picked up the vase she had been dusting. "Ah, I see you have a talent for detail." The corners of his mouth tipped upward in a strange sort of smile as he turned it in his hands. Something about the vase seemed to amuse the man. A knot formed in the pit of her stomach. He put the vessel down and met Anna's eyes for several uncomfortable moments.

"I saw you once before, didn't I? In the hills where all the caves are," he said with a definite smirk on his lips.

Anna could feel each thump of her heart beating against her chest, but she managed to keep her expression neutral. "No," she said. "You must be mistaken."

The man's smile tightened. "I don't think so. You were with the governor of the palace and some others. And how could I forget? You're a fine lookin' woman, with that red-brown hair and those green eyes."

Now Anna was getting angry. "I'm sorry, but you must have seen someone else. And if you have no interest in purchasing a vessel, I must ask you to move on so another customer may take your place." The man paid no attention at all to her request.

"You know, a woman like you shouldn't be keeping company with the likes of the governor. I have private information that he is in poor graces with the queen and is about to be replaced."

Anna narrowed her gaze. She wasn't going to put up with this! "I am a married woman, and I am not keeping company with the governor. But if I were, it would be none of your business. Now I will ask again. Please leave."

The man's hand shot out, grabbing Anna's arm with a grip that was both possessive and threatening. Before she could react, Obadiah appeared out of nowhere, his lips pulled back into a snarl, revealing clenched teeth, as every muscle in his face seemed to tighten with the force of his rage. He seized the man from behind and hurled him to the ground. The man whimpered like a child.

"Touch her again, and it will be the last thing you do," Obadiah growled, his voice low and deadly.

The man scrambled to his feet, humiliated but belligerent. "You … you hurt me! See?" he said, holding forth a barely scraped arm.

Obadiah leaned down, speaking directly into the man's narrow face. "You don't know what pain is, but you will find out if you come near this woman again. And if you ever feign to *borrow* my horse again, I will have you charged with horse theft and you will spend the rest of your pitiful life in the dungeons. Do you understand?"

The man's nostrils flared as he wiped the dust off his robe and straightened the edges. He looked at Anna. "So you don't keep company with the governor, huh?" He threw a backwards glare at Obadiah as he stumbled away, disappearing into the throng of market-goers, many who were looking at Obe with their mouths hanging open.

Anna's heart was still pounding, and she realized she had been holding her breath. "Obe," she whispered, a mixture of relief and confusion washing over her.

Obadiah wiped his hair off his face, concern replacing the fury in his eyes. "Are you alright?"

She nodded, though her hands were still trembling. "Yes, thanks to you. But … how was it that you were here?" He had seemed to just materialize. Was he spying on her? Watching over her? She began to feel uncomfortable. What if someone told Zim about the encounter. Would he think she was inviting Obadiah's attention? Would it cause another rift between these two men that were so dear to her? She looked around the market. Everyone seemed to have lost interest in the skirmish.

Obe flushed. Perhaps he read her thoughts. They had been so close for so long.

"It was about my horse."

"Your horse?"

He raked his hands through his hair. It was then that she noticed that he was not wearing his palace attire, No turban around his head, no fine linen. She had always hated it, as had he. He was so handsome in a plain tunic, his hair curling behind his ears. *Stop it Anna!* She dropped her gaze, forcing the thought from her mind.

"The man has been telling the stable hand that I gave him permission to ride my horse any time he wanted. I had a description of him but didn't know his name or where he lived. It's my day off, and I thought I'd take a ride. When I reached the stable, the attendant told me the man had tried again, and he had sent him away not ten minutes before I arrived. He said the man had headed toward the market. I saw him standing at your booth, and when he grabbed your arm—"

Obe was pale. She started to reach out to touch him, to assure him that she had not been harmed, but she quickly pulled her hand back. She couldn't do that.

Her eyes searched his face. She couldn't help but remember the love they once shared, the future they almost had together. "Thank you," she said, her voice barely above a whisper. "For everything."

Obadiah looked down, his expression conflicted. "You don't need to thank me, Anna. I'm just glad you're safe."

"How have you been?" she asked, not wanting him to leave yet.

Obadiah gave a small, weary smile. "Busy. Jezebel keeps us all on edge. His eyes lit with kindness. It's good to see you … happy."

"I am," Anna replied, feeling the tension between them ease, and a great tenderness take its place. Obe had been more than the object of her love. He had been her dearest friend. He could still be that, even if their paths didn't cross often. "Zim is a good husband. We have a good life together." She started to tell him about the baby, but thought better of it. Zim could tell him.

Obadiah nodded, his eyes reflecting a measure of peace. "I'm glad to hear that. Truly."

They stood there for a moment, the bustling marketplace around them fading into the background.

"I should go," Obadiah said finally, breaking the silence. "Take care, Anna."

"Obe, wait." She had almost forgotten to tell him what the man had said before he grabbed her.

"The man said he had seen me in the hills near the caves, with you and some others," she whispered.

Obadiah's face tightened with concern as Anna relayed the news. He glanced around to make sure their conversation was not being overheard.

"It must have been the day you and the boys came to the cave."

She remembered how angry she had been at Obadiah for demanding she not go to the cave anymore. She knew he had been trying to protect her, but she wasn't going to be bullied into sitting at home while Obadiah and her brothers helped the prophets. But had it been this man that found the cave and directed Jezebel's men to it? She shook the idea out of her thoughts. She couldn't go there.

Obe put his hand over hers. "You must be watchful. The man seems like a fool but he could be dangerous. He removed his hand quickly. It had been an innocent gesture, but she could see he was embarrassed by it.

"I will, Obe. Don't worry."

"I need to go now. It was good to see you, Anna."

"You as well, Obe," she replied, watching as he disappeared into the crowd, leaving her with a mind full of memories.

Anna returned to her pottery, but her hands were unsteady, her thoughts far from the marketplace. She knew she would focus on the future, on her life with Zim and their unborn child. But the past, and Obadiah's lingering presence, would always be a part of her.

CHAPTER THIRTEEN

Jezebel

A knock came on the door of Jezebel's chamber. A loud knock. Surely her handmaid would not dare to be so brazen.

"Enter!"

The girl had better have a good reason for this intrusion. The maid's eyes were wide as she slipped through the door.

"Well? What is it that would cause you to beat down the queen's own door? Spit it out!"

A sheen of sweat dampened the servant's forehead. "The king sent me, my queen! He says to come to the anteroom immediately! Emissaries from Benhadad are waiting on the portico with a message for the king. He said he would not hear it until you were on your throne beside him."

What? Emissaries with a message from Benhadad?

Could it be he had come with some terms of surrender? The queen doubted such was the case. The Syrian king had been defeated soundly the last time he waged war with Israel, but not even a sword had been drawn yet. Why would he surrender before he had begun fighting? Unless … he had come with terms for Israel's surrender. Jezebel ground her teeth. If Benhadad expected Ahab to surrender, he would be sorely disappointed.

"Help me prepare myself," she said, moving to the closet that covered the entire west wall of her chamber, shoving gowns aside until she found the most regal gown she owned.

"But, my queen, the king said not to tarry. That you should come immediately."

Jezebel just looked at the girl, her lips pursed. The maid's face drained of all color in an instant. She bowed her head. "Yes, my queen."

The queen of Israel would not appear before the enemies of the king dressed like a frump, no matter how big of a hurry Ahab was in. Jezebel waved a hand and the eunuch turned toward the door. The maid helped her out of her garment and into the gown she had chosen. A headdress would hide her disheveled hair. The girl's hand was shaking as she tried to apply kohl to Jezebel's eyelids.

"Give me that!" Jezebel snatched the pot from the girl. "I'll do it myself." She had learned the art of applying cosmetics so her appearance would never depend on another. One never knew when one would have to dispose of a maid and how long it would take to get another.

When the girl was finished, Jezebel stood and looked into the polished-brass mirror. Nothing could make her beautiful, but she looked regal. No one would deny her that.

* * *

Ahab's lips pressed into a thin line as the queen approached, his eyes glinting his anger.

"My apologies for the delay, my king. My maid did not come directly to fetch me."

Of course, now she had to dispose herself of the girl. Ahab would expect it of her. Jezebel never tolerated inefficiency. Which reminded her, if the man she'd commissioned to find Elijah didn't soon produce information about the prophet's whereabouts, she would have to do the same to him. Unless she found him valuable as a replacement for that dratted Obadiah.

The queen's gaze turned toward the palace governor, who was standing a short distance from the king. His height and his handsome features made Ahab look all the more pitiable. Jezebel would never have a servant with whom such obvious comparisons could be drawn.

"While you were doing whatever it was you were doing"—Ahab waved his hand, his eyes tracing up and down his wife's robe and painted face—"Benhadad's emissaries wait on the portico to speak to the king and queen of Israel!"

She bowed her head." My apologies again, my king. I'll see that the girl pays for the inconvenience."

They went through the back entrance to the throne room, Obadiah following. When they were seated on their respective thrones, the king nodded and Obadiah opened the door and told the guards to bring in the messengers.

The men, dressed in short leather-belted tunics and sandals laced up their calves, met the king and queen without as much as a bow. Did they have no fear?

The cords in Ahab's neck bulged, and Jezebel could see the blood pulsing at his temple. How dare they approach the king in such a manner!

"Speak!" Ahab spat at the smug-looking toad in the middle.

The man stretched his short neck, lifting his heavily bearded chin. "Benhadad, the heroic king of Syria, sends me to inform the king of Israel that the Syrian army has been joined by thirty-two kings of the city-states from Dan to Beersheba. Our combined armies outnumber the king of Israel's army twenty times over. Israel is like a flock of goats before us."

What? That couldn't be true. How did such a thing happen without the king being warned? The spies would lose their heads for this!

The toad turned his eyes toward Jezebel, a twist of a grin on his pockmarked face, then back to Ahab. "The king of Syria says to the king of Israel, 'Your gold and your silver are mine, as are your most esteemed wives and children. If you do not agree to hand them over, I will send my best men to you tomorrow around this time; they will ransack your house and the houses of your servants; and whatever they see that they desire, they will seize and remove, including your wives and children.'"

Jezebel jerked her head toward Ahab, who was sitting on the throne, stunned, his mouth agape. Fire was licking through her veins. Who did this messenger think he was to come to the throne of the king and queen of Israel with such belligerence! Surely Ahab would have the man run through with the sword! Send his head back to Benhadad on a pike!

Ahab's long fingers gripped the arms of his throne. He said nothing for several moments. It was all the queen could do to keep from ordering their deaths herself!

"I need some time to think about it."

Jezebel's mouth fell open in disbelief. *Time to think about it?*

She started to rise, but Ahab lifted his fingers, a motion for her to stay seated. She stayed in her seat, but every nerve in her body was stretched and ready to snap.

The messenger spoke again. "The king may think all he desires, but tomorrow at this time the men of King Benhadad's army will overtake the palace, the vineyards, the granaries, the storerooms, all of the surrounding buildings, and take what strikes their fancy—and deliver the king's silver and gold and wives and children to the king of Syria."

With that, the man turned and walked out of the room, the others following close behind.

As soon as the heavy doors shut behind them, Jezebel turned to her husband, her body buzzing with anger. "What do you mean you'll think about it!"

Ahab flipped his hands. "Well, the man has given me no choice that I can see."

What! "No choice? You have a choice Ahab! That you would think you have none is ... is unforgivable!"

Had the king lost his mind?

"What do you think my father will do when he hears you had *no choice* but to let his daughter be taken to Syria to service a foreign king!"

Ahab let out a long breath. "I need to talk to one of the prophets."

Now he was coming to his senses. Elijah had eradicated the prophets that had been at Mount Carmel, but there were many who'd not been at the slaughter, and the queen had sought reinforcements from Tyre, which had only just arrived. "I'll call for them now," she said, rising to her feet.

Ahab slapped the air with his palm. "No! I want to speak to a prophet of Yahweh. If you haven't killed them all by now."

Jezebel was taken aback by her husband's sharp retort. He had been happy enough to build her a temple for Baal and worship there himself, but a little pressure, and he runs back to that ragtag bunch of charlatans. But ... some good could come of this yet. She turned her gaze toward Obadiah, who was already anticipating her move, if the color draining from his face meant anything.

"Perhaps Obadiah might be able to find one for you. It's been rumored he hides them in caves and feeds them with the king's own bread."

Obadiah's eyes went wide. Hah! Caught without a defense. Now Ahab would do something about his furtive governor.

"Obadiah?" The king stared at his servant, whose face was now a bloodless gray. "Could you find a prophet of Israel for me?"

Obadiah's whole body seemed to sigh his relief. He bowed. "I will do my best, my king. Although, I'm not certain where to look."

No rebuke? Ahab seemed not to care at all that his governor was stealing from the palace stores. Or he couldn't believe his *loyal* servant would do such a thing. Jezebel's word meant nothing to her husband. And she had no doubt Obadiah knew exactly where to look! Which is why she must find the fool she had hired and have Obadiah followed.

<hr />

Obadiah

I bowed out of the king's chamber, not knowing what to do. I didn't want to take the chance of being followed to the cave. I hurried toward the wheel shop. I needed to talk to Zim.

I looked around carefully before entering. I didn't think I had been followed. Jezebel could not leave the king's side to sic one of her dogs on me—unless—there was someone already commissioned to follow me wherever I went. But I kept looking over my shoulder and saw no one.

Zim looked up from the wheel he was assembling, his face lighting up. "Obe. What are you doing here? It's so good to see you, my brother. I don't see you enough."

A sudden wave of longing swept over me. Zim had been my best friend for all of our lives. I missed him almost as much as I missed Anna. He was the brother of my heart. But things were different now. He had a wife to go home to after a long day's work. I wouldn't cause him to take precious time away from Anna. And what would we talk about? Someday things might be different, but, for now, I served Zim and Anna both best by staying away.

"I need your help."

"Anything, brother," he said, laying aside his tools.

I could see the concern on Zim's countenance as I told him what I had been commissioned to do.

"You don't think it's a trap?"

"Not one that Ahab is setting. But there's always the possibility Jezebel will have me followed. I'd rather not go to the new cave myself. I know the queen has people looking, but it is well hidden." Guilt bit at me. Asking Zim could put him in danger, and I had vowed to protect him and Anna. No one suspected his involvement—that I knew of. But I didn't want to take the chance.

"I will go immediately," he said, reaching for a rag on the table with which to wipe his greasy hands.

I shook my head. "Maybe I shouldn't ask. It could be dangerous, and Anna … maybe she would not approve of my endangering her husband." At that moment I wondered if Anna had told Zim about our meeting at the marketplace. If she had, Zim had taken it well. I was glad. The last thing I wanted was to interfere in their marriage. Anna was Zim's wife. She loved him and he, of course, loved her. I would never wish ill for either of them.

"You must have forgotten, Obe," he said, tossing the rag aside, his eyes lighting with mischief. "If I told her I was going, she would insist on going with me. Which is why I won't tell her."

I was torn. But someone had to go. And if I went myself, I could be leading Jezebel's men to the prophets, whom I had also vowed to protect.

Zim clapped my shoulder and pulled me in for a hug. "Don't worry, my friend. I will be careful. No one will see me, I promise. I have missed you so much."

I fisted his back. "I have missed you as well, my friend."

I turned to go, then turned back. "And, Zim, if he's not stopped, Benhadad's soldiers will be here by this time tomorrow. They have been given permission by their king to ransack the palace, the grounds, anything they wish. Even the servants' homes. Naboth's vineyard does not belong to the king, but I doubt they will ask. If the tide of this war is not turned, escape to the cave yourself with your wife and Naboth and the brothers. Do not be seen near the palace. Do you understand?"

"Yes. I understand Obe. I will heed your warning."

Ephraim asked Ahab and Jezebel to take him to the balcony above the main floor of the palace. We walked through a large sitting room with low couches and tables inlaid with gold and lapis. Ten ivory reliefs, each engraved with one of the ten commandments given to the prophet Moses, adorned the west wall, a large tapestry of a battle between two Phoenician gods on the east. Jezebel had intruded upon the sanctity of the room as she did on everything in the palace.

I followed closely, looking around for Jezebel's lackeys. Surely the queen wouldn't try to move upon a prophet of Israel in the presence of the king. To do so would probably cost her own life. She was too canny for such boldness. But I still worried if the prophet would be safe when he left the palace. And I prayed no one had spied Zim as he'd made his way to the cave.

Yahweh, protect my brother. Protect Anna. Protect this man of Yours who risks his life to speak Your word to the king. Make Ahab listen.

My heart clenched when I looked over the countryside from the balcony. In the distance, Benhadad's army looked like a hundred thousand angry ants waiting for their lunch. How had he gathered such an army? The flags of many provincial kings flew beside the Syrian banner. War horses and chariots at the front of tens of thousands of foot soldiers. The rains had saved much of the king's livestock, but if every animal had survived, there would still not be enough chariots to meet the long line of wooden wheels and flashing swords.

"Well, what does Yahweh speak to you?" Ahab said to the prophet, his voice already angry. Ahab had little confidence that whatever came out of a prophet's mouth would be amiable toward him. That he was consulting a prophet of Yahweh was more than unexpected to me. And Ephraim had not curried the king's favor when he arrived. He had not treated the king with disrespect, but he'd made no pretense of approval of Ahab or his Phoenician wife.

The prophet didn't speak for several minutes, his eyes fixed on something beyond, rather than the armies that lay before him. I knew he was waiting for the still voice of Yahweh. Finally, he turned toward the king, the lines of his sun-browned forehead deepening.

"The men of Syria have counseled their king that the army's defeat last year was because Yahweh is God of the hills, but He is not God of the valleys. Thus they have chosen to meet Israel's army on the plains." He lifted his chin toward the gathering enemy. "This is what the Lord says to Ahab, King of Israel. 'Do you see this vast army? Because they believe the God of Israel to be God of the hills but not God of the valleys, I will give it into your hand.'" The prophet's sharp gaze went to the king, his carriage tall and his voice one of authority as he continued speaking the Word of the Lord. "'And then you will know that I am the Lord and none other.'"

Ahab's neck reddened. He appeared diminished, ashamed before the man of God. He had built a temple to the very gods that his enemies trusted to defeat him. Worshiped in it. With his wife.

Ahab seemed at a loss. He raised his palms and dropped them to his side. "Which soldiers should be at the forefront of the army?" Jehu's men would usually be Ahab's choice. Jehu was a brave and true captain of Ahab's troops. But the two men were at odds a great deal of the time, and Jehu had apparently fallen out of favor with the king.

The prophet answered, "The young men who serve the district officials."

What? Smooth-faced boys, who had barely entered manhood? But Yahweh had used the weak to confound the strong before. David, who killed Goliath with a fast-flung stone. Joseph, the dreamer of dreams, who became second only to Pharaoh and saved his family and the entire line of Abraham from extinction. Gideon, the least in a family who came from the least tribe of Israel. My spirit began to swell within me. Was the God of heaven about to show Himself strong to a king who had shown himself weaker than any king before him?

"But who will lead them into battle?" Ahab asked, his forehead still plowed with doubt.

Ahab knew the importance of a leader to inspire the men to follow into the fray. There was no such commander in Israel at this time. None like those who had led their small armies to victory over mighty enemies.

The prophet pointed his long finger at the king of Israel. "You will."

The king paled for a long moment, but I saw a flicker of determination rise in him. He seemed to stand taller than he had before. My heart filled with hope. Maybe Ahab would rise to the occasion. Become the leader that Israel so desperately needed.

Jezebel stood behind her husband, her face a stone mask. Ahab was going to war on the advice of a prophet of Israel. He had not even inquired of the prophets of Baal that had survived Mount Carmel. Would Ahab finally rescind the free rein he had granted his Phoenician wife? *Let it be so, Yahweh.*

CHAPTER FOURTEEN

Ahab

Two hundred and thirty-two officers of the districts were at the front of Ahab's troops, a mere seven thousand soldiers behind, facing an army that spread over the plain like stalks of wheat waving in the wind. How could Israel defeat such an army with such an insignificant force?

Ahab's heart pummeled his chest as he stood in his chariot. The horses were stock still as they had been trained, but he could see Black's sleek hair almost vibrating with anticipation. The huge white animal the same. They were like coils, waiting to be released. The king had led his armies to victory before—and to defeat. But the prophet said he would prevail. That he would see the hand of the God of Israel. Something stirred inside him. A longing to hear the voice of Yahweh. To be obedient to Him. He let out a huff of breath. That would not settle well with his queen.

Why had he allowed Jezebel to get so out of hand? He shook his head, baffled at how she had almost become a surrogate, to act in his place. If a Phoenician woman could sit on the throne of Israel, she would probably battle him to the death for it. But no. She was powerless without him—and he seemed to be more and more powerless without her. Ahab so disliked the "inconvenient" aspects of ruling, even though he made a show of dispatching a servant on occasion to keep up appearances. A king must not seem weak, even to those closest to him. But Ahab had to admit he much preferred to let Jezebel do what she did so well and give him at least a measure of deniability.

When Ahab took the hand of the King of Tyre's daughter, it was to form a necessary alliance as all his marriages were. But Jezebel had captured his attention. She was far from beautiful like most of his other wives. No. Jezebel wasn't beautiful, but she had a mystique, a presence about her, with her fiery-red hair and obsidian eyes. It was as though those eyes were coals glowing in the midst of dancing flames. They drew you like the devil himself. Ahab shuddered.

Their first coupling had left him feeling like he'd touched a hot stove. It wasn't romantic love he felt for her or a silly infatuation. It was rather the comfort of her strength. But Ahab feared he had become weak in his reliance upon his queen. He hoped he would not regret allowing her such a place. And especially allowing her to propagate the worship of her gods among his people. He hoped to temper her in the matter. But that might be more easily spoken than accomplished.

The noonday sun beat hot upon the small army. Ahab wiped the sweat from his brow with the sleeve of his tunic, waiting for an unction to begin the battle. *God of Israel. Be it as your prophet has spoken.*

∞∞∞∞∞∞∞∞∞

Ahab

Ahab sat astride his horse as two wheelwrights pounded wooden wedges between the hubs and the axels to ensure they were tight enough for the journey home. They were part of a contingent of wheelwrights who always accompanied the king's own chariot and those of his commanders. They had gone into the battle following as closely as possible behind the royal chariots in their carriage equipped with extra spokes and shafts and the necessary tools to repair chariot wheels on the spot or replace them if it came to that. It seldom did. These men were highly skilled. They built the wheels well, so it was only cautionary work they did now. The battle was over.

It had been as the prophet said. Ahab had watched in wonder as seven thousand swords of Israel had annihilated the vast Syrian army; one hundred thousand foot soldiers had fallen in a day. It was as though the metal had found its own way through the Syrian flesh, and the Syrian swords had refused to pierce the hearts of Israel's defenders. Ahab's heart had been filled with wonder and praise for Yahweh.

The news was that the Syrian king had fled into the city to an inner chamber where he cowered in fear. Some of his servants had come in sackcloth with ropes around their necks and a message from the king that he wished to be spared. Ahab had sent for him. Kings conquered in battle weren't supposed to be spared because spared kings could fight another day. Ahab had no intention of sparing Benhadad. He just wanted to see the man meet his end. He would do it himself.

The wheelwrights gathered their tools and bowed before the king. He didn't know these men, but they had done a fine job.

"You will receive an extra month's wage when we return to the palace." The older man grinned a toothless grin, but the younger bowed again. When he raised his head he swiped a lock of black hair out of his eyes. "It is only our duty, my king. We need no more reward than that." There was something about the young man that garnered Ahab's attention. His eyes were clear, as though they hid nothing. Impressive.

"Nonetheless you will have it." The young man bowed again and thanked the king for his generosity.

Ahab stepped into his chariot. The soldiers had returned with the king of Syria who was dressed in sackcloth, standing between two guards. Two soldiers shoved the hobbled king to the ground before Ahab's chariot.

"Unchain him and bring him to me," Ahab said.

The soldiers loosed the chains on Benhadad's hands and feet and lifted him into the chariot. He fell to his knees and bowed his nose to the polished floor. It pleased Ahab to see this enemy of Israel groveling at his feet, but he wanted to see his eyes, not the bald spot at the top of his head.

"Get up!"

The man struggled to his feet and stood, head bowed. His humbled attitude made Ahab embarrassed for him. Ahab would look an enemy straight in the face and dare the man to make him do otherwise. Unless … it served his purpose to appease his captor. The king would keep his eyes open.

"So you are the great Benhadad," Ahab said, raising his eyebrows. "I had expected someone taller. And more handsome. Perhaps with hair that covered his baldness?"

Was that anger that reddened Benhadad's neck? Or embarrassment? Ahab pushed the captive's chin up with the back of his hand.

"Look at me when I'm talking to you."

A small flash of arrogance slid over the man's eyes then quickly gave way to the fear that should attend a man in his position.

"So Benhadad, former king of Syria, why do you think it is that your hundred thousand were annihilated by my seven? And how the thirty thousand who did not feel the sting of Israel's blade and ran back to the city had its eastern wall fall and crush them like so many bugs under a giant shoe?"

The man paled. The story was that the king had fled into Aphek with his cowardly soldiers, barely missing being buried beneath the wall, and hid in a closet.

He had counted on his numbers to secure the victory, but he hadn't counted on Yahweh going out against the enemies of His people. Ahab hadn't counted on it himself, truth be told. The prophet said Yahweh would give Ahab the victory over this pompous king, and he would know that He was indeed the God of Israel. That was a veiled insult. Of course, he knew that Yahweh was the God of Israel. He was the *king* of Israel, after all.

"I would imagine you are no longer of the opinion that the God of Israel is the God of the hills and not the God of the valleys." Ahab chucked the man's chin again. "Do you not agree, great king?"

Benhadad bowed from the waist. "Yes, my king, Ahab. It would appear the God of Israel is indeed the God of all the land."

"Appear?"

He ducked his head again. "With the sword of the king of Israel, your god has prevailed."

Ahab doubted the man's sincerity. Who wouldn't give obeisance to the god of his conqueror? At least in his conqueror's presence. He would probably do the same.

"So what am I to do with you, Benhadad?"

He knew what he was supposed to do with him. The Syrian king had come twice to Israel's borders with a mind to defeat Yahweh's own. He would no doubt come again and again if Ahab let him live. Conquered kings must be dispatched to keep them from fighting another day. It was God's commandment. It was the sin of the first king, Saul, who spared the king of the Amalekites and drew the ire of the prophet Samuel, who finished the job himself.

Ahab drew his sword from its sheath. He would do the deed with his own weapon and carry Benhadad's head before him as he entered the city in triumph. Jezebel would enjoy that.

"My king," the man said, his voice quavering. "If you would allow me just a word? It may be to your advantage to let me live."

The captive king flinched as Ahab wiped his bloody blade on the man's sackcloth tunic.

"Conquering my army was a relatively easy task. But conquering the many cities of Syria could prove much more problematic—and time-consuming—for my lord, the king of Israel." He paused for a long moment, then spoke tentatively. "If Your Highness should choose to spare my life, I am prepared to return the cities that my father took from your father—without a fight. And you can set up your headquarters in Damascus. Open bazaars and sell the fine goods of Israel. You will prosper off my people without lifting a blade. What good is the head of a king in comparison to the great wealth of the cities of the conquered?"

Hmm. The man did have a point. Why shouldn't a king expand his territory and without bloodshed? What could be wrong with that?

A twinge of fear constricted Ahab's chest. This was not the way of Yahweh. Unvanquished enemies always returned to trouble Israel. Which is why the Lord God told Joshua to utterly destroy the Hittites and the Amorites, the Canaanites, the Perizzites and Hivites, and the Jebusites as they conquered the Promised Land.

Ahab rubbed his chin. But that was during the initial takeover of Canaan. Things were different now. If it was possible to expand Israel's territory without even a fight, why would Yahweh not approve?

The king raised a brow. "And what of you, Benhadad? Am I to turn you loose to come back and seek my crown?"

The man shook his head vigorously, his hopeful eyes open wide. "As the God of Israel lives, I will give the king all I have promised and not even the shadow of my foot shall fall on Israel's soil."

Ahab stood for several long moments, watching the beggar king hold his breath. Why should he not profit from this victory, both with the spoils of war and the riches of commerce? It would benefit his subjects, and a king must always do what is best for his people.

Ahab narrowed his gaze.

"Alright. I will covenant with you as you have spoken, then have my men conduct you safely to your borders." Ahab leaned in close enough for his breath to warm the captive's face. "But do not think me the fool, Benhadad. If you do not honor our covenant, or if I see you in Israel again, your head will indeed ride through the gates on my spear. Do you understand?"

A long sigh escaped Benhadad's lips. "Yes, my king, Ahab. I understand perfectly."

"Gather a contingent of a hundred soldiers and escort the king to the border of Syria," Ahab said to the two soldiers who had brought Benhadad to him. He looked back at the pitiful king, a sneer on his lips. "From there he can make his own way."

The men did not move. Their eyes were wide with shock.

"Do what I said, or I'll ride into the city with *your* heads on my spear!"

"Yes, my king." The older of the two came to himself and jerked Benhadad's chain. "Come on you Syrian pig!" the man shouted. "Let's go!"

Ahab's gaze fell on the wheelwrights who had been waiting by the supply wagon to accompany the king's entourage home. The younger man's eyes were filled with what looked like sorrow. And disappointment. He lowered his eyes when he noticed the king's perusal. Something struck at Ahab's heart. For some reason, the wheelwright's opinion mattered.

Ahab battled his thoughts as they rode on toward the palace. What would the people think when he arrived without the king of Syria in chains or his head on a lance? They knew what Yahweh expected. Ahab could explain to them the merits of the deal he had struck with the deposed monarch, but could they understand it? And the holier-than-thou prophets would stir the people up against him. Maybe he should have thought more carefully about his decision. When the king saw the disappointment in the young wheelwright's face, his heart had been pricked. He would never forget those eyes. Like the eyes of Yahweh wept within them. *When will I learn to obey?*

A commotion beside the road ahead drew Ahab's attention from his morose thoughts. A man waved frantically as the royal chariot approached, a bloody bandage wrapped around his forehead and draped over one eye. His face was dirty. He looked to have been beaten. Why was he bothering the king's entourage with this?

"My king! My king! Stop! Please! It is a matter of great urgency concerning the battle!"

The man wasn't a soldier. What urgent matter could he be privy to? But he was alone, and Ahab was accompanied by soldiers. The man could do him no harm. He may as well listen to his story.

Ahab motioned and the chariot rolled to a stop. The horses stood proud, heads held high, in perfect submission to the chariot driver. *Too bad my queen could not be trained so well.*

"Speak, man. The king has no time to waste!" shouted the captain of the guard.

The man bowed deeply. "Thank you, my king. It is a matter of most urgency. Of life and even of death."

Ahab didn't see how it could be a matter of life and death. The man was bloodied but he was not near dead.

"Well, spit it out, man," the king demanded. "Your speech had better not be a waste of my time."

The man bowed his head. "It is not, my king, I assure you. I, your servant, went out into the midst of the battle. I am not a soldier, but I wanted to see how the battle fared."

What was a man not trained in battle doing on a battlefield? No wonder he was bloody.

"I was only looking out on the fray, when a true soldier turned aside and said to me, 'Keep this prisoner, and if by any means he be missing upon my return, your life shall be for his life, or else you will pay a talent of silver.'"

A talent of silver? A man should not be allowed to buy his way out of such a commitment. Ahab said nothing, letting the wounded man finish his tale.

"It was my intention to do as the soldier commanded," he said with a shrug. "But I was busied with one thing and then another, and when I was not paying attention, the soldier beat me and fled."

The man spread his hands. "I am not a wealthy man, my king. I have no talent of silver and no way to procure it."

What? The man was so imprudent as to pay so little attention to a prisoner? Did he really think the king would give him a talent of silver to pay his debt?

Ahab pulled his sword from his sheath. "You are a foolish man! Why would you not heed the words of the soldier who trusted you with a prisoner of war? Do you disregard your countrymen so much you would lose an enemy of Israel and thus endanger others? You will indeed lose your life for such an action!"

The king raised his sword, determined to deliver the sentence himself. The man was a fool, and he deserved what had been promised him. But before he could strike, the man pulled off the bandage and swiped the ash from his face. His eyes narrowed, and his gaze pierced Ahab. He knew the man. Who?

The prophet! He stared at the king. The one who had spoken the Word of the Lord that God would deliver the enemy into Ahab's hands and give Israel the victory over Benhadad. The king's heart juddered. *What have I done?*

The prophet pointed his long finger at the king of Israel. Ahab began to quaver.

"Thus says the Lord, 'Because you let go out of your hand a man whom I appointed to utter destruction, therefore your life shall go for his life, and your posterity for his posterity. Do not think that because your sentence is not executed today or tomorrow that you will escape. As you would have sentenced, so shall you be sentenced.'"

Pieces of the prophet's speech flew around Ahab's head. What did the prophet say? Ahab's life would go for Benhadad's life? His children for Benhadad's children? His knees failed him and he fell to the ground. When he lifted his head he saw the wheelwright's sad eyes.

Jezebel

Jezebel stormed through the palace corridors, her robes billowing around her with each determined step. Fury pulsed through her veins, a palpable force that unsettled servants and courtiers who quickly stepped aside.

From her balcony, she had watched the army return, the King of Israel at its front, with no royal head upon his lance. Not even a chained king stumbling behind his chariot. Instead of wild cheers from the citizens there was confusion. Ahab's attempt to explain that he had freed the king of Syria with a promise that the deposed king would return the cities his father had stolen from Ahab's father, and that he would allow Israel to set up bazaars in Damascus had been met with silence, then whispered murmurs and barely audible accusations. Ahab had entered the palace in defeat.

She waited for him to seek her out, but when he didn't come, she knew where she would find him.

"Is he in there?" Jezebel asked the guard at the gilded door of Ahab's private bath, not waiting for an answer. The man's jaw dropped when the queen pushed the door open without ceremony.

Inside, the polished stone walls reflected the flickering light of oil lamps, casting long shadows across the smooth limestone floor. The large stone bathtub at the center was filled with steaming water, apparently added just moments before by the attendants standing in the corner. The fragrance of olive oil and herbs lingered in the air, a stark contrast to the seething rage Jezebel carried with her.

Ahab was lying back in the tub, his eyes closed. Contempt surged within her at the sight of him. How could he relax when he had shown such unforgivable weakness?

Jezebel pointed her long finger at the door that led to the water tanks. The attendants scampered out like startled roaches fleeing the light.

"What have you done, Ahab?" she spat, her voice shattering the damp calm.

Ahab's eyes snapped open. Seeing his wife's angry face, he slid further into the water. "Jezebel, this is not the place—"

"This is exactly the place!" she cut him off, her voice rising with every word. "You let Benhadad go! You let that dog return to his kingdom with his head still attached to his shoulders!"

Ahab sighed deeply. "He promised to return the cities his father took and allow us to trade in their prime markets. Which is better, Jezebel? A king's head on a spear?—or the cities that were stolen from us and an opportunity to expand our commerce? It was a strategic decision."

"Strategic?" Jezebel's eyes narrowed, her thin red lips curling in disdain. "Strategic?"

"Benhadad insulted you, Ahab. He demanded your gold, your silver, and your most esteemed wives and children. He threatened to ransack the palace and take whatever he desired. And you let him walk away. He insulted me. He insulted us. He should have paid with his life for his arrogance! You had one task, Ahab. One! To bring me his head!"

Ahab rubbed his temples, his head bent. Jezebel only felt her rage grow.

She stepped closer, her hands tightened into fists. "You have doomed us all with your naivety! There is no peace with men like Benhadad. He will see your mercy as weakness and return to take what he desires. You *will* face the man again, and all of Israel will suffer for it."

Ahab sat up, the water rippling around him, his face dark with anger. "You are right, Jezebel. I made a mistake. A grave one for which I will pay a price I cannot even allow myself to contemplate. But you, my dear wife, will pay the price as well. And don't feign any concern for Israel. You have done more to destroy Israel than any enemy. Now leave, and let me bathe in peace!"

Jezebel turned on her heel, her robes swirling around her as she stormed out of the bath. The sound of the heavy door closing behind her echoed in the hall, a harsh reminder of the discord that had seeped into their rule. She was losing sway over her husband. That would have to change. Immediately. She puzzled at his admission of guilt. It wasn't like him. What had happened out there? And what price would he have to pay for the "mistake" he admitted? If he thought she was going to pay for his reckless decisions, he was sorely mistaken.

CHAPTER FIFTEEN

Obadiah

A hab waved me to the table where we took lunch and went over the weekly report. No staring at tiles today, I guessed. And no lunch or report, from the way the king was rising and moving toward me. He had seemed despondent since his victory over Benhadad. He should be in sackcloth and ashes for letting the captive king go. No doubt Israel would have to deal with the king of Syria again. But Ahab seemed revived a bit. I supposed it was a good thing. At least for the people who served him. A despondent king could be unpredictable, and Ahab was unpredictable enough without adding more to it. Zim said that the prophet insinuated that Ahab would lose his own life for sparing Benhadad's. The king had every right to be depressed.

"Are you still on good terms with the master of the neighboring vineyard? It was his daughter you were supposed to marry, was it not?"

Why was he asking? Panic clawed its way up my back, leaving a trail of icy shivers. Had Ahab discovered Naboth's part in feeding the prophets?

"Yes, I had planned to marry his daughter. But her father and I have no quarrel."

"You never told me what happened. She must have been with another man, yes?"

"No!" I didn't want to bring attention to Anna, but I couldn't let the king believe she was an unfaithful woman. "It just didn't … work out. She's married to another man now." I didn't mention that the other man was in the king's employ and that he had accompanied the king into the battle to service the chariots. It worried Zim that Ahab had taken note of him. I didn't blame him. The king's attention is not to be coveted when you're aiding the people his wife hates.

"Well, tell me now if her father holds anything against you. I want you to help me, and if he thinks you've slighted his daughter, he might not be open to my offer."

My heart jerked. What did the king of Israel wish to offer Naboth? This was not good.

"Well?" he said.

I wasn't certain what I should answer. Would it be better to claim Naboth for the friend he was or discourage the king from whatever offer he was about to make and risk reprisals against the man? The truth was probably the best course right now, lest I get tangled in a lie and make it worse.

"No. Naboth holds nothing against me. His daughter's heart was all he cared for, and she wanted to marry another." It was not the complete truth. Anna hadn't wanted to marry another, but she seemed happy when we talked at her booth. A twinge of pain gripped my heart. I couldn't stop the longing for Anna that often came upon me suddenly. But I wouldn't dwell on it. I had vowed to support and protect her and Zim in every way possible. That was my duty, and I would put it before my heart's longings.

"Well, come then," Ahab said and headed for the door.

I held my breath as the king led me through the small gate in the wall that opened to Naboth's vineyard. The vintner's land stretched to the edge of the palace wall. Or better said, the palace stretched to the edge of the vintner's land. When Ahab built his winter palace, he took every bit of space he could without violating the law that granted land by tribe and family. One could not take even a step out of the gate without his sole landing on Naboth's ancestral land. This is the gate I used to spirit bread to the cave where the prophets hid from the king's own wife. Naboth's sons would often meet me here with a wagon and with the help of those few faithful servants who supported our cause unload a few amphorae of wine, as though the steward of feasts had ordered it, and load a few bags of grain or bread already baked and left from one of Jezebel's banquets. The boys would take it to a storeroom at the vineyard, and either they or I or all of us would pack it onto a horse, or in a wagon when there were many prophets in our care, and take it to the mouth of the cave. It was a dangerous business. It was because this gate was seldom used that we had succeeded thus far without being discovered. Was the king about to expose my treason? Tell me he knew what I had been doing and put his sword through my heart?

I was anxious as we walked down the long slope toward the rows of vines stretched out like veins of lifeblood coursing through the vineyard's heart. *Yahweh, set a watch over Naboth's tongue.* I hoped the brothers wouldn't be about. They might react in a way that would make the king suspicious of our treachery.

I saw Naboth looking our way, an amphora of wine on his shoulder, his jaw hanging loose. What could be going through his mind seeing the king of Israel approaching, a lavish cloak like a river of midnight blue cascading off his shoulders, accompanied by Naboth's own accomplice in crimes against the throne?

Joel and Jason and Mikal were working the vines, some distance from their father. The boys could be impetuous at times, especially Joel. I hoped they would have the wisdom to stay in the background and keep their mouths closed. I scanned the rows of vines. Thankfully, Zim was not among the brothers. He was probably already at the wheel shop, but sometimes he would work in the vineyard during midday when the shop was overly warm from the boiling vats of water.

Naboth laid the clay vessel on the ground, bowing deeply. I knew it was difficult for Naboth to do since he considered Ahab a disappointment of a king, but he honored the position as Yahweh had commanded when He said, "You shall not curse God or curse a ruler of your people."

"My king."

Ahab quickly bade Naboth to rise. Naboth gave me a furtive look, then met the king's gaze with obvious unease.

"You have a beautiful piece of property here, Naboth," Ahab said, taking in the rows of knotted vines striping the hillside.

"Thank you, my king. It produces the finest wine in the Jezreel Valley, I'm told. If it pleases the king, I will send an amphora to his table before the day is done."

Ahab nodded. "That would be appreciated, but I wonder if this land, rich as it is, would not be a fine place to grow herbs and vegetables. Do you grow such?"

"Yes, my king. Some. Just for the family's use. Not to sell. We devote most of our time and resources to the vines."

"Yes. Yes. But I have many vineyards. I am interested more in vegetables at this time."

What was the king saying? Did he want Naboth to grow vegetables for him?

"The king is welcome to our garden. I will send the finest as soon as it is ready to be harvested."

"No. I'm afraid I haven't made myself clear at all. I would like to *buy* your vineyard or give you another, better vineyard for it." He waved his hand over the land. "It is in the shadow of the palace. It would be so convenient, and I would enjoy walking through it." He motioned to the vines. "I would leave a few of the grape vines. With the rest of the land I could plant every kind of vegetable. Leeks and eggplants are my favorite," he said, his eyes dancing with anticipation. "I could have some date palms brought in, and hyacinths and lilies to place around the borders. Doesn't that sound wonderful, Naboth?" The king prattled on, not waiting for an answer. Naboth's eyes were two wide orbs, his mouth a gaping hole.

The brothers left the vines and came closer, gathering by the wine cellar, several paces from the king and their father but close enough for Ahab to take notice of them. I wasn't certain they had heard the conversation, but by the looks on their faces they knew something was wrong. I was standing a bit behind Ahab, so I shook my head from side to side, hoping they would have the wisdom to stay where they were and say nothing.

Naboth finally found his voice. "My king, with all due respect, I could not possibly do as you request. It is against the law of our people. Of *your* people. I inherited this land from my father, and I must pass it on to my sons."

"I would give you a vineyard twice this size and money besides."

Naboth bowed his head. "I am sorry, my king. I cannot."

"You would not accept an offer of one of the best vineyards in Jezreel or enough money to never have to crush another grape—from your king?"

Ahab's round face was turning red now. What would I do if he asked me to strike Naboth? I didn't wear a sword, but he could command me to use his own and run it through my friend. Of course, I would not follow his command, but I would be dead before the day was done—Naboth with me, I feared. Sweat was streaming down my back. He wouldn't do that—would he? Naboth's sons would light on him in a minute. I could already see Joel's fists beginning to curl.

I waited, hardly breathing. What would the king do? Ahab seemed not to hear Naboth for a long minute. And then the thing I feared came upon me. Zim appeared on the trail leading from the vats to the wine cellars. *Zim!* I didn't want the king to recognize him. Drawing attention to himself was not a good idea now. Zim's eyes were wide when he joined the brothers. But Ahab's eyes were even wider.

He was looking directly at Zim, his face the hue of a whitewashed wall. He recognized him as the wheelwright who had witnessed his shame with Benhadad and the prophet.

Zim.

"Your sons," Ahab said, eyes fastened to Zim, who was studying the ground. He waved a hand at the four young men. "And these are your sons?"

Naboth hesitated, sensing something was wrong. "Yes, my three sons and my son-in-law."

I saw awareness dawn on Ahab's face. "So this is the one," he whispered. It took a moment for me to realize he was referring to Zim. That Zim was the one my prospective wife had married. My mouth went dry. What was Ahab thinking? Did he think that Zim had stolen Anna from me? That was not good.

"Yes, he is the one, a good friend of mine to this day. He meant me no harm."

Suddenly all the spirit drained from Ahab, and he looked like a little boy who had been refused a new toy from his father. He turned without a word and headed toward the gate.

Naboth's eyes met mine. Would this be the end of it? Or would Ahab act on his wishes and demand Naboth forfeit his vineyard? I took a deep breath and turned to catch up with the king. Surely, the king of Israel would not defy the law of Moses, would he? Why not? He had already built a temple to a heathen god. *Yahweh, have mercy.*

Anna

Anna balanced the basket of bread she'd brought to add to the goat stew simmering on the hearth. She and Zim seldom ate a meal in their own home since none of the men in her family could cook more than gruel and lentil soup. She sometimes wondered if her brothers hadn't yet taken wives because they liked her cooking too much.

A murmur of agitated voices stirred the air as she entered her father's house, the basket under her arm. Father, Zim, and the boys were gathered around the long table. The deep furrows in her father's brow and the angry bloom on her brothers' faces made her wonder what sort of quarrel the boys were engaged in now. It seemed they found some obnoxious pleasure in arguing. It was like a competition to see who could make the better case for his cause. An outsider might think they had no love for one another at all, but they were as close as brothers could be. Zim was accepted as if he were of the same blood—as Obe had been.

It made Anna sad that Obadiah didn't see the brothers or Zim often. She imagined he was giving Zim and her space to become comfortable in their marriage, especially since their meeting at the market. She knew it was a sacrifice since Obe and Zim were like brothers. She appreciated not having to see him often, but she hoped he was not lonely.

Zim rose and met Anna with a kiss to her forehead. He took the basket of bread out of her arms and put it on the hearth, where it would not grow cold before the meal, and stood behind her when she was seated, his hands resting on her shoulders. The weight of them comforted her.

It had been difficult in the beginning—betrothed to Zim and in love with Obadiah. But even before her marriage something had begun to shift in her heart. And now, more and more she found her heart stuttering at the sound of Zim's steps at the door, and her body responding to his eagerly and with tender affection. She felt the affection was leading to … to the foundation of a deep love.

Anna's father looked troubled. The corners of his mouth turned up in an effort to greet her, but the smile didn't make it to his eyes.

"Anna, we have been discussing something that happened earlier today, and I want to include you in our discussion."

Father had always treated her with the same respect he gave her brothers. He never tried to keep her from participating in discussions as some fathers did their daughters. He valued her opinion. Judging from the somber air of the room, they were talking about something important.

"The king and Obadiah came for a visit earlier."

Anna's eyebrows shot up as her mouth dropped open. The king? And Obadiah? *Why would the king come here?*

"The king wanted to buy our vineyard or give us another for it. I believe he brought Obadiah because he knew of our acquaintance."

A rock formed in Anna's chest.

"Why would the king ask such a thing? He knows that land is passed from father to son through the generations," she said, shaking her head in disbelief. "Did he pressure you? And why did he even want it?"

Her father shifted in his chair, his brow still troubled.

"He wanted to plant a vegetable garden. Rip out our vines and plant leeks and eggplant." He shook his head. "No. He did not pressure me. He just dropped his gaze and turned toward the gate when I told him I could not possibly sell my sons' inheritance. He seemed ... depressed."

"He should be depressed!" Joel barked. "He is the poorest king to rule Israel, even worse than his father."

Father raised his palm. "He is the king nonetheless, and we will not scourge him at our dinner table. It is his wife whom we should fear the most. She incites him to evil at every turn." He glanced Anna's way. An acknowledgment that Obadiah was right in keeping her away from the queen? Anna still rejected the notion. She was happy with Zim. She loved him, but she would not have let fear of Jezebel keep her from marrying Obe—had she been given the choice.

"That he wants our ancestral land to plant leeks for his salad is egregious. But that he would even consider asking me to sell is ... well, it suggests something's gone wrong with his thinking. For all his faults, he has never seized what belonged to others except in time of war or forfeiture of property from an executed prisoner, as is the custom. I would like to believe he would not do such a thing, but we should be watchful."

The boys nodded, and Zim squeezed Anna's shoulders.

Anna wondered if there had been soldiers on the other side of the gate waiting for the command to kill all the men if Father refused. She could only imagine what Obe had been thinking at the time. He was probably terrified that some melee would break out and he would have to stop it. Obe would have defended Anna's father and her brothers, even at the peril of his own life. And Zim? Of course he would not allow anyone to lay a hand on Zim.

She looked up at her husband and smiled tentatively. Somehow she didn't think this was the end of the matter.

CHAPTER SIXTEEN

Jezebel

Jezebel looked up and down the grand hallway. No one of consequence was watching. She jabbed her finger at the fool who was standing before her, his body perfectly relaxed, with not even the good sense to be afraid. "I'm telling you—you find those prophets and proof that Obadiah has been aiding them, or you can forget about any future in the palace!" *Or any future at all!*

The man had mocked her long enough. "Find proof of anything that will turn the king against him, and the governorship will be yours!"

The queen could see thoughts of grandeur flitting through the man's mind. He stood taller, a stupid grin stretched impossibly wide on his narrow face. Another bit and it would wrap around his head, corners meeting at the back. The sight made her skin creep. She wanted to signal the eunuch and see his big hand slip around the fool's scrawny neck, but she had no time to enlist another to finish the job. She had to prove Obadiah's disloyalty to the king some way and soon.

It would be difficult because Obadiah served Ahab faithfully before his face, but Jezebel was certain the governor was involved with the prophets' evasion of her vengeance. He was sheltering them and probably feeding them from the king's own bread stores. A servant in the kitchens had said he suspected as much, but his suspicions wouldn't be enough to turn Ahab against Obadiah. She doubted Ahab would even care to punish the administrator if the accusation were proven. The king was skittish about harming Israel's prophets and might even secretly wish for Obadiah's success in the matter. She had to find something that would turn Ahab against the man.

"My queen!" The servant girl was almost running down the grand hallway toward Jezebel.

She waved the man away. "We'll talk later."

"What is it now?" Jezebel said as the girl skidded up to her.

She heaved a deep, raspy breath and panted, "The king! He has taken to his bed and will accept no food. His manservant sent me to fetch you!"

"Why me?" the queen said, taking a step back from the girl's hot breath. "Am I now the king's caretaker? His manservant is to see to his food, not the queen!" These servants were always so worried they would suffer for not doing their duties in a timely manner, they caused more alarm than necessary. Which reminded Jezebel that, in the wake of the battle with Benhadad, she had forgotten to see that this girl was dispatched. If Ahab saw her with her neck not stretched, he would think the queen was lying when she said it was her servant's fault she didn't come at his call.

"Never mind, I will go." She motioned to one of the guards. "Take her out and hang her. She has been unfaithful to her duties, causing harm to her queen." The girl's full lips opened into a perfect circle that matched the shape of her eyes, huge with shock. She was as speechless as the tongueless eunuch who stood by expressionless as always. Jezebel turned toward her husband's quarters, the eunuch two steps behind.

Ahab's manservant met Jezebel at the door of the king's chambers. He was wringing his hands as though the world had come to an end.

"What is the matter?" He had better have a good reason for bothering her with his own responsibilities.

"The king. He lies upon his bed, his head to the wall, and will take no food. I fear he may make himself sick, my queen." *No. You fear you will be blamed if he becomes sick. Which you will, if it is up to me!*

"Move aside!" she demanded. The man jumped out of her way. She pulled the heavy door open and entered the outer chambers without knocking. Maids and servants pressed their gaping lips closed and lowered their heads. Not even the queen entered the king's chamber without being announced and then received by the king himself. Or at least, that was the proper protocol. She strode past them and pulled the doors of his bedchamber open.

The room reeked with the fug of uneaten food and unchanged linens. If Jezebel had her way, the manservant would join the maid, but her husband might not appreciate her dispatching the man, so a reprimand would have to do. He'd allowed the king to sink into his couch, facing the wall, curled into himself like a child.

One of Ahab's soldiers, who provided Jezebel with any information he thought she might find interesting, had told her that some ragtag prophet had chastened Ahab for letting Benhadad keep his head attached to his neck. For once she found herself in agreement with a prophet of Israel. The soldier thought some sort of threat had been delivered because Ahab had been sullen ever since. But it appeared a new wave of depression had overtaken the king. She would have to approach him with some care. He was unpredictable in such situations.

Ahab turned at the pad of Jezebel's slippers on the inlaid tile floor then faced the wall again.

"My husband. What is it that keeps you from your supper?"

"I'm just not hungry, Jezebel. Leave me be."

Hmph! It was going to be like that, was it? She had intended to coddle him, since she had been so forceful at his return from the battle, but he needed prodding, not coddling, today.

"It is more than appetite that keeps my king from food. What is it? Why are you so vexed? Tell me, my husband. Perhaps I can help."

He rolled on his back and stared up at the gilded ceiling.

"You cannot help with this."

You would be surprised how much I can help, Husband. Jezebel practically ran the kingdom from behind the scenes. If it weren't for her, there would be no telling what kind of trouble would come to the throne of Israel.

The queen softened her tone." Forgive me, my husband, but if it steals the king's appetite, it is, indeed, important. You cannot serve your people if you are sick ... and I am at your service."

Ahab looked at her for a long moment. Like he was deciding if he should waste his breath.

"I spoke to Naboth earlier."

Naboth? Ah, yes. Their neighbor whose daughter was to marry Obadiah. All of a sudden her senses were on alert. Maybe she could catch two fish with one worm.

"And what sort of conversation led the king of Israel to take to his bed?"

Ahab sighed. "I offered to buy his vineyard or give him another for it. I want to plant some vegetables. I thought walking among the plants might make me feel better. But he wouldn't sell, of course. It is his ancestral land, handed down from his father, to be left to his sons upon his death. I shouldn't have asked him for it."

Shouldn't have *asked* him for it? He should take whatever he wanted! He was the king! "Do you not govern Israel, my husband? Should you be refused anything you desire?"

"We have laws, Jezebel. Israel does not flit from god to god, looking for a better condition. I cannot break the laws of Moses at will and not expect to hear from the blasted prophets about my sin. You don't understand our ways. Laws govern everything!"

He was correct about that. She had done everything to draw her husband away from these silly edicts laid down by the man Moses, who had been disloyal to his king as well. There *were* laws for everything! How many steps one was allowed to walk on the Sabbath, how long a woman must refrain from intercourse after childbirth, and the worst of all was the mutilation of their male children on the eighth day after birth. Barbaric!

"Rise and eat, my king. I will take care of this. You will have your heart's desire."

The king said nothing. Perhaps he was content to let a grape-grower put him in his place. Finally, he let out a long sigh. "Whatever you do, don't burden me with the details."

Of course not, Husband. I never do.

Jezebel tried to swallow the wide smile stretching over her face as she bowed out of the king's chamber. This couldn't have worked out better if she'd planned it! Not only would she be able to appease her husband and get him the land he was too cowardly to seize, she might be able to use this to rid herself of that pesky Obadiah. Yes. Reason to smile, for certain.

Obadiah

When the door to Ahab's chamber started to open, I stepped behind an ensemble of tall potted plants, their broad glossy leaves stretching toward the lofty ceiling. I had seen Jezebel go in and didn't want to draw her attention. One of the servants had told me that Ahab had confined himself to his bed and would not eat or speak with anyone. That was worrisome. The king didn't skip meals, and he didn't make a habit of lying about. He had been subdued when we left Naboth at the vineyard. He hadn't spoken, except for a short exchange about Zim.

"If you wanted the woman, why did you let the wheelwright take her away from you?" he had asked as we walked back toward the palace gate. I had fumbled an excuse. Now I was concerned that Ahab might think he needed to come to my defense. I had to convince him somehow that Zim had not wronged me and I wanted no vengeance enacted against him. But he had taken to his bed, and there was no way his guards would let me through that door. Ahab was on a downward path. He was depressed because of the prophet's proclamation that he and all his sons would die because he had not obeyed God in the matter of Benhadad, as well he should be. And now Naboth's refusal to give up the vineyard. I feared where this was heading. Ahab was becoming as unstable as water—and a broken dam could be deadly.

Jezebel didn't notice me as she walked past the place where I hid. She was smiling from ear to bejeweled ear. That was not good. Not good at all.

Jezebel

The scribe jumped from his seat at the large ink-stained desk where he wrote missives concerning palace business and scrambled to the floor in an attempted bow, his head hitting the tile so quickly it had to have hurt. Jezebel would normally call him a buffoon, but she needed him not to question her request, so she feigned sympathy. She wished that she didn't have to use a scribe at all, but all communications from the king were written by scribes in that distinctive hand they took so long to learn. She couldn't mimic it, and it was imperative that no one question the letter's origin. Besides that, the letter would require the king's seal, as well as the mark of the scribe. Ahab was too weak and too tied to those rigid laws to do what she was going to do.

"Are you all right?"

"Yes, my queen," he said, his nose still to the ground.

"You may rise." The man scrambled to his feet, his head still bent. "What is your name, Scribe?" she said with as pleasant a voice as she could muster.

"Madat, my queen."

"Well, Madat, the king is not feeling well. He has been confined to his bed and did not want to send for a scribe in such a disheveled state, so he dictated a letter to me, which you will transcribe on the king's parchment and attach his seal upon."

The man paled. "Uh … my queen," he stuttered, "the king has never sent a letter to be transcribed. He has always dictated them directly. I … I have certain protocols that must be followed. I can't just …"

"Just what, Scribe? You can't follow your king's directive?"

"No. I mean yes, but … it must be from the king himself. I am not allowed to write anything in the king's name without being in his presence. It is just not done, my queen."

A man who actually follows the king's orders. If it were not that Jezebel had to have this missive, she might actually have rewarded the man for his loyalty.

"Well, Madat, I shall just have to return to the king's chamber and tell him he will have to wait because his scribe thought his king's request was not important enough to break a tiny little rule."

The man looked Jezebel directly in the eye. "I'm sorry, my queen, but it is your husband who made such a rule and threatened with death any scribe who broke it. I am happy to go immediately to the king's chamber and take his dictation there, or explain and get his permission to do as you have suggested." He shook his head. "But I cannot do as you have asked, my queen. I am very sorry."

She wanted to slice the man's head off there and then, but she kept her composure. "I will relay the message to the king. I am certain he will be appreciative of your loyalty while he languishes on his sick bed." The man paled another shade, but he did not offer to change his mind.

Fortunately there was another scribe who was more afraid of Jezebel than of her weakling husband. As soon as he affixed the king's seal, she accused him of thievery and had him hung. She couldn't leave him alive to dispute the authenticity of the missive. She sent the *would-be governor* to place the missive in the hand of a nobleman she had heard was short on scruples. In the meantime, she discreetly saw to it that the first scribe was given an elevated position to head scribe. Loyalty was so rare in the palace, she couldn't help but reward it.

CHAPTER SEVENTEEN

Kenen

Kenen wiped his brow with a linen cloth he kept tucked in his sash. Every time the temperatures soared and the rains were stayed, he couldn't help but wonder if Elijah had cursed them with another drought. Few people waited for the elders at the city gates today, probably deciding that justice could wait for cooler temperatures.

The other noblemen perched on their stools looked as miserable as Kenen felt. But it wasn't just the heat that pulled their brows into little ditches between their eyes. Lemech was on another tirade about Naboth, the flutes of his sleeves flapping like a chicken running from a hatchet. The man hadn't stopped raging since the night of the wedding when the bride's father asked him to hide the amulet or leave. And now, even more so, since Naboth accused all the city elders of corrupting Yahweh's people by failing to speak against the pollution of the law through the worship of Baal.

Of some, he condemned more than just their silence. Some were found at the temple of Baal, openly worshiping before all of Israel. Kenen couldn't truly disagree with Naboth that it was not a good look for the city elders to be seen doing such a thing, but Naboth took it too far, he feared. A little silence might keep him out of trouble, but Naboth didn't seem to be a fan of silence.

"What do you think should be done, Kenen?" Lemech asked, his tone as pleasant as a snakebite.

Kenen's face warmed another degree. He didn't appreciate Lemech dragging him into these discussions. He had no quarrel with Naboth himself. The man was a decent enough fellow—a sentiment Kenen was certain Lemech did not share. He wished that both Lemech and Naboth would just take a few steps back and let matters work themselves out. The tension was building and could only end badly for everyone involved. And now, this was affecting Kenen's own family.

Kenen's wife had become a patron of Naboth's daughter's work, though he had no idea how that had come about. Their living area had practically become a gallery of the girl's urns and dishes. Not that her art wasn't well-crafted, but Kenen often warned Lillian that she should be more careful of her associations. But his wife was a person who cared little for what people thought. Kenen, on the other hand, cared far too much about what people thought. Navigating the politics of city government was like treading on shards of glass. One should expect to bleed if he tried it. If Naboth could just learn to keep his opinions to himself, he would be better off.

"Well?" Lemech demanded. "Answer my question."

"Be done?" Kenen considered his answer carefully. He hoped to steer clear of conflict with Lemech. The others would likely grumble and let it go, but Lemech had probably never let anything go in his life. He had a lust for justice to be administered to wrongdoers—better said, those he considered wrongdoers—and he considered Naboth to be just that.

"Yes, be done!" Lemech squawked, his voice grating on Kenen's last nerve.

"Well, he's been put out of one gathering. Maybe he'll be put out of this one, and there will be no place left for him to complain."

"I doubt it," Lemech grumbled. "He doesn't restrict his criticism to four walls. He's been known to speak on the streets, calling us all a brood of vipers. And some listen to his rants. Just last week a handful of men accosted me with accusations of being an idol worshiper.

"I am not an idol worshiper! I simply wear an icon so the people know I'm not sitting in judgment of their choices. We have to adapt to our surroundings. The queen has opened the temple of Baal to our people as a sign of goodwill. To insult her with our isolation is not in our best interest as a nation. We have to learn to respect those with whom we disagree."

The irony of it almost made Kenen laugh. Lemech wasn't respecting Naboth's right to disagree.

"I don't know, Lemech. Perhaps time will temper Naboth's fervor."

"Time? In time he could pull us all from our positions. He's a convincing man."

That was true. Naboth's very presence commanded attention. Kenen always felt worse for it when he heard his condemnations. But Naboth was not mean-spirited. He spoke with genuine concern for his fellows. He was known for his philanthropy and his devotion to Yahweh. He didn't seem to be a pretender. Kenen didn't want him to be censured to the point he lost favor with the people.

A man, narrow-faced with sagging jowls, approached. "Who's in charge here?" Lemech immediately raised his hand. The man handed him a scroll.

"What is this?" Lemech said, looking up at the messenger.

"A message from Ahab, King of Israel, for the chief elder of Jezreel."

Ahab? Lemech looked as shocked as Kenen felt. When was the last time the elders had received a message from the king? Never in Kenen's memory.

The man left without so much as taking his leave. The palace must be in dire straits if they hired men like this to deliver missives. Lemech looked around the circle of men, confusion and a blot of worry in his eyes. He opened the scroll, his gaze moving down the parchment.

When he reached the bottom, he stared at it for several long moments. He looked up, a smile slipping over his face.

"I think our prayers may have been answered." He looked at the scroll again and began to laugh. "Yes, indeed."

Something in his voice sent a shiver down Kenen's spine. They hadn't been praying about anything. Hardly. They had been talking about how to solve the problem of Naboth.

<hr>

Anna

Anna saw her father in the vineyard plucking a leaf off one of the vines and bringing it close to his eyes. His vision wasn't impaired, so she knew he was examining the leaf for spots and darkened areas. A pang of worry hit her. A blight had ruined some of the neighbor's vines, and a few others across the Jezreel Valley had suffered some damage. It wasn't unusual, but it was always worrisome. If left unattended it could wipe out an entire vineyard in short order. As she drew closer she could see the depth of the crease between his thick graying eyebrows.

"Good afternoon, Father."

He raised his head, his weathered cheeks lifting, pulling his lips into a wide smile and causing his eyes to crinkle at the corners. His smile always warmed her heart.

"How is my favorite daughter and my grandson?"

Anna felt her cheeks warm. Talking about being with child around her father was a bit embarrassing. It was silly, she knew, but the thought of his knowing she had been intimate with her husband made her blush. Anna loved her father dearly, but since she'd married, her thoughts often wandered to the mother she never knew. How wonderful it would be to have someone to talk with about such things. She definitely did not want to talk to her cousin Zadah.

Zim talked about the baby all the time, asking questions that Anna didn't have the answers for herself. He was overjoyed at the prospect of becoming a father. Anna knew he would be good at it. He was a kind, gentle husband, so she could expect nothing less of him with a child. Affection stirred deep in her heart for her husband. No, not affection. It was love. She loved Zim. She still struggled with her feelings for Obadiah on occasion, but her heart was turned fully toward Zim now.

Anna kissed her father on the cheek. "First of all, I'm your only daughter," she said with a finger raised. "And second," she said, raising another, "I could be carrying a girl, you know. What is it with men and sons and grandsons?"

He chuckled. "You are correct. I would be more than pleased to have a granddaughter. Her mother is the joy of my heart, and the child would be as well."

Anna patted his shoulder and looked down at the leaf in his hand. "No sign that beetles have been at it, I see, or the blight. That is good, right?"

He nodded and drew a deep breath. "Yes, that is good. Praise Yahweh. But others have seen some loss, so we must be diligent to catch any sign of damaged leaves immediately."

Father's face sobered. A fine line appeared in his forehead. He was looking at something over Anna's shoulder. She turned to see two men, obviously of poor estate. One was a big man, tall and on the heavy side. The other was small of stature. There was something about how they approached that gave her a strange feeling.

"Greetings," Father said as they drew closer. "How may I help you?"

The shorter one seemed nervous. The big man dipped his head toward Anna in greeting and spoke to her father.

"We're needin' some work, my lord. Thought maybe you could use a couple of hands in your vineyard there," he said, nodding toward the vines.

Father was silent for a long moment. "Have you worked in a vineyard before? What are your skills?"

"Well," he said, looking at his companion. "We've done some work in the vineyards, yes. Shumani here is good at most all of it."

Father hesitated for a few moments. Anna wondered if the men were telling the truth about their skills. They weren't very specific about their knowledge.

"I do have a job that needs done. One that doesn't require a great deal of experience with the vines and would free up my sons and day workers to continue with their own tasks. Have you ever seen leaves taken by a wilting blight?"

"No." The two men shook their heads in unison, as though they needed to assure Father that they hadn't witnessed any such thing. That seemed strange.

"Well, I want you to walk through the rows and look for leaves that have irregularly shaped lesions. They might be a dull red to a brown color." Father paused. "If they're black, that is very bad. Black rot will cause the entire cluster to collapse in a short time. We have been blessed that our vines are strong and healthy but we need to keep close watch."

He looked at one man and then the other for a moment. Something seemed to be bothering him. The men seemed ... off somehow to Anna. She couldn't put her finger on it, but she sensed some sort of falsehood in their presentation. She thought her father did as well, but he shook hands with them and told them there were blankets in the small shed at the end of the rows and someone would bring them some supper, and to start on the far end of the vineyard and report back immediately if they found anything

The smaller man looked up at the big man with a smile on his face that seemed more like a smirk. Like they had succeeded at some misadventure rather than secured a job. The big man furrowed his brow at the smaller and took him by the arm and started to the other end of the vineyard. Neither of them thanked her father.

"Did that seem strange to you?" Anna asked.

Father watched the men as they walked away. "They did seem a bit ungrateful. We'll see how they work out."

<hr/>

Zim was home from his work early. He was barely through the door when he pulled Anna into his arms. "You look beautiful," he said as he nuzzled the sensitive place behind her ear. They were becoming familiar with one another: the places that made their bodies respond, the things that made them laugh out loud until they had to run to relieve themselves, the words that touched that place in their hearts where love was growing like a vine climbing a trellis toward the sunlight.

He bent down and kissed Anna's stomach. "Greetings, little man. Your mother is the most beautiful woman in the world, and your father the most fortunate."

Anna laughed. "Little man, is it? We'll see."

He took her in his arms again and kissed her in a way that stirred places she never knew existed before her marriage.

But their minds were jerked away from their ecstasy by a noise outside. One of the workers was shouting for Anna's father and the boys to come in a hurry. Zim took Anna's hand, and they bolted out of the house and toward the vineyard where the two men Naboth had hired the day before were standing.

"Right there." The tall one pointed. "That looks like the work of a beetle to me."

Anna's father touched a leaf, his face falling into a worried pinch. "A beetle. I had been more worried about the blight, but it does appear to be the work of a beetle. It's fresh. No discoloration yet around the edge of the leaf from the distress." He observed the two men, who seemed strangely excited at bringing such news. "Is this the only vine you've found that has such damage?"

The big one shook his head. "No, we found several on down at the end. Looks bad, if you ask me."

"Down at the end?" Father said with a frown. "And here? Nothing in between? The insects usually make their way outward from the origin."

"Uh, well ... maybe some of the insects started on one side and some on the other."

Anna saw the frown form on her father's face. He looked up at the sky. "Yahweh, a three-year drought and now this? Blessed be Your name. Help us, or Ahab will get this vineyard for his vegetable garden yet."

<hr />

Anna had prepared the evening meal while the men scoured through the vines for more damage. Zim pecked her cheek as he came through the door, then went to the basin to wash his hands, her father not far behind.

"What did you find?" she said, hoping the news was not as bad as it had seemed.

"Well, that's the strange thing. We found some damage at the end of the row like the men said, but it was confined to one area. We picked a few beetles off the vines. There weren't many, but we kept looking to be certain."

Zim spoke up. "The strangest thing is that the men are gone. Didn't even collect their wages."

What? That *was* strange. "Do you think Ahab sent them to get you to sell, Father?"

"Possibly, but it doesn't sound like something he would do. He seemed resigned when he left, and Obadiah would let us know if the king was raging about it. He didn't say anything yesterday when he dropped off bread for the prophets."

Obe had been here again and Anna hadn't seen him? He must be taking care to avoid her. That was good, she supposed. She hoped he was doing well. She just wished that he could be part of their lives. She missed him. Guilt gnawed at her. Her thoughts felt like a betrayal to her husband. She was Zim's wife and she was happy, but Obe had been woven into the fabric of her life since she was a child. Somehow his absence left her feeling ... like there was a missing piece, an empty spot that nothing else could fill. But she understood that nothing could be the same. It wasn't her and Obe and Zim anymore. And it never would be.

CHAPTER EIGHTEEN

Obadiah

Zim was oiling a leather fitting when I entered the wheel shop. He looked up, surprised to see me. Guilt gnawed at me for not visiting him more often here in the place where we'd shared so many fond memories. Zim's father had always greeted me with a wide smile when I appeared at the doorway hoping Zim would be allowed some time to play with our miniature chariots or take a trip to the creek to catch some fish. I missed the man almost as much as I missed my own father.

Zim must have gotten his lean build from his mother's side because his father had been a man of imposing stature, a towering figure whose frame exuded strength and resilience. I would always miss him.

"Welcome, brother!" Zim wiped the oil off his hands and came to me, pulling me into his chest and pounding me on the back. I loved this man so dearly.

"You have stayed away too long, Obe. I hardly see you." A trace of guilt flashed over his face. He knew how much I loved Anna. I was certain he felt my pain. But we were brothers of the heart if not of the flesh, and the love between us stood on its own merits.

"I'm sorry, Zim. I should take the time more often. I have no excuse to offer."

"That's alright, brother. I know you are a busy man just trying to stay out of Jezebel's way. How goes it in the palace?"

I sighed." It's hard to say sometimes. The queen eyes me like a vulture waiting for its prey to die so it can pick the bones. I know she is conniving to trap me in some way. How's Naboth after Ahab's visit?"

A shadow slid over Zim's face. He ran his fingers through his hair.

"I don't know. Naboth has seemed troubled for a while. Actually I noticed it even during the betrothal period. He seemed better after the wedding. Kind of relieved. But I'm feeling it from him again. Can't really figure out what's going on in his mind, but he seems preoccupied. Maybe worried."

"Truly? Why do you think that is?"

"Not sure. He's had some more run-ins with the city fathers. But he got a notice yesterday that a fast has been called for tomorrow, and they've asked him to lead it. So maybe they're trying to make amends, or at least quiet him—not that it will do any good. Naboth won't be bribed or intimidated to silence."

A fast? I hadn't been told about it. Something didn't quite feel right about this situation.

<hr />

Kenen

Kenen passed through the opening of one of the large chambers in the city wall. The air was thick with the earthy scent of damp stone and the faint, metallic tang of iron. The flickering light of torches cast long, wavering shadows on the rough-hewn walls. He rubbed his arms against the chill.

The backless stone benches were already filled with many of the prominent citizens of Jezreel. The solemn assembly and fast had been called hastily by Lemech and without word of its purpose. All Kenen knew was that Lemech had appointed Naboth to head the assembly, and they were not gathering at the gates, where such occasions were usually held so all who wished to could attend. Kenen wished he had feigned illness, but a solemn assembly was not something he could ignore without garnering Lemech's displeasure, and probably Yahweh's as well. But there was something about this gathering that made him leery. The room was crowded, so he took a seat in the back instead of pushing through the crowd to the long bench at the wall where the other council members were sitting. The hard stone beneath him was cold and unforgiving, a discomfort that mirrored his unease.

Naboth walked through the open doorway with his three sons and his son-in-law. Kenen recognized them from the wedding. Showing humility, Naboth didn't take the upper seat but slipped into one of the stone benches with his family.

Lemech was walking down the aisle toward the back bench. A smile that didn't light his eyes peeked out from his well-trimmed beard. Kenen saw Naboth lean into the son next to him. He couldn't hear what the vintner said but saw a look of concern fall over the oldest boy as he nodded and passed the message to the other three.

Lemech glanced at Kenen and nodded toward the bench at the front where the other noblemen were sitting, then bowed at the waist, and kissed Naboth on one cheek and then the other. Kenen wasn't going to move. He was getting tired of Lemech bossing him around like he was a child. His body stiffened, an involuntary, premonitory response to something in Lemech's demeanor. He was kissing Naboth's cheek in greeting? It was difficult to believe that Lemech would let bygones be bygones.

"Naboth. Elder of Israel. Please take a seat at the front," he said, the smile slipping at the corners. He gestured toward a table set on the stone platform.

There was only one chair. Naboth lowered himself to the seat, his shoulders squared, his back as straight as the solid wood behind him. He was clothed in sackcloth as was the tradition at such an assembly. Kenen looked out over the other sackcloth-clad men and scratched at the place where his own garment rubbed his neck. The tunics were thick, rough, and coarse, a symbol of grief and mourning. They were supposed to be an outward sign of humility and repentance.

Kenen drew a deep breath and let it out slowly. *What is this?*

Lemech stood behind another table at the side of the room and spoke in his deep, grating voice. Kenen winced at the sound of it.

"It is with great regret for the circumstances that have brought us here that we have called this time of fasting and solemn assembly in Jezreel."

What circumstances? Why had he not proclaimed them when the assembly was called?

Lemech looked like a fool with his downturned mouth and his try-ing-too-hard woeful countenance.

"The God of Israel has shown Himself angry by sending a blight upon many of the vineyards across the countryside." He cleared his throat and stretched to his full height. "We fear if no action is taken to stay His hand, Yahweh's judgment will pollute every vine in the land. We cannot sit by and let the cause of Yahweh's anger go unjudged. Only judgment will stay the hand of the Almighty."

Kenen's brows pulled together in question. He had heard of a few vineyards being hit with the blight, but it didn't rise to this sort of alarm. It happened every few years. Kenen had never attributed it to the wrath of God. He imagined that if Yahweh was angry at anything it would be what Naboth was always complaining about.

"Our law says, 'Do not curse the king I have placed over you. Do not curse the God who formed you from the dust of the earth.'"

Curse the king? The man continued, a rise in the tone of his deep voice. Kenen pressed his lips together. "I fear someone in our midst has grievously violated both of these commands." The nobleman gave a nod to a guard standing at the rear entrance of the chamber. "But the Law also says a man cannot be accused by one witness only. There must be two."

Two men passed by Kenen toward the table where Naboth was seated. The smug smile of the larger man was matched by the silly grin on the smaller of the two. Lemech waved a hand, and some men dragged a table to the side of the platform, and set two chairs at it. Kenen noticed their clothing was new. New sandals were strapped on their feet which were not entirely clean and sported broken nails and open sores. Their clothing seemed incongruent with the rest of them.

Alarm began creeping up Kenen's back. This was not a solemn assembly. It was a trap!

"My lords, please say your names so all may hear."

Lords? These men were far from lords. They were men of no worth. Probably paupers and extortionists and maybe thieves.

"Malchus," said the bigger man. "And this is my brother, Shumani. And we heard that man"—he pointed at Naboth—"curse God and the king!"

What? The boys sucked air into their lungs. Kenen felt faint, the blood rushing from his head as the room seemed to narrow around him. This was impossible. Of all people, Naboth would not do such a thing. *Lemech! What are you doing, you fool!*

"Please don't answer questions that haven't been asked yet!" Lemech seemed irritated with the men. But Kenen had no doubt that Lemech was fully aware of what the two were planning to say. These men didn't have the sense to come up with such a plan themselves.

"Before you bear witness, please tell us how you know Naboth of Jezreel."

The tall one raised his bearded chin. "We worked for him at his vineyard."

"So you were his employees."

"Yes."

Naboth's oldest son shook his head and whispered to the others. His face was the hue of a bleached bone.

"And as his employees, you sometimes overheard Naboth and his sons speaking when they were unaware?"

His sons? Kenen knew Lemech hated Naboth for his continuous preaching, but why bring his sons into it? Kenen had paid no attention to the soldiers standing behind Naboth's family. But now he knew why they had been placed there. Nerves stippled his skin and made the hair stand on his arms.

"Yes, happened all the time. People like them don't pay no attention to the folks who work for them. Like we weren't even there. Guess he never thought we'd tell, being like he thinks we was invisible and all."

"And can you tell me what was happening when you heard Naboth and his sons curse God and the king?"

"He was looking at the beetles we ... that were—" The older brother elbowed the younger and looked up to speak to Lemech.

"We saw that the beetles had infested his vines. They were everywhere, just chewing up those leaves like they were never going to get another meal. We ran to the house to tell Naboth since them insects can eat a whole row of vines before you can hardly kill a one of them. Naboth started screaming at us like it was us who had eaten his leaves. He cursed everything in sight. Cursed God for letting it happen and accused the king of trying to steal his vineyard. Said the king was a fool and a greedy son of a ... well, I can't really repeat it, but you get the idea."

There was a collective gasp in the room. A few men seemed uncertain and confused, most nodded their heads in agreement, but Kenen wondered how the story had turned from the blight to beetles. This tale wasn't holding water any better than a bucket without a bottom.

Would these neighbors, colleagues, some Naboth might call friends, take the word of these men against his? By the feel of the room, it seemed so. Naboth had reproved many of them for their neglect of the Law. Many, perhaps most, of the men sitting in this room, sported amulets and charms dedicated to Baal. The murmur of their voices created a rising tide of sound, a cacophony of judgment and suspicion, adding to Kenen's growing sense of foreboding.

Lemech regarded Naboth, a smirk hiding in his beard. "How would you defend yourself, Naboth?"

How *could* he defend himself? Kenen knew it would make no difference what Naboth said.

After the room became still and all eyes were on Naboth, he stood slowly and looked out over the crowd of men. Ashes powdered his gray hair and the shoulders of his sackcloth tunic. His limbs looked as if bags of stones weighed them down.

"I have only this to say. There were but a handful of beetles on my vines, and no blight." He pulled a deep breath. "And these men heard no such blasphemy from my mouth. What I spoke of the king at that moment was no curse. My memory of the moment is vague. I believe I said that Ahab may get his vegetable garden yet. The king had approached me about selling my vineyard to him or taking a larger vineyard in trade so he could use mine to grow vegetables."

Lemech's jaw tightened, his nose in a flare of agitation. "But you say yourself, Naboth, that your memory of the occasion is vague. How can you be sure you didn't curse the king if you don't remember what you said?"

Naboth straightened his frame. "I can be sure because out of the abundance of the heart the mouth speaks." He looked directly into Lemech's eyes. "And it is not in my heart to curse the king of my people. No matter how I may be tempted to do so, the Law forbids it, and I would not do it."

Lemech seemed flustered by Naboth's bold statement. "Two witnesses say you did! And what of cursing Yahweh Himself? What do you have to say on that charge?"

Naboth's gaze turned to the two men sitting at the table. They squirmed in their seats. "What motive these men have for saying such things is lost on me. They will have to answer to Yahweh for themselves." The vintner's eyes narrowed, his chin hardening. "But I would rather suffer any punishment—even one you may impose today in this court—than to curse my God. Yahweh suffers us to ask 'why' when we do not understand. He encourages it. When Yahweh told Moses to go back to Egypt from the wilderness and command Pharaoh to let God's people go, Moses argued that he was unable to speak, and the God of Israel told him to use his brother, Aaron, as his mouthpiece. Even Father Abraham bargained with Yahweh to spare the city of Sodom if ten righteous souls could be found there, but these men were not cursing Yahweh in their questioning. Neither did I curse Him in mine. No! I did not curse God, and if these men say I did, they are lying."

Voices tossed on the cool air of the chamber—a few in protest of the accusations, most demanding Naboth be found guilty.

"But these men are not being judged before this assembly!" Lemech snarled.

Naboth lifted a thick brow. "Perhaps they should be. Better to be judged by man than to be judged by God."

Lemech's face flared an angry red. "You admit you can't remember if you cursed the king, but these two witnesses remember well, it seems. And you twist the words of Yahweh when you say it is no curse to question!"

Kenen looked at the wall where the city fathers sat in judgment of Naboth. What did their faces tell him? Those who hated Naboth would count him guilty, and those who did not—would be too afraid of losing their positions to protest.

Panic began slithering into Kenen's chest. These were no menial charges. And few in this room truly cared if the man was guilty or innocent. The lot had been cast before Naboth walked through the door. Would they seek to put him to death? Kenen let out a long breath. Of course they would; the charges demanded stoning. His stomach rose to his throat. He looked at Naboth's sons and saw the shock stripping their faces of color. Kenen wanted to tell them to run, but it would do no good. Lemech had extended the charges to the sons. Sometimes whole families were executed. And the bridegroom, Naboth's son-in-law. What would happen to him?

CHAPTER NINETEEN

Obadiah

Obadiah!" I turned to see Shadim, one of the servants who helped us with the bread, sprinting down the great hall toward me. I hoped Jezebel hadn't seen him. People had been killed for less in this palace. I put out my palm to keep the man from running me down. "Shadim, stop! What is it? You know better than this." Shadim wheezed like a man choking on a bone as he looked up and down the hallway, then dragged me to an alcove.

"Master Obadiah," he said between snatches of breath.

"What is it, man? Breathe." The servant's face was as white as milk despite the exertion.

"Master, it's Naboth," he said, "And his sons. They're going to stone them."

My head jerked back as though I had been physically struck. That couldn't be. It was not possible that Naboth ... the boys ... "What are you talking about? Stoned? Who's going to stone them? And for what?"

"The elders of the city! They had some kind of meeting this morning. A fast. And someone accused Naboth of cursing Yahweh and Ahab."

Cursing Yahweh? And the king? "Who brought the charge?" Something was very wrong. Shadim must have misunderstood.

"Some men who claimed to have worked for him. Said they heard him curse Yahweh over the blight and cursed the king right along with it! He didn't do it, Obadiah. I know he's outspoken, but he would never curse God, and I doubt he would curse the king out where everybody could hear. You've got to help them!"

The blood drained from my face. I felt faint. "What about Zimiric? Was he with them?"

"I don't know. Eli the blacksmith told me to tell you. It was all over the market. I think it's already too late, Master," he said, shaking his head back and forth, tears gathering in his eyes.

I grasped the man's shoulder hard. "No. It's not too late. If this is true, I'll stop it! Go by the wheel house. If Zim's there, tell him to get his wife and go to the cave." I paused for a moment, not wanting to even entertain the possibility— "And if he isn't, go to the vineyard and take her to the cave immediately. Tell her we'll all meet her there soon." *God, let it be so.*

I took off running down the wide hall. The stream of servants in my path parted like the sea in the days of Moses.

This can't be true. Oh, Yahweh, have mercy.

A groom was outside the stable walking a black mare. She was a fast horse. I'd seen her run. And she was already saddled.

The groom's eyes widened as I ran toward him and took the reins out of his hands. "I need the mare! Move aside!" The boy stepped back, his palms in front of him.

It was a short distance to the field of stones, a swath of ground with scrubby trees and a few large boulders—and a plethora of stones lying loose on the dry soil. There was usually a pile or two already gathered, awaiting their gruesome task. I passed a few men making their way to the place. If I'd had only a minute I would have stopped and beat them bloody for the smiles on their bearded faces.

A group of men dressed in sackcloth were gathered in a large circle. The mockery of the sackcloth made me grind my teeth. Were they looking at the damage their stones had already done, or did I have time to stop this travesty? I saw Lemech. Of course, he was at the root of this!

I dismounted the horse, leaving the reins hanging and rushed toward him, but when he and the man beside him moved apart, leaving a gap in the circle, my feet refused to take another step and I stumbled to a stop. Naboth and the brothers were on their knees, huddled together, each arm extended over another's shoulder—like a braided cord. And Zim, one arm over Joel and one over Jason.

A hand reached into my chest and wrenched my heart out of its place. Zim raised his head, and his eyes met mine. A ray of hope emerged from the fear in his dark eyes. *Zim.* My knees began to buckle. But I had no time for shock. Lemech was praying.

"Stop" I shouted as I regained my footing and lurched forward. "Stop in the name of King Ahab!" Two men caught me by my forearms. Lemech looked up, a fleeting glint of alarm dilating his dark pupils.

"Stop this now!" I shouted. "You will answer to the king for this! I am the governor of his palace! Let these men go!"

The man's wide pupils constricted into pinpricks of dark intensity as he motioned for the men to move away. "I know who you are." He stepped so close I could smell the mint on his breath. He lowered his voice to a whisper. "And you do not speak for the king. We are here at the king's order."

The king's order? "You're a liar! The king did not order this. He would not order this!"

The man laughed, a short, sharp sound that made every nerve in my body fire. He pulled out a scroll, and held it up where I could see the script used only by the king's scribes.

Proclaim a fast and set Naboth at the head of the people. Set two worthless men opposite him, and let them bring a charge against him, saying, "You have cursed God and the king." Then take him out and stone him to death.

My stomach sickened. The king's seal was affixed to it and the mark of the scribe who dictated it. But Ahab couldn't have ordered this. I didn't believe it.

"I wouldn't mention this if I were you," Lemech said in my ear. "The king may not want his orders known among the rabble. If you stir up trouble, the palace may be in need of a new governor."

He was threatening me? Did he think I would withdraw for fear of losing my position? Or my life? I wanted to spit in his fat face.

"I don't believe that the king wrote this missive! Give it to me and I will take it to him and let him confirm or deny it."

Lemech snorted. "Do you think I'm that stupid? I would never see that parchment again. And do you think I would do this if I wasn't certain the order was genuine? It was delivered by a palace messenger. It bears the king's seal and the mark of the scribe who wrote it. It's the king's own business why he wants this order carried out." His eyes narrowed. "And Naboth and his family are guilty of these crimes!"

Lemech lifted bushy brows, giving me a warning that the subject was closed. He turned toward the people standing in a loose circle around Naboth and his sons, about to nod for the execution to begin.

"Stop! Stop!" I grabbed his sleeve. He turned abruptly, about to have me removed, I was sure. I lowered my voice. I didn't know if this would work, but I had to try. "If you have found Naboth guilty of a crime, why destroy his sons? And the man on the right." I looked toward Zim. "He's not a son of Naboth. What right do you have to stone him?"

The man snarled. "You know that sons are called to pay for their father's crimes. It wipes out the bad seed."

Bad seed. The injustice of the claim ignited a wildfire of fury in me. Naboth's sons were not bad seed. They were good, honest men who loved Yahweh. And they were my friends, but I knew I could not convince Lemech on those grounds. I no choice but to let it go and try to save Zim. "But what of the other man. He shares no blood with Naboth. He is not even of the same tribe!"

Lemech looked taken aback for a moment, but he recovered his composure. "Perhaps he's not a son, but the witnesses identified him as one of the young men who cursed alongside Naboth. He is a son-in-law, is he not?"

"Yes."

"Then he will be stoned with the rest of the blasphemers. The wicked seed needs to be cut off from the presence of the Lord."

My blood turned cold. Zim had told me that Anna was with child—the grandchild of the man they were going to put to a painful death. Would they bother a grieving widow with a babe? I would never have dreamed it to be so. But I wouldn't have dreamed they would stone an innocent man either. They couldn't know she was with child, but what of when her stomach began to swell? Would they consider a boy-child from Naboth's daughter wicked seed? And what if Ahab *was* behind this, and it was all about getting the vineyard. Anna or her son could inherit if there were no other male heirs. That would put her at the center of Ahab's focus. I had vowed to protect these people. All of them—and I had failed. *Yahweh forgive me.*

"Just give me a moment with them. These men are my friends. Please!"

Lemech contemplated my request for a long moment, then raised a hand toward the men all too eager to send the hefty rocks to their targets.

"You have two minutes. Let it not be said that this court did not show compassion."

Compassion? I would have laughed in his face, but I wouldn't waste the precious time.

Five sets of eyes fastened on mine as I walked toward them. I could see hope seep out of every one of them as I drew closer. I fell to my knees and joined the braid of hands and shoulders, Zim to my right, Joel to my left, looking at Naboth through tear-filled eyes.

"I'm sorry. I tried. They wouldn't listen."

Naboth nodded, a small smile appearing on his chapped lips.

"I know you did, Son."

Son. A jolt of anger cut through me. "If I am your son, then I'll let them kill me too. Maybe killing the palace administrator will get them the punishment they deserve!"

"No!" Zim looked into my eyes. The words were small when they came out of his mouth. "Who would take care of Anna if you died?"

I felt like one of the waiting stones had hit me squarely in the heart. *Take care of Anna.* Zim was implying that I would marry his widow. No! I would not marry Anna! Anna was Zim's wife! The child was Zim's child! For me to get Anna this way? I shook my head. No. I would see that she was taken care of, but I would not marry Zim's wife.

Zim read my face. He turned to the others. They looked to the hard ground to give us the illusion of privacy.

Zim spoke in just more than a whisper. "Do you think it causes me no pain, my friend?" Tears welled in his dark eyes. "Anna loves me, Obe. Me. I am her husband. Do you think it doesn't gall me to know that she'll become your wife? It does." The tears flowed over the berm of his thick lashes. "But I know you will love her as you have always done. You will love my child, and you will be a good husband to her."

I shook my head sharply. "No, Zim. I will not be Anna's husband. I will see that she is cared for. I will find her a good husband. A good father for your child, but it will not be me." Pain like I had never felt, not

165

even when I lost my father and Anna, filled the empty place where my heart had been. I swiped my leaking nose with my sleeve. "I wouldn't be able to do it, Zim," I said, my voice cracking. "I wouldn't be able to enjoy life with her, knowing that you had to die for it to be so."

Zim pulled me hard to his chest, his mouth to my ear, his shoulders shaking. "You will, Obe. And it will be alright."

The whirl of a stone whistled through the air. It was far afield from us, but a warning that my time was up.

Naboth spoke in a gentle, almost serene voice. "You must go now, my son. Find Anna. Keep her safe. Tell her that I love her." I could see the memory in his eyes of the day he had refused me the time I had begged of him, and said he would give Anna to another. We had both wanted to keep her safe. I hoped that I would not let him down again.

"Your time is up! Move away, or you will perish with your criminal friends!" Lemech shouted.

I pulled these dear men in for one last embrace. "I'm so sorry that I cannot stop this," I said, tears dampening the neck of my tunic. "May Yahweh receive you with the honor you deserve." I put my arms around Zim's neck again. We held each other, weeping, our shoulders shaking. "I love you, Zim. I'm sorry. Sorry for every way I've ever hurt you."

We pulled back, looking into each other's eyes.

He managed a smile through the flood of tears. "I love you too, my friend. My brother."

I couldn't move. I couldn't leave Zim. Moving from his side would unravel the cord that had bound us since our boyhood. It would unleash the stones that waited in the hands of angry men. A moan rose from the deepest part of my soul. I ripped the neck of my tunic and put my head to the ground and scooped up dirt and poured it on my head. *Yahweh!*

A sickening crack, like the splitting of a dry, brittle branch, reverberating with a hollow thud, pulled my head up. Jason's mouth was open, his eyes wide with surprise as blood poured from the wound to his temple.

"Go!" Zim and Naboth shouted at the same moment. In a stupor, I rose to my feet and stepped away. A barrage of stones took to the air and struck the men like heavy hail on a clay roof. Moans of agony assaulted my ears. Zim rocked back from the force of a large stone, then stared, his mouth open, his eyes empty before his head fell to his chest. *Zim.*

I looked at Naboth one more time. His eyes were closed, his mouth moving in silent prayer. Another rock stopped the motion of his lips.

Fear flitted through Lemech's eyes as I approached, the neck of my garment torn, my eyes locked with his. I jabbed my finger at the document he held in his hand. "You had better hang on to that piece of parchment, because when it's made known that Ahab didn't write it, you're going to have to give account for this. And you better hope that the person who did write it doesn't point back at you!"

Lemech's face turned gray.

∝∝∝∝∝∝∝∝

I leaned the brush door back against the entrance to the cave. The silence sent a shiver of fear through me. Was she here? "Anna? It's me."

One of the prophets came around the corner, his arm around Anna's shoulder. Anna stared at me through red-veined eyes, her face white. Her eyes focused on my ripped garment.

"All of them?" she asked, her lips trembling.

I nodded, forcing back the tears. She let out an unearthly wail that cut through the cords of my soul. She swayed and staggered, ready to fall. The old man couldn't hold her, and she started to slip to the floor. In a moment I had her cradled in my arms. I sat on the stone bench rocking her like a child. She clung to me as if letting go would be the end of her. I shouldn't be doing this. I would pay the price when the moment was over. *Oh, Zim. I wish you were here and I was where you are. To be without you and Anna both will be worse than death.*

When her tears dried to a salty stain on her cheeks, I slipped her off my lap and wrapped my cloak around her shoulders and sat on the floor in front of her. The loss of her warmth was excruciating. And by the shudder of her shoulders I could tell she felt the cold truth of the situation.

She looked at me, grief etched in the green depths of her eyes. Her voice a hoarse whisper when she spoke. "Were you there?"

I nodded, pressing my lips together to keep them from trembling. She wiped at her eyes with her sleeve. "I'm glad. I wouldn't have wanted them to be alone."

I choked. "They died with their arms around one another. They were so brave, Anna. Your father smiled, and he was praying when the—" I left the word unsaid.

To my surprise she smiled through her tears. "How like him."

Fresh tears welled in her eyes. She looked at me for a long moment. "—and Zim?"

I drew a deep breath. "His last words were of you. He loved you very much, Anna." I didn't tell her that he expected me to take her as my wife. I couldn't tell her because I couldn't do it. I wouldn't. No matter what Zim said.

Fear mixed with the grief on her face. "What will happen now, Obe? Was this about the vineyard?"

"I think so. I don't know what else it could have been. The ... leader showed me a letter from Ahab that directed the noblemen to call a fast and put your father at the head of it, then have two men testify that he had cursed God and the king." I huffed a breath and shook my head. "I just didn't think he would do it. He seemed to have let go of the notion of getting the vineyard. He knows the law. But I saw the letter. It was in the royal scribe's hand, with Ahab's seal. Maybe Jezebel talked him into it. I don't know, but I intend to find out."

"Father would never do any of that!" Anna said, a flash of anger lighting the pools of green.

"Of course not. Anyone who truly knew Naboth wouldn't believe a word of it," I said, my heart aching for her.

"He didn't think much of Ahab, but he never let us talk disrespectfully of him. And you know he would never curse Yahweh. I just don't understand it. Who were the witnesses?"

"A couple of low-born imbeciles. They said they'd worked for him. The whole trial was supposed to stop the blight. Stop Yahweh's wrath. The men said when they showed your father the beetles they'd found, he cursed at them and then at Ahab and Yahweh Himself."

Anna sucked a shocked breath. "I was there. He gave the men a job. They said they found some beetles, but something seemed off about it. There were just a handful, and the vines were hardly damaged. They didn't even collect their pay."

"They had to have been sent to plant the beetles so the elders could make their case," Anna said, her lips tight.

We talked for a while, until another round of tears choked the words and we wept again. It was just hard to believe. Naboth. Gone. Zim. Gone. The brothers. Gone. All gone in a hail of stones.

I stood. I needed to leave. I had to do some investigating before my regular meeting with Ahab tomorrow. It was hard for me to accept that he had written that missive. But if he had, I would know it when I looked into his eyes. If he did, I feared I would fall upon him with my own sword. But I couldn't do that. I had to get Anna settled somehow, then I could say what I wished to him and let the pieces fall where they may. I wouldn't care what happened to me once Anna was safe. I just had to figure out how to keep her that way.

"I must go. I don't want Ahab to wonder where I am. I want things to seem as normal as possible so I can figure out what brought all this on. There should be plenty of food, and I'll send some extra blankets as soon as possible."

Before I could move a step, Anna was on her feet. "No! You're not leaving me here!"

"I will come back for you soon. I promise."

Anna touched her stomach. "I won't be abandoned again, Obe!"

"Anna," I opened my mouth to tell her that it wasn't safe for her to leave the cave, but she turned a scathing look toward me.

"You can't leave me here!" Her shoulders began to shake as tears spilled down her face again.

"But where can I take you, Anna?" I looked around the cave. "This is the safest place for you. I can't take you back to the vineyard or to the house in Jezreel." I looked at her long fingers as they pressed against her stomach. "I don't think they'll come looking for you, but the baby ..." I didn't want to say it but I had to. "What if they find out you're pregnant? A child, if it's a boy, would be a loose end they would not want to deal with. And you, yourself, could be targeted. If it's proven Ahab didn't write that letter, it would bring up questions they won't want to answer." *Like why they killed your husband when he had no claim to Naboth's land.* Anna chewed her lip, the look of a feral cat on her face as she studied the situation. She knew I was right, but she wasn't going to stay here, no matter how much I argued for it.

"Lillian," she said, her face suddenly animated. "You could take me to Lillian's house! I know she would receive me."

My forehead knotted. "Who is Lillian?"

"She and her daughters helped at my wedding. She bought a vase from me at the market the day you—" She didn't finish the sentence, but I knew the woman now. She had seemed kind enough at the market, and I had been thankful that she and the other young women had been there for Anna. The question was, how could I trust Anna and her baby—Zim's baby—to someone I didn't know?

"You trust this woman?"

"Yes, I trust her. We became friends, and she and her daughters were wonderful to me on my wedding day. She's very kind. I know she will help me."

I didn't want to do it. But what choice did I have? I huffed a breath. "Alright."

Anna ran to the back of the cave to gather her robe and the bag she had hastily packed when Shadim had come for her. In a few moments she was on the mare, sitting in front of me as I held the reins of the animal in one hand. I was careful not to touch her more than absolutely necessary. Everything in me wanted to pull her to my chest and hold her there, but I would not do it.

Oh, Anna. I love you. I will always love you, but I can't be what you need me to be right now. I can't comfort you the way I yearn to. I can't be Zim to you.

CHAPTER TWENTY

Anna

Anna waited beside Obe inside the hallway entrance while an older man with as straight a back as she'd ever seen walked down the wide hall to inquire if the mistress of the house would accept an unannounced visit from a disheveled woman in the company of a palace official.

She was having second thoughts about coming to Lillian. She hadn't thought about Lillian's position. She was a woman of wealth, belonging to a higher class than a vintner's daughter. It had never seemed to matter to her during her visits to Anna's booth. She had become a dear friend. And she had been so gracious at Anna's wedding. But it was quite another thing for Anna to come to *her* home, and especially to seek refuge here. And Anna hadn't even thought about her husband. She had never met him. How did she think he would allow her to infringe on his wife's good graces?

What am I doing here? Maybe she should have stayed at the cave as Obe suggested, but she couldn't. The weight of sadness was too heavy to bear in such a place. And to add the fear of capture with the prophets to her grief was too much to ask.

Obe's posture was almost as stiff as the butler's as he stood upright, putting several inches between them. She wanted the comfort of his hand in hers or his arm tucking her into his shoulder, a place to weep and mourn her loss. Their loss. But it wouldn't be right. It would be a betrayal to her husband to fall into the arms of his best friend, even for comfort, when he was not even buried yet. Then it dawned on her. Zim wouldn't be buried. Nor her father or brothers. They wouldn't rest in

The Struggle for Courage

the family burial cave. Their bodies would lie in the dirt until the wild dogs were finished with them.

The inlaid tiles began to turn beneath her feet. Strong arms caught her as the darkness dragged her down.

∞∞∞∞∞∞∞

Obadiah

I walked the tiled floor of the parlor as I waited for Lillian to return with news of Anna's condition. I had caught her as she slipped to the floor and was bending over her when Lillian entered the room. She had run to where Anna lay, conscious but her face twisted in anguish. Grief? Or was it the child? *Please not the child, Yahweh.*

The man who met us at the door had carried her to a room where Lillian said she should drink a little wine and rest.

"She fell asleep. Or maybe it was a faint. She is not speaking, but she seems to be breathing normally. I have called for a physician," Lillian said as she quietly closed the door to the room where Anna had been taken.

Fear gripped me. Anna came here to hide. A physician might report to someone that Naboth's daughter is with child and recovering in Lillian's house.

"You cannot tell the physician who she is!"

The woman's mouth twisted. A faint line deepened in her forehead. "And why is that, Obadiah?"

She knew me. Of course she did. I was well known, and Anna had probably confided in the woman that I had refused to marry her after years of leading her on.

"She is with child."

Lillian's eyes widened. "Yours?"

What? "No. No! Her husband's child. Have you heard any news today … of a stoning?"

"No." Her faced paled. "Who?"

I stared at a piece of lint lying on the stone floor as I tried to speak over the stony lump in my throat. "All of them. Her father. Her brothers. Her husband."

Lillian moaned. "No. That's not possible. I don't know Anna's family well, but I know her father is a man of good reputation. And her husband—" Her face turned a sickly gray.

I knew my eyes glistened with tears, but I wouldn't let them fall. They would never stop if I let them start.

"There was a trial." Anger welled up in me. "A rigged trial. The elders of the city condemned them on false charges. I tried to stop it, but they wouldn't listen. I had been warned by a friend and sent a servant to tell Anna to take refuge in the—"

I caught myself. I couldn't tell this woman about the cave or the prophets. I didn't know her, and it would be imprudent to trust the prophets' lives to her discretion. "She would not stay where I sent her for good cause. She asked me to bring her here. It is reasonable to think she might be hunted down as well. The child … brings complications that I cannot divulge at this moment. But if a physician realizes she is Naboth's daughter, both she and her child could be in danger."

Lillian's hands were shaking. She stared at me suspiciously for a moment. "And how am I to know you are not out to harm her in some way? I know what you did to her. You broke her heart. What reason have I to believe your intentions are for her welfare?"

My voice wavered as I spoke. "Because I love her. I always have." There, it was said. I prayed Lillian would not take it upon herself to tell Anna. That would not help either of us. My love was of little consequence if I couldn't act upon it. The only way I could love Anna was to see that she and her child were safe.

Lillian's face softened a bit. "I don't think the physician would know her. He has only come to Jezreel recently. The council felt there was not sufficient care here for the ill and enticed him to come from Damascus only a week ago." She took a deep breath. "But there is another problem."

"And what is that?"

"My husband. He is Kenen ben Meshech."

My jaw dropped. The man was one of the elders. He was, no doubt, one who condemned Naboth and his family! I jumped to my feet and started toward the room where they'd taken Anna. She was leaving with me. Now!

Lillian stood in front of me. "Stop! You cannot take her now. She needs a physician. And you needn't worry. My husband is not a cruel man. He would not harm a young pregnant woman. And I'm certain he had nothing to do with this execution."

"And I am to entrust Anna to the wife of a nobleman? And if he is a nobleman, he was there! He took part in condemning Anna's entire family! She's coming with me. I don't want to hurt you, but I will set you aside myself if you do not move!"

"What's going on here!"

Lillian and I turned in unison toward the man standing in the hallway. Lillian's husband, one of the noblemen that had sat at the table with Lemech when Naboth asked them to leave. Why had I brought Anna here?

"Hiding in a cloak closet in my own home! This is an outrage I will not let my lovely wife forget!" Kenen whispered as he pushed a coat off his arm.

I didn't know it was possible to shout in a whisper, but the nobleman seemed to manage it quite well.

I pressed my nose closed with thumb and fingers, trying to suppress a tickle that threatened to erupt into a sneeze. The fibers from the cloaks hanging on pegs all around us were causing a reaction I often had when exposed to certain types of wool.

The physician had arrived, and as a servant was letting him in the front door, Lillian had shoved her husband and me into the closet with a command that we should be quiet and not come out until she came for us. She hadn't had a chance to tell Kenen about the young pregnant girl who had fainted and was at this moment resting in his bed. I could see that Lillian was a woman to be reckoned with, which belied her genteel demeanor.

"You had better have a good reason for being in my home in my absence, Obadiah, because, palace administrator or not, you will answer for any trouble you have caused here!"

"It's you who must answer to me as soon as we are released from …"

The threatening sneeze erupted, and I smothered it with the sleeve of my robe. I listened carefully but heard nothing from the other side of the wooden door.

A short time later muffled voices slid through the cracks: a woman's gentle one and a man's, deep and sophisticated. I couldn't make out the words well, but the tone of the conversation was not urgent. I sighed my relief. At least Anna hadn't died of her faint. She and Zim's baby were probably fine. *Let it be so, Yahweh.*

I blinked against the light that flooded our hiding place as Lillian opened the door, apology ready on her lips.

"I'm so sorry, Husband. I had no choice. You may come out now."

Kenen puffed up like a porcupine. "Oh, may I? Thank you so much. It is so kind of you to allow me into my own living chamber."

The man huffed as he passed his wife and headed for the bar at the west wall of the opulent room and poured himself a drink, not bothering to call for a servant. He plopped down on the mohair couch and stared first at me and then at his wife. "Now can someone tell me why I've spent the last half an hour hiding in a cloak closet?"

Lillian began with what she knew, and I took over from there, telling the story from the place of stoning, where I'd seen the missive supposedly written by the king, to Anna's request to be brought to her friend's home in hope of finding temporary refuge.

"If I'd known"—I slashed a hand toward the man—"that *he* was the master of this house, I wouldn't have darkened the doorstep with Anna!"

Kenen let out a long sigh, sorrow emanating from his dark eyes. "First of all, let me say I was not at the stoning … but I was at the trial. I didn't like how eager Lemech and the others were to bring such charges against a man who had not shown signs of ill behavior before. Except, of course, his constant condemnation of the city fathers, which was aggravating, but not illegal.

"It was a farce. The witnesses were not credible. I left before they gave a verdict. I didn't want to be called upon for my opinion. It wouldn't have mattered. No one would have listened to me."

"You could have tried!" I said, my voice rising.

Kenen's face colored. "You don't understand, Obadiah. Nothing was going to stop Lemech from carrying out his plan."

The man was a coward! I needed to get Anna out of here!

Kenen leaned toward me. "However, I do have some knowledge of the letter that was used as authority for the trial."

My ears pricked up. "Please. Do tell." I tried to keep the sarcasm tempered in my speech. I did not like this man. Or trust him. But I didn't want to make an enemy of him either.

He rubbed at the side of his nose. "Unfortunately, I know nothing of what the letter actually said. It was delivered to Lemech at the city gates a week or so before"—he waved his hand—"all this unpleasantness began."

Unpleasantness. My best friend was dead. All of Anna's family dead, and he called it *unpleasantness?* It was all I could do to keep my seat.

"Lemech read it silently and then said he thought our prayers concerning Naboth had been answered. It grated on me because we had been saying no prayers concerning Naboth. Rather a great deal of complaining." His face reddened as he looked at me. "He could be a very frustrating man, you know. But it was only talk. He said no more, and we went our separate ways."

"Who delivered it?" That was important information. "Did it come from an official palace messenger?"

"I didn't recognize him. But the man did not have the bearing of a palace messenger."

"What did he look like?"

Kenen shrugged. "He had a shifty look about him when he put the parchment in Lemech's hand. No proper greeting. Just said, 'This message is from the king.'"

"His face. Can you be more specific?"

"Hmm. He was heavy-jowled, with a long nose. I really didn't dwell on the man's appearance. It was more a feeling than anything. Then after Lemech replied as he did, I decided I would rather not know more. Better not to know too much sometimes."

Sounded like the words of a coward to me. But the description put me in mind of someone. The man who had grabbed Anna's arm at the market. I should have killed him while I had the chance.

Kenen shook his head. "I'm sorry about all this, but the girl really can't stay here."

"Why?" Lillian leaned forward in her chair.

Kenen stuttered, looking for an excuse that would satisfy his wife. "If … if there's more trouble with the city fathers, I could get dragged into this. It would not be best for your reputation, my dear."

"*Your* reputation, you mean," Lillian said, her voice edged with restrained anger.

"It's alright. We will go." All eyes flew to Anna, who was standing in the doorway of the room where she had been resting. Her voice was weak, and dark circles ringed her emerald eyes. But she was beautiful beyond words. It took all the fortitude I had to keep from going to her and taking her in my arms.

We all rose. Lillian raised her chin at her husband, then turned to Anna. "No, my dear. You will not go. You will stay here with me." She looked back at the man, waiting for a reply. He twisted his lip and nodded reluctantly.

"I think she is right. We should go," I said, making a move toward Anna. Lillian just stared at me. I swallowed the words. She was a formidable woman. Lillian had the same spark that I had seen in Anna many times. I knew it would do no good to protest. And what better place of safety could I offer? But I would be watching the situation carefully. Kenen might be the man he appeared to be. Or he might not.

<hr />

I returned to the palace in haste, eager to begin my search for the truth. Had Ahab actually sent that order? I didn't think so—and that left only one possibility. Jezebel had manipulated the situation some way. I had noticed the mark on the document the leader had shown me. Every scribe had his own insignia. It was a way of making them accountable. If a mistake was found, it could cost the man his position. Perhaps even his life, if the consequences of his error were dire enough.

I knew all the scribes, and I had recognized the mark of Zardak. I assumed much pressure must have been brought to bear on the man, but he had betrayed his duty to the king and in the process gotten my friends killed. The king would have him swiftly executed. I didn't want that to happen, but the man was responsible for his actions, no matter how Jezebel had pressured him. Lives were lost for his cowardice. Precious lives.

"Obadiah."

My head flew up. I had almost run into the queen in my haste. I just stood staring at her in her cerulean robe, the gold lattice headpiece that I always thought looked like an upside-down bowl sitting atop her flaming hair. I couldn't make myself bow.

"You are distracted, I see. Whatever could be on your mind that would cause you not to bow to your queen?" She smiled the most wicked smile I'd ever seen on her over-painted face.

"But don't worry, Obadiah. I'm rather in a hurry. I have some good news that I must deliver to the king right away." She was laughing. I could hear it, though not a sound came out of her mouth. I didn't drop my gaze or step aside. She stared at me for a long moment, a look of amusement on her face. When she stepped past me, the laugh slipped through her lips. It was the laugh that settled it. The way it slithered through the air like a snake, tongue darting in and out. Jezebel had taken everyone I loved and in doing so had left me with nothing to lose but my fear. I smiled at her robe-draped back as she passed. The queen would pay for her crimes. I would see to it.

∽◦◦◦◦◦◦◦◦◦◦◦∽

I entered the chamber where the scribes worked. The quiet scratching of quills was the only noise in the room other than the crackle of flames in the brazier in the corner. Zardak was nowhere to be seen. But Calah was sitting in the alcove reserved for the master scribe, his gray head bent over a document, the former head scribe relegated to a corner of the quiet room. My skin began to warm. This was a recent promotion. I hoped the man had not been involved, because if he had, I would take him to the king myself.

I stood by the scribe's desk silently, waiting for him to notice me. I would not disturb him and cause him to make an error. When he laid down his reed, he looked up, startled by my presence. He stood quickly and bowed.

"My lord, Obadiah. How may I help you?"

"I see you have been promoted," I said, watching his reaction.

"Yes." He shrugged his narrow shoulders. "It was quite a surprise."

"Indeed."

The man looked puzzled at my tone. I would say no more until I gleaned the information I needed.

"Could you show me where I might find Zardak? I need to speak to him immediately."

The scribe's face clouded. "Could you come with me, lord Obadiah? I would rather not speak here," he said in a whisper. His obvious discomfort made me wonder if he was, indeed, involved. But I would hear the man out.

Calah led me into a room lined with shelves of clay tablets and scrolls and all the implements of the man's trade. The metallic odor of the iron salts and oak gulls used to make the ink combined with the grassy smell of the papyrus reminded me of the scroll Lemech had shoved in my face and started the heat rising up my neck again.

Even when we were behind the closed door, the scribe looked around and finally gave a sigh. "He's dead, lord Obadiah."

"Dead?" That did not bode well.

"Some guards came several days ago and took him away. The same day I got this promotion. I was told one of the guards plunged his sword through the man as soon as they were outside the palace walls. His body was delivered to his wife for burial with the excuse he had been caught stealing supplies. But I don't believe that was true."

"Do you have any idea of the real reason for his death?"

The man sighed. "I'm not certain I want to say."

I believed the head scribe was free of guilt in this matter, but he must tell me what he knew. "Don't fear anything from me. I'm just investigating a matter."

The scribe looked around again. "I don't know for certain, but I think the queen had him executed."

That was not a surprise. "For what reason?" The man hesitated again. "Do not fear, Calah. I promise your words will not leave this room."

He took a deep breath. "The queen had approached me about writing a document and ascribing it to Ahab. Which would mean using the official seal and my insignia. Of course, I couldn't do that. She was quite insistent, but I told her the king himself had commanded that any correspondence coming from him had to be dictated in his presence. I was surprised that she didn't have me put to the sword right then. To the contrary, I was promoted a few days hence. But I saw her go to Zardak's alcove after she left mine. I think she gave him the same command. Unfortunately, I think he did not stand up to the queen's insistence. I suspect she killed him to cover her ... indiscretion."

"I think you are correct in your assumption." I clapped his shoulder. "You did well. Apparently even the queen knows an honest man when she sees one. You are fortunate you did not waver in your duty. It would have been you with a sword in your middle."

The scribe nodded. "I don't doubt that."

I bowed in respect. "Do not worry. I will not violate your trust."

CHAPTER TWENTY-ONE

Kenen

Kenen found Lemech already seated at the gate. It was early, and no one else had taken their places as yet, which was good. He didn't want an audience for this conversation.

"I need to see the message that was delivered from the king about Naboth," I said, hoping Lemech had not disposed of it.

"And why is that? The matter is resolved, Kenen. You needn't worry about it anymore."

"I think you're wrong about that. I think *you* have a lot to worry about, and because of our association, I must worry as well."

"And what makes you think that is so?" Lemech said, clearly aggravated that I would even bother him with the matter. He flipped a hand. "The thing is over. Naboth is gone. His sons are gone. Even if they had a legitimate complaint, they cannot speak from wherever it is the dogs deposited them."

"Perhaps not, but Naboth's daughter has taken up residence in my house!"

"What?" Lemech leaned forward, his face white with shock. "In the name of Yahweh, why is the girl in your house?"

"Obadiah himself brought her there. She's a friend of my wife, it seems." He raised a palm. "Don't even ask me how that is so. You know Lillian. And the girl's husband was one of the men you stoned! It would be a stretch of the law to hold the man responsible for his father-in-law's supposed crimes. And, what's more, he was a wheelwright in Ahab's chariot house. And what if there is a child? Maybe the mother can't speak in a court of law, but the palace governor could speak for the rights of the mother, or a son if there is one, and most definitely would do just that! The woman is a childhood friend of his, I'm told. As was her husband!"

Lillian had told Kenen that Obadiah was a friend of the family, but anyone who saw him look at the girl would know he was in love with her. Kenen did not want to complicate the matter so far as Obadiah was concerned. He had the king's favor, another reason the man should have been given a little time to look into the grounds for execution. But Lemech! He had to rid himself of Naboth, no matter the suspicious circumstances that had ordered it.

"If Ahab did not send that missive, then there will be hades to pay for carrying on an execution in his name. And if he did write it, he would not want it brought to public attention. But really, Lemech. Do you think that if Ahab wanted Naboth dead he would have to resort to such a maneuver? He could drag them all into the palace and make any charge he wanted and be off with their heads, and who would challenge him?"

Lemech's face was a deathly gray by now. Good. Kenen hoped he worried himself sick. He had stirred up a nest of hornets, and there would be no way to herd them back into the hive.

"Do you have it in your parchments?" He gestured to the box of recent judgments that had been rendered and awaited permanent entry into the archives. "I want to see it now!"

Lemech sat in shock for another moment. "Do you think I'm crazy, that I would carry such a document in a public box?" He looked around to see if anyone was watching their conversation and pulled the scroll out from a pocket sewn to the inner side of his robe and handed it to Kenen. "Look at it quickly. Before the others come."

Dread took up camp in Kenen's churning stomach as he unrolled the parchment and started to read the letters that flowed into sentences in that distinctive hand of a royal scribe. The insignia seemed genuine, but as his brain translated the symbols, his heart began to race.

The king had not dictated this letter. Kenen would be willing to wager a great deal that someone had bribed a scribe or there was some other explanation for the words he read. The king would not be so foolish as to attach his seal to a command that men bear false testimony against an elder of Israel.

Kenen stood, gripping the scroll in his hand. "The king did not dictate this letter, Lemech. And whoever did has played you for the fool you are. I will dispose of this myself. If Obadiah or the girl get ahold of it and take it to the king, it will be more than enough evidence to condemn whoever is responsible for its contents, and whoever was stupid enough to carry them out!"

Lemech opened his mouth as though to protest, then snapped it closed and nodded.

I turned my back to the man and started down the stone street. Now what was I to do? One thing for certain. That girl had to leave my house. One way or another.

Obadiah

"I would like to speak to Anna privately."

Lillian scowled. "She's napping in one of the guest rooms on the upper floor, and if you think I'm going to let you into a room alone with her, you are sadly mistaken."

"It's all right, Lillian. I'm awake." Anna was standing on the staircase where it made a fluid turn toward the lower floor. She still looked tired and drawn, but she was so very beautiful. She was wearing a lovely blue tunic that flowed gracefully to her slim ankles. It must have been one of Lillian's, or perhaps one of her married daughters had left it on a visit. Would my heart never stop picking up speed at the sight of her? I had tried so hard to put her from my mind, but I may as well have tried to separate the stars from the night sky.

"We will go out to the garden, if that would be agreeable to you, Lillian?" Anna said softly.

The elder woman eyed me again. There was no doubt that Lillian still held my treatment of Anna against me. But she looked back at Anna with a small smile and nodded. "Of course, my dear."

Anna led the way through the wide doors that opened into a lovely garden. The subtle sweetness of jasmine and lilies hung in the air. Stone paths meandered through orderly shrubs, leading to cozy nooks with wrought-metal benches and understated sculptures. I followed her to a bench beneath a bower of roses. I was glad that I had listened to Anna's request to bring her to Lillian. I still had misgivings, but being in the midst of this beauty would surely bring her more peace than the oppressive confinement of the cave.

She lowered herself to the bench and I sat beside her, not certain what to do. I wanted to touch her. A touch to communicate my sorrow at her grief. Isn't that what anyone would do to comfort one who had suffered so much loss? But instead I sat with my hands folded stiffly in my lap.

"How are you feeling?" I asked.

She stared into the empty space in front of her. "I'm not certain. Alright I suppose. I have a hard time keeping my thoughts together." She bit her lip. "Most of the time I'm ... in a fog."

My heart hurt at the sight and sound of her pain. Added to my own, it was almost unbearable.

"And the babe? Is there ... Is everything ..."

"Everything is as it should be, I am told." Her chest rose and fell in a long sigh. "It's strange though, Obe. The physician, Lillian, they talk about the baby, but it's like they're talking about someone else's child. I don't feel ... pregnant anymore. It's as though it was all a dream, and I've awakened and now it's just me. I feel like the recent past has disappeared, and I should be sleeping in the little alcove off the living area in my father's house. Cooking the lamb stew he loved so. Sparring with my brothers. It's as though I had never been Zim's wife. He's an apparition at the corners of my mind." She looked down at her stomach. "I don't know if I can be a mother. I'm terrified, Obe."

"You will be a wonderful mother." My heart broke at her words. She seemed so ... lost. I hesitated, then reached for her hand and held it in mine, hoping she would not misinterpret my motive. But she needed touch, and I could offer her that, if only for this moment.

We sat there for a long while watching a charming fountain featuring a fish as its centerpiece, our fingers intertwined.

"You said Zim's last words were of me. What did he say, Obe?"

My heart contracted. I couldn't tell her the whole of it. She would not understand why I could not grant my brother's request. Why to do as he asked would feel like casting the stones myself. I couldn't have Anna at the cost of Zim's life. I wouldn't.

"He said that he loved you."

She turned back to the garden view, her eyes vacant again. "And that was all?"

No, Anna. That was not all. But what was I going to say? That Zim tried to pass her to me but I refused him? That would not bring her comfort.

"Tell me the truth, Obe. Please."

I drew a shuttering breath. "We had very little time. They only gave me a few minutes before ..." *Don't tell her. You can't!*

"There has to be more. He couldn't just leave me alone to figure all this out myself. I'm lost. I don't know what to do," she said, looking into my eyes, her own eyes pleading and vulnerable. Anna had always been the one to tell the truth. She never vacillated or danced around it. I was the one who buried feelings to keep up the appearance of strength when, on the inside, I felt as weak as the water spewing from the fish's mouth.

But I couldn't tell her what Zim had said. Not right now. I loved Anna, but I had loved Zim first, and he had loved her from a distance for all those years. When I'd put her love aside, Zim had picked it up and nursed it back to health. He deserved to have Anna. I wouldn't take that away from him. Not even in death.

"I'm sorry, but I have to leave now." I jumped off my seat, letting her hand fall away from mine, and left by the side gate without looking back.

───────

Anna

Anna's mouth fell open. What just happened? Obe was leaving her too? A single thought forced its way into her consciousness, ripping any small hope she had to bloody shreds. She was alone. She had no one. No father to welcome her back to his home with open arms. No brothers to act as her protectors and advocates. No husband to love her and cherish her, to help her raise this child.

She had no home. No place to go. She couldn't stay long where she was. Lillian would do everything she could to keep Anna there, but this was Lillian's husband's house, and she could only appease him so long.

Anna covered her stomach with her hands. Fear as she had never known it gripped her heart. *Oh, Obe. You are all I have left in this world. Please don't leave me. I won't survive by myself.*

CHAPTER TWENTY-TWO

Obadiah

H e's ready for you," the guard said.

I heard the words, but I didn't rise from the chair covered in the hide of an exotic cat. The chair I always sat in but hated because the animal had been forced into a corner with no place of escape, an easy target, killed for nothing more than the king's pleasure in the killing of it. The chair had more significance now. Could this king cause the death of an innocent man and his family for the sake of a few vegetables? The sleek fur seemed to testify that he could.

"Obadiah!" The guard whispered a shout and motioned for me to come. I rose from the detestable chair and took a deep breath, not knowing if, after this, the king would be pleased to use my hide to cover another. But I was going to say what I needed to say. No matter the consequences.

Ahab was slouching over his food, barely picking at his plate, when I was let in. Prince Joram was seated beside his father, a large piece of meat on his fork. The boy glared his aggravation at the interruption of his meal. I needed the boy to leave. How was I going to accomplish that?

I thought of Anna. Her hand falling to her lap when I let it go. What Jezebel had done to Naboth, to Zim and the boys—to Anna and her unborn child—was more wicked than all the wickedness she had done before it. She deserved to suffer the grief of her own lost children. If I could lay my knife to their necks I would do it without the batting of an eye. But that was not to be my doing. It would come, as the prophet said, not through anger and retribution but through righteous judgment. But it was Ahab who had truly wrought this evil, by marrying an enemy of Yahweh and allowing her free rein to render such destruction.

I hesitated at the place where I usually kneeled when entering the king's presence. Could I do it? Kneel before such a king as this? Honor the king and despise the man? Was that possible? At this moment I hated both the king and the man. My hands were shaking with the force of my hatred. I made the smallest start to bend my knee to the floor, but Ahab waved me forward. "No. Not today. Just give me your report and be done with it as quickly as possible."

I pulled in a long breath. *I'm afraid it is not going to be that easy, Ahab.* I lowered myself to the cushioned seat across from the king. I allowed the king's servant to set a plate before me but made no move to pick up a utensil. Ahab didn't seem to notice. He *did* notice that I laid no record before him.

"No scroll?" he said with a lifted brow. I always referred to my accounting when I spoke to the king. It was my nature to be thorough. Precise. As good as my memory was, I would not trust it when it came to the king's affairs. But I was in no danger of forgetting my mission today.

"If there's nothing to report, you may be dismissed. I'm not in the mood for accounting anyway." I'm sure he wasn't, but he was going to have to give an accounting of himself today. Whether he liked it or not. He often prefaced my report jokingly with, "Well, who needs the dungeon or the noose today, Obadiah?" Today I would tell him.

"I do have something very important to report. Too important to commit to parchment."

His brows arced higher over his mongoose eyes. He put down his fork and leaned back in his tall chair. "Well. Let's hear it."

I turned my gaze to Joram, who was concentrating on his food. The boy often concentrated on his food, by the look of him. His parents' indulgence was showing in his cheeks.

Ahab caught my meaning and dismissed Joram from the table. "But I'm not through eating, Father," he said.

"Get something from the kitchen. I have need of privacy with the administrator."

Joram plunked his fork on his plate and gave me a not-so-pleasant look. I had interrupted his lunch. What could be worse?

Ahab waved a dismissal to the servant as well, then leaned forward. "Alright. What is such a secret it had to spoil my lunch with my son?"

I drew a breath and prayed for Yahweh's courage.

"Someone has done a grievous thing. It cannot be put right, but I appeal to the king for justice to be administered to the perpetrator of such a heinous crime."

"If the crime is as terrible as you say, the wronged party should bring it before me while I'm holding court. It doesn't sound like a matter to be settled over the dining table."

"I don't think you would want this matter to be addressed in court."

Ahab rolled his eyes. I could see where Joram got it. "Alright, Obadiah. Who is it you seek justice for?"

"For me," I said.

"For you?" Surprise colored his face. "Tell me what wrong has been done to you, and I will see that justice is rendered immediately."

I looked into the king's dark eyes for a long moment, wondering what might await me if I spoke what I intended, but it didn't matter. There was no turning back on this. I started slowly.

"Someone has taken the lives of my dearest friends. An old man who did nothing to deserve death. His three sons—lifelong friends of mine." I pursed my lips, forcing back the boil of anger rising. "His son-in-law—my truest companion since childhood. They left his wife a widow with no one left to care for her."

A knife struck my heart. Her husband had asked me to take care of her, but I could not do it. Even now. Was I better than Ahab?

"She was robbed of all her family in one day. All her possessions." I paused for a long moment, gathering Ahab's full attention before I spoke again. "Including her father's vineyard."

All of the color drained out of the king's face like a sunset swallowed by the evening shadows.

"And what do you expect me to do about this, Obadiah? As I understand it, a verdict has been rendered in this case. A civil verdict. In a city court. And punishment has been delivered. There's nothing I can do about it now. If the verdict was unjust, it is the city fathers who are to blame."

"I suppose I can't expect you to do anything about it. Since you are the one who ordered their deaths."

Shock flooded Ahab's face, morphing into blistering indignation. As I'd thought, he had not written the order, but I had to accuse him to know for certain that he had no involvement. I didn't believe he was such an actor as to accomplish this look of outrage.

"I should deliver you to the guards for execution this minute for falsely accusing the king of Israel! By what evidence do you make such an absurd accusation!"

I knew I was doing a dangerous thing. The king might kill me himself before I could draw him into my trap. But I had to try.

"I saw the order myself."

"You saw what?" he raged, his half-circle brows steepling over his flashing eyes.

"I saw a missive directed to the city fathers, written by the hand of one of your own scribes, marked with the scribe's insignia—and the king's own seal. In your name it directed the noblemen to call a fast and invite Naboth to sit at the head of it. To hire two low-born men to testify falsely that he had cursed God and the king, then take him and his sons outside the city and stone them. But they went one step further. They executed the girl's husband. Naboth's son-in-law. My friend and a wheelwright in your own employ."

Ahab's mouth dropped. "They executed the wheelwright?"

Zim had told me how Ahab had been shamed at Zim's obvious disappointment in him. And I had seen the same shame on the king's face when his eyes met Zim's in the vineyard.

Ahab's gaze bored into mine. "I did not write that order, Obadiah. I swear on the name of Yahweh."

"Then who do you think did? Who could convince a scribe to disobey your directive that no letter from you be dictated unless in your presence? Who would dare to use your official seal?"

Ahab's lips slipped into a terse line. His eyes into narrow slashes.

"You tread on dangerous ground, Obadiah."

"No more dangerous than my friends."

"You are accusing the queen of forging an official document in my name? Using my seal?"

"I am not accusing anyone. That is the purview of kings, not palace governors. And, surely, no king would allow his wife to do such a thing. No king would indulge his queen until she felt the freedom to do whatever she wished, no matter how evil or sacrilegious." Blood was hammering in my head. "No matter what cost to his country or its people. What kind of king would allow his wife such power?"

"Get out!" Ahab was on his feet, his finger quivering as he pointed it at me. "I have always cared for you, Obadiah. I've treated you better than I've treated my own sons. But you go too far! You are relieved of your duties until I sort this out. You are to stay in your suite until I release you or have you hanged. Guards!" Two guards appeared out of nowhere. "Take this man to his rooms and stay outside his door. No one is to go in. And he is not to go out! Do you hear that, Obadiah? And I want that letter! Do you have it?"

"No, I saw it in the hand of one of the noblemen. He obviously would not give it up to the king's governor if it was forged."

"Well, you had better hope he still has it because your life depends on it. Send someone to retrieve it. You are allowed a messenger, and that is all!"

I hadn't thought I would have to produce the letter. I was sure Lemech had destroyed it or had it hidden somewhere. Whatever the case, he would not give it up to me. What was I thinking? Now Anna would truly have no one. I wouldn't be able to find her a husband or a father for her child. She would be on her own. I was such a fool. Would Zim want me to leave her alone to raise a child with no help? It had been difficult for Zim to ask me to take his place. But he loved her. He had thought of her welfare, whereas I thought only of myself and my own pain at the loss of my friend. He was the better man, as always. Anna needed me. Zim knew that she would, and he had used his last words to tell me so. And now I might end up dead also.

Kenen

"Thank you, Jona," Kenen said, handing his robe to the servant. "Bring me some wine, please. Or maybe something stronger." Kenen needed something stronger than wine to cure the headache his exchange with Lemech had given him. The man had no idea what a storm he had let loose. How could he think this would all work out without consequence?

The servant laid the robe over his arm and bowed. All Kenen wanted was to sit on his favorite couch and relax.

His eyes went to Lillian, one slender hand on the rail and one fisting her gown as she padded down the winding stairs. A lump rose in his throat. She was no less stunning than the day he had married her, the delicate lines at the corners of her dark eyes the only markers of the thirty years that had passed.

Now Kenen feared that Lemech was going to bring the whole thing down on his own head and Kenen's in the process. What would that do to Lillian?

And what had the pressure of this too-public life made of his marriage? His beautiful wife, mother of four daughters and no sons.

"She's gone. Did you have anything to do with it?"

Gone? The girl?

"What do you mean, did I have anything to do with it?" Kenen wasn't sure what Lillian was implying. Did she think he'd slipped in and taken the girl from her bed and dumped her in the street?

"I know you didn't want her here. Did you … send her away while I was sleeping? Where is she?"

"No, Lillian. I did not send her away." He didn't mention that it was his intention to do just that, but surely his wife knew he would not be so callous as to slip the girl out in the night. He had been looking for a solution to the problem when he remembered the conversation with Naboth at the wedding about his new son-in-law. A small bit of information had sparked an idea, but who knew if it would work.

Worry tracked in Lillian's brown eyes as she came closer. The crease across her forehead that only appeared when she was anxious or angry was getting deeper.

"I thought nothing of it when she didn't come down for breakfast. I imagined she was still distraught about her meeting with Obadiah yesterday. But when I went into her room and opened the curtains, her bed was made and she was gone." She put her hand to her mouth. "I'm worried, Kenen."

Kenen started to reach for her but held himself back. Their relationship had been strained for a long time and the situation with the girl had only made it worse. He cursed Lemech under his breath. All of this was his fault. If he hadn't gotten Naboth stoned, the girl wouldn't be in Kenen's house and this firestorm wouldn't be threatening them all.

"Please, sit down, Lillian." He gestured toward the couch. "What do you think happened? Where do you think she would go?"

"I don't know," she said, lowering herself to the couch. "I should have gone looking for her, but where would I look? I couldn't go to the palace. Perhaps her father's vineyard? But I thought she would probably return before I could make it so far. So I did nothing." Her worried eyes met his. "She's pregnant, Kenen. And she might be in danger from the king himself. Or, worse, from Jezebel. I know there is a place where she went to hide after the news that her family was in danger—before Obadiah brought her here. He hesitated to tell me where it was. I'm just worried."

Kenen swallowed his fear and reached for her hand. To his surprise, she hung on to it tightly. His heart filled with tenderness for his wife. Lillian was his one love. He could not abide her pain.

"I'll go to the marketplace to look for her. If I find someone I can trust, I'll ask if they have seen her, or if they have any idea where she might be. I will do my best, my darling."

Lillian's gaze held Kenen's for a long moment, then she nodded. "I know you will. Thank you."

At that moment a knock sounded through the cedar door at the front of the house. Lillian jumped up. "Maybe that's her," she said, hurrying to the entry hall. Kenen followed, hoping that it was, indeed, the girl. He would let the girl stay if he had to. He didn't want to see that hurt in his wife's eyes. He wanted her to love him the way she did before he sold his soul to his position.

But it wasn't Anna. Kenen's heart dropped when he saw an official messenger from the palace, dressed in his distinctive knee-length linen tunic, a scarlet robe draped over his narrow shoulders. The messenger looked past Lillian and spoke to Kenen. "I have a message from Obadiah, governor of the king's palace, for Kenen ben Meshech. Are you that man?"

"Yes. I am he." A message from Obadiah? *Why would Obadiah send me a message?*

"And a second message from the governor to Anna, the daughter of Naboth. She is here?" he said, looking toward Lillian.

"No," Kenen said quickly.

"She is not here. She was here, but she is gone," Lillian said, giving Kenen a sideways glance. "We hope that she will return shortly."

"Can I leave the scroll with you? Obadiah was insistent that I make every effort to deliver it."

Lillian held out her hand. "Yes, I will see that she gets it as soon as she gets home."

Home. Lillian would adopt the girl if that were possible. Kenen hoped she wouldn't regret getting involved, but, knowing Lillian, she would not. She was true to the people she loved. Kenen wished that he was more like her.

"One more thing," Kenen asked. "Why didn't Obadiah deliver the message himself?"

The messenger didn't blink. "He's under arrest and confined to his rooms." With that the man turned on his heel and walked out the still-open door.

Lillian and Kenen stared at each other, their mouths agape. Obadiah arrested? He must have opened his mouth when he should have kept it shut. Kenen went to the table and opened the scroll.

> *Kenen,*
> *Come to the palace tomorrow in the evening. Tell whoever is at the gate that you are the messenger the king allowed and to bring you to my rooms. If you have it, bring it with you. My life might depend upon it.*
> *Obadiah,*
> *Palace Administrator*

Kenen cursed Lemech. What had the man gotten him into? He rolled up the scroll and tucked it into his sash before Lillian could look at it. He didn't want her questions at the moment.

"What did he say?" she said, suspicion on her face. Kenen hated seeing it, but he had no intention of going to the palace, and he didn't want her to ask what *it* was.

"He wants me to find a safe place for Anna. I've already been looking into it. I'm going to the market," he said, kissing her cheek. "Would you like me to take the scroll in case I find her?"

She handed him the scroll and, without a word, turned toward the stairs. Kenen's heart hung heavy in his chest. *I'm sorry, my love.*

He headed for the market, hoping to find the girl and ease Lillian's mind. But what of Obadiah?

He couldn't worry about him right now. He needed to save the girl to save his marriage. He was definitely not going to the palace. It was too dangerous.

CHAPTER TWENTY-THREE

Anna

Anna closed the old wooden door behind her and leaned on it, her eyes closed, afraid to open them. Her heart stuttered too fast to catch a proper breath. *Breathe*, she told herself as she forced more air into her starving lungs. *Just breathe.* Finally her chest found a shallower rhythm, and the coil of her muscles began to loosen. She drew a deep breath and opened her eyes, blinking away the blurriness.

The living chamber where she and Zim cooked and ate was in disarray. She had left everything as it was when she fled. The pestle was lying on the table alongside the small bowl of early figs she had been crushing to make fig paste for the evening's meal. The paste would be dry and hard by now. She would have to throw it away, and she had no more figs. She went to the table and grabbed the bowl and scraped it quickly into the clay pot in which she kept scraps of food for the animals. Zim had loved the paste, and Anna had tried to make it for him whenever figs were in the market. And now she had wasted them.

She pulled open a stubborn shutter. Dust particles danced in the shaft of light that illuminated a wide swath of the room. Dust. Always dust. She set about with a straw broom to sweep the stone floor, then took a rag and wiped the table and chairs that Zim had made and the chest he'd carved of walnut wood as a betrothal gift. And every other surface where dust could find a resting place. If Ahab came to claim Anna's home, he would not find a spot of dust in it. She would not have him saying that Naboth's daughter was not a good housekeeper.

She had worried that Ahab had already claimed the land and was relieved to see no sign that he had done so. But he would. Eventually.

She had to come up with some kind of plan. But what? She closed her eyes again. Maybe when she opened them this time Zim would be there with her, smiling over the basin as he washed the day's work from his hands. But he wasn't. He was gone. Dead. Along with her father and brothers. She was by herself, and she had no one in the world.

Coming home was not the safest choice. But she couldn't walk all the way to the cave from Lillian's, and there was no place else. And she had to come. To be where she and Zim had been together.

She didn't trust Kenen. He seemed to be a good man, but even a good man might choose not to harbor the daughter of an executed criminal. Her heart twisted. How could this have happened? *Abba.* Tears flooded her eyes. She sniffed and wiped them with the edge of her shawl. Her father was no criminal. But whoever was responsible for this travesty was, and Yahweh would punish them for what they'd done. *Yahweh. Help me. Be with me, please.*

What would happen to her? To her baby? If it was a boy child, what inheritance would he have? A man had to have land. A man without it would be forced to indenture himself to survive. As a grandchild he would have inherited with her brothers, but now there was nothing to inherit anyway.

Anna's gaze settled on the goat-hair curtain that separated the living area from the sleeping quarters. She had pulled it shut before she left because she didn't want Zim to come home and be greeted by an unmade bed. She swallowed hard. It had seemed so important at the moment.

Anna pulled back the curtain and closed it behind her, all the while staring at the bed Zim had built for them. A deep weariness drew her to where she would not have gone if she could have stood even for a few more minutes. She lowered herself to the straw-filled mattress and laid her head on the pillow. The bed smelled of Zim, the faint scent of oak and oil from the wheel shop, and the harsh soap he used to try to remove the resin from his hands.

She lay there thinking of the first time he'd allowed her in the house. The day of their wedding. She had been amazed by all he'd done in such a short time and frightened at what was going to happen on the bed he had spread with a beautiful embroidered cloth he had purchased in the market. But he had smiled at her with his dancing eyes and his dimpled cheeks and his full lips, and her fear had eased. Anna knew he loved her, and he would be gentle with her. Since that time, she'd come to crave his touch and the tender moments they shared. She turned on her side and could almost feel the warmth of his chest against her back, his arm draped across her. *Zim. Why did you go? Why didn't you stay with me that day? I needed you to stay.*

She'd felt uncomfortable that morning when Zim said he was going to the assembly as soon as he could escape his work. He wanted to be with her father and her brothers. He was proud to be the son-in-law of Naboth the vintner. But something had not felt right with the whole thing. Father should not have gone. None of them.

They all had left her, and now she had no one, not even Obe. He had left her too.

Anna didn't want to sleep. What if someone came? But she was so weary, she couldn't fight the weight of slumber. She settled deeper into the straw pallet and closed her eyes.

<hr />

Obadiah

I saw her from my balcony. Despite the hooded cloak that covered her red-brown hair, I knew it was her immediately. She was hurrying across the grassy field to the long rows of vines that led to the treading vat. She was heading toward her house. Thankfully not toward her father's, which was closer and more visible from the palace. But if I could see her, others could, so I slipped down the stairs that led from my rooms to the garden and walked right through the unlocked gate, shocked that it was open and no one had been commissioned to guard it.

The only problem was, if I had seen Anna, someone looking out an upstairs window could see *me*. I could only pray that no one on the upper floor was in a mood for window-gazing.

I stood in front of the door, pondering if I should knock or just walk in. Considering the shock she had suffered, a knock might frighten her. I didn't want to do that. Walking in could do the same, but at least she would quickly see who it was, and the fear would subside. Maybe anger would take its place, but she wouldn't fear me. She must be angry at me. How could she not be angry? I had left her in her time of greatest need. Regret gnawed at my conscience. I could bear her anger. But I could not bear her pain.

The small house was immaculate, the table and chairs that Zim had built for his bride exquisite in their simplicity shone like they had just had a cloth put to them.

Zim had called me to the shop to take a look, proud of his work and the walnut chest he had made with his own skillful hands. I bit my lips and pulled in a long breath, sorrow gripping my heart. *Oh, Zim, my brother. I miss you so much.* It felt as if my entire being was being dragged into an abyss of grief. But I couldn't think of my own grief right now.

Was Anna still here? "Anna? It's me, Obe," I said as gently as possible. There was no answer, so I carefully pulled back the goat-hair curtain.

Her mouth was open, a small rumbling sound emanating from the back of her throat. Her brow was pinched, even in sleep. The sight of it stabbed at my heart. She was too beautiful to have such care lining her forehead. It did not belong there, and some of it was my fault.

Her eyelids fluttered open, and she fixed that green gaze on me as though I were a specter. Her chin began to quiver, and she pulled herself off the bed, standing on shaky knees.

"Obe?"

I walked toward her, stopping a pace away. "It's me." I wanted to pull her into my arms, but I could not, would not do that. Anna was vulnerable, and I wouldn't do anything that would take advantage of her weakened state. I didn't want her to fall in love with me again when I could not marry her. No matter how much I longed to slip into Zim's place, I would never be able to live with myself if I did. How could I? I would end up being glad that he was gone. Sorry for the tragic way he went but glad he was gone just the same. I would deny it to myself and to others, but it would lie at the bottom of my soul, eating like a canker worm. And it would be the same for Anna. I could not. I would not dishonor my dearest friend that way.

Anna didn't do or say anything. I considered for a nervous moment that she would tell me to leave, but tears exploded from her eyes; her body shook with racking sobs.

"I'm sorry, Anna. I'm sorry," I said, taking her hands in mine. "I will never abandon you again. I will be here for you and your child. I promise." I would worry about my own heart later, but, for now, I would make Anna feel safe. I could never marry her, but I could comfort her and protect her. I could do that much for her and for Zim, no matter how it hurt me in the end.

When the tears eased, I ran an unsteady hand down her arm and settled her on one of the wooden chairs around the table.

"You need to eat. What do you have that I can prepare for you?"

"I can do it," she said, starting to rise.

"No," I stood. "I will do it. Please. You need to rest."

She eased back onto the chair, looking around as though struggling to orient herself. "I was making some fig paste. I had to throw it out." She raised a finger toward a shelf where something lay wrapped in a thin cloth. "There's hard cheese. And maybe there is bread still soft enough to eat in the basket. I haven't had time to bake since … since …"

"Of course not, Anna." She was apologizing for not baking in the midst of all this? She was assuredly not yet herself. But would she ever be her carefree, plucky self again? Losing her entire family and her husband on the same day—how does one recover from that?

I cut some cheese and hollowed out a piece of bread, throwing the hard crust into the scrap pot where the remains of the fig paste lay. She concerned herself with stale bread, and she must have cleaned the house, since there was not a spot of dust when I entered. I felt my brows pull together. I prayed that she would soon recover from the shock of it all.

There was a honeycomb in a small bowl on the shelf, so I spread some on the bread, thinking something sweet might give her a boost of energy. And a small cup of wine to calm her.

"Here. Eat. Drink." I said, setting the clay plate before her.

"You gave me too much." She stared at the meager meal as if the challenge to eat was overwhelming.

"Just eat what you can. You're feeding two, remember."

She sighed, reaching for the bread and honey. She took a small bite and then a bite of cheese and a sip of wine.

"Thank you. I was more hungry than I realized," she said with a pale smile.

I sat in silence, watching her finish her meal and asked her if she wanted another serving. She looked gaunt. I wondered how much food Lillian had been able to get down her. Not enough it seemed, though I was certain the woman had done her best.

"No. That was more than enough. But you should eat, Obe."

"I've eaten. Come. Let's get you comfortable." I looked around. There were some cushions in a corner on the floor. Or I could put her in the bed, but she might be self-conscious, lying in a bed while a man not her husband tended to her.

"I'm fine, really. I feel much better. Thank you."

She did look better. I placed my hand over hers. She intertwined her long fingers with mine and squeezed. It felt like … we were one person. Irrevocably connected by our long history. We had loved each other deeply. Her love had changed, I was certain. But we were still connected by our shared love of her father and brothers, and most of all by our shared love of Zim.

"What course do you want to take, Anna?" I wouldn't impose my will on her again. I would do what she asked. No matter the risk. "I will help you do whatever you decide."

She slid her fingers out of mine and folded her hands in her lap, rubbing one with the other. "I'm not sure, Obe. I'm so confused. It's as though my thoughts can't find a landing place in my head. I didn't feel safe with Kenen, you know," she said, looking at me. "Not that I thought he would harm me in any way. I … just felt he wanted to be rid of me, and I didn't know how he might go about it."

I had felt the same about the man. He was in an awkward position, being a nobleman who sat at the city gate alongside the likes of Lemech. He would want Anna out of his house as soon as possible.

"I know I don't want to go back to the cave." She pulled a long breath. "I can't. I would go mad." She stilled for a long moment, engrossed in whatever it was her mind was concocting. I was becoming nervous. What if she asked me to do something I didn't deem safe? Would I actually follow through? Or would I refuse her again? I should have chosen my words more carefully. But that was what I always did. I was a coward in more ways than I wanted to face.

"What if …?" she clamped her lips between her teeth. "Do you think … could you sneak me into the palace?"

I felt my brows reach for my hairline. Of all the things she could ask. I had given up everything dear to me to keep her out of the palace. I had given up her! I didn't understand why she was asking, or how I could even do it if I wanted to. I had slipped away, apparently unseen, but getting back across the field unnoticed? That was going to be difficult enough for me alone. How could I possibly walk across the field with a woman on my arm and not call attention if someone happened to be watching? But I couldn't refuse her. I wouldn't. I was just going to have to let her come to her own conclusion that this was not possible.

"You don't want to do it. I can tell. I understand. It would be risky. I will walk back to Lillian's," she said, touching my hand. "We're not even certain anyone is looking for me. It may not yet have occurred to anyone that I might be a complication." She stood. "I need to get going. Thank you, Obe. For your help."

"Wait." I raised a palm. "Please, just listen to me."

She lowered herself to the chair again. There was no anger in her face. She was not accusing me with her eyes. They were gentle toward me. But the truth was, she had lost confidence that I would take a risk at all, and I didn't blame her.

"Please, Anna. I'm not saying no, although I have little hope that this plan of yours will work. I just want to hear your thoughts. Why do you think it would be a good idea for me to walk you across a field where anyone might see you? And where would I take you once we were in?"

"To your rooms, of course."

I could feel the warm blood climbing up my neck. Her lips parted. "Oh, I didn't mean …" Her own face flushed. "I only thought, what could be a safer hiding place? And you have closets, don't you?"

"Yes. I have closets, but are you going to stay in my closet all day and night?"

"No, of course not. But if someone should come, I could hide until they were gone."

"There's one thing I don't think you're aware of." I huffed a breath. "I'm under house arrest."

Her mouth flew open. "Why?"

I shook my head. "Because I confronted Ahab about the letter he supposedly wrote authorizing your father's death. The confrontation was a backhanded way to find out if he had actually written the letter—I'm convinced he did not—*and* to clue him in to the probability that Jezebel did. He didn't appreciate my insolence, so he put my position on hold and confined me to my suite until he could sort it out. So, you see, I may not be in my rooms for long. I might, myself, be imprisoned or ... executed. Jezebel would likely invent some special torture just for me if Ahab did not."

The air went out of Anna's lungs. "I'm sorry, Obe. This is my fault."

"No!" I nearly shouted. "This is not your fault! It's Jezebel's fault, or if someone else is to be blamed, let it be me for being so brazen as to force the king's hand, but this is not your fault at all, Anna. None of it." I forced the tears back. "Your father stood against evil. He died a martyr's death, as far as I am concerned. And your brothers and Zim stood with him." I put my hand over her folded hands. "You are blessed to have such a heritage, and you are just as strong as they were." My eyes flooded. "You have always been strong, Anna. Stronger than any of us. Would that I had a small portion of the strength you possess."

Tears dampened Anna's eyes as well. "Thank you. You are right. I have inherited a priceless gift. I am not sure I'm as strong as you say, but I want to be. And I'll entreat Yahweh to give me such great strength. But, Obe, I think you're wrong when you claim to have less strength than I.

She shook her head. "I didn't see it. I didn't understand how you could let me go like you did. I acted like a petulant child. I thought you were a coward. But you were not a coward, Obe. What you did ... it took a strength I can never hope to replicate. You were strong enough to do what you thought was right for me." She pulled an errant lock of hair away from her face. I wanted to touch its softness. How I loved this woman.

"What greater love is there than to sacrifice your own desires for the good of another? I have been blessed with the love of two good men. You have suffered so much at my hand. I'm so very sorry." She wiped her eyes with the corner of her shawl, then covered my hand with hers. "But I ask you to be strong for me one more time, Obe. Please. I will not feel safe anywhere else. I want to go to the palace with you. I have no other option, and I know you will do your best to protect me. And ... it's possible you may fail, but you will give your life trying. Where else am I safer than in your hands?"

The breath went out of me. Anna had just placed her life in my care, acknowledging that I might fail. I couldn't fail. I had failed her too many times. I had to keep my word to her, but how to do it without getting us both killed?

Energized by the plan, Anna gathered a few things into a knapsack and took a long look around the home Zim had made for her.

"I will most likely never return to this house." She looked at me for a long moment. "But it's just a house, Obe." She smiled a tender smile. "You know I love you, don't you? I always have, and I always will. Thank you for what you are doing for me."

I couldn't swallow. "Don't thank me yet."

I told her to don one of Zim's tunics and secure her hair in a tight bun. I found a strip of cloth and tied it around her head as the workers did to keep the sweat out of their eyes. Up close it would trick no one, but from a distance the loose garment might keep a window-watcher from taking a second look. Thankfully, I had changed into a simple tunic. No finery that would give my identity away.

"I hope you don't regret this," I said, looking into her verdant eyes. "When we're out the door we'll slip around to the far side of the house and backtrack to the vines. But you know we're going to have to walk across that field, completely exposed, don't you?"

"Yes," she said, raising her chin.

Now there was the old Anna. The girl who would face down a wild boar without a thought. This was the Anna I had fallen in love with in my youth. The plucky child with the chestnut hair that floated behind her as she flew across the fields—a woman now, of spirit and faith. A woman I would love until the day I died.

I huffed a breath. "Well, let's be at it, then."

I opened the door and took a few steps, Anna close behind.

"Hello, Obadiah."

I stopped suddenly, causing Anna to stumble into me. Several paces away, a man with a drawn sword was facing me, and he was sitting on my horse! It was the man who had bothered Anna at the market. The man who had told the stable hand that I said he could borrow my horse!

"What do you think you're doing! Why are you on my horse?" I demanded. I should have been more concerned about the sword, but taking my horse made my blood boil.

He ran his hand down her silky black mane. "I'm the new palace administrator. Or will be when I get you back to the palace, and I figured the horse came with the position." *The new governor?* The man was laughable, with his flabby jowls jiggling as he talked, but he was brandishing a sword. I didn't want to test his mettle with Anna at my back. I turned toward her.

To my utter amazement, she smiled. "Don't worry, Obe. Everything is going to be fine." She stepped around me, looking straight into the eyes of the idiot, and said, "All right, let's get going." Then turned to me. "We needn't have worried, Obe. See how easy it is to get into the palace," and started walking.

I stood with my mouth agape, then turned to the man and told him, "You had better give me back my horse," and followed Anna.

CHAPTER TWENTY-FOUR

Obadiah

The man dismounted and let the mare's reins fall to the ground. The horse stood tall and steady as she always did, waiting for me to catch up. She had been trained as a war horse but never went into battle. She was the best horse I'd ever owned, and I hoped this clown knew what was coming to him if he abused her in any way.

The man feigned a bow as we approached and gestured to the steps that led to my apartment. "You know the way."

"Yes. I do. And so does my horse," I said as I slapped her rump and said, "Go." She took off in a gallop. The man threw up his hands

"What do you think you're doing?"

I smiled and started up the stairs, Anna on my elbow. The mare would go back to the stables and wait patiently for the groom to rid her of her bit and saddle. The idiot might find her there and take her out again, but at least I had the pleasure of causing him the trouble.

I opened the slatted door for Anna. Now I would have to figure out what to do about the man. I didn't want to kill him, but I would if he was a threat to Anna. Maybe I could tie him up and stuff him in the closet. Then where would Anna hide if necessary? Why was nothing easy? Anna took a few steps then stopped so abruptly I bumped into her. I caught her forearms to steady her. The last thing I needed was for Anna to fall with a babe in her womb.

"Hello, Obadiah."

What? Not again.

Jezebel was standing in the middle of my living space, which looked like a whirlwind had swallowed it and spit it out again: cushions ripped, wool stuffing strewn all over the room, drawers dumped, leaving debris both official and personal scattered to the four corners of the chamber. She was looking for the scroll. Thank Yahweh I didn't have it.

Her eunuch stood like a bronze statue in a sleeveless tunic designed to expose his roped muscles. He could break a neck with one huge hand if told to do so. And I was certain he had been told just that several times.

"My, my. What a surprise," she said, a smile twisting at the edges of her mouth. "Now this is interesting. The palace administrator escapes imposed exile to his rooms and is found with a young woman."

I snapped my gaping jaw shut and tucked Anna behind me, huffing a small breath through my nose. It didn't seem that Jezebel knew Anna was Naboth's daughter. I would try to keep it that way.

The horse thief pushed his way around us, his hanging jowls and the grin on his face making him look like a lop-eared dog bringing his master a bone.

"I found him in the house at the back of the vineyard, with this one," he said, jutting his narrow chin toward Anna. "Been watching the back gate like you said. Seeing if he would head out to wherever he hid those prophets. It was smart to leave it open."

I saw Jezebel's lip twitch as she realized who Anna was. This was exactly what I didn't want. What I'd tried to avoid when I chose not to marry Anna. And here I was anyway. With Anna in danger. After the sacrifice I had made to keep her safe from Jezebel, here she stood in front of the queen, despite all my efforts. *Yahweh, I should have trusted you to begin with.*

"Tried to get away a couple of times, but I threatened him with the tip of my sword, and he straightened right up. Scared out of his sandals practically."

I couldn't help but roll my eyes.

"You may go now," Jezebel said to the man, nodding toward the door through which we had entered. "And if I hear you have mentioned the governor or the girl to anyone, I won't like it. Do you understand?"

"You said I'd be the governor if I found him doing something you could take to the king. Well, I did. He busted out of these rooms without permission. So when do I start?"

I laughed aloud, and the man jerked his head toward me. He truly was a sucker if he thought he was going to take my place as administrator.

"Even if the king decided to strip me of my position—or my life," I said, glancing back at Jezebel, "the king wouldn't let you oversee his chamber pot."

The man snarled. "He would so let me oversee his chamber pot!"

I burst into laughter. Jezebel closed her eyes and shook her head.

The man puckered his mouth into such a tight twist it flared his hairy nostrils. "I told you I was going to be taking your job, and I will. Don't you forget it!"

"We will discuss your *future* at a later date," Jezebel said, pointing a bony finger toward the exit. "Right now I want you to go out that door and keep your mouth shut!"

The man sent another scathing look my way and turned to leave the room. Jezebel was using him. I couldn't believe he couldn't see something so obvious. "I guess I'll go find my horse," he said as he passed. My temperature kicked up. If he hurts that horse—

I turned to Jezebel. "I see you have made yourself at home in my rooms."

"Yes. Thank you, I have," she said lifting her head. "Of course, I might have asked your permission if you had been where you were supposed to be. But"—she shrugged—"alas, you were nowhere to be found. It was fortunate that the fool noticed you going into the vineyard and escorted you back. I wouldn't want to see you get in trouble for disobeying the king's directive. That could be, well, detrimental to your health."

"Did you find what you were looking for?" I said with a smirk. I had left all pretense of honoring this woman's position. The Law said to honor the king. *That* I could feel some remorse for not obeying, but I would feel no guilt for not honoring this wicked woman.

"Not yet. But I can order my eunuch to continue to look if you like. As you can see, he's not exactly tidy. His size hinders such refined movements. But let us save ourselves some trouble. I think you know what I'm looking for. Do you have it in your possession? Remember, Obadiah, I do not tolerate people lying to me. It will not bode well for you if I catch you doing so."

I wondered how Jezebel knew the scroll was floating about. Had

Ahab confronted her? I doubted that he would do so until he had it in hand. But I was certain the woman had spies, even in the king's chamber.

"No. If I had what you are seeking, I would not be detained," he said. "But it is possible that you *would* be, so you should be happy that it is not in my possession."

Jezebel's jaw was clenched so hard, I thought her teeth must be feeling the pain of it.

"You presume much, Governor."

"I presume nothing. I said it was a possibility, which it was."

"And if I believe that you are not in possession of the item in question, how concerned should I be that it might mysteriously appear in the future?"

I wasn't going to placate Jezebel with false assurances. "You should be very concerned. That you are searching so diligently for this … item is a testament that you are, as I suspected, responsible for its creation." I took a long breath, trying to control my seething emotions. "Which makes you responsible for its consequences. So, my *queen,* you can be sure of this. Even if the item does not 'mysteriously appear' to condemn you for your treachery, your judgment has already been decided. You may evade the consequence of your actions for a time, but the prophet has already foretold your future. Not a pretty one. It involves dogs."

I realized that I had probably said too much. But I could not let Jezebel intimidate me any further. I had lived in fear of her too long.

"I see you brought a visitor," Jezebel said, her eyes slipping into two dark slits. "Step out, please. I'd like to get a better look at you."

I was still holding Anna behind my back. She leaned into my ear and whispered. "I'll be alright, Obe. Please let loose of my arms."

Everything in me resisted, but I did as she asked, and she stepped to my side, pulling the rag off her head, wearing a cloak of calm and fearlessness that, for some reason, did not surprise me.

"And you are the vintner's daughter, I presume," Jezebel said, her voice smooth and sinister.

"Yes. I am Anna, daughter of Naboth," she said with pride.

"Ah, I am sorry to hear about your family's misfortune. Your father. Your brothers. And your husband, I believe? Was he not among the convicted?"

"That's enough!" I said, pulling Anna back. How dare Jezebel flaunt the death of a husband to his widow! Especially when she had ordered it done!

"What is it you wear around your neck, girl?"

Anna pulled the necklace from beneath her tunic. It was the necklace Zim had worn. The one he made from the stone his mother gave him. Of course Zim would give it to Anna. An invisible hand squeezed my heart.

"A stone. How interesting. Not of much value, but interesting. What is the story behind it?"

"My husband gave it to me."

"And that is all he could afford?"

"It's of no monetary value. It's a stone his mother gave him before she died. To remind him that Yahweh was the rock of Israel, and that He was always with him."

"Hmm. Maybe he should have kept it," she said with raised brows.

"It was only a reminder. And I assure you Yahweh was with him and my father and my brothers at their deaths. And now it reminds me of the same. The God of Israel is with me. Nothing can separate me from Him. Not life. Not death. Not even you, my queen."

The queen's eyes laughed. She pulled out the necklace that hung around her neck so Anna could see it.

"I also wear a reminder. The gray centerpiece is part of my mother's breast bone," she said, looking at me. "You remember it, don't you, Obadiah? I think I showed it to you on our pleasant walk to the portico one day."

Heat flashed through me as I pictured Jonathan and Martha hanging from those long ropes.

"I wear it to remind myself that I am stronger than my mother, who got herself killed because she was too weak to secure her place in my father's kingdom. I, on the other hand, have secured my place in my father's kingdom—and in my husband's."

I couldn't let that one go. "I wouldn't count on it."

Jezebel shot a venomous look at me. "You would do well to think about your own position, Obadiah. Your own life!" She turned slowly back to Anna. "And the lives of the ones you so obviously love."

Anger flushed through me. I would kill the queen myself if she harmed a hair on Anna's head.

"And you, girl, what do you think of a prophet that would make such predictions as Obadiah mentioned? To wish such an end for anyone is not a very loving attitude. Is it?"

Anna didn't answer at once. She was looking on the face of the woman who had caused the death of her entire family. And what did I see on Anna's face? Anger? Hatred? No. Something akin to compassion touched Anna's eyes.

My lungs expanded and stilled for an impossibly long moment. *Be careful, my love.*

I could see Anna's thoughts displayed as plainly as if they were written on an unfurled scroll. It was as though she was out of her body, standing in the crowd, watching her father's face as he awaited that first rock. Her own face soft with the memory of the man who had taught her the Law alongside her brothers. The commandments of Moses. Thou shalt love the Lord your God and your neighbor as yourself. She was going to forgive Jezebel for killing her entire family. For killing Zim. How could she do that?

Were the words of the Law true? Or were they just some ideal that fathers taught their children to make them behave? No. They were truth. Complete truth. They were written with the hand of God Himself on stone tablets. And Jezebel *was* her neighbor. Quite literally. But I could never do what I knew Anna was about to do. As though releasing the great burden of her soul, she expelled a long whisper of breath and spoke to the queen of Israel.

"When I was young, I sometimes disobeyed my father. Not usually intentionally, but children can be distracted, or they can simply choose to disobey, believing that the parent will forget to punish the infraction.

"My father was a gentle soul. A kind man, but he understood that the seeds of even a small disobedience could grow into a bramble of thorns that would pierce the tender parts of the conscience until scars covered it over completely. It was out of his great love for me and my brothers that he did not let us escape the consequences of our actions.

"Your hardness of heart causes me to suspect that your father did not do the same for you. I pray that your conscience is not so hard that you cannot see the wickedness of your actions and repent, for you will suffer far more than my father and my brothers did—" Tears dampened her eyes. "Than my husband did. And in the end you will regret what you have done—but none of that will bring my loved ones back. So I am left with only one thing, and that is to forgive you."

I tightened my grip on her arm. The queen would not appreciate being told to repent. Jezebel's face was almost as red as her hair. But somehow it didn't seem to matter to Anna. She wasn't afraid of Jezebel at that moment. She would perhaps fear her at another, but, right then, I could see complete peace on her face.

"What would your father say if he could see you, hanging onto the governor's arm when your husband is just a few days dead? Would he think that you had some repenting of your own to do? You are not so pure, I believe! You people! Always judging others!"

It was as if all motion slowed as I saw Jezebel's eyes move from Anna's face downward, to where her hand lay protectively over her stomach. Jezebel stared at the hand for several long moments then raised her eyes, and I saw the mix of recognition and alarm in them. She knew. She knew that Anna was pregnant and that if she had a boy child, a claim could be made by an intercessor for the child's rights if it could be proven Naboth was murdered without cause. If there had been no real danger from the queen before, there was now.

Jezebel looked at her eunuch, some unspoken command passing in the air between them. I shoved Anna behind my back again.

"If you or your henchman lay a hand on this woman, I will rip your throat out of your neck."

Jezebel shook her head and laughed. "Thank you, Obadiah. You have just made things so much easier for me. You've threatened to kill the queen of Israel. Guards!"

Four guards appeared out of nowhere and laid their hands on me. I looked back at Anna, who looked shocked but still calm.

"Trust Yahweh," she said, her eyes moistening. "I will be alright."

Jezebel laughed again. "I wouldn't count on it."

She nodded at the eunuch. "Make the grave shallow. We'll see who is eaten by dogs."

My eyes met the eunuch's, and I saw, or thought I saw, the slightest shake of his huge head. Was he telling me that he wasn't going to kill Anna, or was he warning me that it was useless to fight Jezebel.

∞∞∞∞∞∞∞∞∞

The jailer opened the dungeon door and let me walk through. All the times Ahab had asked me if I needed to report someone in need of the dungeon or the rope, and now I was the recipient of the first and could be the recipient of the second.

"I'm sorry about this, Obadiah. Never thought I'd see the day I'd have to lock you in this rat hole."

Rats. Of all Yahweh's creatures, I hated rats most of all. I had little fear of venomous snakes or wild animals that could be encountered near or in the caves, but rats had always made my skin crawl. They were like tiny thieves skittering through the shadows, their whiskers twitching with mischief. But at the moment, sharing space with rats made no difference at all. Nothing did.

"It's all right, Joseph. You're not the one who put me here. But I would ask of you a favor, if you can do it without endangering yourself. One of the city fathers is supposed to meet me this afternoon: Kenen ben Lehabim. I told him to tell whoever was at the gate to see him to my rooms. But ..." I looked around at the stone walls coated with layers of grime and moisture, a narrow cot covered with a filthy blanket along one wall, "obviously, I am not in my rooms. Could you contact Shadim and ask him if he could watch for the nobleman discreetly and bring him down here instead? It's very important. Perhaps a matter of life and death, but I do not want to endanger any of you."

"Yes, my lord. I would be happy to do that. And I will bring you some better fare than the gruel the kitchens send down here. Is there anything else I can do for you?"

"Some parchment and ink, and a quill please. That would be most helpful. Thank you. And, Joseph, keep an ear out for anything unusual going on in the palace. Anything about a young woman. Or whatever might seem out of the ordinary."

"Yes, my lord. Whatever you did to get yourself in this pickle, I know it wasn't bad. You're a good man. I loved your father, and you've done well by him. He would be proud of you. Yahweh be with you." He pulled the chain with the long key from around his neck as he

213

walked out of the cell and closed the door. The sound of the key in the lock sent a shiver down my spine.

Kenen did not come. I spent the night on my knees entreating Yahweh for Anna's safety. She wasn't dead. I would feel it. Wouldn't I? Jezebel wouldn't commit such a crime when she already risked judgment for so many. But I knew better. There was nothing the queen of Israel would not do if it suited her purposes.

Joseph brought a quill and jar of ink and a few sheets of parchment, and the next day a small rickety table and two chairs he absconded from a storage room. I took quill in hand and wrote a letter to Anna that I knew she would never read. I didn't know if she had received the one I sent with the messenger, but in that one I had not laid bare my heart. It was time to do that. I would likely leave this cell without a head, or with a hole in my chest, my lifeblood soaking the stone floor. So I told her how much I loved her. How much I had always loved her, and that I would never love another. I wished her joy and peace, in life or in death.

When the next day did not bring the nobleman, nor word of Anna, I settled in my heart that she was gone. When King David's child, born of Bathsheba, died, he ceased his prayer and fasting and washed his face, saying the child would not come back to him, but someday he would go to the child. Anna had gone to wherever it was her father and brothers and Zim waited for her.

I wept until there were no more tears to weep, then I set out to remember every image of her stored in my memory. Of Naboth and the brothers. And of Zim. Perhaps I would join them soon. I had no more fear of what Jezebel or Ahab could do to me. I almost hoped for a quick end. I breathed a deep, peaceful breath. *Thank you, Yahweh.* I had vowed that I would protect them. Anna. Zim. Naboth. I should have realized that it was not in my power to protect anyone. Only Yahweh could do that.

CHAPTER TWENTY-FIVE

Ahab

And why was it I wanted this vineyard so badly? Ahab lowered himself to the rough stone ledge of the treading vat. The scent of the rotted fruit and stocks caught in the drain of the slanted floor was at once tart and sweet. The dregs of good wine grapes.

I have a dozen better vineyards.

A hardy breeze arose and made the wildflowers dance with the weeds in the dooryard of the mud-brick house close by. Ahab wondered who lived there. *Had* lived there. It was empty, of course. As was the larger house on the other side of the vines—but he knew who had lived there.

He pressed his fingers against his forehead. He could feel another headache sprouting beneath the surface of his skull.

"Ah, yes," he said, reviving his thoughts. "Vegetables. I wanted vegetables for my salad. That was it. Vegetables. And it is so close," he said to no one as he motioned toward the palace a short walk away. He settled his hands in his lap and took a deep breath. Vegetables.

Ahab smelled him before he saw him. He smelled of the desert and sweat—and vengeance.

"And so you took what you wanted at the cost of five men's lives."

Ahab sighed as he turned toward the voice that came from nowhere. His hair was a wild bush about his head. His beard unkempt, as it had been when last Ahab had seen him. The king supposed a man who lived in the wilderness and ate locusts for his dinner cared nothing of finery or fettle.

He was not surprised to see Elijah. He had half-expected him to make an appearance. The prophet never missed an opportunity to find

Ahab guilty of something. And it was rumored the spirit sometimes transported Elijah from one place to another, so why would he *not* be here now? A satisfying memory popped into Ahab's mind of Jezebel swearing an oath in her anger after Mount Carmel, that the gods were permitted to do to her as had been done to her prophets if Elijah was not dead by the same time the next day.

And here the man stood. Months past. Alive.

Or so Ahab thought. Maybe he really was a ghost instead of a man. Who can kill a ghost?

Ahab sighed. "So you have found me at last, my enemy."

"I have found you. I followed the stench of treachery, and there you were," the prophet said, stretching a palm toward the king.

Treachery! Already he accuses me.

"Now let us not make assumptions, my friend," Ahab said, raising a finger.

"I am not your friend."

The king let out a long breath and nodded. "No. I suppose you are not, but you are a man of law I would think." Elijah didn't answer. Just stared at Ahab through those piercing black eyes.

"I have a right, you know, to the property of a condemned criminal. It is the law of our land. I didn't write it. But I'm entitled to its boon. Entitled, Prophet! I'm not the first king to take advantage of such a law nor will I be the last!"

"But you are not entitled to falsely accuse a righteous man of crimes he did not commit. Nor kill him and his sons," he said, waving his palm in a wide arc, "because he owns property adjacent to your palace."

Ahab burst to his feet. "I didn't do it! I didn't kill them! I wasn't there. I had nothing to do with their fate."

"It was done at your direction."

"No! It was not. I directed no such thing. I am not guilty!" The words swirled through the air as though they couldn't find a place to land.

Ahab threw up his hands. "I offered to buy the vineyard from Naboth. Pay him more than its value or give him a better vineyard. He refused, and I walked away. I walked away!" His heart was thrashing in his ears. *Why did Elijah always speak the worst to me? I'd never heard a good word out of his mouth!* He shook his head.

"You are guilty, Ahab. Because you turned your head to the wall and told your wife not to bother you with the details."

Ahab drew back from the words that slapped the air.

I'm not guilty. I'm not. I didn't do it. His head started to swim, and he lowered himself to the ledge again. *I didn't do it!*

It was the men of Jezreel who had done it. Found the man guilty of blaspheming God and king. And, if Obadiah was correct, Ahab's Phoenician wife had played a part some way. He didn't know the details, but— The breath went out of him. That is what the prophet had just accused him of.

You take things too far, Wife! Jezebel could never leave well enough alone. Ahab rued the day he had married her.

Elijah moved closer. Ahab expected a blast of fury from his lips. But when he spoke, it was in a quiet voice. "You have sold yourself to do everything that the Lord despises, Ahab. As thoroughly as if that were your goal—your planned purpose."

"It wasn't!" he retorted. In truth, he *wanted* to be a good king. A king like David of old. But David wasn't perfect either. The memory of his fall lifted Ahab's spirits for a moment. David had taken another man's wife. Ahab had never done such a thing. *Would* never. And David had ordered Bathsheba's husband, one of his most faithful soldiers, to be abandoned in the heat of battle. David should have been stoned, but the prophet Nathan saw fit to let him go. It was fortunate for David that Elijah was not prophet then. He never let anything go!

And he won't let this go.

To Ahab's surprise, the prophet sat beside him on the ledge, his long fingers rubbing at a place where the plaster had begun to wear away. Ahab's body tensed. The man took a deep breath.

"This is Yahweh's message to you, Ahab. "You have chosen to do evil before the Lord, and now you will be punished. In the place where dogs licked up the blood of Naboth shall dogs lick your own blood. As for Jezebel?" He held Ahab's gaze for a long moment. "The dogs shall eat her flesh within the walls of Jezreel.

"Every man and boy in your household will die. None will escape. Anyone who belongs to Ahab in the city the dogs will eat. And anyone who belongs to Ahab in the open country, the birds of the heavens shall feast upon.

"There is none who has sold himself to do evil in the sight of the Lord like you. You have murdered. But, worse than that, you have incited Yahweh's people to sin against Him."

Ahab pressed his eyes shut. A scene he had not witnessed played on the back of his eyelids. The battered bodies of Naboth's sons. Bloodied stones scattered about where they had met their marks and fallen to the wayside. And another image. The headless bodies of the king's own sons. All seventy. Dead.

Ahab fell to his knees, his head bent backward to the heavens, groaning from the depths of his soul. "Oh, Yahweh. I have sinned against you." He shrugged off his royal robe and gripped his tunic at the neck and tore it.

<hr />

"Where is he?"

"On the portico," the jester answered, his mouth still gaping.

"And he is wearing what?" Jezebel asked.

"Sackcloth. And he is barefoot."

Sackcloth? And shoeless?

"And you're certain it was Elijah's servant he was speaking with?"

"I believe so."

"You believe so?" The man had said it was Elijah's servant that had delivered a small scroll to Ahab.

"Well, was it or wasn't it?"

"Yes. I'm certain it was. The king is acting strangely, my queen. I thought you'd want to know."

The buffoon knows nothing. I will find out for myself.

Jezebel pushed the man aside and walked at a quick pace toward the portico. This was not the scroll she had questioned Obadiah about. She was certain of that, but what was happening with Ahab? She thought he would be happy that she had delivered the vineyard to him. But, as far as she knew, he had not even gone to see it, let alone claim it. He had hardly left his rooms!

The guards pulled the doors open when Jezebel approached. The hair hanging beneath her headpiece swept off her neck in the brisk breeze.

Ahab was standing, staring up at the banner that hung from the bar beneath the upper windows. The rough garment he wore whipped about his bare knees. Jezebel said nothing, waiting for him to acknowledge her presence. At last he turned toward her. His face was pale—and were those tears that had tracked down his face?

"How did you get them up there?"

What? "Get who up where?" Her husband was acting strangely indeed.

He raised his head to the banner again. "The prophet and his wife?"

Bumps raised on Jezebel's arms, and not from the chill in the air. She hadn't realized that Ahab even knew about the couple. And why would he ask her such a question? Since when did he care when she dispatched a nuisance?

The queen fisted her hands in the folds of her robe and schooled her visage. "What is troubling my husband? Tell me please, so I can help."

His face suddenly hardened. The glaze over his eyes sparked into flame.

"You have helped quite enough, Jezebel. I want no more help from you!"

"My king, I —"

"Yes! Your king! Your sovereign! Not your servant to manipulate!"

She pursed her lips, anger creeping up her spine and settling in her neck. Whatever was on that scroll had sent Ahab into this fit of temper. Elijah again! She would be rid of that man if it took her last breath!

"My husband." She gestured toward the scroll. "It is not I that has brought this ill humor upon you. Whatever is written on that scroll has taken you to a dark place. Please. Do not believe the message. Whatever it is, it has been sent to torment you."

He looked down at the scroll he had been clutching as though the weight of it anchored him to the ground. "No. You are wrong, Jezebel. The scroll has been sent to offer me some small comfort."

He met Jezebel's gaze. "I went to Naboth's vineyard today, thinking to make plans for a garden." He paused, some strange emotion touching his eyes. "Elijah met me there. He gave me a message from Yahweh. He said that I had murdered Naboth and his family for the hope of a few vegetables. I told him I was innocent. It was others who had killed the vintner."

The king studied Jezebel's face. His relentless gaze frightened her. She had never seen his jaw so set or the lines in his forehead so deep.

"He said I had turned my head to the wall and told you not to tell me what you did."

The skin on Jezebel's arms began to prickle.

"I tried to blame you, Wife. But the prophet wouldn't let me. We share the blame for what happened to that family. I didn't ask you to have the man stoned. And most especially his sons and his daughter's husband. The man was one of my wheelwrights, you know. I met him on the battlefield. I will never forget his eyes." Ahab pulled a deep breath. "It was disappointment I saw on the man's face. He was disappointed in his king."

The queen's heart froze. If Ahab had this attachment to the girl's husband, what would he think when he found out she had the girl killed?

"But I should have known you would stop at nothing. I don't know the details of how you managed it, because I told you not to tell me. But I will find out. And you should hope you did not cross a line I must keep intact."

Jezebel forced the fear that nipped at her mind to retreat. Fear would make her weak. She could not be weak. Not now.

Ahab swallowed, and this time she was certain it was tears that welled in his eyes.

"Elijah told me that every man and boy from the house of Ahab will die. All of them, Jezebel. Including your own sons."

The words hit her like a sack of rocks. "No!" she shouted. "It's a lie! Stand up and be the king!" Elijah was trying to frighten Ahab. It wasn't true. No one would dare!

"That's what I should have done when you came to my chamber with a promise to get me the vineyard. When you begged me to erect a temple to your gods. But I failed. I've even failed you, Jezebel. I have allowed you to come to this state. And we shall both suffer for it." He looked at the scroll in his trembling hand. "But I fear you will suffer more than I, my dear."

She couldn't speak. He raised the scroll between them. "Yes, it is a message from Elijah as I'm sure you suspected. But the message says that the God of Israel has seen my repentance. And for that reason the prophecy will not be fulfilled until after I am gathered to my fathers. I will not see the death of my sons, Jezebel." He paused for a long moment. "He did not say the same of you."

CHAPTER TWENTY-SIX

Obadiah

I laid my quill down when I heard footsteps in the hall outside my cell. The heavy iron door creaked and groaned as it scraped open on rusty hinges. I stood, wondering who it was. Friend or foe? I was relieved to see Joseph enter instead of Ahab.

"That visitor you've been waiting for is here."

Joseph stepped back, and Kenen ducked through the low entrance. His face was solemn. A wave of sadness rolled over me. Kenen was here to affirm what I already knew. Anna was gone. I motioned to the empty chair tucked into the small table.

"Sit. Please."

He sighed and took his seat, taking care that the old chair would hold his weight.

The man's face flushed. "I'm sorry to see you here, Obadiah. I should have come sooner." He ran his hand through his silver-streaked hair. "I wasn't going to come at all. Didn't want to get involved. I apologize for that."

I felt some compassion for the man, and all the anger I had stored within me had drained away since I'd been in this place. A strange peace attended me. I had lost everything, but I'd also found some things inside these prison walls. I'd found that it takes much more courage to trust than it does to act. I would have faced any obstacle to protect them as I'd vowed: Naboth, Joel, Mikah, Zim, and Anna. I supposed it was a noble aim, but I'd learned here, helpless behind that iron door, that surrender is all a man can really do. So I had surrendered as best I could to the will of Yahweh in the matter.

"I must confess that it is because of Lillian that I am here now. She insisted that I come in person to deliver this," he said, laying a scroll on the table. I stared at it for a long moment. What good would the scroll do me now? I thought about asking Kenen to take it back. It might bring me more trouble and was not likely to make any difference at all. Ahab would believe what he wanted to believe. He had lied to himself too long to stop now. And if Jezebel got wind that a nobleman had come to call, she might abscond it and feel free to dispose of me.

I sat in the other chair and fingered the fibrous missive. I would keep it. It didn't matter what happened to me now, but there might be some way to use it against Jezebel. To keep her from destroying more lives. And I wouldn't allow Kenen to risk being searched by a guard less loyal to me than Joseph and end up as my cellmate.

"Thank you. I know it was dangerous for you to come here at all. You are a good man, Kenen."

He shook his head. "I don't think so, Obadiah. A good man would have come at your call without delaying." He pulled a long breath. "A good man could not ... hurt his wife in the way I have hurt mine."

I wasn't certain what he meant about hurting Lillian, but I had sensed a deep sorrow in her when I took Anna to her house. Whatever the man had done, it had erected a wall between him and his wife that was not easily breached.

"Do you want to talk about it?" I asked, thinking that the man needed to unburden his soul, and since I bore so many regrets myself, I would be as good an ear as any.

He shrugged, letting out a long sigh. "Well, since it's unlikely you will live to tell the tale ..." he said with a sardonic smile that faded into a heaviness around his amber eyes. "I love my wife. Lillian was the light of my soul."

Was? Lillian sent him so she hadn't left. I suspected the man must have fallen into adultery. Perhaps his position had helped him escape being stoned. Perhaps Naboth's and the boys' deaths had brought that to bear on his conscience. Whatever it was, the man carried a broken heart.

"I thought I was missing something. Something I had to have to make me accepted by my peers, to make me feel more of a man. I was wrong. Lillian was all I needed. I let my position and my pride drive me into doing the unthinkable."

His position drove him to a tryst? That didn't make sense. But who knew what went on with the hypocrites who thought themselves above other men because of a political position.

"You've met my daughters, have you not?" he asked.

"Not actually met them, no. I saw them at the wedding. I didn't know who they were then. All beautiful young women. You are blessed."

"Yes. I am. I have come to realize that now. But it wasn't enough a few years ago. I felt I had to have a son. So I took another wife."

Ahh. No wonder the sadness in Lillian's eyes. The conundrum Kenen had faced was a difficult one. One that many men of Israel had faced and borne the burden of. Abraham and the Egyptian slave, Jacob with his two wives. Leah had borne the pain of that plural marriage, but Jacob had borne the consequences.

"And Lillian does not get along with the other woman?" I thought Lillian capable of getting along with anyone.

"It's a little more complicated than that. The other woman was Lillian's maid. A friend, as you can imagine. Lillian considered all the servants her personal friends," he said, lowering his eyes. "And I took the girl before the marriage. I married her a few days later, not wanting to bring shame to her should she be with child. And she was. I have a young son that I do not bring under my roof. Not that Lillian forbids it, but I won't put her through the pain of seeing the child's mother every day. Don't misunderstand. I love the boy. And I am fond of his mother. I have tried to make amends for taking advantage of her youthful crush on an older man. But what I have done to Lillian breaks my heart every day. Who says sons are better than daughters?"

I thought about how much Anna had longed for children. I would do anything to have a daughter of her womb. But who knows if I wouldn't have longed for a son if she hadn't borne me one. Foolish how a son makes a man burst with more pride than a daughter. As though he had done something special.

"I understand. It must be a constant source of pain to you. And to Lillian."

"Yes, it is. But some things in life must be borne, no matter how difficult." Kenen took a deep breath that raised his shoulders half-way to his ears. "That is why Lillian wanted me to come here in person. To tell you that Anna is gone."

Tears sprang to my eyes. So it was true. I had believed it, but Kenen's words still hit me like one of the rocks that had fallen on my friends. "I felt it," I whispered.

"And to give you this." He slid the scroll toward me.

I stared at the wound papyrus, "Thank you, but the scroll means nothing to me now. I care not what Ahab or Jezebel do to me. I'm sorry you endangered yourself to bring it."

Kenen's brow furrowed and then his eyes widened and his lips parted.

"No. You don't understand, Obadiah. This scroll is not the one that Jezebel forged and presented to the city fathers as having come from Ahab. I destroyed that one. I was a coward, and I feared it would fall back on Lemech, and by association on me. I'm sorry for that. Perhaps it could have kept you from this place. When I said Anna was gone, I meant she is no longer in Jezreel. I took her to her husband's family. I'm so sorry, Obadiah. I didn't know what else to do. She found her way back to our house after the eunuch let her go. He was supposed to kill her but he didn't. He wrote in the dirt that she should flee and not show her face in Jezreel again or they would both be dead.

"I had already been considering taking her to her husband's family. I remembered what Naboth had said at the wedding about his son being from the tribe of Ashur and that his ancestral land was not far. Naboth was wrong about that. It was two hard days' journey. When she came to our door again, I didn't want to take a chance on Jezebel figuring out where she was and coming for me and my family. So I took her and left her there with her husband's oldest brother."

"You're saying that ... Anna is alive?"

"She was when I delivered her to her husband's brother, and I was careful not to disclose my plans to anyone. Not even Lillian until I returned. I feigned a business trip. She was used to that. I often said I was going away on business when I went to Megiddo, where I had purchased a small cottage home for my second wife and our son. The city is on the trade routes, so it was never a lie, but it softened the blow a bit. It was our way of avoiding the subject.

"When Lillian discovered I'd taken Anna, she knew I had conceived some plan to hide her. It was better that she not know where at the time."

My heart almost jumped out of my chest. Anna was alive! And she was safe!

"I can't believe it. I was certain she was dead. Thank you, Kenen. Thank you."

The man's face grayed. "I don't think you will thank me, Obadiah. That is why I am here in person. To bear the wrath you may want to lay upon me."

"What are you talking about? If she is with Zim's brothers she is safe, and there is no wrath in me toward you. Only joy and thanksgiving that you have saved the woman I love, and I'm going to stop being an imbecile and marry her as soon as I get out of this place. *If* I get out of this place. And perhaps I won't, but if not, I will die a happy man."

"I'm afraid you don't understand, Obadiah. She wrote it in the scroll. Sorry, but I read it. I couldn't help myself, and it wasn't sealed." He rose to his feet. "I will leave you now. Both to allow you the privacy the occasion calls for and to take my leave before you change your mind and decide to take your wrath out on me after all. You see, I am still a coward, Obadiah. I would that I were like my wife. And like Anna. And even like you. You are a brave man, Obadiah. I wish you all the best."

My mind was swirling with the information, but I had something to say to Kenen. "It doesn't matter what this scroll reveals. I thank you for seeing Anna to safety. And if it turns out you are a coward, you are in good company with me." I reached out my hand. He grasped it with both of his.

"I pray you will find peace, Obadiah. You deserve it." He turned as if to leave, then pulled something out of a pocket sewed to the inside of his robe. "I almost forgot. She told me to give you this. She explains it in the scroll."

He placed something in my open hand. A pretty rock in a pewter setting, a small woven cord threaded through the hole. Zim's pendant.

<hr />

I sat at the table, the pendant lying over my heart, the missive lying on the table long after Kenen had gone, finally garnering the courage to open it.

> *To Obadiah ben Enos from Anna, daughter of Naboth.*
> *Obadiah. I hardly know where to begin this missive.*
> *There is so much I desire to say to you. But I must begin*
> *somewhere, so first I will say that I am alive. Of course,*
> *you knew that when your eyes first fell upon these words.*
> *But I will add that I am safe. By the grace and mercy of*
> *Yahweh. The man that was supposed to see to my death*
> *took me to the outskirts of the city and set me free. He*
> *had no tongue with which to speak, so he wrote in the*
> *dirt that I should leave Jezreel as soon as possible and not*
> *return, lest we both lose our lives at Jezebel's command.*
> *So Jezebel does not cease to be a threat. May Yahweh keep*
> *you from her evil designs.*
>
> *If you have received my letter, it was by the hand of*
> *Kenen, and I'm certain he told you where I am now.*
>
> *Obe, I want you to know that I love you. I never*
> *stopped. You were my first love. My great love. And I*
> *never dreamed that I could love another, but when I*
> *married Zim, my heart expanded to include him. When*
> *you love one soul so completely, it seems impossible that*
> *there would be room enough in your heart for another.*
> *But Zim was my healing love. The love that bound my*
> *wounds, self-inflicted as most of them were. Our shared*
> *love of Zim both drew us together and tore us apart. But*
> *I want you to know that our love of Zim will always*
> *bind us. We share one heart, and it will beat between*
> *us forever.*
>
> *I spoke of this at my house, when you came to find*
> *me, but I will say it again. Forgive me, Obe, for not un-*
> *derstanding that it was your love for me that made you*
> *sacrifice your own desires. How hard it must have been,*
> *and how thoroughly I judged you for it. And I believe it*
> *was your love for Zim that kept you from claiming me*
> *as your own after his death. Although, I am certain that*
> *his last words, the words you said were of me, were to*

instruct you to do so. We are so fortunate to have loved each other and to have loved Zim.

There is another love in my life now, Obe. It's the child that stirs in my womb as I write this letter. This is a different kind of love. A love that demands all. Any sacrifice to keep this little loved one safe and provide a future for him … or her. Were Jezebel to find out that I live, and Zim's child lives within me, she would not rest until she found us. I must make whatever sacrifice is necessary. And so it is with such sorrow that I inform you that Zim's oldest brother, Eber, has stepped forward to do the duty of a brother of the deceased. You know the law, Obe. How God commanded a man take the wife of his dead brother as his own and raise up an heir to his brother's name. If the child I carry is a boy, he will receive Zim's portion of his ancestral inheritance. If it is a girl, Eber and I will have another child. God will honor Zim with an heir. There will be no betrothal period, so by the time Kenen gets this letter to you, I will be Eber's wife. I trust my heart will expand to love him also. In a different way, I'm certain. But he will be a good father to Zim's child.

I hope Zim's pendant arrived with Kenen. I want you to have it. May it remind you as it did Zim and as it did me that the God of Israel is our strength and our protection.

My prayers are with you, Obe. Now and forever. Thank you for the sacrifices you have made to keep me safe. With God's help, you have prevailed.

With love,
Anna

I wept as I set the letter on my makeshift desk. I wept as I lay on the bed that smelled of stale sweat and vomit, the stone in my fisted hand. But when my weeping ceased, I rejoiced. Anna was safe. Her child had a father and a future. *Thank you, Yahweh. Thank you.*

Kenen

Kenen entered his house, the weight of the day pressing down on him like a leaden cloak. Jona approached to take his outer garment. Kenen handed it to the servant with a silent nod. Lillian was standing across the room, her posture rigid, her hands clasped tightly together. The room felt colder than usual, despite the warm afternoon light filtering through the windows.

"How did Obadiah take it?" Lillian asked, her soft voice breaking the thick silence.

Kenen hesitated, his gaze lingering on her. He took in the lines of weariness etched on her face, the sadness in her eyes that seemed to have taken permanent residence there. He thought of all the ways he had hurt her, the trust he had shattered, the love he had taken for granted. Could their lives ever be the same? Could he ever truly mend what he had broken?

"He took it well," Kenen finally said, his voice heavy. "He was relieved to know that Anna was alive and safe. I left him to read the scroll alone. So ..." He shrugged. "But I believe he loved her enough to see that it was the best for her. He thanked me."

Kenen had been deeply moved by Obadiah's declaration that whatever the scroll contained, he would still be thankful for what Kenen had done. Something had changed in Obadiah. Kenen hoped for a change in his own life.

"Did you tell him everything?"

Kenen took a deep breath. "Yes. I told him that I had destroyed the forged scroll. I confessed my cowardice, Lillian. I told him I had been too afraid to act sooner."

He shook his head, still astonished at Obadiah's response. "He forgave me. He thanked me for keeping Anna safe, despite my failings. He ... he even called me a good man."

Lillian's eyes softened, but the sadness remained. "Obadiah is a remarkable man," she said quietly. "He was willing to give her up because he loved her. I didn't understand it at first, but ..." Her voice trailed off.

Kenen nodded, the guilt and regret weighing heavily on his heart. "I wish I could be more like him, Lillian. I wish I had his courage. I let my fear and pride drive me to hurt you, to betray your trust. I'm so sorry for … for all of it."

Lillian's gaze dropped to the floor, her hands trembling slightly. They stood in silence, the distance between them a chasm filled with unspoken words and unresolved pain. Kenen's heart ached with the uncertainty of what she might say next. He felt as if an axe was hanging over his head, ready to drop.

"I have something to say, Kenen," she began, her voice steady but awash with emotion.

A knot of anxiety tightened his stomach. Was she going to tell him she was leaving him? That she could no longer bear to be with him?

"There are things that I have to make right," she said with an unsteady voice.

Make right? It was Kenen who needed to make things right.

"What do you mean?" he asked, his voice barely above a whisper.

"Your son needs you," Lillian said, her voice resolute. "He deserves to have his father in his life."

The axe fell. "What are you saying?" he asked, his voice trembling. Was she going to tell him to leave? To go to Beth and the boy? He wouldn't do it. She couldn't force him to do it. The boy needed him and that broke his heart, but he needed Lillian. He would be of no good to his son if he lost her. He would be of no good to anyone. He wouldn't abandon the boy. He would continue to see him whenever he traveled the merchant route. He would care for him and his mother, but he would not give up his first love. Lillian would have a fight on her hands if she insisted.

"I've sent for your wife and your son," Lillian continued, taking another tentative step closer. "They will live in the guest house."

What? Live here? In their guest quarters? No. He couldn't let her do this. It would destroy her. "You shouldn't have done it," he said, shaking his head. "I can't let you be hurt that way. I will tell her it was a mistake and send her back."

"No. You won't. You will make the best of the situation, as will I." Lillian closed the distance between them. "There are consequences for your actions, Kenen," she said, her eyes meeting his with a steady gaze.

Kenen's heart ached with sorrow. "But if you do this, think about it … how will you feel when I'm … with her? I can't do this to you," he said, his voice breaking.

Lillian's eyes filled with tears. "I will hate it, Kenen. It will tear at my heart every day. But this situation can't be undone. Beth is your wife. She has certain rights that you must grant her."

Kenen's mind raced, struggling to process her words. "But I love you, Lillian. Only you."

She put her finger on his lips. "You love her, Kenen. As you should. As you must. We cannot undo what has been done. I know you are sorry for this, but sorrow won't mend it. I have been wrong. I have let my jealousy and pain rob you of your son and your son of you. You have been a wonderful father to our girls. You must not deprive the boy of the same. We are not the first to be faced with this. It is common in our history. Love stretches to cover every situation. We have to look to Yahweh's love to give us peace in the very worst of things."

Kenen reached out and pulled her to his chest, his heart shredding into little slivers of grief. How was it possible that Lillian could even consider making such a sacrifice? He tipped her chin up and kissed her tenderly, then lifted her into his arms and took her to their bed.

For a long time they lay in each other's arms weeping. His heart was broken. He pulled her long hair from between them and laid it over her back, stroking it gently, his chin resting on the top of her head. He knew she was asleep when her deep breaths fell into a steady rhythm, matching the rise and fall of her chest. He pulled her a little closer and whispered, "I promise you, my love, that I will become a man worthy of this sacrifice. A man you can trust. And I will love you with all my heart and mind and body for as long as we live."

CHAPTER TWENTY-SEVEN

Obadiah

I had fallen into a deep sleep after Kenen left. I was awakened as the door of my cell opened wide, allowing three of Ahab's most faithful servants to enter. Their faces were intense. One of them grabbed the chamber pot in the corner of my dank cell and handed it to the servant standing in the hall. "Argg!" he said, wrinkling his nose. He looked around for something on which to wipe his hands and, finding nothing, wiped them on the hem of his tunic.

"Get it out of here."

The second servant waved a hand at me. "Get up."

What is going on? I thought maybe I was going to be executed, but why then the concern about the condition of my cell? I rose and went to the wall, waiting for some word or reason for this sudden intrusion. The servant turned the dirty mattress over, but the bottom looked worse than the top so he turned it back.

"Nothing I can do about this." He looked me over, settling on my outer garment. I had grabbed it from its peg as the guards took me out of my rooms. I knew the dungeons were damp and chilly and had the foresight to bring it to ward off the cold.

"Give me your robe." I didn't move. "I said, give me your robe! You'll get it back."

"What are you doing?"

"You're going to have a visitor," the man said as he draped the robe over one of the chairs.

"Maybe you should put it on the bed," the second soldier suggested. "That chair doesn't look like it will hold him."

232

"Hold who?" I insisted.

"The king. He's on his way down the stairs now."

Ahab was coming to my cell? What could that mean? Probably wanted to deliver my sentence in person. But he could have summoned me to the judgment seat rather than come to this putrid place.

"Why?"

"How should I know? He could have given us some time to prepare. We had to run ahead of him."

"He's coming!" the other servant whispered.

The man opted to cover the cot. He spread the robe quickly then headed out the door, his face etched with fear. I didn't blame him. Ahab could punish them all for something that was out of their control. He'd certainly done it before, as had Jezebel.

I heard the tromp of feet coming down the hall. Not a large contingent of soldiers. Maybe four? My heart began to pound.

Ahab entered the cell alone, waving at the servants and the soldiers standing outside the doorway. "Go to the end of the corridor, and don't come back until I call for you." That was odd. Ahab always had soldiers at hand, though usually hidden from view. Sending them even a short distance away, while he entered the cell of a prisoner was not something I would expect him to do.

The king and I stood, eyes locked for a long moment. Finally, he pulled out the rickety old chair and sat. I held my breath, praying it wouldn't choose this moment to collapse, but it seemed to be holding. It was stronger than it looked. I hoped I was stronger than I looked because this would most likely be my last day on earth, and the knowledge of that had to be showing on my countenance.

Should I bow? I didn't know how I would manage it, but our God said to honor the king, so I would honor God in doing so. Before I could take a knee, the king settled the matter.

"Sit down, Obadiah. I'll get a crick in my neck talking to you this way." A blade of pain pierced my heart. The words I had spoken to Zim before he delivered the news that drove me to put my fist into his chin. *Sorry for that, Zim.*

Ahab motioned toward the chair across from him. The lines of his face seemed drawn, his eyes troubled and strangely sad. What was going on with the king of Israel?

It was a long minute before he spoke. "I'm a cursed man, Obadiah. You know that, don't you?"

I chose not to comment—or breathe, for that matter.

"The prophet told me what my future holds." He shook his head. "Prophets. They never bring good news, do you agree?"

I didn't answer. The king was right that prophets seldom brought good news, especially to kings, but it wasn't a choice. They spoke the words the Lord put in their mouths, and few kings were to be commended for their actions. There was something about power that watered any corrupt seeds lying dormant in a man's soul. Few rulers in our history had escaped the stain of it.

I found myself unafraid of Ahab as he sat at my absconded table on a seat that could drop him to the floor at any moment. I felt a strange pity for the man, despite the things he had done. He was right. He had sealed his destiny with his disobedience in the matter of Benhadad. Yahweh prizes obedience in His people. And then he finalized it by abdicating his duty to keep Jezebel under control.

"The prophet visited me again. In the vineyard," he said, expelling a long sigh. "If I thought it possible that I would escape judgment for my actions with the king of Syria, I know now I will not escape from the matter of the vintner and his family. I would like to place the blame on my wife, but mine is the greater sin."

I was stunned. It was hard to fathom that the king of Israel was accepting responsibility for wrongdoing. It was not the way of kings to do such. Especially in the presence of someone who had accused them openly, as I had. I wondered if Ahab was aware that Jezebel had ordered Anna's death. Perhaps not. Jezebel would have kept it secret that she'd buried a young woman in the palace gardens.

Ahab was staring at the floor by the wall. I followed his gaze.

The scroll! It must have been knocked to the floor when Ahab's men were making their preparations. If he asked for it, he would know that Anna was alive. Jezebel would know, and her fury would drive her to the ends of the earth to right the eunuch's wrong.

"Is that it? The letter you accused Jezebel of forging?"

The banished fear tried to return, but I calmed myself with the newfound peace that had begun to rule my heart.

"No. It no longer exists." I wondered if Ahab would deny it had ever existed and use the opportunity to condemn me.

"Hand the scroll to me."

My heart beat like the heavy clop of a dozen horses in my chest. I had no choice. I picked up the scroll and laid it on the table in front of the king and stood in the middle of the room, praying he would not open it.

"You can trust my word that it is not the scroll of which I spoke. That scroll has been destroyed; I am certain. It is only a missive from a friend who wished to comfort me. You did say I could have a messenger. It was delivered by one yesterday."

Ahab picked up the scroll and rubbed his thumb along the coarse parchment. Anna had, no doubt, procured it from Zim's brother. It was of poor quality. Eber would have little use for writing materials beyond the occasional missive he had sent to Zim and the infrequent need of correspondence concerning the workings of his farms. Zim and I had joked occasionally about the parsimonious nature of his oldest sibling.

"And you swear it is not the scroll you said you saw?"

"Yes, I swear it."

He held it in his hand as he spoke. "It must be nice to have friends. True friends. I don't think I've ever had one. I know you would not consider me a friend, especially after I left you in this place," he said, looking from ceiling to floor at the dank dungeon that had been my home for several days, "But you are the closest thing I've ever had to one. At least I could make believe that you cared for me as such."

I felt my cheeks redden. I had never been Ahab's friend. That he thought of me as such was disconcerting. I had tried to serve the king with loyalty and honor, but friendship was not for men who defiled Yahweh's children. Or allowed their wives to do it.

He drew a deep breath. "The message is of no consequence now. I'm certain you were correct in your assumption that Jezebel was responsible. I need no convincing. I know my wife only too well. It might have been necessary to bring a case against her, but I can't do that; it would start a war with her father." He laid the scroll on the table and moved his hands to his lap. I tried not to show the relief that swept over me.

"I do not deny my culpability in the deaths of Naboth and his family, so I do not say this to absolve my guilt. I simply want you to know the facts. When the vintner refused my offer of money or a better vineyard, and we returned to the palace, I had no intention of forcing the issue. He was right about the Law and ancestral land, and although it was a great disappointment, I had let it go. When Jezebel found me moping about the outcome, she said she would get the land for me, that I was the king and nothing should be denied me."

The old Ahab showed a peek of his face. "It's true, you know. A king should be able to take what he wishes, if he fairly compensates the loss. Sometimes our laws …" He caught himself and took a deep breath. "I turned my face from Jezebel and told her not to tell me the details."

He looked directly into my eyes. "I did not tell her to have Naboth killed. Nor his sons. Nor the wheelwright. Especially not the wheelwright. I expected her to manipulate the situation in some way, but the thought that she would actually kill a whole family"—he bit his lip—"well, I'd like to believe I would have stopped her if I'd known what she was up to."

I hated to think it, but I doubted he would have stopped her. He would have turned his head as he always did.

Ahab heaved a sigh.

"The prophet would not accept that as an excuse, and I do not offer it as one to you. I turned my back, Obadiah. I closed my eyes, and for that my sons and I will pay dearly. But the prophet saw my repentance and said it would not happen in my lifetime." He let out a huff of breath. "But my lifetime will not be a long one, I fear," he said, his eyes downcast.

Ahab's forehead furrowed, then lifted, his eyes brightening. "The wheelwright. He was the one your woman married, was he not?"

I hoped Ahab had forgotten the subject, but he had not. How was I going to handle *this?* I didn't want to sully Zim's memory by letting him seem the villain here.

"Yes. She married him because I waited too long. I was friend of the groom at their wedding. Her husband remained my dearest friend until … until he met his death with the rest of the men."

"I am sorry for that, Obadiah. There was something about the young man that caught my attention."

That was what Zim had tried so hard *not* to do—catch Ahab's attention. But Zim had an aura about him with his bright eyes and wide smile, with his kindness, that made people notice him and like him. Zim was the pollen that drew the bees.

Ahab's brows pulled together. I could see something clicking in the king's consciousness. He raised his head.

"The girl. You can marry her now. So it worked out for your good after all!" he said, a big smile on his face.

Every nerve in my body fired. I wanted to slam my fist into Ahab's jaw as I had Zim's, but ... Ahab's words might actually work for my good. *Yahweh, give me wisdom.*

"I'm afraid that is not possible, my king," I said, letting the genuine emotion of losing Anna show in my face.

"And why is that, Obadiah? Her husband is dead. She will need another, and if you still love her as I felt you did before, it seems a perfect situation for you both."

How was I going to say this in a way that protected the eunuch that set Anna free? I had no desire to bring trouble on his head if Ahab was looking for someone to punish.

"Because Jezebel ordered her death. She is gone." Both statements were true. Jezebel did order her death, and she *was* gone. Just not gone to her grave. I was trying not to break out in a grin. This was perfect. Perhaps Ahab would do something about his wicked wife now.

Ahab jerked to his feet. "Jezebel killed the girl too? How do you know this?" It seemed the queen had not seen the need to provide the details surrounding my threat to her person.

"Because I heard her give the order. My reaction is what landed me in this place."

Ahab tipped over the table and threw the chair across the small room. "How dare she!"

Boots beat a quick path to the cell and gaped through the open door. "It's nothing. Go back to where I sent you!" the king said with a wave of his arm.

The men looked at the broken furniture and at me—no doubt thinking I had provoked the king some way. They turned and retreated, probably expecting an edict from Ahab to hang me in my cell.

I would have loved to have been a fly on the palace wall when Ahab confronted Jezebel. And what could she say? For all Jezebel knew, the girl was dead indeed. She couldn't produce Anna to prove her innocence. She wouldn't try, anyway. She saw little wrong with dispatching whomever she pleased. The queen would have no reason to look for Anna. Now or in the future. *Thank you, Yahweh.* As hard as it was to receive Anna's farewell missive, it gave me the freedom to formulate this plan.

"I'm going to let you out of here, Obadiah. Tomorrow I will tell Jezebel to leave for Samaria and to take Ahaziah and Joram with her. That's what I came here to tell you. She will not return to Jezreel while I am alive. But when I am gathered to my fathers"—he swallowed hard—"which may be sooner than I hope, you should leave the palace immediately. Leave Jezreel. Find Jehu or one of the generals and ask for their protection. Ahaziah is as bad as his mother. He will kill anyone he considers disloyal. You are a formidable man. You would be one of the first."

I wasn't certain what I should do. Thank him? Even now, that would be difficult. I trusted Ahab only slightly more than I did Jezebel.

"And you, my king. Will you be going to Samaria with them?" I hoped he would go to Samaria and never come back, but I knew that would not be the case.

"For now. I will return when I feel Jezebel and the princes are truly settled. Jezebel will hate it," he said, a smile peeking out of his well-groomed beard. "She has many enemies among the other wives in Samaria. And I'm certain they will do their best to make her life miserable. As well as the lives of her sons."

Ahab's gaze locked on my face. "And, Obadiah, if you are still hiding prophets in caves, feel free to steal bread from my ovens. As you have been doing for the last few years."

"My king …" I searched for something to say that would not be a complete untruth.

"Do you really think I did not know? Not the extent of your escapades, I am certain, but that you were absconding bread from Jezebel's banquets as well as grain from the storehouses was not something you could easily hide. I must say, feeding Israel's prophets with bread prepared for the prophets of Baal has a ring of irony about it."

I stumbled for words, but in the end just stood, staring at the king.

"The prophets have tormented me with their ill will, but I fear Yahweh too much to wish them dead."

I wanted to laugh. *But you don't fear Yahweh too much to worship Baal in the temple you built for your wife. And you certainly sought Elijah's death.*

Ahab called the guards, and I walked up the stairs and out of the dank prison to the smell of fresh air and a tenuous freedom.

∽∾∽∾∽∾∽∾∽∾∽∾

The next morning Ahab called all the servants and lords to the throne room.

Jezebel looked like she had swallowed a ball of fire and it was burning its way from the inside out as she sat on the throne to Ahab's right, her eyes spitting sparks as she saw me standing in the king's presence instead of rotting in the dungeon beneath her feet.

The two princes stood against the wall opposite me, glaring their anger and humiliation. Ahaziah's jaw hard on his handsome face. The heir had never liked me. Why would he? His mother hated me, and the king favored me, treated me like a son. The boy had taken every opportunity to put me where he thought I belonged, but to no avail.

Ahab raised his hand, and the room settled into a tense silence. Not looking at his wife or sons, he spoke in a voice of authority.

"I have gathered you here for an announcement. Queen Jezebel and I, with our sons Ahaziah and Joram, will be departing for Samaria by noonday."

Jezebel jerked her head toward the king. Apparently he had not forewarned her of his plans to relocate her and her sons to the Samarian palace.

"The princes and their mother will not return to the Jezreel palace for some time. I will travel to and from the two seats but will govern primarily from the city my father built."

Jezebel's mouth fell open, then snapped shut with a force that had to jar her teeth. The boys stared in shock.

"I hereby place the palace governor, Obadiah ben Enos, in charge of the Jezreel palace in my absence. He will keep me informed by messenger of all the daily workings of the palace and will inform me of any who dare to defy his authority. For that, I will make a special trip to Jezreel—a trip such persons would not welcome." Ahab paused to look over the audience. Most had smiles on their faces, but many tried

239

without success to hide their aggravation. The imbecile who had stolen my horse looked worried. I would deal with him soon enough. In fact, I had a job for him. I would make him the stable overseer's assistant. He could muck out the stalls all day since he loved horses so much.

The shock of Ahab's proclamation still juddered through my being. Ahab hadn't told me of his plans. Hadn't given me a chance to protest. I wasn't certain if this was good fortune or bad.

I knew that I had enemies: friends of Ahaziah and Joram. Those few with loyalty to the queen, most of it purchased, of course. Even with the queen and the princes gone, I would have to watch my back.

∞∞∞∞∞∞∞∞

A few hours later I watched from the portico as the royal family took their seats in the carriages that would convey them to Samaria. Jezebel turned her head toward me, too far away for me to see the glint that I knew was in her black eyes, but the set of her jaw told me she wasn't through with me yet. Strangely, I wasn't worried. I had stopped fearing Jezebel when I thought Anna was dead. And since her missive assured me that she was safe with Zim's family, peace had replaced fear in my heart—for the most part. My mind sometimes ran wild with thoughts of retribution from the queen or her sons, or someone acting on their behalf, but I called the thoughts in, refusing to borrow trouble when none threatened. If such trouble presented itself in the future, I would deal with it then.

I had struggled for the courage to protect Anna and the others that I loved. But I now realized that courage is not something we accomplish on our own. It, like all good things, comes from Yahweh. Yahweh wanted me to trust Him. Even when it seemed the enemy had won, I would trust God to do His best for me. For all the people I loved.

Help me not to forget, Lord.

CHAPTER TWENTY-EIGHT

Obadiah

Three years later

I walked down the wide hall, the floor beneath my feet a giant puzzle of mosaics crafted from the finest marble and precious stones. The opulence of the Samarian palace always made me thankful I was governor at Jezreel instead of this monument to excess. The intricate designs depicted maritime motifs, many paying homage to King Omri's exaggerated voyages across the seven seas. Kings of all the ages had used palace art to embellish their exploits. From the entry hall to the balustrades of the grand staircase leading to the upper chambers where Ahab held court, the palace was adorned with intricately carved ivory panels. I sometimes wondered how many animals had lost their tusks to decorate Ahab's ivory house.

Three years had passed. I had thought all was lost when I entered that dark dungeon. But Yahweh had been with me there, and although my heart still yearned for Anna, I had been able to let her go, knowing that she and her child were safe. I had never tried to contact her or even check on her well-being. One slip of the tongue from a messenger or a servant could land in Jezebel's ear, and she would not hesitate to do what the eunuch had not done. And it would be the eunuch's life as well as Anna's. But I often lay awake at night wondering if she had a boy-child, or a girl with green eyes and chestnut hair. Did she have other children now? Was she happy with Eber? Had she come to love him as she hoped she would? As I hoped she would?

Ahab had called me to the Samarian palace to see that all was properly prepared for a visit from Jehoshaphat, the king of Judah.

The king had sent for me a few times during the years when he entertained royal guests. He didn't seem to have great confidence in the governor in charge of his ivory palace. It was obvious to me the man was capable and faithful to his duties. But trust was hard-earned with Ahab. It was strange because I had violated the king's trust many times, many of which he was aware, but for some reason he overlooked my indiscretions and trusted me in spite of them.

But I would not be fooled. The king was still the king, and he was a volatile man that could erupt into deadly anger at any moment.

After settling into my rooms, I took the walk to the governor's office. He was leaning over a list.

"Obadiah." The man stood and bowed at the waist.

"Levi. Bowing is not necessary. I've told you that before. We are equals. In fact, your position is the greater since you serve in the principal palace and I in the secondary."

The man smiled, his eyes crinkling at the corners. "Ah, but it is you who the king calls for on such occasions as this. And that is fine with me. If something goes wrong, it will be your neck that is stretched, not mine," he said with a chuckle.

The man had a point.

I looked at the list lying on the governor's desk. "May I?" I said, stretching out a hand.

"Yes, certainly. Sit."

I perused the menu and seating charts, nodding. "All looks well. You don't need me."

"Ah, but I do." He pointed at the seating chart for the banquet that would be held to honor Jehoshaphat. "The queen of Judah will not be attending with her husband, but the royal prince will accompany his father. Of course, Jezebel will sit in the place of honor beside her husband, but I have chosen to seat the three princes together."

I raised an eyebrow.

"Exactly." The man nodded. Ahaziah and Joram will not like that. They will be expecting a place above the prince of Judah, but I will not dishonor the king of Judah by giving his son a lower seat."

"You have chosen well, my friend. Don't worry about it. Put the blame on me. The princes and their mother will do that anyway."

"Believe me. If it becomes a problem, I will be more than happy to lay it at your feet," he said, laughing. "And that the youngest prince of Israel shares the same name with Jehoshaphat's youngest son is a disaster waiting to happen. Prince Joram is likely to insist that Judah's prince change his name."

I snickered. "I wouldn't be surprised."

I spent some time with Levi, making a few suggestions and asking questions about the royal entourage.

"Do you know the purpose of Jehoshaphat's visit?" The king had sent an envoy to accompany me to Samaria to help with preparations but gave no further information to his soldiers. Of course he wouldn't. It wasn't uncommon for the kings to exchange visits, especially since they ruled two parts of one divided country, Ahab the northern half and Judah the southern, but for some reason I had some trepidation about this one.

Levi looked around to see if anyone stood near and lowered his voice. "I have no official word, but we were informed that Jehoshaphat's army would be billeting in the hills nearby."

The hair rose on my arms. So this visit was the precursor to a war. A war that could only be with the king of Syria. I knew Ahab was nettled that Benhadad had not kept his word. The city of Ramoth-Gilead had not been returned to Israel as Benhadad had promised when he was trying to save his neck three years prior. Would this war be where Ahab would meet his end? It was for not dispatching the king of Syria that the prophet pronounced Ahab would lose his life. The king's repentance had won him a reprieve. God said Ahab's sons would not be killed in his lifetime. But his life could come to a quick end in another war with Benhadad.

<hr/>

The banquet had gone as I thought it would. Ahaziah's lips were as tight as a strung bow. He clearly didn't appreciate the seating arrangement, thinking himself worthy of more honor since he was heir apparent of his father's throne. Ahaziah had always been haughty like his mother. He had none of his father's complacency. He would not be the type to acquiesce to his wife's demands when he took one.

The next morning, escorted by four palace guards, I made my way through the city gate to the large open area where the two kings would consult with four hundred prophets of Israel. Since I'd made enemies of the queen and her sons, Ahab probably thought to avoid an inconvenient accident along the route by providing me protection.

The air was cool on my face. I looked at the sky. It had transformed from a serene blue to a brooding gray since I left my rooms. Clusters of clouds, their bellies touched with silver and gray, meandered across the sky. I never complained about rain. Three years without it had cured me of that.

Two golden thrones sat on a grand carpet that had been removed from one of the wide hallways in the palace and spread across the dry ground. Made of finely woven wool, its surface was a mix of rich purples, deep blues, and lush greens forming a repeating pattern of interlocking geometric shapes, threads of gold and silver woven throughout. All I could think about was how difficult it was going to be to clean if it rained. I pitied the people tasked with the job. A canopy of deep purple supported by tall wooden poles swelled and settled in the breeze.

I found Levi and took my place beside him, standing behind and to the side of the king. Jezebel had apparently not been invited to attend or chose not to stand before such a number of Israel's prophets. Probably both. I didn't think she'd dare to show her face here.

The prophets of Israel stood in the field before the thrones, dressed in fine robes, a glint of gold about their necks. Elijah had never seen the need of such finery. But these men were not of the same stature as Elijah.

Jezebel was no longer able to convince her husband to listen to the false prophets of Baal, but I had not found these prophets of Israel to be faithful to Yahweh's words either. These were the kind of prophets Jonathan had talked about that sought safety in the finer schools and meeting places, never stirring the pot of the king's displeasure. Ahab had heaped together men that would prophesy what he wanted to hear.

Zedekiah, the son of Chenaanah, who led the compromising seers, was wearing a headpiece sporting two iron horns. He stood before Ahab, superiority in the set of his sharp jaw, and thrust the horns toward the sky. "Thus says the Lord," he shouted in a voice that could be heard all the way to Syria. "With these horns will you push the Syrians, until you have consumed them."

The man looked ridiculous. I was embarrassed for him. Ahab looked happy, but Jehoshaphat's brow cut deep at the center of his forehead as the prophets all shouted the refrain. "Yahweh will give the king victory! Like a bull he will trample the enemies of Israel until they are destroyed! Go up to Ramoth-Gilead and prosper; for the Lord shall deliver it into the king's hand."

Jehoshaphat hardly moved a muscle. It was obvious that he was appalled that Ahab took counsel from such men. "Is there not here a prophet of the Lord besides these, that we might enquire of him?" the king asked.

Ahab's face fell into a pout. "There is one man, Micaiah, the son of Imlah, but I hate him." He slapped his hand on the arm of his throne, causing the king of Judah to flinch.

"The man never prophesies good concerning me. It's always evil."

Jehoshaphat shook his head. "Do not say such a thing."

Ahab threw up his hands. "Alright, alright!" He looked around the room and motioned an officer of the court to come forward. "Do you think you can find the prophet?" The man would have no trouble. Micaiah was not in hiding. He lived in a small village on the outskirts of the city. None of the prophets were in hiding now that the queen was confined to the Samarian palace. Since Jezebel had lost her hold on her husband, the prophets had returned to their homes or their itinerate ministries. I still would not trust her, but there's a time when we have to leave fear behind and do what Yahweh has called us to do.

The wind was picking up as I saw the messenger and Micaiah walking towards the group, the messenger throwing a stern sideways glance at the prophet. I imagined that the man had entreated Micaiah to follow the lead of the other prophets who spoke only good to the king, but the look on Micaiah's face said what I knew would be true: Micaiah would not be deterred from speaking what he heard from Yahweh. Four guards escorted the prophet to where the two kings sat.

"Well?" Ahab said, a growl in his voice. "Shall we go against Ramoth-Gilead, or shall we forebear?"

Micaiah simply shrugged a wide shoulder. "Go and prosper, for the Lord shall deliver the city into the hand of the king."

Jehoshaphat's forehead furrowed. I could tell he was questioning Micaiah's verity as a prophet of Israel. Ahab let out a breath and sliced a hand through the air. "How many times have I adjured you that you should tell me nothing but that which is true in the name of the Lord?"

Micaiah's dark brows rose. "The truth? You wish to hear the truth?"

Ahab was getting angrier. "Yes! I wish to hear the truth! What good is a prophet that doesn't tell the truth!"

Micaiah turned to the four hundred prophets spread over the ground before the gate. "Indeed. What good is such a prophet?"

I could see the streaks of red climbing up the king's neck. Micaiah feared nothing from the king. I wondered if I would be so brave if I were in the prophet's position.

"So if you wish to hear the truth," Micaiah said, his dark eyes sparking, "this is the truth. As I entreated the Lord on my way to the palace, I saw a vision of Israelite soldiers walking around in the hills like sheep with no shepherd to guide them. The Lord said to me, 'This army has no leader. They should go home and give up the fight.'"

Ahab turned to Jehoshaphat. "Didn't I tell you that he would prophecy no good thing concerning me? Evil! That's all he ever speaks!"

The prophet pointed a long finger at Ahab, his eyes glinting with anger. "I'm not through, Ahab. I saw the Lord seated on his throne with all the host of heaven gathered around Him, and the Lord said, 'Who will trick Ahab, that he may be persuaded to go up and die at Ramoth-Gilead?' And one said on this manner, and another said on that manner. But then there came forth a spirit who stood before the Lord and said, 'I will persuade him.'"

The hairs on my arms were standing at attention. The king's fingers gripped the arms of his golden throne. "The Lord asked the spirit how he would do that. 'I will go forth, and I will be a lying spirit in the mouth of all his prophets.'"

There was a pregnant pause as the prophet's gaze bore into Ahab's.

Micaiah stretched his arm at the prophets who were red-faced angry. "The Lord has put a lying spirit in the mouth of all these, your prophets, and the Lord has spoken evil concerning you."

I could see the king was shaken by the prophet's words, but the words weren't driving him to repentance as the words of Elijah had. Ahab was furious.

There was a sudden movement. Zedekiah, wearing the absurd horns, took long strides toward Micaiah. He raised his hand and smote the prophet hard on the cheek. Micaiah stumbled then straightened himself with dignity.

Zedekiah was far from dignified. He was shaking like the leaves of a tree with a wild boar butting at its trunk as he shouted in Micaiah's face, spittle flying.

"Who do you think you are that Yahweh would speak to you and not to me? I am the leading prophet in the king's court! And you!"— loathing contorted the man's face as he sneered at Micaiah—"are a renegade like Elijah was before you!"

Micaiah raised a bushy brow. "You'll find out who I am when you have to hide in the backroom of some house."

The man stepped back, his face blotched with fury.

Gesturing to his guards, Ahab pointed a shaking finger at Micaiah. "Carry him back to the city and tell the jailer to put him in the dungeon, and give him nothing but bread and water until I come back in peace!"

Quiet settled in the air for several long moments. All eyes were on Micaiah when he spoke.

"If you return at all, then the Lord has not spoken by me."

I sucked a breath. The prophet's words felt like thunder, and I was afraid Ahab would feel the lightning strike. At that moment I felt drops of rain touching my face, and then the clouds let loose their load. Rain pelted the field and the thrones—and the wool rug beneath them. The prophets pulled their shawls over their heads and ran, while servants tried to secure the canopy covering the two kings.

I expected Jehoshaphat to stand and say that he was going back to Judah with his army—but he didn't. He had committed his armies to recover Ramoth-Gilead, and he would not go back on his word. But I could see the worry on the man's face. He was going into a war that the prophet of God said would be lost. Jehoshaphat was a good king. I prayed he would return from the battle in safety because I felt in my heart I would never see Ahab alive again.

CHAPTER TWENTY-NINE

Ahab

Inside the opulent battle tent, King Ahab and King Jehoshaphat sat at a wooden table strewn with maps and scrolls, the flickering light from an oil lamp casting dancing shadows on the canvas walls. The king of Judah was leaning over the maps, his brow furrowed in concentration, tracing potential strategies with a ringed finger. The battle would begin at dawn.

Ahab watched the Judean king. He knew the man was concerned by the prophet's words. *Ahab* was concerned by the prophet's words, but he thought perhaps, even now, there might be a way to escape Benhadad's sword. He lamented that he didn't kill the conquered king when he'd had the opportunity. It would have been so simple then. And Ahab might have lived to be an old man.

"King Jehoshaphat, I would ask you a favor."

The king of Judah looked up at Ahab, anger seething in his eyes.

"And what favor do you seek, King Ahab? I have agreed to join with you in this war. Is that not enough?"

Ahab was shamed by the king's words, but he would ask anyway. He had to. He swallowed, trying to force some spittle into his dry mouth.

"When we get to the battlefield, will you wear your royal attire?"

The king crinkled his forehead in confusion and let out a puff of breath. "Of course I will wear my royal attire. What kind of king would enter into battle without making himself recognizable before his enemy? How would my men know to follow me if I was dressed like a common soldier?"

Ahab fidgeted in his seat, taking a long breath before he spoke to the Judean king. "I have decided not to wear my own kingly garb. I would ask you to wear yours and understand why I choose not to do so."

The king of Judah shook his head. "Why would you choose to dishonor yourself in such a way?"

"It is not a matter of honor, Jehoshaphat."

Or was it? It was something the prophet had said. He said that every man would leave the battlefield and go home because they had no one to lead them. That sounded like the prophet expected Ahab to lose his life, and that the people would not lose theirs but return to their homes in peace. That could only mean one thing. Benhadad would not make war with the soldiers. He would be looking for Ahab only. And if the king of Judah wore his royal attire and Ahab did not, perhaps Benhadad would think that only Jehoshaphat led the armies. Maybe he could yet escape the future that had been foretold by Elijah. And now by Micaiah. Maybe he could still live.

"It is me the king of Syria is bent on destroying. If I am not so visible, perhaps he will not recognize me."

"And you have no thought that Benhadad might mistake me for you and kill me in your stead? That would be convenient for you, wouldn't it?"

"No. No. Of course not. How could he mistake you for me?" Jehoshaphat was a big brawny man. Ahab was much leaner. But that was a possibility. Ahab didn't wish for the king of Judah to die in his place. He just didn't wish to die, and perhaps the confusion might keep him safe from his enemy.

"I will wear my royal battle attire, Ahab. You may do whatever you wish," the king snapped as he returned to studying the map before him.

King Ahab surveyed the battlefield from his chariot. The scene stretched out before him was a blend of tense anticipation and eerie stillness, reflective of the state of his own mind. What would this day bring? His lungs were as still as the air around him.

The king watched the early morning light cast long gold-gray fingers across the rolling plains. He tried to remember the last time he had paid attention to a sunrise. Would this be his last? No! He would find a way out of this mire pit. He would not die today!

The cool air carried the faint scent of dew-soaked earth mixed with the distant tang of sweat and leather from the assembled forces. Rows of soldiers stood in formation, their armor glinting dully in the growing light. Spears and swords were at the ready, a forest of deadly points aimed at the sky. It was time.

As the battle progressed it was obvious that Ahab had been correct in his assessment of the prophet's words. The opposing army didn't seem interested in killing the army of Israel *or* the army of Judah. He saw few Israelites fall. He was thankful for that. Then there was a flurry of soldiers charging toward the place on a knoll where Jehoshaphat overlooked the battle, his bronze flat-topped crown upon his head, a short red cloak over his shoulders, and bronze breastplate and greaves covering his chest and legs.

Ahab's breath caught in his lungs. They were almost upon King Jehoshaphat, when the man shouted that he was not the king of Israel. When they heard his cry, they left him alone and continued their search.

Ahab wiped the sweat flowing into his eyes. What was he thinking? He had endangered the king of Judah. At that moment Ahab knew he would not escape his fate. A strange calm attended him, and he let out a long, stuttering sigh. Fate cannot be avoided. Even when one knows it's coming, one cannot evade it. It teases with thoughts that there might be another outcome if one can just outsmart it. But no one could outsmart the God of Israel.

Ahab's shoulders began to relax. He would meet his fate as a king, not a coward.

Syrian Archer

The Syrian archer stood atop a windswept hill, his gaze fixed on the strange clash of the armies below. He was unhappy to have been left near the rear of the battalion and had climbed the hillock to get at least a glimpse of the battle. Benhadad wanted only swordsmen at the front. He was not a swordsman. He was an archer. The king didn't want a stray arrow to fell a soldier—Israel's or his own. "Fight with neither small nor great, but only Ahab," the king had said to the thirty-two captains of his chariots. Only to defend themselves were they to raise their swords at other than the king of Israel. All those chariots in the pursuit of only one man.

When the Syrian army was defeated in the most recent war with Israel despite having a daunting advantage in chariots and men, Benhadad had been brought to Ahab's chariot in ropes. He had covenanted with Ahab that the shadow of his foot would not fall on Israel's soil if the king would spare his life and grant him safe passage back to the Syrian border.

But here he was. This war was personal. Benhadad had been humiliated and would have his vengeance only on the king.

Swords flashed but seldom drew blood. The Israelites seemed confused that the Syrians were not trying to kill them, only to push them out of the way. Many of them stood on the battlefield, their swords hanging limp in their hands.

The archer grew tired of watching the pitiful battle. He would not meet a soldier face-to-face on this battlefield, but he would not go to his home without sending an arrow into the sky. He pulled his bow off his back. His father had formed this bow with his own patient hands. Crafted from the heartwood of a yew tree, the bow bore the weight of a father's love.

Horn strips, painstakingly affixed by his skillful touch, lent the bow its distinctive curve, while sinew harvested from his own beasts bound the layers together, infusing the weapon with strength and resilience.

Slowly the archer reached over his shoulder for an arrow. Touching one then moving to another, he drew the third from his quiver. The arrow's shaft was straight and smooth, carefully carved and polished to reduce the pull of the air and ensure a true aim.

He balanced the arrow atop the bowstring, ensuring it rested snugly against the nock, then slid it into place, the familiar click of wood against string resonating through the thick silence that had settled around him, separating him from the sounds of war.

As he drew the string taut, tension playing out in his muscles, the sinewy resistance of the bowstring yielding to his strength; with each length of pull, he could feel the bow bending against the weight of his resolve, the steady thrum of the string vibrating through his fingers like a heartbeat.

And then, in a moment of sublime release, he let the arrow fly.

He did not avert his eyes as the glint of the sun lit the arrow like a thin bolt of fire.

Go, arrow. Find your target. A smile dawned on his face.

<hr>

Ahab

Ahab saw it coming. The arrow that would take his life. His eyes locked on the iron-tipped shaft as it arced above the lines of swordsmen. He knew it was this arrow that would slip between the joints of his armor and slice into his chest. Not the heart. It would not pierce his heart. For to do so would be a sudden death, and Ahab would not die for several hours. His men would prop him up in his chariot so he could watch the battle, and he would bleed into the bottom, dark-red puddles that the dogs would lick, as the prophet had spoken.

It was strange, the things Ahab remembered as he waited. And the things he didn't. He remembered the wheelwright's eyes, abashed for him and disappointed. For some reason the man's opinion of the king mattered, and Ahab had felt the young man's disappointment keenly. To know that the wheelwright had been caught in Jezebel's web was the greatest sorrow. The king grieved for the life that had ended in such a needless way.

What Ahab didn't remember was the names of all his sons. Nor could he recall all their faces. He tried to remember them by their mothers, but could only go through a few before the faces blurred into a maze of forgotten features. But Ahab grieved their deaths. His lineage would stop with their hearts. There would be no more house of Ahab. Perhaps that was a good thing. What good was it that the house of Omri had survived?

As the king of Israel stood in his chariot, awaiting the implement of his death, he thought of Benhadad in this same chariot, begging for his life. *His life for yours*, the prophet had said. If Ahab had obeyed the law, Benhadad would be dried bones by now instead of leading an army whose only goal was to take Ahab's life. The king had disobeyed. He did not honor the God of the kingdom of which he was the king. And he would pay the price for his disobedience.

Deep sorrow settled in his spirit. How was it that a man met his God? Face-to-face? Or was there any meeting at all for a man who had spurned his Creator? A moment of panic sped up his heart. That would be the worst punishment of all.

The arrow spun toward him. Its sharp black tip was close. He almost felt he could reach out and snatch it from the air, but his arms would not. And he would not try. This was his fate. He watched the arrow as it slid into his body.

"The king has been hit!" Ahab heard the soldier shouting from somewhere above him. "We must get him back to the palace!"

"No!" he said, gasping. "Turn the chariot around and take me out of the fray, but I will not leave while my men still fight."

The soldiers tried to staunch the flow of blood with strips of their own garments, but the wound wept as Ahab watched the battle from his chariot. As dusk descended upon the battlefield, the vibrant hues of daylight gradually faded, giving way to softer shades of lavender, amber, and indigo. Wisps of clouds, tinged with the last remnants of sunlight, stretched across the horizon.

The air grew still as daylight relinquished its hold on the world. Shadows lengthened, stretching across the ground like cold fingers reaching out in the fading light.

The boundary between day and night grew indistinct. Ahab pulled a deep, last breath.

<hr />

Obadiah

Ahab's bier had been met at the gates by the queen and the princes. None of the fanfare due a king of Israel had been spared as it made its way through the narrow streets. The city seemed to mourn in earnest for its fallen monarch. Somehow I could not help but grieve for the king I had served. I had seen his sorrow for his sins. His repentance, though shallow and short-lived, was genuine. He had lived for some time on the battlefield. I wondered what went through his mind in those hours he awaited his death—and I wondered what would happen in the first days of his son's reign. Would Jezebel's first order of business as Queen Mother be to settle old scores? I would soon find out. Two palace guards were striding down the ivory hall, their eyes set on me.

The guards delivered me to the new king, who was sitting on his father's gilded throne in a most relaxed manner. He hadn't wasted any time.

I bent to the ground before Ahaziah as I had before his father, waiting for his call to rise. He was not slow in giving it.

"You may go," the king said, waving a hand at the guards. "I think I'm safe in the governor's presence," he said with a sardonic smile. "Aren't I, Obadiah? Should I fear you have a sword beneath your robe?"

"No, my king. No sword."

Ahaziah stared at me for several moments before he spoke again. Like he was sizing me up for a shroud.

"What do you think will happen, now that I am king in my father's stead, Obadiah? You were a favorite of the king. My mother always lamented that my father treated you better than he did his own sons."

So here it would begin. Ahaziah would seek vengeance for his mother and for the favor Ahab had shown to me. I did not care. I had no one to worry about. Not Anna. Not Naboth. Not Zim. My heart wrenched a little. I was happy for Anna, although I missed her every day. I would never stop mourning Zim. And Naboth's death was a stone that always sat heavy in my chest.

"I believe the king will do whatever he has a mind to do," I said with a slight bow of my head.

Ahaziah burst out laughing and slapped the arm of his throne. "That is right, Governor. I will do whatever *I* have a mind to do."

And that would likely be to dispose of me as soon as possible.

"My father was a weak man, Obadiah. I'm sure you would admit that if you dared. Well, Governor, I am not like my father. I am more like my mother. I don't like anyone to tell me what to do. Even her. Especially her. Before my father was even buried, she was giving me a list of people to dispatch. And you, Obadiah? You were on the top." He leaned back on the throne, his eyes dancing with sardonic mirth.

"I am not surprised, my king."

"No. I'm sure you are not, Governor. The two of you have danced around this for years. To hear her tell it, you and you alone are responsible for her exile to Samaria. She hates it here, you know," he said, laughing again.

I didn't answer, but Ahaziah's father had said the same. He was delighted at the thought of Jezebel being caught in the other wives' web.

"So," the king said, as he leaned forward in his royal chair, "what am I to do with you, Obadiah. The gallows perhaps? Or should I let you rot in the dungeon beneath our feet?"

I winced. I hadn't feared death, but I did hope the Samarian dungeon had fewer rats than the prison that had been my home in Jezreel.

"Ahh, a reaction at last. It should be the dungeon, then?"

I wasn't going to let the king's toying get the best of me. If it was prison, it was prison. The rats might even become my friends if I was down there long enough.

"As I said, King Ahaziah, you will do whatever you have a mind to do."

"You're a strange man, Obadiah. I'm beginning to see what my father saw in you. Well, I had already made up my mind before I had you brought to me. It will be neither death nor dungeon, Obadiah," he said, "Unless you give me a reason to think differently, you will return to Jezreel as governor of the palace. It will make my mother unhappy, which will give me some entertainment. She will stay in Samaria, so you shouldn't see her face again unless I summon you to the capital for some reason. You are an able steward. You are worth more to me alive than dead. Who would I get to replace you?"

I knew my face must have looked ridiculous with my jaw hanging open like a gaping hole in an old blanket.

"Go now. Return to Jezreel. The place will go to pot without you."

I closed my mouth, bowed, and left the throne room, thankful for Yahweh's mercy.

Two years passed, and Ahaziah proved to be yet a worse king than his father. One day, the balustrade that surrounded the roof of his upper chamber gave way, and he fell to the floor beneath. He did not die from the fall, but fever took him and he became very ill. So ill that he sent messengers to inquire of Beelzebub, the god of Ekron, whether he should recover from his malady.

But the angel of the Lord spoke to Elijah and said to arise and meet the messengers on their way.

"Is there not a God in Israel, that you go to enquire of Beelzebub the god of Ekron?" he said in a message to the king. He prophesied to Ahaziah that because he had not chosen to inquire of Yahweh, he would not get up from his bed. And he did not. Ahaziah died soon after, and Prince Joram became king.

I carefully considered leaving, as Ahab had suggested. Maybe I should. If Jezebel wanted me dead, she would get her desire, for Joram was his mother's pet and would, no doubt, follow any command she gave. But, again, I chose to stay, and to my surprise, Jezebel chose to stay in Samaria, returning to Jezreel only on occasion. After Ahaziah's death, she was on top of the pile again where wives were concerned. Joram married the most important treaty wives. Others returned to their homelands. The rest remained as far away from Jezebel as possible. As Queen Mother, she could sway her son whatever way she wished.

I could see the hatred that still tainted her painted face when we met in the hall, which was not often. The queen was seldom in the palace, but when she was, I made a point to stay out of her sight if at all possible. Not as much out of fear but because every time I saw her, I would see the faces of my friends. Naboth, a man true to his God until the end. Joel and Jason, Mikah, and Zim, arms over shoulders praying as cruel stones unjustly struck them down. And Anna. Always Anna. I had found a measure of forgiveness in my heart for Ahab. And I lived in peace with losing Anna. She was safe. But I still hated Jezebel. The sight of her left me sickened at my core.

In the beginning I waited for her to remove my head from my shoulders, or at least remove me from my position. To send me to the rat-infested prison or banish me from all of Israel. But the years slipped by and she didn't do so. I remembered her tales about feeding her childhood friend to the crocodiles, and the maidservant and butler that she had killed after throwing them a grand wedding feast. I sometimes wondered if she kept me around because she liked to toy with me, like the cat she had carried about so long had loved to toy with the palace mice.

But, at the bottom of it, I believed she knew her youngest could not run the palace without me. And since she was so seldom in Jezreel, it was somewhat out of sight, out of mind.

But all of that changed when Joram was injured in yet another war with Syria and came back to Jezreel to recover. Of course, his mother came with him. Jezebel moved about the palace in a flurry of fluttering robes, seeing that the cooks prepared the proper foods to strengthen her son. That the physicians did all that was possible to speed his recovery. I had felt sorry for the sober-eyed men. It would not be well for them if the young king took a turn for the worse—or if he died. Fortunately, the king was soon up and moving about. But not for long.

CHAPTER THIRTY

Obadiah

From my balcony, I had watched Joram fall, Jehu's arrow protruding from his back like a fork buried in a piece of meat.

Elijah had sent a prophet to anoint Jehu, a captain of Joram's army, as the new king of Israel. Moving quickly, before word that Joram had been deposed could reach the palace, Jehu and those who had pledged their loyalty to him gathered a short distance from the palace gate.

The watchman ensconced in his tower sent a message to the king, concerning a large company of soldiers, led by a man resembling Jehu seated in a chariot. The king had sent a messenger on horseback to ask Jehu if he had come in peace. The messenger did not return, neither did the second messenger, so Joram had mounted his own chariot and asked the question himself. I was told by one of the men who had ridden with Jehu that the new king had responded that there could be no peace as long as Jezebel's whorings and sorceries were unchecked. Joram had reined his chariot about, but he could not outrun his fate. Jehu drew an arrow and put it between the king's shoulders.

Jezebel's sons were dead, and it would soon follow that every male of Ahab's household would be destroyed. The meting out of justice had begun in the house of Ahab.

I knew there was something I had to do.

∞∞∞∞∞∞∞

There were no guards at the gilded door of Jezebel's quarters. All had fled at the sight of the army amassed outside the palace gates. Only a young eunuch stood at the entrance, his eyes darting back and forth, pupils dancing like trapped birds.

"Why are you still here?" I asked him.

"I was told to guard the door," he said, his voice quavering.

"Leave," I told him. I couldn't believe he hadn't fled like most of the servants, rats on a rope, abandoning ship as fast as their legs would take them. "If you don't, you'll die when they storm the gates."

"But ... I was told to stay."

"By whom?" I asked.

"By the queen's head bodyguard. He said if I left, I ... I would be executed as a traitor."

I shook my head. "Where do you think *he* is? Get out now. Do not be found near the queen's quarters."

Relief rolled over the man's face. "Thank you. I will go. Thank you." The man scurried away like a mouse released from a trap.

I opened the doors to the wide corridor and walked the marble pathway to Jezebel's private suite. I didn't knock. I had no worry that she might be unclothed. Jezebel would be in her finest, even as she faced a certain death.

There were two eunuchs in the room that opened to the balcony. The big Philistine stood tall and stoic as he always did. Not even a twitch of an eyelid as I stared at him. I would find a way to thank the man when this was over, for what he had done for Anna. He had killed many at Jezebel's command, but there was something good about the man. I wondered what his story was. Where he had come from. What he had been before he was robbed of his tongue and his dignity.

The room was thick with the scent of perfumed oil burning in a shallow dish atop a tall golden stand. Jezebel was sitting at her ivory-inlaid dressing table applying powdered lapis to the creased lids of her eyes. A polished bronze mirror reflected a woman aged beyond the help of cosmetics. She looked up, the smallest flash of surprise on her face. Jezebel had always been a master at schooling her emotions.

"So, it's you he's sent," she said. "That would-be *king*." Her lip snarled around the word.

She didn't turn toward me. She spoke to my reflection and I to hers. That is probably what we had always done, spoken to a semblance of each other, never letting our true faces show. But, today, I would hide nothing from the woman.

"No one sent me." The air between us hung heavy and uncomfortable, like a wool blanket on a summer day. "I have come on my own."

Her freshly painted brows rose. "Wanted a better view of the spectacle. I see."

I reflected for a moment. Something in me did want to see Jezebel get what was coming to her. She had destroyed so many lives. It was difficult to understand how the woman could do such evil. But that is not why I had come.

"I've come for another reason, Jezebel, and to say my piece."

Her mouth tightened, forcing a pucker of deep creases to appear above her lip. "*Queen* Jezebel. Don't forget it," she said, opening one of the alabaster jars of color. Her hands stilled, and the creases deepened. "Queen Mother until Jehu put an arrow through my son's back."

Was that the shimmer of a tear or the lapis that brightened her black stare?

I felt the muscles in my jaw stiffen in resistance to pity for the woman. "Ahh, but no. You are neither queen nor Queen Mother now, Jezebel. Not even a princess, since your father died. You are a widow and an orphan. A mother who's lost her children. Like the widows and orphans and childless mothers of the prophets you destroyed."

The line of her shoulders hardened under her scarlet gown. I remembered the embroidered flowers on the hem of Martha's red robe as she hung beside her husband on the palace portico. A knife turned in my heart. I still wept for Martha and Jonathan. And for all the others. Naboth. Joel. Jason. Mikah. Zim.

Zim. I miss you, my brother. I would never stop missing Zim. Every childhood memory had Zim at its center. And the memory of his horrible death would never leave me. I didn't want it to. I didn't want to forget him, even if remembering brought pain.

"So, you came to watch me pay the price for my crimes, eh? Can't say that I'm surprised."

"No. That's not why I came, Jezebel." I let the words hang in the space between us. Could I say what I'd come here to say? I knew I had to say it, or I would never be fully free of the woman whose reflection stared at her bejeweled hands.

"I came to tell you that I forgive you."

Her head shot up. She laughed. "That is difficult to believe."

"Now that I'm here, I'm not certain that I can, but I came to try."

"And what do I have to do to secure your forgiveness, Obadiah? If I repent my errors, what then?" she said with a jerk of her chin. "Jehu will pull his army back and leave me to my grief?"

"No, that will not happen. Ahab repented, but it did not make null the prophet's words concerning his death. Only that he would not have to see his sons' deaths."

Jezebel pursed her lips. There was a small quiver in them. She had, no doubt, been standing at the window as Jehu's arrow sliced through Joram's back.

"A small mercy. That's what my husband said when he read in the scroll that he wouldn't see his sons' deaths. Very small indeed. I think I would rather see and know the murderer, so I can curse him with my last breath."

She dipped her long finger into the alabaster pot and spread a small swath of the rosy blend on her sharp cheekbones. "I don't think your god would welcome my repentance anyway, Obadiah. Even Baal has closed his ears to me."

"Perhaps not. Repentance must be sincere, and it would not annul the prophet's words concerning the destruction of the house of Ahab. It has begun with your sons, but it will not end there, Jezebel. There will be no survivors of Ahab's line. And what the prophet spoke of you will be fulfilled as well—today."

"Then why would I want to repent?" she snorted. "What good would it do me?"

"Perhaps you could go to your death with a clearer conscience, but … time is running out."

The sound of the army, now inside the city wall, attested to the truth of my words. Shouts and curses mixed with the snorts of horses pawing at the ground beneath the queen's balcony, the queen's name rising above it all. The army of Jehu was here to send Jezebel to her prophesied end.

Jezebel pushed back the cushioned chair and rose. There was a slight tremor in her hands. She saw that I noticed and fisted them into the folds of her robe.

"Well, I may as well get it over with. I will meet this rebel king with my head high." She took a step toward the balcony, then turned to look at me again.

"I am sorry for one thing, Obadiah."

I raised a brow, wondering what she would say. Her long painted lashes closed over her black eyes for a flick of a moment. "I'm sorry about the girl. The one you were in love with. She was brave. I think about her from time to time. I wish I had let her live."

I deliberated about what to say next and decided that no one could be harmed by telling the truth. "Anna. Her name is Anna. And she is not dead. She lives."

Jezebel's head jerked to the eunuch. "You too!" she said, eyes blazing. "Can no one be trusted to do their duty?" She caught the contradiction of her words. She had just said she was sorry for Anna's death, then berated the eunuch for not killing her. She let out a huff of breath. "I'm not sorry she lives. But I'm disappointed that you did not follow orders." The eunuch didn't move a muscle. How the man held himself so still seemed almost unearthly.

She stood for a long moment as though unable to make her body move. I didn't know why I did it, but I walked to her and offered my elbow. Shock inundated her face. She stared at the curve of my arm, and I knew she was thinking about the other walk we took to the portico where she had hung Jonathan and Martha from the upper windows.

She gave a small shake of her head. "No. But thank you, Governor. It is a kind offer."

Pulling herself to her full height, she walked out on the balcony, to the balustrade, the two eunuchs following behind, one on either side. The noise lowered so all that could be heard was the sounds of horses pawing the ground. I assumed Jehu had raised an arm to quiet the gathering crowd.

Jezebel shouted over the wall. "Murderer! You so-called king! You murdered your master!"

Jehu's thunderous voice could be heard plainly above the din.

"You men up there? Are you with me, or are you loyal to a wicked queen?"

Jezebel shouted an obscenity and cursed the man who killed her youngest child.

The eunuch turned to look at me. He wasn't asking my permission, but his eyes told me he was going to throw the queen over that wall, and he wasn't sorry. He had suffered much at Jezebel's hand, and I suspected he had suffered at the hand of others as well. I knew how he felt. I could have thrown her over myself at one time, but I had come to the conclusion that Jezebel would one day give an account to one more righteous than a palace governor.

The man nodded at the other eunuch, and together they grasped Jezebel by her arms and legs and tossed her over the wall. She didn't fight the men or scream, just fell to an ignominious death.

I heard the sound of horse and chariot picking up speed, and the cheers of the soldiers, and imagined that Jehu was running his chariot over the queen. I wasn't sure what I thought of that, but I couldn't blame Jehu. He was the instrument of Yahweh's vengeance upon a woman who had incited the children of God to sin.

The eunuchs didn't try to leave the room. They feared no retribution from me. I nodded at the big Philistine.

"Thank you. For saving Anna. I am indebted to you for the rest of my life. I will speak to the new king for you. He will be inclined to reward you. Anything you need, I will gladly give. If you want to return to Philistia, I will take you there myself. Help you find your family if you have one. Sadness filled the dark eyes, and I knew the man had nothing to go back to. I would talk to Jehu. We would find this man a place.

Jehu was sitting at the table where Joram had been taking his morning meal when he learned an army was gathered within a bowshot of the palace. The same table where I shared a meal with Ahab once a week with my report. I took a knee and lowered my head, staring at the tiles I knew by heart.

As I knelt before the new king, my thoughts were an eddy of relief and anticipation. The departure of Ahab and Jezebel marked the end of an era plagued by corruption and idolatry. Now, with Jehu ascending to the throne, there was hope for a new era of righteousness in the land. Jehu had served valiantly in Ahab's armies. I hoped that same valor would be matched in his service to his God.

"Long live Jehu, King of Israel."

"Rise, Obadiah. I'm not used to people bowing before me yet. I'm a soldier at heart. Perhaps someday I'll enjoy it, but right now I'd rather have you sit and eat some of this cold roast duck with me. It's good to see you."

I stood to my feet and tipped my head. "It's good to see you also." I prayed Jehu would never get too comfortable with the trappings of power. He was a good man, but good men had fallen prey to pride before. But he was a man who honored Yahweh and eschewed false gods, so I had great hope for him.

"So it's almost over, Obadiah. Soon the house of Ahab will be gone. It will take a while to finish the task, but there will be no heart to fight. Just flee. And there's nowhere any of Ahab's seed can hide from Yahweh."

"Indeed, there is none, my king. I want to speak to you for the eunuchs that threw Jezebel over the wall." I winced at the memory of the men lifting the queen headfirst over the wall, her long uncovered legs like twigs in their large hands. The ignominy of it would have killed her if the fall had not.

"The big Philistine especially. He aided Naboth's daughter, Anna, when Jezebel commanded that he kill her. He has no home to return to."

"Yes, of course. Whatever you suggest. He's welcome to serve in the palace, or if you have something else in mind, consider it done."

"Thank you, my king."

Jehu took another bite of duck and wiped his mouth with the sleeve of his tunic. He would definitely need some royal robes, or he would be mistaken for the kitchen help.

"And what about you, Obadiah? I hope you will continue as palace governor. No one could do better."

I thought for a moment. I had been the governor well over twenty years. Did I really want to continue? Serving Jehu would be nothing like serving Ahab or his sons, but I wasn't certain if I wanted to be part of palace politics anymore.

"Of course, it would be a great honor, my king. But if you would give me a little time to consider it, I will speak to you soon."

"Yes, of course, Obadiah. You've served faithfully, and you've protected Yahweh's prophets. You may choose your path with any help I can provide."

Suddenly something dropped into my mind from nowhere, it seemed. Something that might serve me and the Philistine both.

"Thank you, my king. That is most gracious of you."

"Speaking of being gracious," Jehu said, leaning back in the high-back chair. "I don't feel very gracious toward the dead queen. I could never honor her as such. But she *was* the daughter of a king, and I suppose I should get someone to see to her burial. Joram's body will need to be recovered as well. I told the men to dump it in Naboth's vineyard as a testament to what his father did to the vintner and his family."

He motioned to a couple of young soldiers. "Find some shovels and bury the queen. It won't be pleasant. Her blood is all over the wall, and she wasn't in very good shape before I ran my chariot over her. Probably a real mess now."

"I'd like to supervise, if you don't mind. I know it's not possible, but I'd like to see for myself that she hasn't gotten up and walked away. I'll rest better at night." I laughed.

"I assure you she is going nowhere, but whatever you wish. You may regret it. It won't be pretty."

I didn't have any true thought that Jezebel had escaped her judgment, but for some reason, I wanted to see her body, and I wanted her to have a proper burial.

I could hear the dogs snarling in the distance as the two soldiers and I walked toward the road that separated the outer wall from the palace, shovels in hand. I was startled. Of course I knew the prophesy, but hearing the animals sent chills up my spine. I was not prepared for what I saw.

The dogs had almost completely devoured the body in the time it took for Jehu to eat his lunch. There was nothing left but two bare feet and two hands, still bearing several rings, including the ruby ring I had compared to Martha's robe. The pack was trotting away, one dragging a flesh-stripped bloody skull by a hank of red hair. My stomach turned over.

I thought about Ahab. At least he'd had a proper burial, but there wasn't enough left of Jezebel to bury. No one would visit the grave of the queen of Israel.

The glint of a gold chain winked in the sunlight. I leaned closer. Jezebel's pendant. I looked around and found a stick and fished the chain out of the bloody mess where it lay. The bone was red with blood. Jezebel had claimed that her mother had been murdered because she wasn't strong enough to secure her place in her husband's kingdom. Now Jezebel's blood covered her mother's breast bone. She thought she was stronger than her mother, but maybe her mother was the stronger one. Who knew what choices the woman had made? Better to be murdered than to be a murderer.

I tossed the pendant back into the bloody mess and stood. My hand went to the place where the simple stone on a tightly woven cord lay beneath my robe. I hadn't removed it since I'd slipped it on when I found it in Anna's farewell missive, over thirteen years ago. Zim's mother had given it to him as a reminder that Yahweh was the Rock of Israel, and Zim could rest upon that rock, unafraid.

Both Elijah and Jonathan had told me that courage and fear could live in the same heart at the same time, and I had finally begun to understand what they meant. Being afraid was not a signal of cowardice. The true test of courage is found in placing our trust in God. Giving up control, and that can be the most frightening thing of all.

I had vowed to protect the people I loved: Naboth and the brothers, Anna, Zim. But I hadn't taken into consideration that I did not have the power to protect them. I did what I could, and that was commendable by any man's standard. But now I'd begun to understand that true courage is to trust God. To give him permission—not that He needs it—to do what He deems best. Trust is impossible without surrender.

Yahweh, may I continue to learn to live without fear, surrendering my will to Yours, trusting You with all I hold dear.

"Should we recover the rings?" one of the soldiers said, his face a sickly yellow.

I took another look.

"No. Leave them. Leave it all."

CHAPTER THIRTY-ONE

Obadiah

I looked over the rows of vines stretched out in disciplined lines, heavy with clusters of deep-purple grapes. Our first harvest. I had requested that Jehu allow the eunuch and me to stay at Naboth's vineyard and do what we could to recover at least a portion of the vines that had lain neglected under the young king's care. For all that Jezebel had done to obtain the place, she wanted no part of it after Ahab's death. It was a curse to her, to her family. I wondered if that was the reason she had spent so little time at the Jezreel palace. The view from her balcony was a constant reminder of a future she could not evade.

Jehu had given me complete oversight of the vineyard. "Consider it your private enterprise. Run it as you will, and for the first season the profit is yours for all you have done for Israel. You may hire all the help you need at the expense of the palace. When the vineyard is restored, you will give the palace half, after expenses, and you will keep half for yourself."

I had no intention of keeping the profit. I didn't need the money. It was Naboth's vineyard. I would find some way to get the money to Anna for Zim's child. The solace and peace of tending the vines was reward enough. I had never worked so hard or felt so good.

In the winter months we had pruned the vines, carefully cutting back the previous year's growth. We mended the trellises and checked the stakes for stability, making certain everything was in place for the growing season. The soil was turned and prepared. We hauled manure to nourish the vines. That wasn't my favorite part, but I had grown to appreciate the odor for the good it did. I wondered if that wasn't true of other things in our lives. The things that stink in our nostrils cause us to bud and grow and eventually bear fruit.

As spring arrived, the vines started to awaken, and we focused on training the new shoots. We tied them gently to the stakes and posts, guiding their growth upward. The days grew warmer, and the vineyard was alive with the scent of blossoming flowers. We vigilantly inspected for pests and diseases and channeled water carefully to ensure each vine received the moisture it needed.

In the heat of summer, we spent our days thinning the canopy, removing excess leaves to ensure the grapes got plenty of sunlight and air to prevent mildew and other diseases. We trimmed the vines, ensuring they focused their energy on the developing grapes. Come autumn, the vineyard was a sea of ripening grapes, heavy on the vines.

We would harvest carefully, selecting the clusters ourselves to ensure only the best grapes were brought to the wine press, where the fruit of our labor would begin its transformation into wine.

My hands were stained and scratched, as Naboth's had been, but I had connected with this land, and Yahweh had tended to my heart like a master vintner. He had lovingly tied me to the stake so I would look up instead of wallowing on the ground where I would get no sun and bear no fruit. He had inspected my heart and plucked out the pests and healed the disease of bitterness and anger. I had submitted to his trimming. I had allowed Him to remove the excess leaves that look so good on the outside but served no purpose but to block the light from reaching the innermost parts of a man's soul. I had come to trust His pruning as an act of love that prepared me for a better harvest.

My life had been spent seeking courage, but what I found in the end was trust and surrender, which brought me to a place of peace.

I rolled my shoulders, feeling the muscles stretch then release, my stiff joints popping and clicking like dry twigs underfoot. "Do you think we should hire a few more men for the picking?"

The eunuch shook his head, then made a series of simple signs that told me he thought we had enough. We could always hire more later.

Our method of communication was efficient, born from months of working side by side. For more complicated conversation the eunuch carried a tablet and a stylus. I had learned his name was Samson, after the Israelite judge whose eyes were put out by his Philistine captors.

I wondered why his parents would name him after the man who had destroyed so many of their ancestors.

Jehu had given the eunuch to me. I had immediately given the man his freedom and offered again to see him to his homeland if he so desired. In perfect script he wrote that he had watched his wife and child die in the raid on his village that landed him at Jezebel's mercy and had nothing to go back to. We were two men stripped of our loved ones, but our comradery gave us company, and we enjoyed working together.

I pulled a long breath. The air was filled with the earthy scent of the soil and the sweetness of ripe grapes. I loved the aroma the merging of the two presented. The vineyard, once a place of sorrow and loss, was slowly becoming a sanctuary of peace and productivity under our care.

I saw Kenen coming down the road in his conveyance, the wheels kicking up a lazy plume of dust. He stopped by from time to time with his son, to let him experience the vineyard so the young man would know that grapes didn't just appear in the marketplace or on their dining table. It took a great deal of work to get them there. We had become friends. Or, at the least we were no longer enemies. He had helped Anna, and that made him a good man in my eyes. Kenen had unseated Lemech and become head elder. Lemech had lost favor with the people for his bent to settle his personal grievances with abuses of the Law. The court had become more conservative in its judgments, slower to pull out the stones. Kenen was a different man. A better one.

The cloth-covered carriage pulled up, the wooden wheels creaking to a halt, but Kenen's son was not the one sitting on the raised seat, reins in hand. His son was lighter-haired, older, and heavier than this boy of thirteen or so.

"I brought you a visitor," Kenen said, grinning from ear to ear. The lad slipped off the seat and stood before me, a lock of dark hair hanging over one eye. He swiped it away and smiled, a grin that lit up his dark eyes.

I started to sway, the blood draining from my head. *Zim?* I must have been hallucinating. But it was him. The same dimples in his cheeks. The same sparkle in his eye. I shook my head, trying to force my thoughts back into focus.

Kenen hopped down and opened the door. A woman's shoes

touched the ground with a soft thud. When she rounded the door, I saw chestnut hair and emerald-green eyes. It was Anna.

"Hello, Obe."

I didn't reply. I had no breath in my lungs with which to do so.

"Well, aren't you going to greet me, Obadiah?" she said, her eyes twinkling.

"Anna?" I spoke to my own ears, as though they would tell me if it was truly her.

"Yes. *Anna*. In case you've forgotten my name."

Forget? Not a day had passed in more than thirteen years that I hadn't thought of her. Spoken her name in the quiet of my heart.

She turned toward her son. "Looks like his father, doesn't he?"

To say the boy looked like his father was a colossal understatement. He was the very image of his father at that age. I let out a breath and shook my head. "I've never seen one person so precisely resemble an-other." I walked toward him with the intention of shaking his hand, but I put my arms around him and pulled him to my chest. He seemed startled, but he accepted my embrace. I took him by the forearms and looked into his dark eyes, my heart overwhelmed with both pain and joy.

"Your father was my best friend in the world."

The boy beamed. "My mother has told me about it. I'm so happy to finally meet you."

I looked at Anna and laughed. "It's hard to believe. I thought I was seeing a ghost." As soon as the words were out of my mouth I regretted them.

Anna's eyes glistened. How she must have missed Zim all these years.

"Forgive me," she said. "I haven't even introduced you. This is your father's best friend—and mine, Obadiah ben Enos." She paused for a long moment, a mischievous grin playing on her full lips. "Obadiah. This is my son, Obadiah ben Salmone. We call him Di."

My jaw dropped. She had named Zim's son after me? I didn't know what to think. It was a great honor, but why not name him after his father? Especially since Zim was gone.

"It was Zim's idea. Before I was even pregnant he said if we had a son we should name him after you."

I swallowed hard, the lump in my throat refusing to go down. It sounded like something Zim would do. Zim always deferred to me. Not because I was the dominant person in our relationship, although … there was that, but because he was a man of absolute selflessness. The young man standing before me was his father's image, and I could see that he carried his father's heart inside that lean body.

"I am … honored beyond words."

A huge grin spread over the boy's face. "I've heard so much about you, but I want to hear more about you and my father when you were both young. I'm sure my mother doesn't know it all."

I laughed and looked at Anna. "No, she doesn't know it all. Some things can't be shared with girls, no matter how good a friend they may be."

Anna's eyes lit with laughter. "I knew you boys were holding out on me. You always had your secrets."

Yes, we had secrets. Even from each other. We were both in love with you.

I looked back toward the carriage. "Eber? He didn't come with you?"

Sorrow slipped over Anna's beautiful face. "Eber passed when Di was only three. I miss him. He was a good man. We had no other children, but he loved Di. Nathor looked after us both. He was a surrogate father to Di. His wife was a wonderful friend."

I could fill in what Anna wasn't saying. Nathor already had a wife, and since Zim had an heir, there was no need for the younger brother to fulfill the duty prescribed by the Law. So Anna had lived without a husband all these years. I was sorry that Eber had died and that she was alone. I knew as well as anyone how difficult being alone could be, but she had Di, and I could see how close they were. The boy had been a comfort to her. I was glad for that.

My eyes flicked to Samson still standing in the row where we had been working. Anna's gaze followed mine. Her mouth opened wide.

"Is that …?"

"Yes."

She walked toward the rows of vines, slipping through a gap to the giant of a man and taking his huge hands in hers. "Thank you." Her voice cracked, and I knew tears were spilling down her face. "Thank

THE STRUGGLE FOR COURAGE

you for what you did for me. It was so brave. My son and I wouldn't be here if it wasn't for your courage."

The big man had slipped into that stoic demeanor he had perfected in Jezebel's service, but I saw a hint of moisture in his eyes.

Kenen climbed back on the carriage. "I suppose you won't mind bringing them back, Obadiah? Lillian is preparing a feast, and she's instructed me to buy out the entire market. You are invited, of course, to share the afternoon meal with us. And you, Samson."

The eunuch nodded his thanks, but I doubted he would go with us. He hadn't yet become comfortable in his role as a free man. I hoped someday he would grow into it.

"Of course. We'll be there in a few hours."

Kenen reined the carriage around and headed back toward Jezreel.

Anna wanted to see the place where she and Zim had lived, so I walked her and Di down the path that led to the little stone house. The door juddered as I opened it and stood aside so she could enter. The door swelled in the summer, causing it to catch on the wooden frame. I would have to fix that. I had moved into Naboth's house, but this place was sacred ground. I had one of the maidservants clean it and keep the little yellow flowers that grew in the dooryard watered.

Anna ran her fingers over the dustless table that Zim had built.

"Does someone live here?" she said, looking at me. "It's fine if they do. Really. It's just so well taken care of it made me wonder."

"No. No one has lived here since—" I stopped short, but she didn't seem to notice.

She walked around the house touching everything, including the mortar and pestle still sitting on the counter with a double-handled clay bowl she had made with her own hands. She paused before the curtain that provided privacy for their sleeping chamber. Finally she pulled it open and looked at the bed where she had lain in Zim's arms. Where her son had been conceived.

I had to turn away. I called Di's attention back to the table. "Your father was a very talented man. Give him a fine piece of wood and he could turn it into a work of art." By the boy's solemn demeanor, I knew he was moved to be standing in the place where his father had stood. Touching the wood his father had meticulously shaped and smoothed and coated with linseed oil to bring out the grain and leave a polished gleam. He nodded, his face filled with a reverent sadness.

"I wish I could have known him."

I wish you could have too. I would have done anything to make it so, if it had been in my power. But it was not. I laid my hand on the boy's shoulder. "Your father loved you from the moment he knew your mother had conceived. He would be proud of the fine young man you've become."

A thought budded in my mind. I reached for the fine cord around my neck and pulled Zim's pendant over my head and placed it in Di's hand. "I want you to have this. It belonged to your father. He made it from a stone his mother gave him before she died. Your mother can tell you the story behind it."

The boy held the stone in his hand for a long moment, his face soft, his dark eyes shimmering.

"Thank you."

Anna was more talkative as she showed Di the house where she had lived as a child. She talked about the boy's grandfather and uncles with a smile on her face, as though she refused to enter into the grief of their loss in front of Di. She opened doors and cupboards, touching mementos tenderly. She shared funny stories with her wide-eyed son, and we all laughed, making the burden of the memories seem lighter.

When we went outside again, Anna turned to me. "Obe, I would like to go to the cave. Could we do that now?"

I hesitated a moment. The cave had been the last place Anna wanted to be after Zim's death. But perhaps she wanted to face her fear. I had a *different* sort of fear.

"Mother, I'd like to stay here with Samson, if you don't mind. Maybe he could show me more about how wine is made from the grapes." He stood up straight. "I assume my mother will be safe in your company, Obadiah?"

I wasn't certain it was a good idea, but Anna begged with those huge eyes.

"Yes, Obadiah. Your mother will be safe in my care." I hoped.

"Samson, would you saddle Gray and one of the other mares please?"

"Oh, that won't be necessary. We only need one horse. I can ride with you, Obe."

My blood began to heat. Anna and me on the same horse? *Help me, Yahweh.* Anna had obviously ceased to think of me as a man. Not as a man but as a man who would find her close proximity uncomfortable. I was her friend. She had told her son that I was her best friend, and I was thankful for that, but Anna was more than my friend. She was the woman I had loved most of my life.

I stood looking at Gray, wondering how I should do this. If I put her in front of me, I might see a portion of her legs as her belted tunic rucked up. She hadn't come prepared to ride in trousers, as she did when we were younger. Or I could put her side-saddle, but she would have to lean into me.

I decided to mount and pull her up behind me, but it wasn't any better because she had to hold on, and that required putting her arms around my waist.

It was going to be a long ride.

<hr/>

Anna pulled a deep breath and let it out slowly as we entered through the narrow opening. She had to be remembering the last time she was in the cave. The day she learned her entire family had been brutally murdered. I remembered how I held her on my lap after she fainted. My heart breaking with hers. How I refused to honor my brother's last words because I couldn't bear being married to my best friend's wife when he'd had to lose his life for it to be so.

Anna touched my arm. "You did a wonderful thing here, Obe. Risking your life for Yahweh's prophets."

Her touch sent my heart racing again. "You did your part."

"You didn't make it easy for me," she said, that little line I loved appearing between her shapely brows.

"No. I didn't. I'm sorry for that." I *was* sorry. I had not given Anna the dignity of choosing for herself. I had tried to impose my will on her, and that had not gone well. Anna had deserved my respect of her courage and her willingness to trust Yahweh with her safety.

"I know you did it because you …" She didn't finish the sentence. *Because I loved her.* Those were the words she didn't say. I wondered if she had any idea how much I had loved her. I hoped she didn't sense how much I loved her still, because I didn't dare to hope that she might feel the same.

She asked me if I still saw any of the prophets I had housed here. I told her it had been a long time. They had no need of my help since Jezebel seemed to have lost the lust for their lives when Ahab died.

She tapped her foot lightly, something she had always done as she thought, then straightened and looked me in the eye. "Obe, will you marry me?"

What?

She scratched her head. "I didn't intend to say that. Not yet. But … I've been waiting a long time, Obe. Jezebel is dead. There is no more danger. You'll probably have some kind of excuse to offer," she said, waving a hand through the air. "But don't say you can't marry me because of Zim. If you do, you're an idiot and you didn't know Zim at all."

I was in shock. Anna was asking me to marry her?

"I love you, Obe. I always have and I always will, and that doesn't make my love for Zim any less true. My love expanded to include Zim, but it didn't diminish my love for you. Just changed it for a time." She took a step forward. "I have honored Zim with my love and loyalty. He would want this, Obe. I want it."

I was frozen. My body wouldn't move, including my tongue, which was lolling in my gaping mouth. Anna had asked me to marry her? It was … surreal. Was this some fantastical dream my mind had concocted? Would I awaken from my sleep in a moment and realize she wasn't here at all? No. She wasn't a vision or an apparition come to haunt me. I could smell the faint odor of sweat from the warm day. She smelled like sunshine and the sprig of mint … she had picked from the dooryard of her home.

"Anna … I … I don't know what to say."

She shook her head and looked at the floor.

I cleared my throat, dispelling the silence that hung between us. "Marrying a woman your age. How old are you now? Let's see. You were twenty when I asked you to marry *me*. So you're at least thirty-three now. Right?"

Her head popped up, her eyes narrowing into little green slits. "You are still the same infuriating man."

I shrugged. "I mean, you could be a grandmother."

"Yes!" she retorted. "If you hadn't been so stubborn, we could have had grandchildren by now!"

I took a step toward her. "I don't know what it would be like to be married to a grandmother."

A small smile played at the edges of her mouth. I could see the effort she was making to contain it.

"Anna. I have a few conditions if I'm going to marry you."

"Conditions?" she said with no small amount of sarcasm. "And what might they be, Obadiah ben Enos?"

I raised a finger. "No mud pies. Absolutely no mud pies."

"I haven't made mud pies since I was a child, Obe."

I placed my hand over my heart. "Perhaps, but I was deeply scarred by the last one you made for me."

She shrugged. "Is there anything else, Master?"

I took another step forward, my pulse picking up speed. "No leaving me. Ever again."

She folded her arms over her chest. "And I would require the same of you. If you remember right, it was you who left first."

I winced at the truth of her words. "I know, Anna. I've wrestled with that decision all these years. Played it over and over in my mind. Everything I ... gave up."

The weight of it, made in the name of duty and protecting her, now seemed hollow. Every moment without her had been a void, a chasm that no amount of duty could fill.

Anna reached out and touched my hand. "It was the right decision, Obe. The brave decision. I know that now. You did it because you loved me."

"Yes." I took a deep breath, trying to steady my heart and my mind as I said the words I had so longed to say. "I did it because I loved you—and I have loved you every moment since."

Her eyes filled with tears as she spoke. "Only death could make me leave you again."

I reached out and pulled Anna into my arms, my lips meeting hers with all the love and longing of a lifetime. She was here. In my embrace. I wasn't dreaming or imagining it. Her body was next to mine. Her arms around my neck. *Oh, Yahweh. Thank you. Thank you.*

Anna pulled away for a moment. "Now *I* have a question. When? When do you plan to do this? Because if you think I'm going to stay on the hook while you delay again, you're wrong."

I laughed, something she didn't appreciate by the depth of that line between her brows.

"As soon as we can have a contract drawn up. I promise, my love."

Anna pulled a paper out of the fold of her sash and handed it to me. It was old and …

I looked up at her. "Is this …?"

"Yes. I told you my father had probably had a contract in a basket somewhere since I was twelve. That's exactly where I found it. In a basket in one of the cupboards. And it's already signed."

I burst out laughing. "Well, then, how does tomorrow sound?"

"No. Tonight. Lillian's already preparing a feast. As head elder, Kenen has the authority to marry us."

"And Lillian is preparing a feast for what occasion? It couldn't be that the two of you have been conniving, could it?"

She blushed. "Why would I do that? It's not like I could depend on you to give the right answer if I asked you to marry me."

I couldn't stop the grin that was stretching from one end of my face to the other. "Then tonight it will be."

She threw her arms around my neck and kissed me with a passion that set my blood on fire. Tonight couldn't come fast enough. It was I who pulled away next. "I promised Di you would be safe with me. Maybe we should take a break."

She kissed me again. With a softer, safer touch. My heart was overflowing with love, with thankfulness, with abandoned joy. As we stood, her head against my chest, wrapped in one another's arms. I thanked Yahweh that through this most convoluted path He had brought us together again. Our struggle had been long and difficult. It was a struggle for the courage to do the right thing no matter how much it hurt. The struggle to surrender our will to Yahweh and to trust that He had not abandoned us.

I held her to my chest, her arms around my waist, and silently told Zim that I would take good care of her—until we all met again.

Obadiah

Anna and I were married that same evening, under the rose arbor in Lillian's garden. In the place where I had left her in her greatest need. I had been given a second chance to honor Zim's last words. I felt his approval as Anna and I vowed our unending love.

Anna wore a lovely emerald gown that Lillian had loaned her. It matched her eyes perfectly. I had asked Samson to be my friend of the groom. He looked regal in one of my best robes. The usually ascetic man cried unabashedly as we walked toward Anna, who was radiant, her arm tucked into Di's elbow, accompanied by Lillian's daughters and granddaughters and Kenen's second wife. I fought with my own tears, but I lost the battle.

We spent our wedding night back at the vineyard. I had taken my bride to the room I had chosen when I took over Naboth's vineyard. Her father's room. She refused to make love to me in her father's bed, so, laughing, we moved to another chamber. Our coming together was full of tenderness and passion and the most exquisite joy.

Anna conceived on that first night. She bore me a daughter, whom I adored beyond measure. She was the image of her mother, as Di had been the image of Zim. A son followed within a year. He was an amalgamation of us both, with my build and eyes and Anna's chestnut hair.

Eventually, Di returned to his father's ancestral land, married, and made Anna and me grandparents. Anna asked me a question when we heard the news.

"So, do you think you'll mind being married to a grandmother?"

I shrugged, chewing on my bottom lip for a long moment. "I don't know. I'll have to think about it."

She slapped my arm, and I pulled her close and kissed her soundly.

A NOTE FROM THE AUTHOR

When I finished my first novel, *The Struggle for Love: The Story of Leah*, I wasn't sure what to tackle next. I had been writing that story for a long time. I don't want to say how long, but here's a hint: some authors I follow had written enough books to fill a shelf by then. So, what was next? I had a few ideas, so I took my three favorites, wrote them on small pieces of paper, folded them, prayed, and drew one. I supposed that if the apostles could cast lots to replace Judas, it was all right to cast lots to see what book I was supposed to write next. LOL. I do believe that *The Struggle for Courage: In the Days of Jezebel* was a timely pick. Courage is something we all need these days.

The challenge of writing biblical fiction is filling 300-plus pages with gripping drama and emotion while being faithful to a few short scriptures. I try to stay true to both the letter and the spirit of the Bible when I'm writing. I do take creative license, occasionally rearranging timelines to fit the narrative, or adding extra-biblical characters and events, but I never deliberately contradict the Word. If you find such a contradiction in my writing, it was an oversight, and I sincerely apologize.

The important thing to remember is that stories presented as biblical fiction are just that: fiction. They are windows that allow a peek into the culture of the ancients and a glimpse of God's faithful dealings with them—and an opportunity to learn from their mistakes! They are not meant to replace the Bible. I think one of the greatest benefits of biblical fiction is that it whets the appetite for the Word. I've found that reading fictional accounts of Bible characters and events makes the Bible come to life. I hope you have that experience with *The Struggle for Courage: In the Days of Jezebel.* Thank you.

ACKNOWLEDGEMENTS

First, of course, I want to acknowledge the Lord Jesus Christ. I was 14 when He came into my heart. I'm thankful that He knew me before He made the heavens and the earth. He had a plan for me, which included writing stories.

My husband deserves more than a few words of acknowledgment in this book. He has to pick up the slack when I can't keep up. He's always looking for some way to make my life easier so I can do what God called me to do. Thank you, sweetheart. And thanks to my children, who are proud that their mama is an author and aren't ashamed to promote me to their friends. That says a lot!

Special thanks to C.S. Lakin, the best editor an author could have. I've learned so much from her through the years. She's truly made all the difference in my books. She holds nothing back but is a great encourager as well. Thank you, Susanne. And thanks to Roseanna White, who has done most my covers. She's so patient with me when I can't make up my mind about what I want.

I can't forget my great friend, Judy Campbell. She has the eye of an eagle when it comes to proofreading. Thank you, Judy. And, of course, thanks to all my wonderful readers. Without you, this would all be in vain. You're the reason I write. Bless you all.

Discussion Questions

1. Do you think it was ethical for Obadiah to abscond food from the palace to feed the prophets? How would you justify it by scripture?

2. Which of the five senses did the author use in the opening chapter? Give an example of each and share how it helped to set the scene. How did the opening scene in the cave make you feel?

3. How did you feel when Obadiah told Naboth he couldn't sign the betrothal contract? What do you think of the culture that gave the father the right to choose a husband for his daughter? What are the positives and the negatives of such a culture?

4. What did you think of Obadiah and Zim's friendship? Do you think it would have survived if Zim hadn't died? How do our friendships define us?

5. When the prophet told Ahab all of his progeny would die, did that mean that God commanded it? Or was it God's foreknowledge? In your opinion, why was violence such a part of the Old Testament? Why do you think that changed in the New Testament?

6. How do you feel about Obadiah refusing to honor Zim's request that he marry Anna? How have you seen this scenario play out among your friends or family? Would it make you feel guilty to marry

your best friend's husband, knowing that your friend had to die to make it possible?

7. What did you think about Obadiah going to Jezebel's quarters to tell her he forgave her? Do you think we should forgive people who do horrifically wicked things? How did Obadiah's forgiveness affect Jezebel? Did his forgiveness in any way absolve Jezebel of her sins?

8. Obadiah's goal was to protect the people he loved: Anna, Zim, Naboth, and Anna's brothers. How did his attitude change when he was locked up in the dungeon and had no power to protect them? What were the two things he said he learned during his incarceration? They are the real lessons of this novel.

9. What do you think of Anna's sacrifice in marrying Zim's brother to provide for her child? Why was it so important in ancient Israel that land was passed from father to sons in the same tribe? What do you think happened to men who didn't have land in those days?

10. Were you satisfied with the ending of the story? As you read the novel, did you fear that Obadiah and Anna would never be together, or were you confident they would be reunited? What was the one thing that had to happen before they could be together again? Why do you think Obadiah was able to marry Anna in the end without guilt? What had changed in Obadiah's heart?

Sign up for my newsletter and get all the latest news about my upcoming books, contests, and lots of fun stuff. You'll have access to my blog: Persevering Women (men welcome!). AND get a free copy of *Where It Began: Prequel to The Struggle for Love: The Story of Leah*. Thank you so much for signing up. It means a lot.

ALSO BY MARILYN T. PARKER

The Struggle for Love: The Story of Leah

Non-Fiction

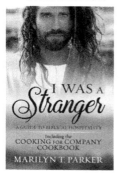

I was a Stranger: A Guide to Biblical Hospitality
(with image and QR for print, link for ebook)

The Surviving Child: Living With My Mother's Grief

HOW TO HELP THE AUTHOR

Thank you for reading *The Struggle for Courage: In The Days of Jezebel*. I hope you enjoyed it. If you would like to help, it would be great if you would leave a review on Amazon and Goodreads. More than any other thing, reviews help authors to spread the word about their books. And they help readers find the books they love. The review doesn't have to be long or fancy. Just an honest expression of how the book made you feel. Please create your review for *The Struggle for Courage: In the Days of Jezebel* here.

For the print version, please scan the QR code with your phone camera. It will take you directly to the product page. Click the link for the ebook.

BOOK
CLUB
KITS

PW
PRESS

Have a book club?
Check out the book club kit on Marilyn's website
for discussion questions, author Q&A, and more!

https://marilyntparker.com/book-club-kit/

CONTACT ME

I absolutely love to hear from my readers. You can contact me at
marilyn@marilyntparker.com
I promise to get in touch.

Social Media Links
Facebook
https://www.facebook.com/marilyntparker

Instagram
https://www.instagram.com/marilyntparker/

BookBub
https://www.bookbub.com/authors/marilyn-t-parker

Website
www.marilyntparker.com

ABOUT THE AUTHOR

Marilyn has worn many hats: pastor's wife, mother of four God-loving children, school teacher, singer/songwriter, author and blogger—to name a few. Four years after becoming a widow, she married Peter Parker. She thinks being Mrs. Spiderman is pretty cool! When Marilyn and her superhero husband are not out RVing they reside in Arizona with their monster dog, Mimi (don't let the cute name fool you!). Marilyn's greatest desire is that her work reflect the glory and goodness of God.

Printed in Great Britain
by Amazon

55648901R00169